## WHISPERS OF THE HEART

At midnight when he kissed her, Diana trembled at his touch and at her own fears. Was she strong enough for this? She was almost whole again, but still quite vulnerable. And he was just-wounded and so very vulnerable, too.

"What are you thinking, Diana?"

"That you're a lonely man and I'm a lonely lady."

"What else?"

"That this has disaster written all over it."

"Even if we're very careful with each other?"

"Probably." Diana gave a soft laugh. "Probably."

Their loving began with smiles and teases and laughter. But as the teases faded, the emotions that replaced them were very dangerous. Because now when he whispered, "So beautiful, Diana, so very beautiful," he wasn't whispering about her sapphire eyes or the softness of her body. Now when he told her she was beautiful, he was whispering about the way his heart felt about hers . . .

# KATHERINE STONE

# LOVE SONGS

**ZEBRA BOOKS**
**KENSINGTON PUBLISHING CORP.**

ZEBRA BOOKS

are published by

Kensington Publishing Corp.
475 Park Avenue South
New York, NY 10016

First printing: April, 1991

Printed in the United States of America

Part One

# Chapter One

The appearance of Paige Spencer at the entrance of the Azalea Room halted conversations midsentence, drew admiring stares, and raised intriguing questions.

What was Paige doing in the elegant dining room of the Southampton Club on a Monday noon? On a Saturday evening, yes, of course, Paige would be here hostessing a celebrity dinner for charity, a black-tie gala for the Art Museum, or a lavish reception for the maestro of the Symphony. But on a weekday for luncheon?

What — who — was important enough to take Paige away from her busy schedule for a leisurely gourmet lunch?

Paige Barclay Spencer was a glittering symbol of the new generation of women, not just Southampton women — although Paige was one of them, and Southampton was proud to claim her — but all women. Paige so artfully balanced her roles of wife, mother, stylish society hostess, champion of worthy causes, patron of the arts, and successful Manhattan architect that the balance appeared effortless.

But everyone knew that to make such an intricate balancing act appear effortless took great effort and

7

discipline—discipline that had not before, in the memory of the women in the Azalea Room, included leisurely weekday dining at the Club. Usually Paige spent the hours while Amanda was in school in the tranquil privacy of her study at Somerset, designing the buildings of exceptional elegance and taste that would become sublime counterpoints to the edifices of glitz and gilt that, too, were reshaping the skyline of Manhattan. Paige sketched the magnificent works of art and Chase Andrews transformed her visions into breathtaking reality.

Perhaps Paige was meeting Chase today. Perhaps she and Chase would begin their luncheon with a bottle of Krug champagne, gently touching crystal to crystal in a toast to the success of their next marvelous venture. Paige Spencer, architect extraordinaire, and Chase Andrews, stunningly successful and critically acclaimed real-estate developer, meeting for luncheon in the Azalea Room at the Southampton Club. How interesting. How *wonderful!* The scenario could get even more delicious . . . perhaps Chase's wife, the famous heart surgeon Diana Shepherd, would be joining them.

And even if Paige was dining alone, that was still intriguing, more insight into the remarkable woman. Maybe she simply felt like pampering herself with a gourmet luncheon elegantly served, a peaceful respite from her busy life, the talented artist drawing inspiration from the Club's luxuriant gardens and vistas of the wind-caressed sea. Perhaps she had swirled her honey-blond hair into a graceful chignon, artfully accented her sky-blue eyes, touched pale-pink gloss to her lips, and clothed her slim figure in soft folds of azure silk just for herself, a celebration of *Paige.*

Whatever the reason for her presence in the Azalea Room, it was fascinating . . . it was Paige.

Paige sensed the sudden hush that greeted her and saw the expressions of curiosity and surprise. She cast

8

a brief glance toward the window table she had reserved to be certain that Julia had not yet arrived. Then, because the table was empty, she turned her attention to the women in the room, weaving among them slowly, greeting each by name, the gracious hostess always.

Once seated, Paige sipped a dry martini and gazed out of the window at the splendor of the June day. The gardens below the window bloomed in a bountiful pastel bouquet of azaleas, roses, and lilacs. In the distance, Peconic Bay shimmered beneath a cloudless pale-blue sky that was backlit in gold, a promise from the just-born summer sun that a warm summer lay ahead.

The day was perfect — soft, gentle, golden. A day to match the warmth and happiness Paige felt not just today but all days.

*I'm content,* Paige mused. *I'm forty-two years old, deliriously happy, euphorically content.*

A soft smile touched her lips as she remembered a time when "content" had been an enemy of dreams, a symbol of complacency. Paige was a veteran of the sixties, a foot soldier in the struggle for women to be whomever they wanted to be, to dream impossible dreams and then to live them. Paige began as a foot soldier, courageously and tirelessly engaging in the all-important battles, and now she was a general. Now, a conquering heroine, she was living her dreams, living more than she had ever dared to dream. Now "content" was a wonderful ally, a word gift-wrapped in happiness and joy.

"Content" had been an enemy once and so had "age." But forty-two was wonderful. Paige had never felt younger, more beautiful, or more creative.

Born in Southampton, a Barclay, Paige's blood was blue, her lineage impeccable, and there was and al-

9

ways would be vast wealth. At fifteen Paige had made the momentous decision to become an architect. Her ambition wasn't small. She was an artist, and she was going to sculpt elegant structures of stone that reached for the sky.

After graduation from Yale, Paige had moved to Manhattan. The first years were difficult, but her belief in her own talent was strong and relentless. Slowly but surely her stylish, elegant, tasteful designs began to make small statements and attract attention.

Paige's boldly traditional architectural style caught the attention of Edmund Spencer. Edmund was a bright, talented, uncompromisingly ethical Madison Avenue attorney. Edmund needed "something done" with his drafty loft. Paige transformed the cavernous space into a cozy, livable work of art. And sometime during the late-night hours when Paige and Edmund sat on cushions on the loft's hardwood floors, sipping wine and poring over her sketches, they fell in love.

Paige and Edmund were a perfect match. Armed with energy, talent, dreams, and now love, they set out together to conquer Manhattan. And conquer they did. As Spencer and Quinn became one of New York's most respected and prestigious law firms, Paige's magnificent architectural statements grew from delicate splashes of taste on the colorful easel of Manhattan to elegant strokes that redefined the city's skyline.

Then ten years ago Paige and Edmund left the vibrant energy of Manhattan for the tranquility of country estate life in Southampton. The decision to leave was trivial compared to the reason *why* they left. Paige and Edmund heard it at precisely the same moment: the soft chime of the biological clock. They wanted a baby. It was so simple, so easy, so amazing. Each believed that there could be no deeper or stronger love than what they felt for each other. And each learned with their precious Amanda new things

10

about love. Priorities were set without hesitation. Amanda was the priority. The rest fell into place.

Edmund commuted into the city. Paige remained at Somerset, sketching still and being with Amanda. At home with Amanda, the fatiguing strain of battle, the persistent vigilance despite her remarkable success magically vanished, and Paige mellowed, like the finest of wines, better with age.

*At ease, soldier.*

Paige was at ease although her life was busier than ever before. She designed her magnificent buildings— more grand and celebrated every year—carefully selecting projects and finally choosing to work solely with Chase who shared her unwavering commitment to classic elegance and style. Paige was an architect, the talented sculptress she had dreamed she would be; and a loving and beloved wife; and a mother, the dream she had never even known to dream.

So very content. And so very lucky.

Paige was pulled from her thoughts by a sudden change in the Azalea Room. The soft hum of voices had stopped with a gasp, a sharp drawing of breath followed by breath-held silence as another impeccably dressed, beautiful woman appeared beneath the arched entrance. But this time the curious eyes didn't fill with admiration and the lips didn't curl into welcoming smiles as they had for Paige. And this time intriguing questions didn't dance and twirl. Instead, the questions thundered.

What was Julia Lawrence doing here? Who could she possibly be meeting? Jeffrey, of course. But Julia's stunningly handsome and powerful husband, the nation's leading network anchor, would be at the television studio in Manhattan preparing his evening newscast. Yet who in Southampton other than Jeffrey would choose to dine with *her?*

11

The answer came swiftly, shockingly, as Julia's lavender eyes found Paige and flickered briefly with relief. *Julia was meeting Paige.* The answer triggered another round of even more perplexing questions.

Why? Why in the world would Paige take time away from her busy schedule—her important work—to dine with Julia of all people?

True, there were reasons why Paige had to associate with Julia, reasons they all had to. Jeffrey Lawrence's name appeared at the top of every guest list for every party in Southampton. Jeffrey and Julia were always invited. And although the couple rarely attended, the number of invitations didn't diminish, because even a brief appearance by Jeffrey Lawrence virtually assured a party's success. Just as Julia's appearance could ruin it.

For Paige there were additional reasons to associate with Julia, other ties—the girls. Merry Lawrence and Amanda Spencer were best friends. Naturally, because of the friendship of the girls, Paige had to associate—*communicate*—with Julia. But plans for the daughters could be discussed over the phone. There was no need for Paige to meet with Julia for a leisurely luncheon at the Club, as if she approved of Julia, liked Julia, as if she and Julia were friends, too.

Was it possible?

*No!* But . . . but Paige was smiling, a fond, friendly smile—for Julia.

Paige was smiling, but inside she churned with anger at the unconcealed disapproval that greeted Julia as she wove between the tables as just moments before she herself had done. Her reception had been warm, appreciative, admiring. And Julia's reception? Icy, silent, laced with contempt.

Julia wove gracefully, her lavender eyes slightly downcast as if she were Hester Prynne and her astonishing beauty and style were as shameful as the scarlet letter A.

Julia was unwelcome in Southampton, *still*. Paige simply hadn't realized it. Paige was the hostess of the most splendid parties in Southampton, but her busy schedule kept her out of touch with the day-to-day socializing and the gossip. Paige hadn't heard the gossip, but she could guess the reasons why Julia caused such wariness. The reasons that weren't reasonable. The reasons that had nothing to do with reason, just emotion and passion and fear.

At the very heart was the chilling belief, apparently held by most of the women in the Azalea Room, that Julia Lawrence had the power to take everything away from them if she wanted to . . .


When Julia had arrived in Southampton six years before, she was only twenty. By then, by the time she moved into Belvedere with Jeffrey's grandmother, Meredith Cabot, twenty-year-old Julia had been married to thirty-year-old Jeffrey for almost three and a half years, and she was the mother of his three-year-old daughter. And by then, even before she arrived, there were those in Southampton who knew all about Julia and her crimes against their patrician sensibilities.

The crimes committed by the daughter-in-law she refused even to meet were relentlessly recited by Jeffrey's mother, Victoria Lawrence, from her Beacon Hill mansion in Boston. Victoria had lived in Boston for thirty years, but her wicked, influential tentacles still reached to her girlhood Southampton home.

Julia had no pedigree whatsoever, Victoria informed her Southampton friends. Julia's blood wasn't blue—it was red and hot and very, very *common*. Julia had seduced Jeffrey and forced the marriage because of the child. *The child,* Victoria whispered, as if speaking the words aloud might be lethal. Without providing reasons, Victoria strongly implied that Julia's trickery and deceit were even more scandalous because the child wasn't even Jeffrey's. Julia had deceived Jeffrey, then she had tricked Meredith Cabot, Southampton's revered and beloved Grandmère.

Julia and *the child* lived with Grandmère at Belvedere during the four years that Jeffrey was a correspondent in the Middle East. While Jeffrey risked his life in Beirut, Cairo, Damascus, and Tripoli, Julia had charmed Grandmère, somehow convincing the gracious and lovely dowager to teach her how to behave like a lady—the wife of an aristocrat like Jeffrey and the mistress of an estate as grand as Belvedere. The years in the Middle East were dangerous for Jeffrey, but he returned victorious having captured the coveted plum of network anchor. The years were triumphant for Julia, too. Her victory, the ultimate trophy, was Belvedere, because when Grandmère died she left the magnificent estate to Julia.

Victoria successfully convinced her friends that her daughter-in-law was an unscrupulous seductress. But Victoria's friends were of a generation, cloistered in an elite society of their own. Most of Southampton didn't even know of Julia's crimes against the Cabot family. They were left to form their own conclusions about Julia based on what they saw: Julia herself. She was so very different, and so very threatening.

Julia never wore fur. Her only jewels, worn always, were the elegant wedding band from Jeffrey and the delicate diamond-and-sapphire earrings from Grandmère. Julia's clothes had been modest—*homemade*—until Jeffrey returned from the Middle East. Then, when Julia needed a wardrobe to match Jeffrey's celebrity, her clothes were different still. Stylish, yes, but not always the creations of Dior, St. Laurent, Givenchy, or Chanel. Sometimes the splendid satin-and-sequin gowns she wore were Grandmère's, tastefully modernized by Julia.

14

And there was more. Julia redecorated Belvedere and made it a showcase without the help of de Santis or Buatta or Hadley. Julia cooked and gardened and cleaned. She never escaped to a spa for a day or a weekend or a week, never escaped at all, never needed to be away from her husband or her daughter. Julia simply stayed in Southampton and made a beautiful happy home for Jeffrey and Merry.

Was domesticity such an unforgivable crime? Was it unspeakable to depart at all from the traditions of wealth and leisure and privilege? Couldn't Julia Lawrence be a superwife and supermother without incurring glacial stares every time she entered a room?

Of course! If only . . .

If only she weren't so young—twenty-six!—and so astonishingly beautiful. If only the innocent lavender eyes and black velvet hair and rich creamy skin and lovely soft voice weren't magic to children and seduction to men.

All children were welcome always at Belvedere. Julia made the stately mansion a fairy-tale castle fragrant with baking cookies, warm with roaring fires, and enchanted because of the make-believe stories spun from Julia's remarkable imagination and told to the mesmerized children in her soft voice. The children flocked to Belvedere every afternoon, the moment school was out at Southampton Country Day, and they flourished at Belvedere with Julia. Shy children bravely joined in games, bullies relented under Julia's gentle wide-eyed gaze, and there was no conflict, only harmony and peace.

Fine, let her be the Pied Piper of Southampton!

But there was more, a threat greater even than the adoration of the children. The men, the husbands, wanted her.

Julia stirred something very primal, some essential ingredient in the lingering mysteries between men and women, something that all the legislation in the world

15

would never change. Julia sent bewitching messages of sensuality and vulnerability, fragility and passion, the desperate need to be possessed, taken, and conquered by a man and then to join in the ecstasy of the conquest.

Men's eyes filled with hunger at the sight of Julia, and later in their beds with their wives the hunger lingered, painful, gnawing, unable to be satisfied by anyone but Julia.

Julia was a tigress. Her fangs and claws were hidden now, but when she decided, when she chose, she could devour the traditions of privilege and leisure, and the affections of the children, and finally, most treacherously, the passions of the husbands . . .

Not a tigress at all, Paige thought as Julia approached. Just a serious young woman who tirelessly devotes every moment of her life trying to make a happy home for the man she loves and for his precious child.

And succeeds? To the wary eyes of Southampton, Julia succeeded in spades and went on to conquer other children and other men. But Paige knew that Julia wasn't even confident of her success with Jeffrey and Merry. Julia struggled, an uncertain pilgrim, unwelcome and shy in the midst of the disapproving descendants of the *Mayflower.*

"Hello, Paige," Julia whispered softly when she finished the icy journey across the Azalea Room.

"Hi, Julia. Welcome." *Welcome!*

"I'm sorry I'm late."

"It's all right." Now Paige knew why Julia, who was never late for anything, not even fashionably, was late today. She hadn't wanted to arrive first.

Anger swept through Paige, familiar anger whenever she encountered something that was unfair. The foot soldier was within her still, ready and willing to

16

bear arms to fight for a worthy cause. What worthier cause than her dear friend Julia who had been so misjudged from the very beginning?

Paige wanted to right the wrong. She would talk to every woman in the room, to every woman in Southampton if need be. Paige knew them, liked them, knew them to be nice, reasonable women.

*Did you ever visit Julia at Belvedere when Grandmère was alive?* Paige would ask. She knew they hadn't. No one had visited except her. Paige visited because Belvedere and Somerset were adjacent estates, because she had heard the stories and worried about Grandmère, because there was the little girl exactly Amanda's age, and because Paige, being Paige, had to see for herself. And what she had seen at once was that Victoria Lawrence's malicious accusations were simply untrue. There was great love at Belvedere, not treachery, not seduction, not deceit.

Paige could swiftly dispel the myth of the unscrupulous fortune huntress. The rest—who Julia really was—would be more difficult.

*Have you ever seen Julia trying to seduce your husbands?* Paige could query, knowing the answer would be no. Julia didn't *try* to seduce or enchant. She had no wish to be loved by any man but Jeffrey. At the parties where she caused such lingering hunger, Julia never left Jeffrey's side, and her lavender eyes sent intimate messages only to him. She didn't try to seduce but it happened anyway. When Julia entered a room there was magic. It was who she was, as much a part of her as her instinct to protect and nurture, and there was nothing she could do to change it.

No, they would admit truthfully, but it didn't lessen the hurt, or the fear, or the damage. Then, turning the tables, they might ask Paige pointed questions: *How would you feel, Paige, if Amanda preferred being with Julia to being with you? How would you feel, Paige, if Edmund wanted her?*

17

How would she feel if Amanda preferred her aunt Julia to herself? Or if Edmund's eyes filled with hunger for Julia? Whatever Edmund had felt when he first saw Julia—and surely he had felt something—he had suppressed it quickly and then vanquished it. What filled Edmund's kind eyes when he saw Julia now was warmth and fondness, never lust.

But what if Edmund *was* distracted by her? What if Amanda *was* happier at Belvedere? Wouldn't Paige's calm rationality evaporate, too? Wouldn't her sky-blue eyes view Julia warily? Wouldn't she become a tigress in return to protect her family?

She could tell herself, reasonably, that Julia wasn't trying to steal the children and husbands. Not a tigress, just a kitten—soft, innocent, defenseless. Somehow that image was little comfort. In the end, Julia's magic would still be there, menacing, threatening, beyond reason.

Paige could fight the fight for Julia. She might melt the iciness of the stares, but even a resounding victory would be hollow. No genuine friendships would emerge. And, Paige knew, Julia wasn't looking for more friends in Southampton. Her circle of love and friendship—Jeffrey, Merry, Paige, Edmund, and Amanda—was enough, bountiful. Julia wished for no more.

*At ease, soldier. Don't force this war of principle on Julia. Julia doesn't care if she is liked or feared, welcomed or ostracized. She has other worries, other struggles.*

"So, Julia, how many times were the words *riding lessons* spoken this morning before Merry left for school?" Paige asked, smiling fondly as she addressed the worry that loomed far larger in Julia's mind than her icy reception in the Azalea Room.

"A million trillion," Julia answered with one of Merry and Amanda's favorite numbers. She smiled softly at the memory of Merry cantering around the

18

mansion before school. "The girls really want to learn how to ride this summer."

"I know. Beginning the second school is out. Five days and counting. What do you think, Julia?"

Paige and Julia needed to reach the same decision about the daughters who were best friends. Paige and Edmund had already decided. Of course Amanda could take riding lessons.

It worried Paige a little, naturally, as every new step in Amanda's life worried her. But Paige was willing to take the risks mothers needed to take. It seemed much more difficult for Julia to take the same risks, as if she had no right to take them, as if Merry wasn't really her daughter, just a precious child for whom she had been given the immense responsibility of caring until her real mother came to claim her.

With each new decision, Julia gathered all the data she could, then carefully weighed the knowns against the unknowns. For Julia there were mostly unknowns. Her own childhood had been so different from Merry's, without a glimmer of luxury or wealth. Swimming, sailing, ice-skating, riding were all foreign to Julia, foreign and somehow terrifying.

Every decision was a struggle for Julia, and the struggle was solitary because Jeffrey took no role in the daily decisions about his daughter. Paige tried to help, guiding gently and reassuring but never pushing. She never said, "Trust me, Julia. I'm sixteen years older than you. I know this will be fine." Paige had so very much more life experience than Julia, valuable lessons she could have shared, but as mothers of nine-year-old daughters, Paige and Julia were equals, equally experienced, equally inexperienced.

"We meet with the riding instructor at one-thirty?" Julia answered Paige's question with one of her own. She hadn't made a decision yet because there was more data to gather. The final piece was meeting with the man who would teach the girls. Then she would

19

have to decide.

"One-thirty, yes. Julia, the Club manager is always very careful about who he hires and he says this man is an excellent instructor." Paige's calm reassurance didn't erase the worry in Julia's eyes. Paige would have liked to have had a nice relaxed luncheon with Julia in the Azalea Room for all to see, but she knew Julia couldn't relax until the decision was made. After a moment she suggested sympathetically, "Would you like to go to the stable now? Perhaps he's free. If not, we can look around until one-thirty."

"Do you mind, Paige?"

"No, not at all." And after, Julia, if you like, we can have lunch — sandwiches on the terrace — at Somerset.

# Chapter Two

Their high heels clicked noisily on the cobblestones in the stable courtyard. The courtyard was empty on this Monday five days before school was out for the summer, but by next week it would be bustling with horses and their eager young riders. In the distance Paige and Julia heard soft whinnies, the splash of water, and the rustle of hay — signals that the grooms were busy caring for the large stable of valuable horses.

Paige and Julia crossed the empty courtyard to the stable office. The riding instructor was there, seated at the desk, reviewing the leather-bound lesson-schedule book. The sharp clicking of high heels, so distinct from the familiar soft thud of leather riding boots, alerted him to their approach and he stood when they appeared.

This is the carefully selected and excellent riding instructor? Paige wondered the moment she saw him. Paige had expected, at the very least, neatly trimmed hair, spotless ivory jodphurs, a teal-blue turtleneck, and leather riding boots polished to a mirror shine. She had expected the image, or at least the comforting illusion, of a proper country gentleman, and she had imagined even more — a distinguished-looking man in his late fifties with a slight British accent.

This man was about thirty, Paige guessed. He wore

a denim shirt rolled to his elbows, threadbare faded jeans, and battered cowboy boots. The sartorial look was rodeo, not fox hunt; bronco-busting, not dressage; dude-ranch chic, perhaps, but certainly not Southampton Club elegant.

His clothes were rugged, unrefined. And the man himself? He was handsome, very handsome, but there was a wildness about the coal-black hair, the fearless gray-green eyes, and the lean body that sent a strong yet graceful message of tightly controlled power. As if poised and ready to spring.

Like a panther, Paige decided. Wild, powerful, majestic. The panther eyes really were a blend of gray *and* green—granite and forest, emerald and steel . . . a violent winter storm tossing the Atlantic.

The panther eyes that met hers were polite, calm, and inscrutable, but Paige imagined he could will the eyes to seduce. She imagined that he, like Julia, could stir fiery passions and gnawing hungers. But, unlike Julia, this sleek panther surely was not oblivious to the effect of his sultry sexuality and his predatory gray-green eyes.

"Hello. How may I help you?"

His voice was another surprise. Hardly the voice of a cowboy! Accent-free, the voice was refined, aristocratic.

"We were looking for the riding instructor," Paige answered as she searched her memory for the name the Club manager had given her. Patrick, he had said. Patrick James. "Patrick?"

"I'm Patrick."

"I'm Mrs. Spencer, and this is Mrs. Lawrence. We have an appointment to meet with you at one-thirty."

"Yes, but now is fine, Mrs. Spencer."

After Patrick replied to Paige, he shifted his gaze to Julia in well-mannered acknowledgment of the introduction that Paige had made. Paige watched, wondering how the panther eyes would respond to Julia's magic. Would there be the silent recognition of predator meeting prey, conqueror meeting temptress, Adam meeting Eve?

But the gray-green eyes remained inscrutable, flickering no more than a polite hello and then returning calmly to Paige.

"You were interested in riding lessons, Mrs. Spencer?"

"For our daughters this summer. The girls, Merry and Amanda, are nine."

"Have they ridden before?"

"No."

"Did you want private lessons, or with a group?"

"Private—just the two of them, I should think."

Patrick nodded, then looked down at the lesson-schedule book. "I could give them a first lesson this Saturday morning at ten. After that I would like to schedule their lessons for midweek, if that's convenient for you. I should keep the weekend times open for adults who can't come on weekdays."

"That would be fine," Paige said.

As Patrick started to write "Merry and Amanda" in the lesson book at ten on Saturday, the decision made, a *fait accompli,* Paige realized Julia hadn't spoken, hadn't agreed.

"Julia?"

"Is it safe, Patrick?" Julia answered Paige's question with one for Patrick. "Is it safe for nine-year-olds to ride?"

Patrick turned to Julia, surprised by the softness of her voice and the worry in it. He wondered if the concern was false, a pretension, but the lavender eyes were serious and the astonishingly beautiful face frowned, losing none of its beauty with the frown but instead enhancing its fragility.

"It's safe, Mrs. Lawrence." That was the truth. It was all Patrick needed to say. But he revealed a little more about himself in the words he spoke and in the

23

gentleness of his reassurance. "Horses are just big gentle creatures."

"Merry and Amanda are just little girls," Julia countered quietly.

"It's safe. Really. I will watch them very carefully."

"Would it be all right for us to watch, too, during the lessons?"

"Of course. If you like."

"Yes. Thank you."


As Paige and Julia walked from the stable back to the parking lot and lunch at Somerset instead of the Azalea Room, Paige asked Julia what she thought of Patrick.

"Oh," Julia replied absently, still preoccupied with the decision she had made and with the hope that it was right. "He seemed nice, didn't you think?"

"Yes." *I guess,* Paige amended silently. Nice, but a little menacing. What did Patrick do with the primal passions he stirred? Paige wondered. Did he satisfy the hungers? Or did he simply torment and tease and play with his prey? Did the panther prowl and devour? Or was he pure—provocative yet innocent—like Julia? Did he give his heart and his passion only to one true love, as Julia gave herself only, always, to Jeffrey?

Paige played with the questions briefly, then dismissed them. It mattered little to her whether Patrick James was an amoral panther, a noble savage, or an aristocratic cowboy. It didn't matter how he spent his private hours outside the riding ring. Even if he was this summer's seduction, as Paige imagined he would be, the season's most irresistible and intriguing sport for the ladies of Southampton, it didn't matter. All that mattered was that Patrick was a careful riding instructor. And she would be at the riding lessons, watching, making sure. And, because the first lesson was scheduled for Saturday, Edmund would be there, too.

"Maybe Jeffrey will be able to watch the lesson on Saturday," Paige suggested as they reached the parking lot.

"Oh." Julia's lavender eyes looked hopeful for a moment and then a little sad. "I don't know if he can."

"I hope he's not going to be out of town. Edmund and I are planning a small dinner party for Saturday evening."


"Paige and I are planning a small dinner party for Saturday evening." Edmund Spencer spoke the same words to Jeffrey Lawrence ten minutes later.

Edmund and Jeffrey were at Lutèce in midtown Manhattan for a business meeting over lunch. The business discussion had lasted almost the entire meal. At Jeffrey's request Edmund had reviewed the script for a soon-to-be-taped documentary on the Iran-Contra hearings. During lunch they had considered Edmund's questions and concerns point by point. Together they made small but critical changes in wording and added "alleged" in several places. Finally, as they drank coffee at the end of the meal, Edmund pronounced the script libel-free, not destined to be a repeat of the Westmoreland fiasco.

Business completed, the conversation shifted to other topics, personal ones, like dinner at Somerset on Saturday.

"I hope that you and Julia are free. I know you'll need to check with her," Edmund added with a smile. He and Paige had the same system — neither agreed to a social commitment without discussing it with the other and reaching a joint decision.

"That's the code, Edmund, but it hardly applies to seeing you and Paige. Julia and I always look forward to it."

"Thank you. Likewise."

"A small dinner party?" Jeffrey asked, curious. The Spencers and Lawrences had dinner together frequently, often at the last minute, casual get-togethers, not parties. The "parties" Paige and Edmund usually gave at Somerset or at the Southampton Club were always very grand and very elegant—black tie, satin and sequin gowns, hundreds of famous guests, silver fountains splashing vintage champagne. A *small* dinner party was unusual.

"It may be just the four of us and the newest member of my firm, a sensational trial attorney from California. This summer, while she studies for the New York Bar, she'll be living at our beach cottage."

"At SeaCliff?"

Jeffrey knew the small cottage perched on the cliffs very well. Somerset and Belvedere were adjacent estates, forested along their common border until the cliffs, where the forest opened to a spectacular panorama of sky and sea. As a boy, during the wonderful summers Jeffrey spent with his grandparents at Belvedere, he often made the long walk through the lush forest to the sea. When he reached the cliffs he would gaze at the vastness of the ocean and the sky, inhale the fresh salt air, and dream about the adventures that beckoned to him from beyond the azure horizon. Then he would scamper down the steep trail to the white sand beach and stand close enough to the water's edge to be splashed by the thundering waves.

Jeffrey never swam in the surf, never dove into the crashing waves, nor did battle with the powerful undertow. As a small boy he gave his grandparents a solemn promise that he never would. But later, when he was fifteen and won blue ribbons for the swim team at Exeter, he was very tempted. The surf was treacherous yet seductive, and he was such a strong swimmer! But Jeffrey resisted the temptation.

He had given his word.

Jeffrey had boyhood memories of SeaCliff, and he had a more recent one, a mature one, the most wonderful memory of all . . . an afternoon in May three years ago making love to Julia in a meadow of wildflowers above the sea.

"SeaCliff," Edmund echoed. "I'd forgotten the cottage had a name."

Edmund had almost forgotten about the cottage itself. The beach and cottage were in a distant corner of the huge estate, a corner he and Paige avoided because of Amanda and the lethal surf.

"Does she know about the surf?" Jeffrey asked.

"Yes, and promises not to swim."

"Good. So, Edmund, who is this sensational import from California?"

"Casey English."

"I don't recognize the name. Should I?"

"Not yet. But you will."

"Sounds impressive."

"She is. Very." Edmund smiled and added, "Casey's been impressive all her life. Through high school she attended the Carlton Academy in Atherton, just south of San Francisco. Carlton's a small school, very exclusive, academically rigorous, terribly expensive. But you've lived in the Bay Area, Jeffrey. Have you heard of it?"

"Yes. Some of my classmates at Stanford attended Carlton. As I recall, they did quite well."

"I imagine all graduates of Carlton do quite well. The academic requirements for admission are extremely rigid. No matter who you are, or how much money you have, you can't buy your way in. Because of the expense, most of the students are quite wealthy in addition to being exceptionally bright. But there are occasional scholarships for extremely gifted students who couldn't afford to attend otherwise."

"Like Casey?"

"What? Oh, no. Cost wasn't an issue for Casey, though I imagine she would have gotten a scholarship had she needed one. She graduated first in her class."

"The best of the best."

"Yes. She had similar academic success as an undergraduate at Berkeley and as a law student at Hastings. She clerked for our San Francisco office in the summer during law school. My San Francisco partners were dazzled, eager to keep her, but they assumed she'd join English and McElroy when she graduated."

"English?"

"Casey's father is Kirk Carroll English."

"A name I *have* heard of." Jeffrey smiled slightly at the understatement. Who hadn't heard of Kirk Carroll "K.C." English? The powerful high-profile attorney and his precedent-setting legal triumphs were legendary.

"Indeed. Anyway, Casey graduated first in her class from Hastings Law and surprised everyone by joining the San Francisco D.A.'s office."

"Altruism?"

"I'm not sure. I know she wanted rigorous trial experience. She felt what she'd learned in law school was a bit academic, more ivory tower than real world. But it may have been altruism, too. Casey is passionate about justice."

"Justice? Edmund, I thought justice was for judges and juries and the attorney's job was to . . ." Jeffrey searched for a tactful phrase.

"Win? No matter what?" Edmund smiled. "The euphemism, Jeffrey, is 'to provide the best defense.' "

"Ah, yes."

"Well, while she was in the D.A.'s office, Casey managed to do it all—provide the best defense, get justice, and win. Her record was truly remarkable. She won a number of very big cases, although none that could rival her final one. The defendant was a prominent and politically influential San Francisco

28

attorney."

"That sounds tricky."

"Tricky and potential professional suicide. The D.A. assigned the case to Casey assuming, I imagine, that she would review the evidence, decide there was little hope of winning, and recommend that it not be pursued. Especially given the charge."

"Which was?"

"Rape. Not a middle-of-the-night assault on a stranger, where you at least have the hope of concrete evidence, but *acquaintance* rape. At best a million shades of gray and virtually impossible to push beyond reasonable doubt."

"But Casey decided to try it."

"She met with the plaintiff and was convinced by her story. And, as she made abundantly clear in her opening arguments, Casey English doesn't see shades of gray in rape. As she eloquently explained to the jury, sex in which both parties aren't wholly, *enthusiastically,* consenting is rape, pure and simple. Casey defogged the issue. All the jury had to decide was if the plaintiff was consenting or not."

"And Casey prevailed."

"Actually, justice prevailed. As the trial progressed, other women — other victims — came forward. Just before the closing arguments the defendant changed his plea to guilty."

"That must have been dramatic."

"Yes, and an immense victory for Casey. The perfect swan song. As soon as the trial was over, she decided to leave the D.A.'s office and made it known that she wanted to join an East Coast firm. The trial of the Nob Hill Rapist may not have made the evening network news, but in legal circles it was quite important. Casey English was suddenly in great demand."

"And you got her. And she gets to spend the summer in one of the most idyllic settings on Long Island."

"I do hope she finds it idyllic," Edmund said thoughtfully. "Although she won't admit it, I think the trial took a bit of a toll on her. Many attorneys — perhaps even K.C. English himself — criticized Casey for taking the case. She was in the spotlight for months, and it was a harsh, glaring spotlight that only softened into limelight at the end. I've assured Casey that she'll have complete privacy at the cottage. I hope she'll find it a peaceful break." Edmund smiled enigmatically and added, "I am also glad that she'll be stretching her long legs on our secluded beach rather than along Fifth Avenue where she might be spotted by Eileen Ford."

"What?" Edmund was afraid that Casey might be spotted by a top New York modeling agent?

"You'd begun to form a mental image of Casey English, hadn't you, Jeffrey?"

"Well . . ." Jeffrey replied sheepishly. He *had* formed an image. The Casey English he imagined was prim, no-nonsense, a smart, unglamorous woman who was a little tough and a little — maybe a lot — rigid. "Tell me."

"In addition to being a brilliant attorney who is passionate about justice, Casey English is also model beautiful. And very charming."

"I look forward to meeting her."

"As I said, you and Julia and Casey may be the only guests, but Paige is going to call Diana to see if she and Chase can join us. You still haven't met them, have you?"

It had become almost a joke. Over the past two years, despite careful scheduling and best intentions, Jeffrey and Julia and Diana and Chase had still not met. Invariably one of the two couples had been unable to attend whenever Edmund and Paige hosted one of their grand affairs at Somerset or the Club. And every dinner for six planned weeks in advance at Le Cirque, La Côte Basque, or Lutèce had faltered at the last moment. Jeffrey would have to fly to Chernobyl or Manila or Lockerbie, or have to be in the studio covering a fast-breaking catastrophe; Edmund would be in the midst of a trial, encounter a surprise twist, and need to work into the night to plan the new strategy; Diana would have to perform emergency heart surgery even though she wasn't on call; Chase would have a crisis with a hotel he was building—Chase and Paige; and when Merry had the measles, Julia didn't want to leave her—and four hours later, when tiny red spots appeared on Amanda's fair skin, too, Paige and Edmund were glad that the evening out had already been canceled.

"No, I still haven't met either one. I do, however, have an appointment with Diana at three this afternoon."

"An appointment? With Diana? Jeffrey, are you all right?"

"What? Oh, yes, of course. I guess I should have said I have an interview with her this afternoon. It doesn't feel like an interview because it's just the two of us, no lights, no camera, only fifteen minutes. She doesn't have time for anything more than that today, and today is when I need to see her."

"Because of the heart surgery she's doing tomorrow on the Soviet ambassador."

"Yes. Naturally it's big news. Very much in the spirit of détente and *glasnost*. I'll be doing live reports about the operation so I want to learn as much as I can about the Shepherd Heart and its creator before tomorrow. Which means, if even briefly, at last I will meet the famous Queen of Hearts."

"I don't think Diana likes being called the Queen of Hearts." Edmund frowned uncertainly and admitted, "Of course, she's never actually said so, not to me, but I get that impression."

"Really? It seems so apt."

"It is. And it makes wonderful headlines. Diana

and Chase, the Queen of Hearts and the man who would be King. All of Manhattan could be their kingdom except for . . ."

"The Trump card."

"The Trump card," Edmund repeated quietly, solemnly acknowledging the monumental battle being waged by the two real-estate magnates. It was a battle of giants, stylistically so different yet each wanting to etch his signature, a permanent imprimatur, on the skyscape of Manhattan. It was a battle for Manhattan and a battle for immortality. "Anyway, since scheduling dinners together weeks in advance hasn't worked, we're trying the last-minute approach. Of course Diana may be on call Saturday and that will be that."

"This is quite a party you're planning, Edmund," Jeffrey said as he thought about the guest list. The men were impressive enough, but it was the women who truly dazzled—a famous heart surgeon, a brilliant trial attorney, a gifted architect . . . and Julia. Julia, who had left high school a month before graduation to marry him and have her daughter.

Would Julia feel uncomfortable—inadequate?—with these stunningly successful women? She wouldn't feel uncomfortable with Paige, of course, but with Diana and Casey . . . ? Jeffrey didn't know. He did know that his terribly bright wife, who *could* talk knowledgeably and insightfully on virtually any topic, would be silent as always. Would Julia spend the next few days dreading the evening? And when it arrived, would it be an ordeal for her? Jeffrey didn't know that, either.

He only knew that Julia wouldn't tell him.

"I'm particularly eager to have Casey meet Julia," Edmund said after a few moments of silence.

Jeffrey looked at him with surprise, wondering if kind and thoughtful Edmund had sensed his worry about Julia. But he was obviously quite serious.

"You want Casey to meet Julia?" Why? What

could Casey and Julia have in common? Clearly they were both very bright and beautiful, but Casey's summer would be spent studying for the New York Bar so that she could dazzle New York as she had dazzled San Francisco. And Julia's summer would be devoted as always to Merry.

"Yes. I don't know how much free time Casey will have, or will allow herself to have. She's brilliant, passed the California Bar with ease, but doubtless will study compulsively anyway. If she does allow herself any leisure time, though, I thought she might enjoy spending it with Julia."

"With Julia? Why?"

"Well, they both grew up in northern California. And they are practically the same age."

"The same age?" Jeffrey had revised his image of Casey to include beautiful and charming, but the sensational trial attorney whom Edmund was so pleased to have joining his prestigious firm was only Julia's age?

"Practically. Casey is just a year older than Julia."

When Jeffrey returned to the television studio at two-fifteen he learned that Dr. Diana Shepherd's secretary had called to cancel the three o'clock interview.

"The message," the booker told him, "is that Dr. Shepherd is still in the operating room and will be until at least six."

"Terrific," Jeffrey muttered sarcastically.

That morning, after the booker had met with immovable resistance, Jeffrey had personally spent a great deal of time and patience talking to Diana's secretary. He had politely listened to how busy Dr. Shepherd was today, then countered with how flexible he was, that he could see her at any time except during his evening broadcast. Diana's secretary had been polite but firm. Jeffrey had been polite but even more

33

firm. He didn't know if Diana was a silent participant in the negotiations—sending messages from the operating room—but finally he and her secretary had agreed to "fifteen or twenty minutes" beginning at three. And now . . .

"Her secretary said Dr. Shepherd would be willing to meet with you in her office after your broadcast, at eight, if you want."

"I want. Will you get a message to her that I'll be there?"

"Certainly."

"Good. Thanks."

Jeffrey walked into his office and pulled the door behind him. He noticed the folder on his desk—background information on Diana Shepherd M.D. assembled by his research team over the past few hours. Jeffrey now had plenty of time to carefully read the file before the eight o'clock interview—assuming it happened. Plenty of time to learn about Diana Shepherd and to prepare the evening newscast. Time to spare, time to call Julia.

Jeffrey called Julia often, if only for a few minutes, just to say hi, just to hear her voice.

"Hi, Julie."

"Jeffrey." Julia's soft voice filled with surprise and joy as it did every time he called. "How was your lunch with Edmund?"

"Very nice. Did Paige talk to you about a dinner party Saturday night?" *Does it terrify you?*

"Yes," Julia murmured, trying to recall what Paige had said, realizing that most of her thoughts had still been on the decision about Merry's riding lessons. "Something about a woman attorney who is joining Edmund's firm and will be spending the summer at the beach cottage . . . Jeffrey?"

"Yes, darling?" He heard the soft worry in her voice. *Tell me, Julie. If you don't want to go to the party, it's fine with me.*

34

"I just arranged for Merry to take horseback riding lessons at the Club. Do you think that's all right?"

"Why wouldn't it be?" Jeffrey heard the sudden sharpness in his voice and felt a stab of pain in the part of his heart that was a raw open wound. The conversation had shifted from his gentle worry that Julia might feel uncomfortable at Paige and Edmund's party to a discussion of Merry.

*Merry* . . . Julia's precious daughter, the living symbol of Julia's greatest deception, the ever-present reminder that he could never really trust the woman he loved with all his heart.

"I just thought it might be dangerous," Julia answered softly as she fought tears and anger. The tears were old and familiar, but the anger was new. Julia knew anger of course, anger at herself, but recently she had felt the beginning of anger toward Jeffrey. Jeffrey, whom she loved so very much, but who refused still, after all these years, to love his daughter.

Jeffrey heard the hurt in Julia's voice and reminded himself of the promise he had made to her three weeks before on their tenth wedding anniversary: *All right, Julie, yes. If that's what you want. We will be a family.* And he reminded himself of the vow he had made to himself: *I will try.*

"It's probably not dangerous, darling," Jeffrey said gently. "Especially if she's taking lessons at the Club. When does she start?"

"Saturday morning at ten."

"Would you like me to go with you?"

"Would you, Jeffrey?"

"Of course."

"Thank you."

*You're welcome, my Julie. I love you, and I made a promise to you.* Jeffrey wanted the thought to stop there, but after all these years the taunting thought had a life of its own. It continued defiantly, *Just as you promised me — ten years ago! — that there would be no more lies.*

Jeffrey took a breath, banished the rogue thought, and returned to his loving worry about her.

"Julie? About the dinner party."

"Oh, yes." Julia frowned, searching her memory, trying to recall what Paige had said. She didn't remember Paige's words, but she remembered her enthusiasm. "I think we should go, don't you? I got the impression from Paige that Edmund is delighted to have her joining the firm."

"Yes. He is. Did Paige tell you that she's about your age?"

"No. Really? She must be very impressive."

"Yes." Jeffrey sighed softly. If it bothered Julia, even if it terrified her, he would never know.

She would keep her fear hidden, nestled beside the other secrets of her heart.

## Chapter Three

The data assembled on Dr. Diana Shepherd by Jeffrey's research team included articles written about Diana, scientific articles written by Diana, and a copy of her curriculum vitae. Jeffrey read the articles with interest and made a surprising discovery when he read the C.V.

Diana Elizabeth Shepherd and Jeffrey Cabot Lawrence were born on exactly the same day thirty-six years before, she in Dallas, he in Boston. Who, Jeffrey wondered, had entered the world first on that distant November eleventh? And had the stars and moon and sun pulled with invisible strings on the just-born infants and mysteriously instilled similar traits in each?

Jeffrey Lawrence did not believe in astrology. "That proves you're a Scorpio!" Julia teased whenever he made the aloof pronouncement.

Jeffrey didn't believe in astrology, but his observant journalistic mind could not ignore the similarities between himself and Diana Shepherd.

Something deep inside had driven the two infants to set lofty goals, accomplish them, and then set new goals, loftier and more challenging, and accomplish *them*, too. Jeffrey knew the strength of his own ambition, and he saw the proof of Diana's in her impressive C.V. They both had abundant ambition and the other ingredients necessary to convert dreams and visions into reality: ability, determination, and drive.

Diana Shepherd was an achiever and so was he. Jeffrey guessed that, like him, she was demanding and perfectionistic, unused to failure and intolerant of it. *So?* So was almost every successful man or woman Jeffrey knew. Lofty ambitions, stunning successes, and intolerance of failure didn't make the celebrated Queen of Hearts his cosmic twin.

But there was the other similarity, the one in the photographs . . .

True, the rich sable-brown hair, intelligent ocean-blue eyes, and classically sculpted features conspired differently in each—softly in beautiful Diana and powerfully in handsome Jeffrey. Different, yet somehow the same. As Jeffrey studied a photograph of Diana, he decided the similarity was in the eyes, a resemblance beyond the darkest shade of blue, a sameness in the direct yet appraising way they viewed the world.

Did her serious sapphire eyes ever sparkle? Jeffrey wondered. Was there warmth in the deep-blue depths? He knew that his relentless drive and demands for perfection were softened by humor and love. Was there softness in Diana Shepherd, too? Was there a private place in her heart for laughter and love, a core of gentleness at the center of the steel?

Jeffrey couldn't answer those questions by looking at Diana's photograph. He wondered if he would find out when he met her tonight.


Jeffrey's driver brought the limousine to a gentle stop at the main entrance of Memorial Hospital at seven-fifty. The limousine and driver were provided by the studio and would be waiting to take him home to Southampton after the interview.

Jeffrey entered the hospital against a stream of humanity as the day's visiting hours came to an end. Once the visitors vanished, the hospital could settle into its quiet nocturnal routine. Even as Jeffrey approached the bank of elevators, the lights dimmed — nights lights replacing bright lights — a signal that the hospital and its overnight guests were going to bed.

Diana's office was on the tenth floor of the Heart Institute. As Jeffrey walked along the dark, deserted corridor, his footsteps eerily loud, he wondered if she would be in her office and how he would find her in this vast shadowy maze if she weren't.

In the distance he saw a golden beam, a beacon of light guiding him through the darkness. The light came from Diana's office. The door was ajar to enable the bright light to illuminate the shadows. Jeffrey heard voices from within — no, not voices, just one voice, soft, with the faintest trace of a Southern drawl . . . a voice that was smiling.

Jeffrey knocked softly and moved so that she could see who was knocking. Diana was at her desk, talking on the phone. She smiled a warm hello and waved a hand for him to enter.

"Thank you again, Paige. It will happen sometime! Please give my best to Edmund and Amanda. Good-bye." Diana replaced the receiver, then looked at Jeffrey.

"Dr. Shepherd," Jeffrey greeted her formally.

"Mr. Lawrence," she replied, matching his tone and formality. This was a professional interview, after all, and they had never met. But that was almost a technicality. Only a series of flukes — their busy careers and the illness of a little girl — had prevented their meeting before. Diana's dark-blue eyes sparkled as she added, "We meet at last."

"At long last. Please call me Jeffrey."

"I'm Diana." The hand Diana extended to Jeffrey, her handshake hand, was jewelless. On her other hand she wore a gold wedding band crowned with a glittering four-carat diamond.

As Jeffrey shook her hand he marveled that it was the hand of a virtuoso, and he was touching the talent. Guided by her brilliant mind and resolute determination, Diana's graceful and agile fingers had carved great fame for her—top honors at Harvard Medical School, a surgical residency at Massachusetts General Hospital, the "Heart" Fellowship at Memorial Hospital, her extraordinary reputation as a cardiac surgeon. Over the years Diana's fingers had shared their magical gifts with countless patients, but that wasn't enough, the fingers couldn't rest. When Diana wasn't operating, her fingers were hard at work writing the scientific papers that had won her international acclaim.

And—the most astonishing accomplishment of all—Diana's remarkable vision, brilliant mind, and talented hands had created the Shepherd Heart. Her creation was a giant step beyond heart transplantation, beyond the Jarvik Seven, beyond what medical science had dreamed even for the next decade. The Shepherd Heart was a twenty-first-century invention created by a woman of the eighties.

"Will we see each other again on Saturday?" Jeffrey asked after they had shaken hands. From what he had overheard when he arrived, Jeffrey guessed the answer was no.

"I'm afraid not. I'm on call this weekend." *And my husband left me three weeks ago, to think, to decide.* Diana frowned briefly, then forced away the painful memory with the hopeful thoughts she had held ever since Chase left: *Chase will come back. He will decide to spend his life with you. Believe it.*

"Too bad."

"Yes." *Yes. Chase will come back.*

"Sometime . . ."

"Please excuse my attire," Diana said suddenly, shifting the topic and gesturing gracefully at her outfit.

The top layer, a crisply starched white coat with the words *Diana Shepherd M.D.* embroidered in green, gave her the familiar professional appearance of a physician. But underneath the white coat Diana wore royal-blue surgical scrubs. The pajamalike cotton scrubs were loose-fitting except where she had cinched the drawstring of the trousers tightly around her slender waist. The Adidas running shoes she wore perfectly completed the image of fitness and energy and health. At a moment's notice, Jeffrey imagined, Diana could shed her white coat and dash off for a three-mile jog, or teach a class in advanced aerobics, or expertly navigate a sailboat in a brisk breeze on Long Island Sound.

"You look fine."

"A little informal. I was in my civvies, all dressed up for our interview, until one of my colleagues started a very tough case and asked me to be available. I'm sort of on stand-by." After a moment she added, feigning worry, but in fact sending a challenge, "Oh, I said 'case,' didn't I?"

"Yes."

"A medical term made distasteful by the media."

"And it shouldn't be distasteful?" Jeffrey asked. Diana's dark-blue eyes smiled but gave deeper signals, little flickers of annoyance and impatience, turbulence beneath the calm. She was multilayered, complicated, *critical*—as was he.

"Perhaps."

"And perhaps not. Tell me. Educate me, Dr. Shepherd."

"There seems to be a perception that simply ut-

41

tering the word 'case' instantly depersonalizes the patient and thereby compromises his or her care. However, whether I refer to you as a 'case', or even a very *tough* case"—a dark-blue sparkle told him she knew he could be tough—"or call you Jeffrey, I will always give you the best care I can possibly give."

"Maybe you're unique among physicians."

"I *know* that I'm not," Diana replied emphatically. Then, lightening her tone, she added with a slight smile, "However, media-bashing is just as bad as doctor-bashing, so that's the end of my minilecture."

"Except?" Jeffrey sensed there was more.

"Well, as long as I'm grinding an axe, and so far you don't seem too offended . . ." Diana tilted her head as she waited for confirmation.

"So far the sound isn't too grating. I'll let you know when I begin to feel steel splinters."

"OK. Speaking of depersonalization, the news media has made a 'case' of the Soviet ambassador. Witness the fact that although I have been putting new hearts in people—nice, everyday folks—for almost six months, only when the patient happens to be a V.I.P. does the nation's leading anchor want to meet with me. The ambassador has been depersonalized completely into a symbol of détente."

"It's a very big story," Jeffrey murmured quietly. Diana was right, of course. Not that her observation was a newsflash for him. It was something he thought about, worried about, and tried to improve. Jeffrey knew well that the feelings of victims and their families were all too often sacrificed for the "story" and that dramatic and explicit pictures of bodies and carnage frequently filled the airwaves in living—dying—color long after the tragic event was over.

"Yes, well, the real story is that the ambassador

is a fifty-six-year-old man who, like the fifty-six-year-old machinist I operated on last week, will die very soon without a new heart. The surgery may be an important step in Soviet-American relations — but for the ambassador it is a simple yet profound issue of mortality. Perhaps after tomorrow there will be more goodwill between Washington and Moscow. But all the ambassador cares about, and all *I* care about, is that perhaps after tomorrow he will have a chance to see his grandchildren."

"What can I say?" Jeffrey asked the intense sapphire eyes. "Point well taken, Doctor."

"Thank you . . . Anchor." Diana smiled. "Now, what would you like to know about tomorrow's surgery? I have a model of the Heart over here, fact sheets, brochures, visual aids. You're welcome to take everything, including the model, if it would be helpful for tomorrow's telecast. I do need the Heart back."

"Of course. That would be wonderful."

"Good." Diana closed the office door and led the way across her expansive office to a large oval oak table in front of a wall of windows that gave a panoramic view of Manhattan.

Jeffrey silently admired the magnificent view as they crossed the office, but when they reached the table his concentration focused entirely on the model of the Shepherd Heart. Diana's creation was made of clear plastic and was the size of four small clenched fists. Delicate wires were embedded in the plastic, webbing it with gossamer threads more fine than spun silk.

Jeffrey stared at the invention that was decades ahead of its time. It was so stark, so sterile, so clinical. What had he expected? Crimson plastic, heart-shaped, Diana's loving Valentine to the world? Filled with blood, of course, the Heart would become red. And, Jeffrey noticed, the wires connecting the model to the small boxes — the energy source and the tiny computer — were red and blue, small concessions to nature, wires the color of arteries and veins.

If his own heart failed would he want this webbed plastic placed inside him? Would he trust it to keep him alive? Could this stark, sterile creation beat with passion and love? Could it weep with pain and joy?

Jeffrey realized that Diana was waiting for him to ask questions. But the questions that filled his mind were philosophical, not technical.

"So, Dr. Shepherd, can you mend a broken heart?" he asked finally, frowning slightly, suddenly off guard, wondering if she would understand.

"No," she answered quietly. "It's a little scary, isn't it? A little nervy to remove a flesh-and-blood heart and replace it with a plastic one. I have to do that, though. I have to take out the entire native heart to make room for this one. I worried in the beginning about what I would be taking out with it."

"And?"

"The emotions and passions stay behind. All I do is replace a pump." Diana spoke softly, reverently, well aware of the profundity of what she did. "And I never call it an artificial heart. I call it a new heart. I call it . . . off the record, Anchor?"

"OK."

"I call it the Heart Nouveau."

"That's nice. Off the record, really?" Just like Queen of Hearts is off the record? The name was so perfect. Diana was so regal, even in her scrubs, her *royal*-blue scrubs.

"Really." Diana gazed at Jeffrey until he nodded agreement. Then she began to tell him how her Heart Nouveau worked, why it worked, all about the tiny computer in the wallet-size box that enabled the recipient to go anywhere, unencumbered by a machine, just like a normal human being — free. "The native heart responds to a complicated network of physiological impulses. It has been possible to simulate most of the physiological responses in the computer."

"Most, but not all? What's missing?"

"The mysteries beyond science. Like the inexplicable quickening of a heart as it falls in love. I don't know where that nerve synapse is. It's not programmed in a human being. How can I program it into a computer?"

They were interrupted by a knock at the door.

"Oh, dear," Diana apologized in advance. "That's probably someone from the O.R."

Jeffrey smiled. "They need help with the *case*."

"Yes. I'm afraid so."

"It's not a problem. I'm happy to wait."

Jeffrey watched as Diana crossed the office and opened the door. It was immediately obvious from her expression that it was not a messenger from the O.R. The intrusion was altogether different . . . and surprising. Jeffrey couldn't see the man, but he could hear his words as well as Diana's.

"Dr. Diana Shepherd?"

"Yes."

"Mrs. Chase Andrews?"

"Yes. Has something happened to Chase?" Diana's tone shifted swiftly from polite curiosity to sharp concern.

"This is for you, ma'am."

"What . . . ?" Diana took the envelope the man handed her. The engraved return address was a law firm on Park Avenue, not the familiar Madison Avenue address of Spencer and Quinn. Diana didn't finish the question because she already guessed its ominous answer; the clues were suddenly obvious and terribly painful.

"Divorce papers, Dr. . . . uh, Mrs. Andrews."
The process server answered Diana's unfinished
question anyway. His mission was accomplished:
she had been served. His tone conveyed a mocking
message. *How can you be surprised, Doctor? Here
you are at eight o'clock at night working instead of
being at home, and not even bothering to change
your name.* "The papers will be filed with the
court tomorrow morning."

The process server vanished quickly, leaving Diana with the envelope and its painful message.
Chase had made his decision.

For a long, silent moment Diana's heart and
mind were suspended between the new pain and an
ancient one—when she hadn't been enough for a
man she loved once before. Finally the disciplined
part of her that helped her go on always, no matter how deep the anguish and loss, pulled her back
to the present.

Diana slowly shut the office door and turned to
Jeffrey.

"I guess you heard."

"Yes."

"I would appreciate it if you would keep this off
the record."

"Once the papers are filed with the court it will
be in the public domain." *And it will be a very big
story.* "The court reporters are paid to check."

"I know. I'm just asking you not to mention it
tomorrow in your coverage of the surgery."

"I'm not a tabloid journalist, Doctor." Didn't she
know he wouldn't consider mentioning her private
life—ever—in his newscast? Realizing that his tone
had sounded harsh, Jeffrey added gently, "You
have my word."

"Good. Thank you. Now, where were we?"

*We were talking about the mysteries of the
quickening of a heart as it falls in love, Jeffrey*

46

thought, but he said, "You were telling me about the programming of the physiological responses."

"Oh, yes."

Diana put the unopened envelope on her desk as she walked back to the oval table by the window. She resumed the explanation of her remarkable invention, but her eyes no longer sparkled and her voice was like the plastic heart — stark, sterile, clinical.

*What is she feeling?* Jeffrey wondered. *Does she want to scream with pain? What kind of heart beats inside the Queen of Hearts? A heart of ice? No heart at all?*

*A wounded heart,* Jeffrey decided as he listened to her mechanical words and glanced carefully into her cloudy sapphire eyes. *A deeply wounded heart.*

"I'm sorry," Jeffrey said quietly and sympathetically.

"It's . . ." Diana didn't finish the sentence, but her eyes communicated her thought, her warning, quite eloquently: *Stay away.*

Jeffrey understood the warning and the emotion behind it. Diana was reacting just as he would. Private grief, private rage, resentful of intrusion.

*Just as he would react.* That was what was so eerie. Before his eyes Diana was living the nightmare that haunted him, the secret fear that someday Julia might do this to him. *I'm leaving you, Jeffrey. It's over. There is someone else. There always has been.*

The scene would be just as it had been for Diana. One night, while he was still at the studio, a man would arrive with divorce papers. The blow would stun, but Jeffrey would recover quickly on the surface as Diana had. And in those anguished moments when the nightmare became a reality, he would not want the soft sympathetic voice of a stranger. He would want to be alone, face-to-face

47

with the truth, face-to-face with his loss, his emptiness, his *failure*.

So leave Diana alone, Jeffrey told himself sensi-
bly. But his heart had an emotional answer, an
urge to help the bright, beautiful, wounded
woman.

*Besides,* he reminded himself. *Who says Diana
and I are really alike? The stars?*

"Chase could have picked a better time," Jeffrey
offered very quietly.

"What do you mean?" Diana reflected on her
own question for a moment and then finding an
answer, she continued coolly, "Oh, I see, sometime
when I had surgery scheduled on someone not so
*important* as the Soviet ambassador? Just another
*case* instead of a media event? You weren't listening to me earlier, were you?"

"Yes, I was. I meant that Chase could have
picked a time when you would be able to have
some privacy."

"You think I'm going to unravel, don't you?"

"No." Jeffrey hadn't even considered it. If he was
presented with divorce papers ten hours before his
newscast—or even ten minutes—he would be able
to go on, a mechanical presentation, perhaps, but
he would function. Of course Diana's situation was
quite different. In ten hours she had to remove a
dying heart and replace it with a new one. Could
she really operate ten hours from now? *Should*
she? If Jeffrey gave a lackluster and distracted telecast, he might get a few critical letters. More likely,
the letters would be sympathetic. Had the nation's
favorite anchorman been ill? The flu, perhaps? But
a distracted performance in the operating room
could be lethal. "Are you still . . ."

"Going to operate on the ambassador?" Diana
finished Jeffrey's question and stared at him with
eyes that were suddenly alive with anger.

48

"Yes," he replied quietly.

Diana fought to control her rage before speaking again. It was a legitimate question, of course, but not one she needed him to ask. She would ask herself that question, find her own private answer, and act accordingly, ethically.

"For the record, Mr. Lawrence," she whispered finally, a whisper of ice, "I would *never* jeopardize the welfare of my patient. If I am not prepared, for whatever reason, to give my very best, then I do not operate."

Jeffrey was about to apologize. He owed her an apology. He had assaulted her integrity. His attempt to help, to sympathize, had only offended. But the phone rang as he started to speak and Diana turned away to answer.

It was the operating room. She was needed.

"I have to go," she said flatly after she hung up. "The brochures and fact sheets should cover any areas I didn't discuss. Please close the door when you leave."

Then she was gone without a good-bye and before Jeffrey could offer either an apology or a thank-you.

As he put the brochures in his briefcase and the model of the Heart in its white cardboard box, he realized that Diana had been the first to leave, but he was the one who had been dismissed.

It was the Queen of Hearts who had decided when his audience with her was over.


The aching feeling that he had been the unwitting witness to a death—the death of a love—clung tenaciously to Jeffrey as the limousine made its way from Manhattan to Southampton. He guessed that Diana had been a little prepared; the divorce was something she feared even though she hoped it would never happen.

But even if Diana had been *completely* prepared, expecting it, the actual moment, like the moment of an expected death, was achingly somber, irrevocable, the end of hope—the empty forever end of all the joyous promises of love.

The eerie feeling clung and ominous thoughts taunted. Beautiful, successful, talented Diana had been unable to prevent the death of her marriage. Couldn't the same fate befall him? One night, perhaps tonight, he would return to Belvedere and Julia would be gone. She would leave a note, an apology: *Merry is not your daughter. She and I need to be with her father. I am so sorry, Jeffrey, please forgive me.*

Jeffrey fought the ominous thoughts with reason. The aching he felt was for Diana, *her* loss, *her* pain. What happened tonight wasn't a message from the stars, an astrological augur of things to come for him and Julia.

Still . . .

When Julia opened the mansion door Jeffrey felt his heart quicken—the wonderful and mysterious flutters of love that even the brilliant Queen of Hearts could not define.

"Julie," Jeffrey whispered softly, a joyful, relieved whisper of love.

"Hi." Her lavender eyes shimmered, happy to see him, relieved, too, as always, that Jeffrey had come home to her. "Is this the Heart?"

"Yes."

Jeffrey set his briefcase on the floor in the foyer and removed the plastic model from the cardboard box. He held the Heart for Julia and watched as her fingers delicately traced the webbed contours and her eyes became thoughtful and serious as her mind filled with the philosophical questions that he, too, had pondered.

"Will you tell me about it?" Julia asked. She hoped that even though Jeffrey was home later than usual they would sit in the great room as always — Jeffrey with a glass of Scotch and she curled against him — and talk. Like lovers resentful of any moments apart, they would share the events of their days, lovingly filling in the gaps of life when they couldn't be together.

"Yes, I will tell you about it. . . ." Jeffrey hesitated, frowning slightly. He was home and she was here and her eyes glowed with love . . . but the fears still lingered.

"Jeffrey?"

"Just let me hold you a minute first." *Let me hold you and touch you and know that you are real and my fears are only imagined.*

Jeffrey put the model of the Heart on the marble table in the foyer. Then, not so confidently, he extended his arms to her.

Julia went to him swiftly, joyfully. *Just hold me always, Jeffrey. There is nowhere else I would rather be.*

The delicate, gentle hug became a strong, tight one, as close as they could be. Julia responded eagerly as his arms wrapped tighter, molding to him, her soft loveliness kissing his lean strength. Jeffrey's lips brushed the top of her silky black hair, caressing, nuzzling, whispering her name.

Julia looked up, saw the desire in his dark-blue eyes and felt a wave of trembling heat sweep through her. Smiling softly, she raised her lips to his.

Like the hug, the kiss began gently, softness touching softness, but, like the hug, the kiss gained strength and energy. Jeffrey was hungry for her and Julia was hungry for him. The kiss became warmer, deeper, closer, but it was still not enough.

"More?" Jeffrey whispered finally.

*More* was a word in the intimate vocabulary of their loving. From the very beginning of their love, a kiss had never been enough. They had always wanted more of each other, *all* of each other.

"More," Julia breathed.

They walked, hands entwined, up the sweeping circular staircase, beyond the room where Merry lay sleeping, to the master suite. The balmy night air floated gently through the open windows, carrying with it the fragrance of roses from the garden below. The perfume of a hundred roses came in through the windows and so, too, did the golden glow of the full summer moon.

Neither Jeffrey nor Julia moved to close the windows or drapes. Only the moon could see them, and neither wished for darkness while they loved.

Jeffrey made love to her slowly, a leisurely, sensual loving despite the powerful waves of desire that wanted all of her *now*. His hands explored gently, delicately caressing her graceful neck, her creamy shoulders, her soft, full breasts . . .

Jeffrey's gentle hands led the way, and his hungry lips followed. Hungry lips, talented lips. Rough and gentle, loving and teasing, whispering and probing, Jeffrey sensed her trembling desires and lovingly, expertly, answered them.

No part of Julia's naked loveliness was a secret to him. She gave all of herself to him, a joyous and unashamed gift of love and passion. No part was secret, no part forbidden. After ten years of loving, he knew her so well. And yet discovering her anew still held such mystery and such wonder.

Jeffrey made love to her and Julia made love to him. She knew his desires, too, and all the lovely ways to make him moan so softly. She loved to give him pleasure, loved to kiss brave, delicate, exquisite kisses until . . .

"Julie, darling." *I need you, all of you,* now.

"Jeffrey." *I need you, too*.

The wandering lips found each other, exploring there, deep and warm. And then they were together, where he belonged, where she wanted him to be. He stopped the kiss, but not the rhythm of their loving, to gaze into her moonlit eyes and whisper to her.

"I love you, Julie."

"I love you, too, Jeffrey."

They held the loving gaze as long as they could, until the crescendoing waves of desire took control, forcing their lips to join again and even their eyes to close. Then, swiftly, *swiftly* and together, they melted into a molten golden river of joy. And they were one, forged together by the fire of their passion and their love . . . so close that there was no room for secrets.


Julia fell asleep in Jeffrey's arms, nestled close, warm and lovely. She breathed softly, delicate whispers of contentment, and a gentle smile curled her lips. Jeffrey gazed at her and marveled at the perfection of this moment.

Sometimes—most of the time—their love was so perfect, like a brilliant diamond bathed in sunlight, a glittering kaleidoscope of color, ever-changing, ever-wondrous, always breathtakingly beautiful.

Perfect, glittering, and flawless—to the naked eye.

But their magnificent love, like all but the rarest of diamonds, wasn't free of flaws. What marriage, what love, was flawless?

None, of course. Jeffrey knew that. But their flaw, the tiny flaw in their almost perfect love, could be a fatal one.

The flaw was so tiny, so trivial compared to the immensity of his love, but, like the tiniest flaw in a

53

beautiful diamond, it could destroy. The virtually indestructible stone could be shattered by a soft blow placed just so. The glittering gem could crumble into a million pieces, the wonder gone, the brilliance a mere memory, the rainbow of dazzling colors clouded to gray.

The flaw was Julia's lie to him about Merry. Jeffrey knew he wasn't Merry's father—he could not be—but Julia had told him, her lavender eyes so innocent, so bewildered, so unflickering, *You are her father, Jeffrey. There has never been anyone else.*

And all these years she had resolutely continued the charade, protecting the secret lover she defiantly claimed didn't exist. So many times she could have told him the truth! He encouraged her, gently, lovingly, and sometimes angrily, but Julia steadfastly maintained the ancient lie. Jeffrey didn't know the reason she kept her secret still, and that was what terrified him . . .

Because, from the very beginning, Julia had only deceived him about the important things.

# Chapter Four

San Francisco
February 1979

The day was perfect, the winter sun warm, the sea breeze invigorating, the sky bright blue and cloudless. As Jeffrey wandered through the Saturday-afternoon activity of Ghirardelli Square he was amazed by the rush of nostalgia that swept through him. It was his last day in San Francisco, and his last day, too, as a local reporter. Soon the camera crew would arrive and Jeffrey would tape his fond farewell to his loyal viewers. Then, once the taping was over, he would drive to Los Angeles and his new job as a network correspondent. He was eager to be on his way; the prospect was exhilarating, thrilling, but still . . .

He would always remember this elegant, stylish, sophisticated city. And he would remember this perfect day. He would etch today in his memory and recall its gentle sunny images on future days in distant cities ravaged by war; cities whose children didn't scamper across emerald-green lawns trailing silver-tailed kites but cowered instead on sun-parched grass splattered red with blood; cities whose daytime sounds weren't laughter and music but rather the thunder of mortar and the anguished cries of death. He would recall the memory of this flawless day as a gentle antidote when the new visions of his life became too grim.

He crossed the park in front of Ghirardelli Square to the edge of the Bay and watched the sleek sailboats gliding swiftly across the sparkling whitecapped water, etching those graceful images, until a bell sounded, signaling the hour and drawing him from his reverie.

As Jeffrey turned to join the just-arrived camera crew, he saw her. She sat cross-legged on the grass, her long black hair dancing in the wind, her lavender eyes gazing serenely at the sea, and her full lips curled into a soft smile.

He added her image—a beautiful San Francisco woman—to the other images of the day. Not that he needed an image of a San Francisco woman. He had known many. But she was a perfect symbol of all the others he had known, so serene, so elegant, so beautiful.

As he was making a permanent memory of the lavender eyes, midnight-black hair, and sublime beauty, she turned her remarkable eyes from the sea to him. The lavender flickered with surprise, as if she had recognized him, then confusion, as she realized he was a stranger. Suddenly shy and embarrassed, she looked down, her long inky-black lashes delicately closing over her eyes like tiny fans.

Jeffrey felt surprise, and recognition, and confusion, too, but he didn't become embarrassed nor did he look away. Instead he stared at her, willing her to look at him again. When she obeyed his silent command, bravely lifting her magnificent lavender eyes to him, there was surprise, still, and recognition, again, but now the confusion was replaced by wonder.

She had recognized him, but it wasn't the familiar recognition—"Oh, you're Jeffrey Lawrence from Channel Four News!"—it was deeper, and he felt it, too.

It was a recognition of the heart.

Jeffrey suddenly felt the immense relief of being found, even though he had never known he was lost. And he suddenly felt full, a joyous, bountiful fullness, even though he had never for a moment in his splendid successful life felt empty. And he felt the triumph that accompanies the discovery of the missing piece in a puzzle, the piece that instantly makes the confusing picture crystal clear, even though he hadn't known there was a puzzle much less a missing piece.

For an astonished moment Jeffrey was lost in the wonderful-and-so-powerful feelings and lost, too, in her magnificent eyes and their seductive invitation: *Come be with me forever.*

The moment felt like an eternity, but in fact it was brief. Jeffrey's disciplined mind intervened, willing control over his racing heart and swirling thoughts, forcing a perfunctory spell-breaking smile on his lips, and commanding his legs to continue walking away from her and toward the crew and his future.

Jeffrey walked away, but he was shaken, and the inquisitive mind that had already won so many awards in investigative journalism sought answers.

*You simply gift-wrapped her in your surprising nostalgia about leaving San Francisco,* he told himself.

The explanation seemed sound. Emotion and sentiment had played very small roles in his life, cameo appearances, well scripted in advance. Today the sentimentality and emotions he felt about San Francisco had caught him by surprise. Those unfamiliar feelings, used to dormancy and suddenly awakened, had become rogues, awakening other fantastic feelings.

Fantastic feelings like falling in love? Of course not! His emotions had simply gone awry on this sentimental day. It had to do with him, not her.

Still, as Jeffrey taped his adieu to San Francisco, his gaze drifted to where she sat and he sent a silent command: *Don't leave*. As soon as the taping was over he would speak to her and prove that it was nothing to do with her, only his own surprising emotions, and he would be on his way to Los Angeles.

*Don't leave,* Jeffrey silently commanded the beautiful woman with lavender eyes. *Be there, so I can say hello and good-bye.*

Julia didn't leave. She was sitting on the grass still, even though the winter sun had set, taking the gentle warmth from the air and leaving in its golden wake an icy chill. As Jeffrey approached, closer than he had been before, he saw that she was even more beautiful, more bewitching, but less sophisticated. Her loose-fitting jeans bore no designer label. Her pale-yellow cotton blouse was faded from many washings. Her V-neck blue sweater was threadbare and not cashmere. She didn't have an elegant purse fashioned by Gucci or Coach, in fact no purse at all, and no jacket. And on her lap, its title turned from his view, she held a book. The book was like her clothes, threadbare and tattered, its navy cloth cover frayed and showing cardboard.

"Hi. I'm Jeffrey."

"I'm Julia."

A gust of wind swept a strand of her long black hair into her eyes and across her lips. Julia's fingers trembled as she pulled the strand away.

"Are you cold?"

"A little, I guess," Julia admitted, although she had been trembling ever since she first met his dark-blue eyes, long before the sun fell into the sea.

"Would you like to go somewhere warm?" *Like to Southern California?* one of the frolicking rogues taunted. He reminded the frisky thought that he was only going to say hello and good-bye, to prove there was nothing. But there wasn't nothing. Her lovely eyes, her soft voice, her well-worn clothes had hold of his heart and wouldn't let go.

"Yes. Thank you."

*"Jane Eyre."* Jeffrey read the title of her tattered book as she stood. "A favorite?"

Julia nodded. She was proud to admit that the wonderful romance was a favorite. Proud and fond. Strong, patient Jane and handsome, troubled Rochester were beloved friends. Julia almost told Jeffrey that she hadn't damaged the book—she wouldn't do that to her friends!—despite the many times she had read it. Others had caused the damage, reading carelessly, but because of their carelessness the precious volume had found its way to a used bookstore and had been marked with a price just short of nothing, a price that Julia could afford.

"Here. Wear this," Jeffrey said as he draped his jacket around her slender shoulders. "So, shall we get a drink? Hot buttered rum? Irish coffee?"

*He thinks I'm at least twenty-one,* Julia realized with a tremble of excitement and fear.

59

"Just coffee would be fine."

"How about chowder? It's turned into that kind of day."


The Chowder House on Fisherman's Wharf was a warm sanctuary for others who sought escape from the sudden chill of the winter twilight. The popular restaurant was crowded and noisy, but Jeffrey and Julia were lost in their own world, in a wooden booth scarred by the initials of a hundred young lovers, enveloped by the warm scent of fresh-baked sourdough bread, the steaminess of the restaurant, and the magnificent feelings of being together.

"You're an actor," Julia said softly, stating it as fact even though she wasn't sure. It was what she had deduced from watching the stunningly handsome man standing before camera crews and surrounded by admirers. He was probably a famous movie star. If she had had money to spend on movies, she might have known for certain.

"You really don't know who I am?" Jeffrey asked gently, not wanting to embarrass her and quite pleased that she wasn't a fan.

"No, I'm sorry, I don't."

"For the last four years I've been a reporter with Channel Four News. The segment we just taped was my final one. I begin work with the network in Los Angeles on Monday. How about you, do you live here?"

"I live in Berkeley." She added quietly, apologetically, "I don't watch television."

There was a television in the tiny house in Berkeley where Julia lived with her aunt Doreen, but it was in her aunt's bedroom and off limits to Julia.

60

*You don't watch television and you must not read newspapers, either,* Jeffrey mused. In the past few weeks all the Bay Area papers had run pieces about him, his summa cum laude graduation from Stanford, his extraordinary career at Channel Four, the excellence-in-journalism awards he had won, his promotion to the big leagues of network news, and his never-before-disclosed pedigree . . .

Jeffrey Cabot Lawrence was one of the truly wealthy. He wore his heritage of generations of wealth and privilege the way the forever wealthy do, quite casually, like a coat slung over the arm in case of rain. But close examination of the raincoat would reveal it was the best, perfectly tailored, just as close examination of Jeffrey revealed his perfect manners, his impeccable taste, and his love of the expensive and rare.

Jeffrey's appeal, his elegance and style, was suddenly explained. He was an aristocrat. It had to do with breeding, not money, although Jeffrey's personal fortune was already immense. Still, he worked for a living, worked very hard, and no blue-blooded strings had been pulled to get him the job at Channel Four or the important promotion to the network. Jeffrey Lawrence was a rich kid who could have done nothing, but chose to make his own way and create his own success. The facts about Jeffrey made his devoted fans even more devoted.

Most of the Bay Area—the viewing and reading public—knew all about Jeffrey Lawrence.

But Julia did not.

"You are famous, aren't you?" she asked, remembering the crowd that had assembled to get his autograph after the taping.

"Not really. A little local fame."

61

"But you *will* be famous."

"Yes, I guess, if I accomplish what I hope to accomplish. The fame doesn't matter."

"Only the dreams."

"Yes," Jeffrey whispered, stunned by her choice of words. They *were* dreams, of course, and he thought of them that romantic way, but to others he had always referred to them as "career goals," not "dreams." Until now . . . "Only the dreams."

Jeffrey told Julia about his dreams. He used the words he always used when he talked about his plans, but Julia understood as no one ever had before.

"I love being at the heart of a news story as it unfolds, being an eyewitness and reporting what I see. So far I've just done local stories, but I hope to travel overseas and report from politically turbulent places."

*That will give you a lot of camera time, won't it, if you're in the Middle East or somewhere?* the beautiful and sophisticated women who had been Jeffrey's lovers would ask when he told them. Then they would smile knowingly and add, *And you'll become famous and return as a network anchor.*

That all might happen, of course, but that wasn't Jeffrey's reason.

"That's very important," Julia replied quietly.

"I think so," Jeffrey answered even more quietly. That was his reason, because he believed it was important, not because it was a path to celebrity or fame. The planet was small, so small. Little political fires in distant places could spark destruction for all of mankind. That was Jeffrey's reason for his dream. The lovely intelligent lavender eyes knew his dream was important, but did they know why? Part of Jeffrey didn't want to ask, didn't want to hear Julia say, *It's important because you'll get a lot of camera time and then you can return as a network anchor.* But part of him, the part that was beginning to believe that unbeknownst to him his heart had been searching for her all his life, wanted to know. "Why do you think it's important, Julia?"

"Because the planet is so small."

As they curled their hands around the bowls of steaming chowder, feeling the warmth but not eating because their mouths had better things to do — talking and smiling and falling in love — Jeffrey softly told Julia, who already knew, the truth about his dreams.

Jeffrey told Julia the truth. Julia told Jeffrey some truths, too, and she told him some lies.

"You said you're from Berkeley. Are you a student?"

"Yes." Julia *was* from Berkeley and she *was* a student. But she knew that Jeffrey was asking if she was a student at the university and that with her Yes she was deceiving him.

"What year are you?"

"A senior." True, too, in a way. Julia was a senior in high school, even though she was only sixteen, a year, two years younger than most of her classmates.

"And what will you do when you graduate, Julia? Tell me your dreams." Jeffrey watched the lovely lavender eyes become confused. "Julia?"

"I . . . I don't know."

"When I first saw you today you were gazing out at the Bay and smiling. What were you thinking about then?"

63

"Just a make-believe story."

"A story about what?"

Julia looked at the wonderful, handsome man who made her feel so safe, magically luring her from her painful shyness, encouraging her to speak and welcoming her quiet words with a gentle smile.

"About love."

"Love," Jeffrey echoed softly. "Are you going to be a writer, Julia? A modern-day Charlotte Brontë?"

Julia considered his question, testing that dream, and finally said quietly, "I don't think so."

"What then?" Jeffrey pressed gently. "What is your dream?"

He thought she wouldn't answer. Her cheeks flushed pink and her eyes were confused again. He waited, smiling and sending silent messages: *Tell me, Julia. Trust me with your secret dreams.*

Julia had never dared to dream, but she had lovely wishes that lived in a part of her heart hidden even from her, a delicate, fragile place where hope and love lived still despite all the losses of her young life.

Jeffrey discovered that delicate, fragile, hopeful place.

"My dream is to make a happy life for someone I love," Julia whispered bravely. "It's not very important." *Compared to risking your life to save mankind.*

"Yes it is." Jeffrey spoke from a hidden place in his heart, a place of tenderness and love that Julia had discovered. "It is very important." *Nurturing a precious love may be the most important dream of all.*

\* \* \*

"I love the sea," Jeffrey told her as they walked along the Wharf beneath the starry sky. The fishing boats creaked in their moorings, rocked by the brisk wintry wind and the whitecapped waves.

"It scares me."

"It does?" Jeffrey looked with surprise into the lavender eyes that hours earlier had gazed so serenely at the sea as she imagined stories of love.

"It's very beautiful when the sunshine glitters off it, but at night it seems so dark and cold." Julia could overcome her fear of the sea—she was teaching herself to overcome it, in the daylight, from a distance, by gazing at the sparkling blue and thinking about love. But at night, this close to the swirling water was terrifying. It would take longer to overcome the nighttime fears . . . because it was at night that the plane carrying her parents became a coffin of fire and fell into the dark cold depths. "And I don't know how to swim."

Julia's soft shrug became a tremble as an icy chill of fear swept through her. Jeffrey wrapped his arms around her, pulling her close, protecting her from the turbulent sea, wanting her never to be afraid.

And wanting more . . .

Her soft lips were cool at the surface because of the winter wind, but beneath, just beneath, there was fire and passion.

Julia had never kissed anyone before, but her lips discovered his instinctively with caresses that were timid and brave, gentle and ravenous. Timid and gentle with wonder. Brave and ravenous from a lifetime of hunger. Julia's hands explored instinctively, too, curling around his neck, weaving into his hair, and her body kissed his, pressing softly against him and trembling.

Jeffrey felt Julia's trembling and stopped his tender kisses to look at her. Her shivering was desire, not the winter wind, just as he trembled with desire for her.

"More?" he asked softly.

"More," she whispered, not knowing what she was agreeing to, but knowing that she couldn't say no.

Jeffrey got them a room at a motel on the Wharf. While he pulled the curtains and hung the jacket he had given her and turned the thermostat for heat and hooked the Do Not Disturb sign on the door handle, Julia searched for answers to the questions that swirled in her mind.

What was she supposed to do? What did he expect? She wanted to give him pleasure, but she had no experience. The romances she read were wonderful fantasies of love, not guide books of loving. But if she told Jeffrey the truth—how young she was and how innocent—the night would be over, wouldn't it? His gentle blue eyes would darken with disappointment, or perhaps even anger, that she had deceived him, and he would tell her to leave.

And, oh, how she didn't want to leave him! The thought filled her with emptiness greater than all the losses of her young life. *I have to* act *experienced,* she told herself. But how?

With trembling fingers and a prayer that it was right, Julia began to undress. By the time Jeffrey turned to devote his attention to her for the entire night, Julia had removed her threadbare sweater and pale-yellow cotton blouse and folded them neatly on a chair beside the bed. Julia had worn no bra that day, so with the removal of her blouse

66

and sweater she was naked above the waist.

Naked and so beautiful, her skin rich and white, her full breasts high and proud. Julia stood before him, shy and brave, awaiting his appraisal and praying his eyes would fill with approval and desire.

"Julia. What are you doing?" Jeffrey asked gently as he moved toward her.

He had wondered if there had been a flicker of lavender uncertainty when he suggested a motel and had almost told her then that they could kiss all night, or talk, or sleep . . . but now she stood before him, half naked, the most beautiful woman he had ever seen.

"Oh." Julia frowned. Isn't this what I am supposed to do?

"You are so beautiful."

Jeffrey kissed the lovely frown away. Then his lips found hers and his gentle hands found her nakedness and Julia didn't have to worry about her inexperience because loving Jeffrey was as instinctive as kissing him had been. And for the first time in his years of expert, skillful lovemaking, loving was instinctive for Jeffrey, too. Always before, in the midst of pleasure, Jeffrey's mind was engaged, *Now I should do this*. His lovers proclaimed him *the best,* but that was simply Jeffrey, excelling at whatever he did.

He had made love many times before, with elegance and finesse, but never until Julia had he *loved*. Never, until Julia, had there been a purpose to the intimacy except pleasure. Now, beyond the exhilarating pleasure of touching her, was an urgent need to be as close to her as possible, to be part of her, to be one with her.

Jeffrey explored her exquisite, sensual body,

touching hello, kissing hello, wanting to be all places at once. He was hungry for all of her, but he forced extraordinary control over his own desires, discovering her desires, savoring each new discovery, returning often to her eyes and her lips. Julia's perfect body responded without shame, arching to him, hiding nothing, keeping no secrets. She gave him all of her loveliness, a breathless trembling gift of joy.

Julia heard the lovely soft sighs of joy and realized with astonishment that they came from deep within her, carried from her heart to her lips on rushes of happiness. And she heard, too, the wonderful soft deep sighs that came from him.

"Julia?" Jeffrey whispered finally when he could force control no longer, when he needed so desperately to be one with her.

"Jeffrey." She welcomed him and there wasn't any pain, not even a little, even though she was a virgin, because he had been so very gentle . . . as if he knew.

"My darling Julie."

"No one has ever called me Julie," she said quietly as she lay in his arms and his lips caressed the tangle of her silky black hair. No voice had ever before softened with affection for her. She had always been Julia, a serious name, not Julie, a tender loving one.

"Never?"

"Never."

"May I?"

"Oh, yes."

"Julie," Jeffrey whispered again.

He whispered her name over and over as he

showed her his love. And sometime during their astonishing night of loving, Jeffrey embellished her name, speaking aloud what he already knew in his heart, a joyous, confident, wondrous knowledge . . . words he had never spoken before. "I love you, Julie. I love you."

Ten hours before he was to begin his new job with the network in Los Angeles, Jeffrey left Julia at the Telegraph Avenue entrance of the Berkeley campus. He left her reluctantly, missing her in advance, dreading already the twelve days until she could visit him in L.A.

As soon as his car was out of sight, Julia began the two-mile journey to the dilapidated house where she lived with her aunt Doreen. Her journey took her far away from the bright lights of Telegraph, but she was unafraid of the dangers that lurked in the remote dark streets of Berkeley. She had spent her life roaming streets filled with menacing strangers and she had survived.

And tonight, even if she had been afraid, her fears would have been vanquished by the magical words that echoed in her mind: *I love you, Julie.*

No one had ever loved Julia, not her parents, not her aunt, certainly never a man. Julia didn't know why she was unloved, only that she was. As a little girl she reached the only conclusion she could: something about her made her undeserving of love. Was it her shyness? Her seriousness? She didn't know. And she had no way of knowing that it had merely been her great misfortune to be born to parents who were too flawed and self-absorbed to love their daughter.

Julia's parents had been flower children. She was

an accidental bud, a fragile blossom who should have been cherished but was only neglected. She became a wildflower, delicate but hardy, surviving the elements without protection. Until she was ten Julia and her parents lived in a commune in Haight-Ashbury. Her parents were two of the many would-be acid-rock musicians of the sixties. Her father was very talented and his star might have shined brighter than the rest, but he discovered he could make money more easily by selling drugs than by struggling for success.

Julia's parents were phantoms that floated in and out of her life, frequently away, erratic in the attention they paid her even when they were at home, unreliable, out of her reach—but so important to her!

She fought the loneliness of her life by creating wonderful fairy tales. In the lovely stories of her imagination, Julia was a princess, so very loved by her adoring parents. How they hated to be away from her! But they had to be away because they had to share the magic of their music with children less fortunate than she was.

There was no death in her fairy tales, or sadness or violence; and there were no villains, either, no wicked witches, evil sorcerers, or terrifying monsters. Julia's imaginary lands were populated by wonderful creatures like Puff—gentle magical pastel dragons that soared in the sky on gossamer wings and breathed soft mists of perfume, not swirls of fire.

Julia preferred her lovely happy fairy tales to the ones she read, but reading was still a wonderful escape. She taught herself to read, and one day someone emerged from a drug-fog long enough to realize that four-year-old Julia was intently reading

70

an article from *Rolling Stone* magazine. That discovery precipitated a flurry of attention. How bright *was* she? How much knowledge was stored in the quiet, serious head? They discovered the truth about her—she was brilliant, gifted—and for a while she became a prized specimen. The interest in her remarkable intelligence eventually faded, but not before she was enrolled in kindergarten, the youngest student by over a year.

Julia's small heart pounded with joy at the sudden attention and ached when the interest waned. It was more proof that there was something about her that couldn't hold love. A new pattern developed—joy and pain. Joy when there were flickers of interest from teachers and classmates because she was so very bright, and then pain as the interest died because she was so quiet and so shy.

When Julia was ten, her parents left for the last time. " 'Bye, kid. Be good," they murmured as they left, although her imagination, as always, made it a loving farewell. Her parents never returned from whatever enchanted kingdom they were visiting because their small plane exploded in midair, a kiss of death from a fire-breathing dragon, and fell in a ball of flames into the cold, dark sea.

Julia never knew that her parents had been smuggling cocaine from Cartagena and that the fiery explosion had been caused by a bomb placed by a drug lord who resented intrusion in his not-so-enchanted kingdom. She never knew, either, that there was sixty thousand dollars of drug profit in her parents' bank account.

Her only living relative was her aunt Doreen, her father's sister. Doreen Phillips shared with her brother a genetic package of destruction—a compelling addiction to drugs and an associated addiction to finding the easiest way to survive even if it meant ignoring talent. Doreen didn't want Julia. A deep instinct had prevented her from having children of her own or even marrying. Doreen didn't want Julia, but the ten-year-old girl came with a sixty-thousand-dollar bank account.

Small compensation, Doreen decided, for the imposition of having to care for Julia. Not that Doreen cared for her more than anyone ever had. Long before she squandered all the drug money, Doreen told Julia that they were very poor and that Julia had to "earn her keep" by doing household chores in the neighborhood until she was old enough to get a real job.

The wonderful fairy tales that had sustained her during her lonely, loveless childhood died when her parents fell to the sea in flames. For two years following their death, Julia lived in constant pain, unnumbed by fantasies. When she was twelve, a little girl becoming a young woman, she read the romantic stories of Jane Austen, Louisa May Alcott, and the Brontës. The wonderful romances sparked her imagination and she began to invent her own stories of love.

As a little girl, by pretending that *she* was the beloved princess in her fairy tales, Julia had bravely convinced herself that one day her parents would love her. But the fantasy that her own life would be filled with such happiness had been brutally shattered when her parents died, and Julia vowed never to delude herself again. The heroines of her stories of love were other young women, women deserving of love, not her, never her . . . and she never allowed herself to dream that a man would ever say "I love you" to *her*.

*I love you, Julie*. She believed Jeffrey meant it

for the moment, as others had shown flickers of interest in her before. But Julia, the terribly bright girl who had learned well the painful lessons of her young life, knew with absolute certainty that eventually he would lose interest in her. Jeffrey loved her beautiful body, her unashamed passion, *something* about her for now. But it wouldn't last.

It would be her fault, not Jeffrey's, when he left because it was she who could not hold on to love.

As Julia emerged from the last dark alley and walked up the creaking stairs to her aunt's tiny house, her heart whispered a gentle plea, *I love you, Jeffrey. Please love me for as long as you can.*

## Chapter Five

*Los Angeles*
*May 1979*

Jeffrey knew he would love her forever, and he was restless to make definite plans for their life together. Restless, and a little afraid. Before he could ask Julia to spend her life with him, Jeffrey needed to tell her a very private truth about himself. He needed to tell his brilliant love, who could be anything she wanted but whose dream was simply to make a happy life for those she loved, that he could never give her children. It would just be the two of them. Was that—just him and all his love—enough for her? Or would he lose her?

Jeffrey's heart quickened as he neared his apartment on the first Friday evening in May, quickening with eager anticipation because Julia would be there, waiting for him, and quickening, too, with apprehension because this was the weekend he would tell her.

She was in the living room, gazing at the garden beneath the window, so lost in thought that she didn't hear him come in.

"Hello, darling."

Julia spun at the sound of his voice, and when she did, Jeffrey's loving smile faded to gentle worry. Her lovely lavender eyes were dark-circled and troubled, and she didn't rush eagerly into his arms.

"What's wrong?"

"I've come to say good-bye."

*"Good-bye?* Julie, why?"

"Because . . . there are things you don't know about me."

"Tell me," Jeffrey whispered calmly even though his heart raced with fear. *Tell me your secrets, my love, and I will tell you mine . . . and we will say hello forever, not good-bye.*

"I'm not a senior at Berkeley, Jeffrey. I don't live in a dormitory on campus. I live at home with my aunt. She's my guardian."

"Your guardian?"

"Yes. My parents were killed when I was ten. The small plane they were flying from Cartagena exploded in midair and fell into the sea."

"Oh, darling, I'm so sorry. Now I know why you are afraid of the sea."

"I'm not afraid when I'm with you," Julia replied swiftly, distracted from her confession by the concern and gentleness in his eyes. *Oh, Jeffrey, please look gentle still when you hear the truth.*

"I'm glad. You should never be afraid when you're with me." But she was afraid now, afraid of what she had to tell him, and he was afraid because she had come to say good-bye. Jeffrey urged gently, "So your aunt became your guardian after your parents died."

"Yes." Julia sighed softly. "Jeffrey, that was six years ago."

"*What?* You're telling me that you're only sixteen?"

"Yes. I know I should have told you. I'm sorry."

"*Sorry?*" he echoed harshly, stunned by the truth and angered by the lie. He had assumed, because she told him she was a senior in college, that she was twenty-one or twenty-two. But he had wondered if she was older, closer to his age, because of her insights, her serenity, and the maturity of her passion.

*Sixteen?* Sixteen-year-old girls had never appealed to Jeffrey, not when he was sixteen, or fifteen, or even fourteen. Even then the silly giggling, the pretense at sophistication, the false maturity had made him restless.

But Julia didn't giggle and her eyes didn't sparkle with the foolish expectation that life would glitter always with happiness. Julia's beautiful lavender eyes were serious, thoughtful, wise—eyes that knew about the sadness of life. Julia didn't giggle, but she smiled a smile that filled him with such desire. And her laugh was so soft . . . and when they made love it filled with wonder as if amazed that such joy could come from within her.

Julia wasn't sixteen, except in years.

She looked young now, younger than she had ever looked to him, as she bravely met his angry glare. Young, and so beautiful, and so lost, and so afraid. Jeffrey wanted her never to be lost or afraid! And, as that wish of love magically melted his fury, his spinning mind spun to an amazing conclusion: he could live with the truth—he loved her no matter what her age—and he could forgive the lie. It had been a necessary deception, hadn't it? Because if Julia had told him her age on that enchanted afternoon in Ghirardelli, he would have walked away, run away, wouldn't he? *Wouldn't he?*

76

Yes . . . maybe . . . *no*.

"So you're sixteen," he whispered gently with a soft loving smile. "It doesn't change the way I feel about you. I still love you, Julie."

Julia's lavender eyes shimmered with disbelieving joy. She had only come today because she believed she owed Jeffrey the truth. She knew he would be angry at first, but she prayed that their inevitable good-bye would be gentle. Yes, of course their relationship had to end now that he knew how young she was, he would say. But then maybe, her greatest wish, he would tell her gently that he *had* loved her. If only she could spend the rest of her life believing that for two and a half months she had truly been loved by this wonderful man . . .

That had been her wish, and it had seemed so foolish, such an impossible dream. She had never for a moment dared to dream Jeffrey would want her still. If she had imagined that, she might not have come at all, because there was the other secret, something she had never planned to tell him, the reason she had to stop seeing him now before he noticed the new softness of her sleek body.

"Julie?" Jeffrey asked gently. His anxious heart had calmed when he saw the joy in her eyes, but it raced again, suddenly worried, because now there was new lavender fear. "Another secret?"

"Yes." Julia frowned, hesitating, wishing she had a chance to think about this first. But the gentle eyes that had always been able to lure the innermost secrets of her heart urged her now and Julia heard herself say, "Jeffrey . . . I'm pregnant."

Her voice was soft, her words barely audible, but they echoed like thunder in his brain and plunged into his heart with excruciating pain as his

77

mind filled with vivid images of Julia with another lover, a man whose loving had given her something he could never give.

As the images swir'ed and his heart screamed, Jeffrey's blue eyes darkened, emptying of all warmth and gentleness and filling with a stormy turbulence that was beyond anger. Julia watched the transformation and felt an icy chill as she read the dark and eloquent message.

*Jeffrey didn't want their baby.*

There was no room for children in Jeffrey's important dreams. If she'd had a chance to think she would have known. Now she knew and it caused such pain . . . new pain for the innocent life growing inside her, a tiny life she already loved so much, and old pain for another unwanted child, an unloved little girl with lavender eyes who had survived on fairy tales.

The little girl was a woman now. And for the past few months she had lived a fairy tale of love, an enchanted fairy tale that almost had a happy ending. Because Jeffrey loved her, wanted her . . . but he didn't want their baby.

"Jeffrey, I'm sorry," she whispered helplessly, hopelessly to his angry dark eyes.

The soft sound of her voice registered above the thunder in his brain, but as he focused on her apologetic eyes, another devastating revelation, perhaps the most devastating of all, swept through him . . . the real reason she had come to say good-bye.

"You're leaving me to be with the baby's father, aren't you?"

"No, Jeffrey, *you* are the father." Her eyes widened with astonishment that he could imagine she had ever had another lover. "The first night we were together I wasn't using any birth control."

"I can't be the baby's father, Julia."

"But you are," she countered softly. *I can see how much you don't want to be, but you are!* "Jeffrey, there has never been anyone else."

Her soft confession caused even more turbulence in his dark-blue eyes. How she wished she had known not to tell him about the baby! How she wished she could have had a gentle memory of their good-bye! But all gentleness had vanished from his eyes and voice, and Julia's breaking heart couldn't wait to see if it ever returned.

"I have to go. Good-bye, Jeffrey."

*Let her go,* reason urged as he watched her gather her tattered knapsack and begin to cross the room toward the door. *She is sixteen. She lies to you. She has lied from the beginning and is lying still. Let her go to her other lover! Your life can be yours again, your privacy, your freedom, your dreams.* To assume the responsibility of Julia and her lover's baby would be sheer insanity.

Jeffrey's heart made different pleas. *You love her. She is the other half of your heart. Can you really live your life without her?*

"Do you love me, Julie?" His voice stopped her, and when she turned and he held her lavender eyes, he added quietly, "Please tell me the truth."

"Oh, yes, Jeffrey, I love you."

"Then marry me."

"Marry?"

"Yes, marry. I love you, Julie. I want to spend my life with you."

"Jeffrey," she whispered softly, a whisper of hope and pain. "The baby."

Jeffrey fought the stabbing ache that swept through him and smiled a wobbly smile. "I want you, Julie, and I want your baby."

*Your* baby. Julia knew that the little life inside her had been created because of her lies, because she had deceived him into believing that she was experienced and prepared when in truth she had been so very innocent and so very desperate for his love, but it was still the precious child of *their* magnificent love. The part of Julia's bright mind that was firmly tethered to the lessons of her life warned her to flee to protect herself and her baby from further pain. But the defiant corner of her gifted mind that in gentle collaboration with her heart had imagined wonderful stories of love urged her to stay. Because not even her remarkable imagination had imagined a love as wonderful as Jeffrey.

Julia believed in Jeffrey. She believed in the kind, gentle, loving man to whom she had so joyfully given her heart. He had had every right to be angry that she had deceived him about her age and innocence, and of course he had been shocked and enraged to discover that those deceptions had created a little life he might never have chosen to create. But someday Jeffrey would love his baby, wouldn't he? How desperately Julia needed to know the answer to that so important question. She couldn't know now, but still her loving heart gave a confident reply, *Yes, he will. And until then, while Jeffrey follows his important dreams, you will love your precious baby.*

"Do you really want to marry me?"

"More than anything in the world."

\* \* \*

80

Yes, Julia admitted softly, she had done well in school. But graduating from high school, or going on to college, didn't matter. What mattered, all she wanted, was to be with him as soon as possible. And that was what Jeffrey wanted, too.

As soon as possible was a week, they decided that weekend as they made joyful plans and gentle promises of love. They promised to love each other forever, and never to be afraid to tell each other the truth, and Julia whispered with glowing, hopeful lavender eyes, "No more lies, Jeffrey, I promise."

Julia promised no more lies, and she told him the secrets of her lonely, loveless childhood, shyly sharing those painful truths, and Jeffrey listened, holding her gently and loving her all the more, and waiting so patiently for her to confess to the words he knew to be untrue: *There has never been anyone else, Jeffrey.*

But Julia never confessed to that lie. She only met his expectant loving gaze, blushing finally because his blue eyes appraised her with such intensity. And Jeffrey didn't force her confession by telling her why the baby she carried could not be his because sometime during the weekend of joyful plans and promises of forever the most astonishing, most wonderful thought began to dance in his mind.

What if Julia was telling the truth? What if, in the past eleven years, everything had changed? What if the woman he loved so very much really was carrying his child?

* * *

81

"When I was fifteen I had mumps complicated by mumps orchitis," Jeffrey told the fertility specialist at UCLA five days before he and Julia were married. "My sperm count following the infection was extremely low, and the doctors said they didn't expect it to change."

"It hasn't," the specialist confirmed.

"Oh," Jeffrey said quietly. He had been so hopeful.

"I take it you have been unable to conceive?"

"I've never actually tried."

"So we don't know."

"We don't?" Eleven years before, despite occasional admonitions to practice birth control just in case, the solemnity of the specialists, the eloquently descriptive terms "sterile" and "infertile," and his mother's grim horror had sent a message that was abundantly clear: Jeffrey Cabot Lawrence was *never* going to pass his blue blood on to heirs. "Some of the doctors did recommend contraception unless pregnancy was desired, but frankly I thought that was because my mother tended to have a kill-the-messenger look every time we were given the prognosis."

"Perhaps it was," the doctor said with a wry smile. "As you know, although only a single sperm ultimately fertilizes the egg, the reality is that millions of sperm seem to be required to create an environment in which conception can occur. However, as long as any sperm are present, I, too, would advise contraception unless pregnancy is planned."

"You mean there actually *is* a chance?"

"A chance, yes, although it is vanishingly small."

"But not impossible."

"Doctors never say never. We believe in miracles like everyone else."

"So it would be a miracle."

"Approaching one. But, Jeffrey, your chance of fathering a child using the new technique of in vitro fertilization isn't vanishingly small. We once thought that test-tube babies would forever be a fantasy of science fiction, but just last year Louise Joy Brown was born in England."

Jeffrey knew, of course, about Louise Joy Brown and the remarkable advances in medical science . . . but what he needed now was a miracle.

And Jeffrey Lawrence didn't believe in miracles. At least, the journalist whose logical, disciplined mind was trained to deal with hard facts and incontrovertible data didn't believe in miracles. But wasn't that the same Jeffrey Lawrence who hadn't believed in falling in love—until it happened?

Jeffrey's heart had fallen swiftly, joyfully, confidently in love with Julia, and now that heart proclaimed with swift and joyful confidence: the miracle has already happened.

The fact that Julia's baby *could* be his was miracle enough, wasn't it? He simply had to accept it, to believe her baby was his and vow never to challenge that belief.

*Simply* . . . but it would be simple, as simple as falling in love with her, as joyous, as wonderful, as right.


Jeffrey and Julia spent the weekend before their wedding in romantic Carmel, making love in their charming room at the Pine Inn, strolling along

83

Pebble Beach, laughing at the antics of the lively otters, and wandering through the quaint shops on Ocean Avenue.

Jeffrey had suggested Carmel because Julia had never been there. He knew she would love it, and he had memories of the unique gold jewelry crafted by talented local artisans. Julia had told him she didn't want a diamond, but her lovely eyes had filled with soft hope when he suggested a very special gold wedding band.

Jeffrey wanted something very special, a worthy symbol of their love; Julia was overwhelmed by just plain gold. Still, when she saw the matching rings, elegant swirls of white-and-yellow gold, her eyes filled with wonder. Delicate ribbons of the two golds had been woven together and then flamed by fire and melted together . . . forever . . . into one.

The smaller of the two rings was unusually small, as if specifically made for Julia's slender finger. When Jeffrey slipped it on her, it fit perfectly; and that was how it looked—perfect, elegant, designed precisely for her. And the larger matching ring fit Jeffrey's finger perfectly, too, as if it, too, had been designed precisely for him.

"You're going to wear a ring?" Julia asked as she watched him put the ring on his finger.

"Of course, darling," Jeffrey gently told her surprised and hopeful lavender eyes. "Don't you know how proud I will be for the world to know you are my wife?"


"No more presents, ever, Jeffrey," Julia said twenty minutes later. They were in a secluded park

84

two blocks from Ocean Avenue. The magnificent wedding bands were in Jeffrey's coat pocket and his arms gently circled her waist as they stood beneath an arch of wisteria the color of her eyes. "We'll just give each other ourselves and our love."

"As your soon-to-be husband, I reserve the right to lavish you with presents." His eyes grew serious as he added softly, "But you never need to give me any because you are all I want. You are the greatest gift."

"*You* are."

"No, *you*." Jeffrey kissed her, and after a moment began to talk to her between kisses. "Someday I want to take you on a magnificent honeymoon. Maybe a three-week romantic meander through Europe?"

"Won't every day be a honeymoon?"

"Of course."

"So, we don't need to go to Europe."

"Julie?"

"I've never been on an airplane."

"And you're afraid to fly."

"Yes." Julia gave a soft shrug.

"We have a lifetime, darling. Someday, when you're ready, we'll fly together." Together, someday, they would conquer Julia's fear of the sky, but there was a more important fear to vanquish first—the lingering uncertainty he still saw in her lovely eyes when he told her of his love. As if she really didn't believe he would love her forever. "You're the romantic, but I've been thinking about the words to engrave on our rings anyway. On the ring I'm giving you, I thought, 'Julie, I will always love you, Jeffrey.' "

"You're the romantic."

"Because of you. So, what do you think?"

"I think that after you put the ring on my finger tomorrow I will never want to take it off."

"I will never want to take mine off, either. But that means they won't be engraved."

"It doesn't matter. I know the ring is from you. And besides," she added softly, "the words are engraved in our hearts."


Meredith Lawrence was born on September twelfth, twenty-four hours after Jeffrey left for a ten-day assignment in Vietnam. Merry had respiratory distress and her skin was jaundiced, but her tiny lungs matured quickly outside her mother's womb and the yellow of her pale skin responded nicely to the bili lights.

Eight days after she was born, the day before Jeffrey returned, Julia took her baby daughter home.

*Her baby daughter.* Julia had loved the little life from the moment she knew she was pregnant, but she was unprepared for the immense joy and wonder she felt when she first held Merry in her arms and greeted her small, beautiful face. And since that first moment the joy and wonder had only increased.

How eager she was for Jeffrey to see his daughter, this most astonishing of all gifts of love.

How excited she was to have him hold Merry and be swept away by this wondrous joy that was beyond all words . . .


The miracle had already happened, Jeffrey had

decided when he learned that it was possible for him to be the father of Julia's baby. His heart accepted the miracle that day, a decision of love, and his mind had embraced it, too, with a vow simply to believe and never to challenge. But when he saw the infant curled in Julia's arms, the disciplined mind that was anchored to truth and reality could not be silent.

Because it was so obvious, so painfully obvious, that the golden-haired brown-eyed baby girl could not be his.

It wasn't, of course, the fact that the genes that colored eyes blue were strong on both sides of Jeffrey's family and Julia's baby had eyes the color of mink. That was the softest of science, easily dismissed. No, it was the hard science, his own except-for-a-miracle-infertility and the indisputable fact that this infant had surely been conceived before he and Julia even met.

When Jeffrey did his award-winning story on the Neonatal I.C.U. at Children's Hospital in San Francisco, he spent many hours in the I.C.U. gazing into incubators, looking at babies who were a month premature, and two, and even three, and learning about the prognosis of each group. Babies born two months prematurely *did* survive, but after weeks in the I.C.U., and Jeffrey had only been gone ten days and Julia's baby had been born and was already home.

"Here's your baby daughter, Jeffrey. I named her Meredith, after Grandmère. Oh, Jeffrey, she is such joy, such wonder." Julia stopped, was stopped, by the look of great sadness in his tired blue eyes. "Jeffrey?"

"All you all right, honey?"

"Yes, Jeffrey, I'm fine." Julia smiled lovingly, trying to erase the sadness that was surely because he had been away when the baby was born. "We're both fine. Would you like to hold her?"

But Jeffrey didn't reach for Merry. Instead he sat down across from Julia and gazed at her with sad and gentle eyes.

"Who is her father, Julie?" Jeffrey's heart, the heart that orchestrated the magnificent deception, the miracle that was now hopelessly shattered, had long since banished thoughts of Julia's other lover. The thought of one other man loving her and creating this precious little new life with her was almost too much to bear. And what if there had been many lovers? What if Julia had no idea who the father was? "Do you know?"

"You are her father, Jeffrey."

"No, darling, I'm not." Jeffrey sighed softly and smiled reassuringly at her. Of course Julia knew this baby could not be his. She had hidden her other lover, praying the baby would be Jeffrey's, or at least be born at a time when they could believe she was. Julia had been protecting him, just as Jeffrey had protected her by hiding his infertility. But now they needed to admit the truth, share the disappointment they felt, and swiftly go on together to share the wonderful joy of loving the little girl cradled so carefully in her mother's arms. Jeffrey said quietly, his voice apologetic because perhaps he should have told her before but . . . "When I was fifteen I had a mumps infection with complications that make it virtually impossible for me to father a child. I didn't tell you before because I didn't want to dampen your joy. I'm so sorry, Julie, but it would have been truly a miracle for her to be mine."

As Julia gazed at him with bewildered eyes, she tried to fight the ominous worry that Jeffrey's eyes first had filled with sadness, not wonder, when he saw his daughter, and that now he was searching for distant reasons why Merry couldn't even be his.

"But she *is* yours, Jeffrey," Julia whispered finally, quietly. She added softly, "And she *is* a miracle."

Jeffrey drew a soft breath and felt icy ripples of fear wash through him. *No more lies, Jeffrey, I promise,* Julia had vowed. But she was lying now!

"Julie, when was she due?" he pressed almost urgently. *Please don't lie to me!*

"You know that, Jeffrey. She was due on your birthday, November ·eleventh." How thrilled she had been when she told the obstetrician the date of the first time she and Jeffrey made love and he had calculated the due date.

"And she was born when?"

"September twelfth."

"And she's home already and healthy. That's not a baby born two months prematurely."

"We were very lucky, Jeffrey," Julia whispered softly.

Jeffrey stared at the woman he loved with all his heart and felt an immense sense of dread. He didn't believe her, the facts wouldn't allow him to, and Jeffrey knew Julia knew the truth, too. But she was maintaining the lie. She was going to protect the secret of her other lover. *Why?* Was she still ’ not confident enough of his love to tell him the truth? Or was it something else, something worse . . .

Julia's lies had only been necessary ones, and she had only deceived him about the important things. Was this a necessary deception that was more important to her than their love?

Jeffrey stared at her with eyes that were stormy reflections of the turbulence in his heart. Julia returned his gaze, her lovely lavender eyes bewildered and innocent . . . so innocent, so unflickering, just as they had been when she had told him the other necessary and important lies.

"It's late, Julia," Jeffrey said finally, heavily. "I've been traveling for twenty-four hours and I'm exhausted. I have to be at the studio early tomorrow morning to begin editing the tapes. I'm going to bed."


Julia remained in the living room, nursing her hungry daughter and fighting the pain that swept through her. This summer she had begun to believe that Jeffrey wanted the baby. He had been so gentle, so loving, and he had taken such wonderful care of her. But he hadn't greeted his daughter with wonder and joy. In fact, he had searched for reasons that Merry couldn't be his, and when she had insisted that Merry was his, his eyes had darkened to the stormy turbulence beyond anger she had seen when she first told him of her pregnancy.

Jeffrey didn't want Merry. He didn't even want Merry to be his. Why? So that he could justify ignoring her? So he would feel less guilty about the career that already, because he was so talented, frequently took him away? So he wouldn't be torn between his dreams and the immense responsibility of a child he would never have chosen to have?

As Merry's tiny, eager lips nursed her full, creamy breast, Julia kissed gentle kisses on the silky blond head and silently renewed the vow she had made the day Jeffrey asked her to marry him. She would love her lovely little girl, as she already did, and she would ask nothing of Jeffrey, never pressure him, never make him feel torn or guilty. And someday . . .

*Your daddy will love you, my little Merry,* Julia promised with soft kisses. *But he is restless now, and has important dreams that he must follow. I believe in your daddy's important dreams, and someday he will believe in mine. You are the most important dream, my little love. Someday your daddy will know that.*

When Merry finished nursing, Julia carried her into the room where Jeffrey slept and put her in the cradle next to her side of the bed. As Julia crawled quietly into bed beside Jeffrey, she made more promises. *I love you, Jeffrey. I promise I will make this right. Merry and I will never interfere with your dreams.* And then because the confidence of their summer of loving had been so shaken and because there would always live within her the little girl who believed she could not hold love, she made a silent plea, *Oh, Jeffrey, please don't leave us.*

At three A.M. Merry awakened with a cry. The night before, on her first night home, Merry hadn't cried at all. Perhaps she would have cried if Julia hadn't been awake watching her sleep, watching her breathe, whispering soft reassurances to her whenever she stirred. But this night Julia wasn't keeping her vigil because fatigue had overcome her.

She quickly lifted Merry from the cradle, curled her into her arms, and walked out of the bedroom into the living room as Merry's cries became screams.

"Oh, Merry, please be quiet. Your daddy has to sleep. Be quiet, honey, please, please be quiet." Julia's soft tone wasn't comforting because Merry heard the panic in her mother's voice, and Julia's soft warm breast didn't calm her, either. Julia's hot tears spilled onto her infant daughter and her voice trembled, "Merry, Merry, please, Daddy has to sleep."

"Julia, what's—"

"I'm sorry, Jeffrey," she whispered as she looked up at his glowering eyes. "I'm so sorry."

Jeffrey's anger was intercepted by the fear on her lovely face. How could she be afraid of him? It was he who was afraid, afraid of losing her, afraid of the secret that was too important to reveal.

*Don't be afraid of me, my lovely Julie!* Jeffrey had vowed to vanquish all her fears, beginning with the most important one—her fragile uncertainty about his love. And he had almost succeeded during their magnificent summer of love, but now she trembled and looked as lost as she had looked on the evening he asked her to marry him.

He had known on that warm spring evening that she lied to him, that she was carrying another man's child, and that the secret of her other lover might remain hidden in her heart forever.

And he had chosen to marry her.

And now? Now the baby had been born, and his mind wouldn't allow his heart even to pretend the miracle had happened, and Julia was going to maintain her secret . . .

But nothing had changed. He loved her with all his heart.

Jeffrey carefully took Merry from Julia's arms and spoke very gently to the baby's crying face. "Merry, you're making your mommy cry. How come? Your mommy looks so tired."

Magically, Merry's screams became whimpers and then curious coos as her attention shifted to the deep voice and the strong arms that held her so securely.

"That's better," Jeffrey whispered. He looked from Merry to Julia. "Julie, did I hold you and kiss you and tell you how much I missed you and how I love you?"

"No."

"Why don't I do that after this little one falls asleep?"

"Is it all right that I named her after Grand-mère?" Julia asked as the autumn sky began to lighten with the dawn. Merry was asleep now and they had been whispering gentle words of love between kisses.

"Of course," Jeffrey answered, his voice soft with love for Julia and for Grandmère. His beloved grandmother had been very lonely in the years since his grandfather's death, but Julia, loving Julia, had magically restored Grandmère's joyous laugh and youthful spirit. Their relationship had begun with letters, because Julia was so timid on the phone with the elegant voice she didn't know, but now there were frequent phone calls, and Grandmère, who had announced four years before that she was too old to travel, had come to visit for ten lively days in July. Julia loved Grandmère, and Grandmère loved Julia. And Grandmère was so excited about the birth of her first great-grandchild. "Grandmère will be thrilled. Why don't we call her right now? You tell her, Julie."

"Grandmère?" Julia asked moments later when a sprightly voice answered the phone a continent away.

"Julia? Are you all right?"

"Oh, yes. Jeffrey's home and we wanted you to know that our baby has been born. She's a beautiful little girl and we've named her Meredith."

"Meredith?" Grandmère's voice trembled.

"We call her Merry."

"Oh, my dear, there was a time, a lovely time a million years ago when Jeffrey's grandfather used to call me Merry."


Five hours later Jeffrey placed a call to Merry's doctor. It was a call he had to make, a call from a loving heart that was still searching for a miracle, and a call from a disciplined mind trained to double-check all the facts.

The doctor confirmed what Jeffrey already knew. Merry *was* premature, perhaps as much as four weeks, but certainly not almost nine, and she had done remarkably well for a baby born that early.

Merry wasn't his baby. Julia was going to maintain the lie. Those were the facts. In the middle of the night Jeffrey had told himself that nothing had changed. But it wasn't true. He loved her, yes, always, but now mixed in with the immense strength of his love were other powerful emotions—hurt, anger, fear. If he used the power of his love he could surely tranquilize the swirling emotions, couldn't he? But wouldn't they rage inside him still, in some hidden corner of his heart, burrowing deeper and deeper until they caused a festering wound that would contaminate all of their love?

Could he really simply forgive Julia's deception, and protect their love by living her lie, as he had once joyfully planned simply to accept the miracle?

Jeffrey didn't know. He only knew that he had to try.

But Julia didn't ask him to live her lie. As if in silent admission of the truth she could not speak aloud, she did not ask of him that he be a father to the daughter that was not his. During the increasingly infrequent times that Jeffrey was even home when Merry was awake, Julia very carefully kept her infant daughter far away from him.

Julia cared for the golden-haired little girl she loved so much, and she loved Jeffrey as joyously as she always had. And their magnificent love survived, flourished, because Julia, whose generous heart had lived for so long without love, had more than enough love for him and for his very precious daughter.

95

## Chapter Six

Before Jeffrey fell in love with Julia, television viewers had been enchanted by his sincere, intelligent eyes, his aristocratic handsomeness, and his elegant charm. But after, there was something new, something more, something breathtaking.

No one could accurately pinpoint what the something was. It was very subtle, a subtext from the heart, a tender smile, a soft inflection, a gentle apology in the sensual blue eyes when there was tragic news to share. Jeffrey knew that his love for Julia lived inside him always, a magnificent fullness, a joyful warmth, but he had no idea that his joy overflowed from his heart to his face. It did, however, and whenever he spoke to the camera he was speaking to his love, and the viewing public became an unwitting yet willing recipient of the wondrous intimacy.

The viewers had ample opportunity to see Jeffrey. The extraordinary quality and impeccable honesty of his work advanced him with astonishing speed to the top of the very elite group of foreign correspondents. By Merry's third birthday Jeffrey had become the network's first choice to cover the most important news events throughout the world. A month later the network assigned him to the place it judged to be among the most critical to the survival of the planet . . . the Middle East.

It was an important assignment, one Jeffrey could not refuse, but one that was far too dangerous to have Julia and Merry to accompany him. So it was decided that he would go to Beirut and commute to New York by Concorde whenever he could and that Julia and Merry would live with Grandmère at Belvedere. Two weeks before he left for Beirut, Jeffrey drove Julia and Merry from Los Angeles to Southampton. He worried a little about being cooped up in the car with three-year-old Merry for the five-day drive. Julia worried even more because she didn't want Jeffrey to be annoyed by the chatter that to Julia was joy, a sparkling fountain of happiness from her bright little girl.

But the trip was wonderful.

Jeffrey drove, and Julia entertained Merry. Mother and daughter talked and played quiet games and watched the world speed by. And Julia told Merry the most magnificent fairy tales Jeffrey had ever heard.

"The beautiful little princess was so sleepy," Julia whispered lovingly to her daughter, who was in need of a nap but struggling to stay awake, "but she had to make a decision. Should she fall asleep on a soft cloud in the sky? Or on a gentle wave in the ocean?"

As Jeffrey listened he marveled that his lovely Julia, who was afraid of the sky and the sea, made them magical places for Merry. Julia wanted no fears for Merry and gave her daughter only gifts of happiness and love.

"Where do you think she wanted to fall asleep, Merry?"

"The sky. On a cloud. Daphne could take her there."

"Yes, she could," Julia answered softly. "So the little princess called to Daphne, and Daphne scooped her onto her back, and they flew to a cloud that was pink and so very soft. And Daphne stayed with the little princess, because Daphne was sleepy, too, and together they wished sweet dreams to the golden moon and fell asleep."

"Who's Daphne?" Jeffrey asked after Merry had fallen asleep.

"A dragon."

"And who are Robert and Cecily?"

"Twin sea serpents."

"And Andrew?"

"A unicorn."

"You made up these stories, Julie?"

"Yes."

"They're wonderful, darling." After a moment he said quietly, "You never told me any of your stories of love. Will you tell me? Will you write them to me?"

They had promised to write, every night, during the hours when they should have been holding each other and loving each other and sharing the events of their days.

"I don't make up love stories anymore, Jeffrey. I don't need to because our love is more wonderful than anything I ever imagined."

"Oh, Julie. Will you write to me about our love then?"

"Every night. I promise."

\* \* \*

"Moo cows, Mommy! Moo cows! Mommy! Mommy!" Merry exclaimed with breathless glee the next afternoon as they sped past the animals she had only seen before in books.

Julia cast an apologetic glance at Jeffrey, but Jeffrey laughed softly at Merry's enthusiasm and asked, "Would she like a closer look, Julie? Should we stop?"

"If you don't mind."

"Of course not."

A mile later Jeffrey pulled to the side of the road beside a pasture where a herd of cows was grazing. Jeffrey held an excited Merry above the top of the wooden fence so she could see without obstruction, and when Julia moved beside him he whispered lovingly into her ear, "Moo cows, Mommy."

Julia's life at Belvedere with Grandmère and Merry was filled with great happiness. A perfect life, except she missed Jeffrey so much! He called often and came home to her whenever he could, but sometimes she didn't see him except on television for weeks, even months.

As promised, Jeffrey and Julia wrote to each other every day.

Jeffrey was an eyewitness to the important history of the world and he faithfully reported what he saw to a nation that increasingly relied on his vigilant eyes and intelligent mind. Jeffrey reported the news to the nation, and in the private words he wrote to Julia every night he shared his feelings about the tragedies he saw.

As Jeffrey was an eyewitness to the important history of the world, Julia was an eyewitness to the important history of Jeffrey's daughter. And in reporting the news of Merry's life, Julia was as good a journalist as he, reporting the events faithfully and without editorializing. Julia always wrote *Merry,* never *your daughter* or *our daughter,* because she had vowed not to pressure him ... even though her heart cried restlessly, *Oh, Jeffrey, you are missing such joy, such wonder!*

Julia wrote about Merry and their happy life at Belvedere. And, in bold unashamed passages that were as magnificently intimate as their loving, she wrote bravely of her love, her passion, her desires, and her fantasies.

The daily letters and frequent phone calls prevented gaps in their love, their feelings, and their most private thoughts, but no number of intimate words of love could ease the pain of the physical separation. As weeks became months, the need to touch and to hold and to love—to be one—became almost desperate ...

Between October 1985 and May 1986, Jeffrey was unable to return to Southampton at all. Beginning with the hijacking in October of the *Achille Lauro* the events were relentless—the fleeting but hopeful rumors of peace in Lebanon ... the meeting of special envoy Terry Waite with the captors of four kidnapped Americans ... the hijacking of the Egyptian airliner to Malta that ended in the death of fifty-seven passengers and crew as commandos stormed the plane ... the simultaneous massacre of civilians in the Rome and Vienna airports at Christmas ... the subsequent arrest warrant issued for Abu Nidal ... the military police riots in Cairo . . . the clash of Libyan and U.S. forces over the Gulf of Sidra . . . the terrorist bombing of the TWA flight from Rome to Athens and the averting of a similar attempt at Heathrow . . . the United States' attack on Libya in retaliation for the bombing of La Belle Discotheque in West Berlin . . .

The events were relentless, and all the while, in a crescendo chorus, there was escalating violence in the civil war in Beirut.

Jeffrey could not leave. He had become almost as indispensable to the network and the viewers who trusted him as a general in a war. In a way he *was* indispensable. His fame, the common knowledge that his reports were respected, trusted, and viewed by a large segment of the free world, gave him access to places and people that other reporters did not have.

For over six months each planned trip to Southampton was postponed and ultimately canceled. Then, at last, Jeffrey came home. He called Julia from each milepost in his journey home to her, swiftly reassuring her, "I'm leaving Beirut." Then, "I'm in Athens." Then, "I'm at Charles de Gaulle. The plane is on time, darling. I will see you in four hours."


He was like a wanderer too long in the desert and dying of thirst . . . and Julia was the oasis. He walked through the door of Customs and into her arms. They just held each other, without speaking, unable to speak, overcome by the immense relief of touching again and the wonderful feeling of life returning to their lonely bodies as

101

they became whole.

"Oh, God, how I've missed you," he whispered finally. "Shall we go home?"

Julia had told Grandmère they would be home by dinner and Merry was with Paige at Somerset. She had made the decision weeks ago that she wanted to be alone with him in a private place. Still, suddenly uncertain, she almost drove past the hotel where she had already booked a room. But when she pulled the car into a parking space near the room and removed the key from her purse, her uncertainty vanished because she saw such joy and desire in his eyes.

In the motel room at Fisherman's Wharf Julia had undressed herself, and her clothes had been threadbare, and she had worn no bra. Now Jeffrey undressed her, as he had always after that first time, and she wore expensive linen and silk, and beneath that elegance her lovely breasts were clothed in satin and lace.

Jeffrey's hands trembled as he undressed her and his mind filled with the brave words she had written about her fantasies. He knew how she dreamed of him undressing her so slowly, his tender, talented lips lingering and loving each newly revealed patch of her white, silky skin. Jeffrey had spent months dreaming about doing just that and much more, but . . .

"Oh, my lovely Julie," he whispered against her naked breasts. "I need you too much."

"Jeffrey . . . I need you too much, too."


"What would you like to do today?" Jeffrey asked three days later when Julia rejoined him in

bed after Merry had left for school and Grandmère had gone to visit a friend in East Hampton.

"Whatever you want."

"What would you do if I wasn't here?"

"I would miss you."

"What else?"

"Transplant the roses."

"Let's do that in a while."

Two hours later Julia led the way to a sun-
drenched island of rich dark earth and pointed to
a cluster of six rose bushes.

"I think these are all ready to come out of the
I.C.U."

"The I.C.U.?"

"This is the I.C.U. I put the plants that haven't
done well over the winter here because it has the
best sunlight. Once they're healthy, they can go
over there, beneath our window."

Jeffrey smiled at her. She was such a nurturer,
so loving, so gentle, giving intensive care always to
those she loved.

Jeffrey first dug six holes in the ground beneath
the window of their master suite. Then, very carefully, he began to remove the once frail but now
healthy bushes from Julia's I.C.U.

"Oh, wait," Julia said as Jeffrey began to put
one of the newly well roses beside an established
bush. She looked at the metal tag on the bush.
"That's Smoky. Smoky can't be next to Mister Lincoln because the colors will clash."

"What colors will Smoky and Mister Lincoln
be?" Jeffrey's question was an innocent and interested one, but it caused his lovely Julia great pain.
"Julie? What, honey?"

Julia shook her head. She had made a solemn

103

vow never to interfere with his important dreams.

"Tell me." Julia was silent, so Jeffrey made a hopeful guess from his heart. "Is it because I won't be here when they bloom?"

Julia looked at him and nodded a soft apology. But it was an admission that filled Jeffrey with happiness.

"You always seem so calm when I leave."

"I cry after, Jeffrey. You're calm, too."

"But I cry, too, darling." That was the truth, and the other truth, what had been spinning in his mind, was that he couldn't do it anymore. He couldn't leave her knowing it might be seven months again. He *wouldn't*. "After we get these roses out of the I.C.U., let's go for a walk. I want to talk to you."

They walked along deer trails through the dense, lush forest that led to the bluff overlooking the sea. The bluff was an artist's palette of spring wildflowers, and in the distance was a charming cottage perched on a cliff. Jeffrey led her down the winding trail to the white sand beach. The surf was high and the waves crashed angrily on the sand. Jeffrey looked from the treacherous surf to the azure horizon and remembered the words his grandfather, Hollis Cabot, had spoken to him in this very place. *Always follow your dreams, Jeffrey, wherever they lead, no matter what anyone else says*.

Jeffrey had spent so many hours here dreaming about the adventures that lay beyond the horizon, loving the danger of the waves and the vastness of the sea, restless to follow the beckoning waves beyond the horizon to his dreams.

But now his dreams were here, beside him, and he looked into her lavender eyes and saw that the powerful waves frightened her a little even though he held her. Jeffrey drew her even closer, and after a few moments led her back up the cliff.

"I have to go back to Beirut, honey, until they find a replacement for me," he said when they reached the crest of the cliff and sat on a warm patch of grass in the meadow of wildflowers. "It shouldn't take very long. Then I'm coming home to see your roses."

"Oh, Jeffrey . . . but what will you do?"

"I thought I'd follow you around all day every day."

"You'll get bored and restless."

"I don't think so, but if you get tired of having me underfoot I could probably find a job as a reporter at a local station."

"Probably." Julia smiled, but her lips trembled and her eyes filled with tears of joy.

Jeffrey kissed the tears, and her trembling lips, and her tears again. And when the hunger of their kisses demanded more, he undressed her very slowly and tenderly caressed all the wonderful places of her lovely body with an exquisite gentleness that was beyond any fantasy Julia had ever imagined. Only the springtime sun watched as they loved in their fragrant ocean of wildflowers, and on that perfect day in May even the crashing surf in the distance became a soft splash, a gentle rhythm that matched their tender loving, a soft sigh in an endless afternoon of soft sighs of joy.

* * *

"Hello, Frank." Jeffrey smiled a warm greeting to the bureau chief on his return to Beirut three weeks later.

"Jeffrey. Welcome back. How was your month?"

"Very nice." Jeffrey took a soft breath. "Frank, there's something I need to discuss with you."

"I have something to discuss with you, too. Come on in." Frank opened the door to his office, but before either man could enter the room they were distracted by a commotion in the newsroom.

"Was anyone inside?"

"No."

"What happened?"

"An explosion in the school inside the diplomatic compound. Thank God school had already let out for the day."

"How the hell did they get inside the compound?"

"Who knows?"

Jeffrey quickly scanned the newsroom. He was the only reporter. He beckoned to a cameraman and said to Frank as they rushed out, "Drinks later, Frank?"

"You bet."


The diplomatic compound, the sanctuary for dependents and families from all foreign countries, was quite close to the bureau. A dark plume of smoke stretched into the sky above the flaming four-story building whose lower three floors served as a warehouse and whose top floor was a school.

A crowd had assembled in front of the burning building and watched helplessly as it was consumed by flames. At first the crowd was expectant, waiting to hear sirens pierce the fire-hot air, strident signals that help was on the way. But then they remembered. This was war-torn Beirut, not their homeland. No shiny red fire engine would arrive to douse the fire and send its long silver ladders up the scorched stucco walls.

It was so lucky that no one had been in the building.

Jeffrey interviewed several bystanders, quickly determined that no one had seen anything, then began his live report. As he spoke, he gestured at the flaming building, turning toward it and then freezing as he saw a glimpse of gold.

It was just a flame, wasn't it? Or the hot sun glinting off a pane of glass?

No, it was golden hair and it belonged to a little girl. She had gone to the classroom to get a book she had left and had cowered beneath a desk after the explosion until the flames and smoke drove her to the window.

No fire engines with long ladders would arrive, no hoses would douse the inferno, no nets would be held beneath the window so that she could jump to safety . . . it was too far to jump anyway.

Without a moment's hesitation Jeffrey ran into the blazing building. He made a few false turns but finally found the stairs and dashed up them, holding his breath and praying he could inhale something not so lethal as the dense smoke before he began the return trip with the little girl in his arms.

The golden-haired girl was about Merry's age. She was at the window, safe still, when Jeffrey reached the flaming classroom. He smiled a friendly hello before leaning out the window to take a much-needed gulp of air.

*I need one of Julie's wonderful flying dragons,* he thought as he gazed at the ground four stories below. *Daphne, where are you?* The silent question came with rush of emotion. *Julie.* And then confidence. *I am coming home to you, Julie.*

"Hi," Jeffrey said gently to the terrified little girl. "I'm going to take you out of here, OK? Put your arms around my neck. Good. Now hold very tight because we're going to be moving fast. When I say 'three' take a deep breath from outside the window and then hold it until we're out of the building. OK? Ready? One. Two. Three."

Jeffrey couldn't see a thing because the smoke had become a heavy black veil. He moved in a direction that he believed was the opposite of the way he had come, a retracing of steps, and finally, gratefully, found the stairs. When they reached the second level there was a loud crash and a falling beam of fire. The beam struck Jeffrey, shattering his collarbone. As he gasped with pain he inhaled a lungful of smoke.

But their journey continued, and then they were outside, and the little golden-haired girl—who had held her breath and had been protected from the beam by his arms—was fine. Jeffrey was taken to the hospital.


"I just spoke to Julia," Frank told Jeffrey two hours later. "I told her that you're in good shape— broken collarbone and smoke inhalation notwithstanding. She wants to speak to you, naturally, so I've asked the staff to get some portable oxygen and arrange for a phone line. While we're waiting,

I want to tell you about a call I got *before* you became a national hero. The network wants you to be the new anchor for the nightly news. The president of the news division called about an hour before you returned, looking for you, I assume, although it was a courtesy to let me know he was going to recruit you away."

"What did you tell him?"

"That I thought you'd been here long enough." Frank smiled wryly. "That it was dangerous for you here; although the willingness of all the factions to speak with you is wonderful for the network, your high visibility makes you a prime target for kidnapping. I told him I thought it was getting too risky for you to be here, and that was before I knew about your tendency to rush into blazing infernos to save little damsels in distress."

"I hadn't known about that one, either."

"Anyway, the network is looking for serious journalistic talent, like you, having at last decided to get rid of the celebrity anchor who has the misguided notion that *he's* the real news. They wanted you before you became a national hero, and were probably prepared then to offer you some editorial input. But now you can demand absolute editorial control, which, knowing you, you'll go crazy if you don't have."


Jeffrey had planned to come home and simply be with Julia, but he couldn't turn down the position of network anchor, and she didn't want him to.

And it was such a luxury to be close to her, to be able to call her a hundred times a day if he wanted, to hold her when he returned home late at night and as they shared the events of their days before going to bed.

Jeffrey began as the anchor for *The World This Evening* in August of 1986. By the following spring his newscast had gone from a distant third in the ratings war to a solid second. By October of 1987 the popularity of *The World This Evening* began to rival the number-one show, and long before the nation went to the polls in November 1988 and elected George Bush to the presidency, Jeffrey Lawrence had become the anchor from whom the majority of Americans chose to hear the news.

Christmas of 1988 was marred by two international tragedies—the devastating earthquake in Soviet Armenia and the terrorist bombing of Pan Am Flight 103 over Lockerbie. Six weeks after 1989 began, on a snowy night in February, Grandmère died. She had been a little tired that evening, nothing more, and Merry and Julia had taken turns reading one of Julia's fairy tales to her. Grandmère fell asleep with a soft smile on her face, and sometime in the night she died, very peacefully, smiling still.

"I don't want Merry to go to the funeral, Jeffrey."

"All right, darling." Jeffrey pulled Julia's tense body close to his and lifted her grief-stricken face to meet his eyes. He didn't need to know why Julia didn't want Merry to attend the funeral, but he needed Julia to talk to him. Grandmère's death had been devastating for Julia, but she hid her grief and focused her energy on her nine-year-old daughter. Julia was helping Merry, and Jeffrey wanted to help Julia. "Honey, tell me why."

"Because it's winter and the ground is so cold . . ."

The tears spilled then, finally, and her body began to shake. When she could speak she told Jeffrey about the horrible memory she had of her own parents' funeral. Then she sobbed softly and Jeffrey held her and kissed her and wished, as he often wished, that he could vanquish all the silent agonies of her heart.

"Julie. I don't want you to go to the funeral, either. Grandmère would understand why you weren't there. In spring, or whenever you want, we can take flowers to her grave."


Meredith Cabot's fortune was immense. Her will gave generous gifts to charity and to her loyal servants and equitably divided her liquid assets among her children and grandchildren. To Julia, she left Belvedere, a sum of fifteen million dollars, and the diamond-and-sapphire earrings that had been a gift from her late husband. And for Merry, her great-granddaughter and namesake, she left a trust fund of five million dollars.

Grandmère also left two very private letters, to be shared with no one else, not even each other, for Jeffrey and Julia.

Julia read the loving letter written to her as she knelt beside the grave where she had come alone to place a dozen winter roses and to say good-bye.

My beloved Julia,

Don't worry about me, my darling. I am in a heaven as wonderful as the enchanted kingdoms of your lovely imagination and I am happy because I am with my Hollis. My years on earth without him weren't so happy until you and your precious Merry came into my life. Since then there has been *such* joy!

Belvedere is yours, Julia, as it should be. Victoria will huff and puff, but Edmund has put in clever stipulations that will prevent her from even attempting to contest my will. Perhaps if I had been a mother like you, perhaps such stipulations would have been unnecessary. But I digress . . .

I know you would have worried about dismissing the servants—even though you could never have instructed them to serve you—so I have made them all millionaires! Belvedere is yours, and so are the earrings. They were a treasure from Hollis to me, and I want them now to be a gift from him to you. I left the rest of the jewels—of great value but none so precious as the earrings—to Victoria, since I know you would never wear them.

Wear my gowns, though, Julia. Plunge the necklines and raise the skirts! You are too timid to do this, I know, but you will make them enchanted as you do everything you touch.

Dearest Julia, I think you don't know how wonderful you are, how rare and precious are your gifts of love. You give so much, Julia, but you should take. My dearest grandson loves you more deeply than you will ever know. I knew the man Jeffrey was before he met you—a fine and magnificent man before, of course, but a little selfish. His love for you has changed him. He is so gentle now and so filled with love.

Believe in Jeffrey's love, my precious Julia, and believe in yourself.

Jeffrey read his letter in the privacy of the Manhattan apartment provided for him by the network. The apartment was two minutes from the studio, a place for the tailor-made suits, laundered shirts, and silk ties he wore on the air, and a place to sleep on snowbound nights or when a world crisis required that he stay in town.

Jeffrey rarely used the apartment for sleep, preferring to return to Julia no matter how late, but he used it now for privacy to read Grandmère's letter and privacy for the emotions he had kept tightly reined because of his worry about Julia. Jeffrey's dark-blue eyes had misted in the past few days, but he hadn't cried until now . . .

My darling Jeffrey,

Are you crying? Don't cry for me, Jeffrey, but be happy that you can cry. You never really knew about tears or laughter or love — Oh, yes, my darling, you did love your Grandmère! — until lovely Julia came into your life. She found a part of your heart that no one else could, the most wonderful part.

Forget about mumps and an army of doctors, Jeffrey, and let Merry be yours. You thought your mother had spared me the details? No. I know that you cannot have children, Jeffrey, and I know that I greatly preferred an era when science wasn't so involved in our love. But do the genes really

113

matter so very much?

Let yourself love that precious little girl, my darling, as much as you love her mother. Let yourself share that wonderful joy with Julia!

And there is something else, my dearest grandson. Sometimes when I look at Merry I see your grandfather. His eyes were dark brown, do you remember? And when she smiles in a certain way it is as if Hollis has returned from heaven.

I know Merry cannot be your daughter. But you *can* love her as your own as I have cherished her as my great-granddaughter.

The only obstacle, my darling Jeffrey, is in your heart.

Jeffrey held Grandmère's letter in his hands, his eyes blurred with fresh tears, his mind swirling with the loving wisdom from Grandmère. *You're right, Grandmère, it would be better not to know the truth. It would be better for me simply to believe that Merry was mine.* But Jeffrey knew the truth. He and Julia both did. And even though he had told Julia it would be virtually impossible for him to father a child, she was so careful with their birth control, not wanting to make a mistake, not wishing for any child except the lovely daughter she still kept so very far away from him.

Grandmère's letter caused rushes of pain—grief because Jeffrey loved Grandmère and would miss her terribly and other pains, ancient quiescent ones from a deep wound he believed had long since healed.

But as rushes of hurt and anger at Julia's deception swept through him, Jeffrey realized that the old wound wasn't healed at all. It had simply been bandaged by the thick, soft, protective covering of his love. Beneath the balm of love the wound was open still, unhealed and unhealing, raw, evergreen, and able still to cause great pain.

Until Julia trusted him with the secret of her heart the ancient wound would never heal. But until then, as he had done ever since Merry's birth, Jeffrey would gently and lovingly dress the gaping wound, covering it, hiding it, burying the pain far away.

And he and Julia would go on with their almost perfect love.


*No more presents, ever,* Julia had told him beneath a lavender arch of wisteria in Carmel moments after they had bought their perfect wedding rings. *We'll just give each other ourselves and our love.*

In memory of that spring day, the day before their marriage, Jeffrey and Julia never exchanged gifts—*things*—on their wedding anniversaries. Instead, they gave themselves and their love. Usually in response to the question, "What would you like for this anniversary?" each simply replied, "I only want your love."

But on their tenth wedding anniversary, in May, three months after Grandmère's death, each wanted other gifts of love.

"I'd like to take you on the honeymoon I promised you ten years ago," Jeffrey said quietly when Julia wished him Happy Anniversary and asked him what he wanted on this special day.

It was only the beginning of Jeffrey's wish. He wanted much more. He wanted Julia to accompany him when his work took him to safe, wonderful places. He wanted to show her the treasures of the greatest cities in the world, to see the beautiful places, marvel at them as he knew she would, and enjoy the luxurious surroundings of the fabulous hotels where he always stayed. Not that in all his travels Jeffrey had ever found a place as beautiful and luxurious as Julia's Belvedere, or rose gardens as lovingly tended and bountiful, or decor as tasteful and elegant, or suites as lovely and romantic, but still . . .

"It's time for me to outgrow my fear of flying, isn't it?"

"I think so, darling, with me to help you. You've made great headway. You used to seem frightened whenever I flew, and you don't anymore."

"I've just become a better actress." Julia sighed softly. She had tried not to let it show, part of her vow never to interfere, but Jeffrey had known anyway, so now she told him truthfully, "It terrifies me when you fly. I'm so afraid you won't come back."

"I will always come back to you, Julie." Jeffrey sealed the promise with a gentle kiss. "So, my love, will you think about it? Sometime in the next ten years, may I take you on a romantic honeymoon in Europe?"

"Yes."

"Good." Jeffrey decided not to push any further for now. He knew that Julia's fear of flying was far more than fear for herself. Her residual girlhood terror had another component, perhaps the greatest fear, the fear of orphaning her daughter as she had been orphaned. Jeffrey didn't push. Julia had heard his wish and he knew that she would try. He kissed her lips and whispered, "Now tell me what you want."

Jeffrey expected Julia's usual swift reply, "I only want your love," but her lavender eyes told him that she, too, had a special anniversary wish.

"Tell me," he whispered.

"I want us to be a family, Jeffrey." Julia's voice was soft, uncertain, laced with apology and hope.

He heard her hope and a rush of hope swept through him, too. At last she was going to tell him the truth and the ancient wound could finally heal.

"I know how busy you are, Jeffrey, but if there could be times when we could plan to do things together . . ." Julia's eyes grew timid under his intense gaze. Timid but resolute because it was time. Her lovely little girl needed her father. There were fathers far less busy than Jeffrey who ignored their children, Julia knew that, but that wasn't what she wanted for their daughter. Julia gave Merry all the love she could give, and it had been enough when Grandmère had been there, too, covering Merry in a downy comforter of love. But now Grandmère was gone, and Merry's best friend's very busy father always made time to be with his daughter, and Merry needed Jeffrey as much as Amanda needed Edmund. Julia asked softly, "Jeffrey, please?"

The hope that had filled Jeffrey's heart, the hope that the wound could finally heal, faded as the realization settled. Julia wanted to change the rules by which they had lived the last ten years of

117

their lives, but she wasn't going to tell him the truth.

Now, after all these years, she was asking him to live the lie . . . and she was asking him to become a father to a little girl he didn't even know.

Jeffrey didn't know Merry, not the girl inside. He only knew the visual images his talented journalistic mind had made as he had observed from a distance the drama of a tiny baby becoming a little girl. Merry as an infant, cooing softly as she cuddled in Julia's arms . . . Merry as a sunny, lively toddler galloping on sturdy legs to Julia and laughing with glee . . . Merry as the little girl whose limbs had lengthened gracefully and whose white-blond hair had darkened into lustrous gold and whose soft voice, so very much like Julia's, spoke now in full, quiet sentences, not excited bursts of words.

Jeffrey knew from a distance the ever-changing cover of the lovely sunny book, but he didn't know *Merry*. He always had a warm smile and gentle hello for her, of course, and he wished happiness for the precious daughter of his precious love. When she was very young Merry had eyed him with obvious interest and curiosity, clinging to Julia but quite bold, peering at him and then erupting into gleeful laughter like a game of hide-and-seek. More recently, in the rare times that Jeffrey had even seen her since his return from Beirut, Merry's dark-brown stares ended with an embarrassed rush of pink in her cheeks when he caught her eyes and smiled at her.

When Merry called Jeffrey by a name she called him Daddy, and that had bothered him at first. But for almost ten years Daddy had just been a name without expectations . . . from Julia or from Merry.

Until now.

Now Julia expected him to embrace her lie.

On this tenth wedding anniversary, Jeffrey had asked of Julia that she conquer her fear of flying. And now she was asking of him that he conquer his fear of the ancient secret that was still too important to share.

Could he do it? Could he pretend to be the father of a little girl who wasn't his?

Jeffrey didn't know. But as he gazed at Julia's lovely, hopeful eyes he heard himself whisper quietly, "All right, Julie." *I promise I will try.*

When the old wound had been exposed by Grandmère's wise and loving letter, Jeffrey had quickly hidden it deep beneath thick, soft layers of love. Now the wound was exposed again, but this time it couldn't be so easily hidden because now they were living the painful lie.

Julia's wish that they become a family was a wish of love that promised forever. Jeffrey should have felt hope, and he did, but the old, unhealed wound came with old, unhealed emotions. The ancient emotions of hurt, anger, and betrayal surfaced from the depths, and now, after a decade of confident and joyous love, Jeffrey suddenly felt brittle, precarious, and raw.

It would take him a little time to conquer the ancient emotions, but he *would* conquer them.

The emotions were still swirling very near the surface three weeks later, however, when he returned to Belvedere after the interview with Dr.

119

Diana Shepherd that had been disrupted by the arrival of her divorce papers. That night, ominous thoughts had taunted and he had been so relieved to find Julia waiting for him, so relieved to see the familiar love and joy in her eyes. After they made love, as she slept gently in his arms, Jeffrey thought about Julia's deception, the tiny flaw in the brilliance of their love. And as he drifted off to sleep, he wondered what flaw had shattered the love of Chase Andrews and his beautiful Queen of Hearts.

# Part Two

# Chapter Seven

Diana stood on the balcony of the luxurious Park Avenue penthouse that she and Chase had shared for five years and watched with relief as the summer sun began to lighten the sky. Diana's night had been so dark, her sleep disrupted by nightmares and her wakefulness haunted by ghosts. Some of the ghosts were new — fresh, vivid phantoms of the marriage that had lived and died in the fabulous penthouse. But there were other ghosts, old ghosts — painful shadowy memories of Janie and Sam.

The night had been long and dark. With dawn came the promise of escape to the sanctuary of the hospital and the even safer haven of the operating room.

*Are you still going to operate on the Soviet ambassador?* Jeffrey Lawrence had asked her last night. The nation's leading anchor, excellent journalist that he was, posed the question evenly, without bias, but the question itself was a challenge to her ethics. Not that it wasn't a legitimate question . . . but Diana didn't need *him* to ask it for her.

123

Was it ethical for her to operate today? Her sleep had been fitful, her night long and tormented, but Diana was accustomed to sleepless nights and she knew from years of experience that her ability to concentrate in the operating room was absolute.

No ghosts were permitted in the O.R. No ghosts, no memories, no emotions. Diana was confident of her ability to keep the ghosts out. She had years of practice. When Diana operated, every corner of her brilliant mind was focused on the surgery. She was safe and so were her patients.

Safe and at peace.

Diana loved the peace of the operating room, its magnificent stillness interrupted only by the necessary sounds of surgery—the soft sighs of the ventilator, the rhythmic beeps of the cardiac monitor, the gentle whoosh of suction, the whispered snips of scissors clipping suture, the crisp snap of instruments, and the creak of rubber gloves moved by expert fingers.

Sometimes necessary words joined the other sounds, but most of the communications between Diana and the members of her team were silent. Diana didn't need to say "scalpel" or "clamp" or "sponge" or "forceps" to her scrub nurse because the highly trained nurse already knew. And she didn't need to ask the other heart surgeons who assisted her for "retraction" or "suction" or "cautery," nor did she need to tell them to hold the delicate leaflet of the mitral valve gently so that she could place a suture just so, because they knew that, too.

When Diana operated, the sounds were the necessary sounds of surgery only. She operated in absorbed and reverent silence, and because she was the leader of the team, her team members followed suit. There were no discussions about the weather,

124

no light banter about politics, no mention of books or movies or the theater. Diana's team assumed, incorrectly, that she disapproved of casual conversation in the operating room. But she didn't disapprove. She knew perfectly well that surgeons could talk and operate at the same time.

Talk . . . or listen to music.

Talking wouldn't have distracted her, but *music* might have. Music might have permitted emotions that had no place in the operating room; it might have reminded her of the songs of love that had been written for her, and sung to her, and of a precious love that had died.

But music wasn't allowed when Diana operated and the ghosts stayed away and her talented hands worked their magic.

Would she operate today?

Yes. It was ethical.


Five minutes after leaving her Park Avenue penthouse Diana was in the surgical dressing room at Memorial Hospital. She hung her dress on a metal hook, exchanging mauve silk for royal-blue cotton scrubs, then reached for the four-carat diamond and the gold wedding band on her left ring finger. The gesture was reflexive, almost an instinct.

How many hundreds of times in the past five years had she removed the rings and secured them to her scrubs with the solid-gold safety pin Chase had given her for just that purpose? Surgeons couldn't wear rings when they operated—and Diana had doubts about wearing a flawless four-carat diamond ever—but the diamond was an Andrews family treasure and Chase wanted her to have it. And, he had asked lovingly, weren't her talented fingers skillful enough to remove and replace a priceless diamond without dropping it to the tile floor? Yes, she had replied with a sapphire sparkle, Of course.

Diana reached for the rings now, but her finger was already bare. She had removed them last night when she was called to the O.R., thankfully ending the interview with Jeffrey Lawrence, and after she couldn't force herself to wear the glittering symbols of the marriage that was over. Instead she had carried them curled in her hand as she walked back to her penthouse. Once there she had hidden them between layers of silk in her dresser drawer.

Diana sighed softly as she touched her already bare ring finger. She would have to teach herself to abandon the ritual of reaching for her wedding rings . . . just as she would have to learn about living her life alone again, perhaps this time forever.

"Good afternoon, I'm Jeffrey Lawrence. We are interrupting regularly scheduled programming to bring you this special report. The surgery to implant the Shepherd Heart in the Soviet ambassador has just been successfully completed. We expect to go to a live press conference at Memorial Hospital very soon. Although the eyes of the world are focused on this major advance in Soviet-American relations, one should not ignore the major advance represented by the Shepherd Heart itself. I would like to spend the next few minutes sharing with you what I learned in a conversation I had last evening with Dr. Diana Shepherd about her remarkable invention. This model was generously loaned to me by Dr. Shepherd for this telecast . . ."

Holding a model of the Heart to the camera, Jeffrey explained what he had learned from Diana and from the brochures she had given him. He had written the copy as he always did, and when he ran out of script, because the live press conference hadn't yet started, he embellished effortlessly until the producer signaled that they were ready to switch to the hospital.

Jeffrey watched the live press conference on the studio monitors. The conference room was crowded with radio, television, and newspaper journalists from around the world. Diana arrived with an entourage—her team of three nurses, two other cardiac surgeons, and an anesthesiologist. After introducing the members of her team, Diana gave a brief summary of the surgery and announced that the ambassador was recovering uneventfully in the I.C.U.

"The ambassador is in the I.C.U.," a reporter reiterated when Diana asked for questions. "What does that mean?"

"All patients who receive the Heart are 'recovered' in the I.C.U. It's quite standard."

The questions continued for twenty minutes, questions about the surgery, the Heart, the length of time on cardiopulmonary bypass, the ambassador's anticipated convalescence in the hospital, and his life expectancy. The reporters asked medical questions, and political ones. Did Dr. Shepherd expect a call from President Bush? From Gorbachev?

Diana listened to each question carefully, her intelligent blue eyes focused and thoughtful, and answered each appropriately—the medical ones seriously and the political ones with a slight twinkle.

The press conference could have gone on all afternoon. Diana had them captivated and was quite happy to answer their questions. But she brought the session to an abrupt close after a reporter from a local affiliate of Jeffrey's network asked a question that was neither medical nor political, simply private.

"Dr. Shepherd, was it more difficult for you to operate, to concentrate, in the wake of your personal news?"

"I beg your pardon?"

"The news that your husband, real-estate mogul Chase Andrews, has just filed for divorce."

Jeffrey couldn't hear Diana's answer. Whatever she whispered was lost in the hubbub that suddenly erupted in the conference room. But he saw her reaction. For an astonished moment she simply stared at the reporter with glacial disbelief. Then, quite elegantly, quite regally, the Queen of Hearts led her court from the room.

Jeffrey gave the nation a pleasant and eloquent recap of the special report, and then, as soon as he was off the air, he demanded with quiet rage, "I want to know *now* how that reporter knew about the divorce."

"Tough news, Diana."

Diana glanced up from the progress note she was writing. Dr. Thomas Chandler looked down at her, his face carefully composed to appear genuinely concerned.

"Has something happened to the ambassador, Tom?"

"I meant about Chase."

"Oh." Diana gave a frown that she hoped looked authentically confused. Then she said sweetly, resurrecting her Dallas drawl, reminding Tom that he might be a bigger-than-life Texan, but so was she,

"It's not tough news, Tom, but thank you for your concern."

"You're good, Diana."

"You mean the surgery on the ambassador?"

"You know what I mean." That was Tom's parting line, his parting shot, and his voice hardened slightly as he delivered it.

Then he was gone and Diana was left to calm her racing heart and control the rushes of anger that pulsed through her.

In eight months Diana and Tom would be vying for the prestigious position of director of the Heart Institute at Memorial Hospital. They were both deserving candidates—heart surgeons of impeccable skill and extraordinary talent, capable administrators, academic scholars—and each wanted the appointment very much. It would be war, but the battle between the two had begun literally the moment they met. Diana was unused to enemies. Even when she had critical opinions of others she usually concealed her true feelings artfully beneath layers of gracious politeness. But the antipathy between Tom Chandler and Diana was so apparent and so mutual that it was pointless to pretend it didn't exist.

Tom looked like Tom Cruise, or, as admirers were fond of saying, Tom Chandler looked the way Tom Cruise *might* look at forty-one if the handsome young actor aged magnificently. Tom Chandler was indisputably handsome and fully expected that when he arrived at Memorial Hospital he would be Top Gun. Diana had been quite prepared to defer to the newly recruited cardiac surgeon, willingly admitting that Tom's experience and credentials should place him at a level above her, but the other surgeons at Memorial viewed Tom and Diana as equals. All of which simply aggravated the dislike at first sight.

"He's such a typical heart surgeon!" Diana had exclaimed to Chase.

"You're telling me that he's incredibly sexy, incredibly bright and has hypnotic sapphire-blue eyes?" Chase had countered lovingly to his heart surgeon wife.

"No," Diana had replied with a smile. "I'm telling you he is impossibly arrogant and egotistical."

Tom Chandler *was* impossibly arrogant and egotistical, but his talent in the operating room could not be denied. Not that Tom and Diana ever operated together—each had their own teams—but she knew of his work just as he knew of hers. Diana garnered attention and publicity for her Heart, but long before that remarkable invention she had been recognized nationally and internationally as a top pediatric heart surgeon. Tom achieved public notoriety for his research in heart transplantation, but like Diana he had long been recognized in the surgical community for the magic he worked on pediatric hearts.

Tom and Diana shared talent, dedication, and special expertise in cardiac surgery in children. They should have been respected colleagues, but instead they were engaged in a war of nerves, steel against steel, a war in which the strikes on the enemy camp were made with exquisite surgical precision and finesse.

Tom had a reason, of course, for being in the nurses' station on the pediatric ward tonight. He was making post-op rounds on his youngest patients just as Diana was. But he had no reason to engage in conversation with her except as a test to see how she was coping with the viewed-by-millions live announcement that her husband no longer wanted her.

130

Diana knew it was a test. She knew that Tom wanted to see if her rock-steady hands were trembling or if there were indications in her eyes or voice that she was shaken. *Tough news about Chase.* Tom's voice had implied that the news might be tougher than just the emotion of a failed marriage, as if her divorce from Chase might disqualify her as a candidate for the directorship. Because her happy marriage to extraordinarily wealthy and influential Chase was as important to the appointment as her own stunning credentials? Because with Chase, Diana could hostess phenomenally successful fund-raisers for the Institute?

Did Tom really think the announcement of her divorce might influence the board? Yes, obviously he did. And maybe it would. The board of Memorial Hospital was conservative, proper, and acutely aware of public image.

Diana sighed, finished the progress note she had been writing, and checked her watch to record the time in the chart. Seven P.M. All her patients were fine, stable, and in the more than capable hands of the on call doctors.

Time to go home.

Time to go home *after* the errand she had been planning ever since the end of the press conference.


Jeffrey was in his office, the evening broadcast just completed, preparing to leave when Diana appeared at his doorway. Jeffrey had no warning that she was coming. The studio's security guards recognized her from the special report and she mumbled something about needing to get the model of the Heart she had loaned the star anchor. Not that Jeffrey needed a warning. Had the guards called, he

131

would have said, "Of course, send her right up," and he would have been waiting at the elevator to greet her. But no one called, and she was let in, and it was a security breach. "Crazies" tried to get into the studio and on the air all the time. Last year there had been a murder, live, at a station in D.C.

What if Dr. Diana Shepherd had been carrying a gun? The ice-blue eyes that met Jeffrey's looked as if they would be perfectly happy to kill him. Of course the Queen of Hearts didn't need a gun to assassinate. She had all the ammunition of medical science in her arsenal. Perhaps she had a syringe of curare or potassium concealed in the pockets of her stylish silk dress.

Diana's eyes blazed with sapphire rage. And, Jeffrey noticed in the few seconds between the time she appeared at his door and he spoke his greeting, there was another symbol of her iciness and perhaps her rage: Diana's left hand was ringless now, the dazzling crown jewel gone. Had the immensely skilled cardiac surgeon so swiftly excised Chase Andrews from her heart?

"Good evening, Doctor."

"You are really a bastard."

"Thank you. What have I done?" Jeffrey should have known not to feign innocence. He knew why Diana was angry. He was angry about it, too. Still, it annoyed him that she assumed he was the cause of the on-the-air revelation about her divorce.

"If I even intimated a confidential detail about a patient, I could be sued, censured, maybe lose my license. In medicine, it's called ethics, an essential inviolate code to protect privacy. But you journalists have that wonderful First Amendment. Anything goes, anything to increase the ratings. Let's see if we can get her to unravel on national televi-

132

sion! Let's see if the Queen of Hearts is heartless after all! I don't need it, you bastard. I don't want it, and, dammit, I don't deserve it."

"I don't want it for you."

"Really? Then why did you do it?"

"I didn't."

"I don't believe you. The man was a reporter from your network."

"From a local affiliate, not this studio."

"How very convenient. Just far enough away from you to shift blame but close enough to boost the ratings!"

"Last night this journalism-bashing was tolerable, even intelligent, and your holier-than-thou attitude had a certain charm. But now, *Doctor,* you are questioning my integrity and that is not acceptable."

"Not *acceptable?* Your integrity is beyond question?"

"Just like your ethics. For the record, the divorce papers were filed first thing this morning. The court reporters from the local station made the discovery about ten."

"And you're telling me they weren't tipped?"

"Not by me."

"Perhaps by someone you know?"

Jeffrey had given Diana his word that his unwitting knowledge about her divorce would be off the record. Now was she actually accusing him of *planting* the tip? Yes, apparently she was.

"I am not responsible for your divorce, Dr. Shepherd," Jeffrey paused, his dark-blue eyes silently communicating the unspoken, *You are.* "Neither am I responsible for the information becoming available to the press. If the court reporters were tipped, and I have no reason to believe they were, perhaps

133

it was by your husband or someone who is his friend."

The implication of "friend" was obvious. Jeffrey meant *mistress*.

Diana stared at him, her eyes shining with rage. Or was the shininess tears, a sign that the ice could melt? Jeffrey almost apologized, he should have, but . . .

"I repeat, Mr. Lawrence," Diana hissed softly. "You are a bastard."

With that she left his office. The box containing the model of the Heart remained on Jeffrey's desk. He would send it to her by courier. With a message? With a dozen red roses and an apology? There had been a veneer of ice tonight, but Jeffrey remembered the way Diana looked last night. She had been deeply hurt, and now that hurt would become public, the reasons for the decay of the marriage a matter of energetic and intriguing speculation. Were there other lovers? Was the iciness sexual, too?

Diana was wounded. She lashed out at Jeffrey from pain. Jeffrey understood it. But he resented it. Maybe someday, if she reflected at all, Diana would realize how insulting her remarks to him had been.

Jeffrey decided he would return the Heart without a message. He wasn't proud of what he had done — his lack of control and his cruelty — but his integrity meant as much to him as Diana's ethics meant to her.

*Because we are so much alike?*

*No!* the answer came swiftly. As Jeffrey began to search for differences — proof that he and Diana weren't alike at all — reason promptly intervened and called off the search.

It didn't matter. Very likely, hopefully, he would

never see Diana Shepherd again. He already knew that she wouldn't be at the Spencer's small dinner party at Somerset on Saturday. He assumed that Chase wouldn't be there, either, and he imagined that because of Chase's work relationship with Paige it would be Chase, not Diana who received invitations to future galas hosted by Edmund and Paige.

Jeffrey would probably never see Diana again. And that was just fine because he had absolutely no desire to.

# Chapter Eight

"Grrrr."

"Grrrr?"

"My zipper's stuck. Would you zip it up for me?"

"You're asking me to dress you?" Jeffrey moved behind her and kissed her bare shoulders. "I would *undress* you in an instant, Julie, but aiding and abetting in concealing this body, I don't know."

Julia turned in his arms and tenderly kissed his lips, smiling as she did, so happy with the memories of this wonderful day. Jeffrey had been at Merry's first riding lesson, and he had watched, really watched, smiling encouragement to Merry and Amanda, not seeming the least bit restless or bored.

"Thank you for this morning, Jeffrey," Julia whispered as her soft lips caressed his. "It meant so much to Merry."

Julia didn't see the slight frown that clouded Jeffrey's handsome face, because he was returning her kiss. He had been at the stable for Julia, because it was what *she* wanted. Jeffrey couldn't imagine it mattered at all to the golden-haired little girl he didn't know. Merry had been shy and distant with him, as always.

"I'm glad, darling. So, do I get to undress you?"

"Not now. We're due at Paige and Edmund's in ten

minutes."

"But later? If I zip you up now, do I get to unzip you the moment we get back?"

"Oh, yes."

"Welcome." Paige smiled warmly as she greeted the Lawrences ten minutes later. Focusing on Merry, who was spending the night at Somerset because the dinner party would probably not end before the girls' bedtime, she asked, "How is my favorite overnight guest?"

"I'm fine, Aunt Paige."

"Still pretty excited about your first riding lesson?"

Merry answered Paige's question with a vigorous nod of her blond head. In the hours since the riding lesson had ended, for Merry and Amanda their long golden hair had taken on new symbolism. No longer were they Alice in Wonderland or Goldilocks or Rapunzel. Now they were palominos with wonderful flowing manes.

"So is Amanda. She's in the day room."

Before cantering off to join Amanda, Merry said to Julia, " 'Bye, Mommy." And then lifting her face bravely to Jeffrey she whispered, " 'Bye, Daddy."

"I think we know where our girls are going to spend their summer," Paige said. "It's a full-time occupation, as I recall, helping the grooms with the endlessly intriguing tasks of raking hay, pouring oats, and cleaning stalls."

"Patrick may not want them there all the time."

*Oh Julia,* Paige thought fondly, marveling at her friend. Didn't she know that what Patrick wanted didn't matter? Patrick was a servant. He was paid, and probably not very much, to satisfy the whims of his employers — the wealthy mistresses of the great estates. All the whims, Paige mused. She had been struck again today by the alluring yet menacing sensuality of Patrick James and wondered about the whims that his mistresses would command him to satisfy.

Julia was one of the wealthiest mistresses of one of the greatest estates in Southampton . . . but because she was Julia, she considered Patrick's wishes not her whims and would never dream of making a command.

"I'm sure Patrick won't mind, Julia, but if you like we'll ask him. So, shall we go outside? Casey and Edmund are on the terrace."

En route to the terrace, Julia remembered the seventeenth-century Belgian tapestry Paige and Edmund had just acquired from Sotheby's. As Paige and Julia made a brief detour to the dining room to admire it, Jeffrey continued on to join Edmund and his dazzling new associate.

Casey English was looking forward to meeting Jeffrey Lawrence. Casey knew, of course, that Jeffrey was married. Although the private life of the nation's leading anchorman had eluded the pages of *People, Portrait,* and *Vanity Fair,* Casey, like most of America, had noticed the elegant wedding band he wore. Paige had told Casey that Jeffrey was *very married,* but the conversation had wandered to a new topic before Paige had had a chance to tell Casey about Julia.

Not that Casey was interested in details about Jeffrey's wife. Jeffrey was the one who appealed, as all handsome and powerful men appealed. Casey did not have affairs with married men — she did not need other women's husbands! — but she loved the provocative games, the innocent seductions, the way their eyes wanted *her.* She was very much looking forward to seeing flickers of appreciation and desire for her in the dark-blue eyes of the handsome and so sexy

138

anchor.

"Oh, Jeffrey, here you are. I'd like you to meet Casey English. Casey, this is Jeffrey Lawrence."

"Hello, Edmund. Casey, how nice to meet you." *She really is model beautiful,* Jeffrey mused when he saw Casey's forget-me-not blue eyes, flawless smile, sleek, perfect figure, and dazzling golden-blond hair. Tonight the long spun-gold hair was even more magnificent because the setting sun caressed it with glittering flickers of red. No, Jeffrey realized after a moment, the streaks of fire were part of the spectacular hair, not reflected brilliance.

"I watch you every night," Casey purred. Her eyes told him with unashamed blue-violet candor that she watched *him,* not the news, and sent a playful-and-wistful message: *I know you are married, Jeffrey Lawrence. Too bad. We might have had fun, mightn't we?*

"I understand you are wonderful to watch in the courtroom," Jeffrey replied politely, marveling at her beauty, her confidence, and his lack of interest. Jeffrey was used to appreciative smiles from beautiful, confident women, although few as truly beautiful as Casey English, but his heart never quickened, never fluttered even for a moment. That mystery was reserved for only one woman, the most beautiful one of all, one who was not so confident . . .

One who appeared on the terrace now and whose lavender eyes quickly found his. Jeffrey smiled a loving welcome and said, "Casey, I'd like you to meet my wife."

*"Julia,"* Casey whispered. It only lasted for a fraction of a second—the sun behind a cloud, the frown on the flawless face, the radiant confidence struck a staggering blow. Casey recovered quickly, although her voice was strained when she spoke again, and she barely heard her own words above the thundering pulse in her brain. "Julia Phillips."

"Casey. How lovely to see you. I had no idea." Had Paige mentioned Casey's name? If she had, she must have been so preoccupied with the decision to let Merry take riding lessons that it simply hadn't registered.

"You two know each other." Edmund stated the obvious.

"Julia and I were in high school together. How long has it been?" Casey asked casually, but of course she knew, knew exactly. "Ten years."

"Well, what a wonderful coincidence," Paige said. "Edmund, why don't you supply drinks while I get the hors d'oeuvres? Then we'll get acquainted and re-acquainted."

"Let me help you, Paige."

"No, Julia. Stay here and catch up with Casey."

"We didn't really know each other very well," Julia said quietly, hoping that would end the discussion.

Julia saw the subtle shift in Jeffrey's eyes, the ominous darkening of the blue to the shade *beyond* anger she had seen only twice before . . . when she told him she was pregnant, and four months later when he first saw their baby girl. The darkness terrified her, a symbol of how much Jeffrey didn't want Merry. Was that why he was angry now? Because she and Casey had known each other in high school and that was a reminder of the time when their passion created a baby he didn't want then and didn't want still?

No, Julia reassured herself swiftly by filling her mind with images of today at the stable. Today was the beginning, the fragile beginning, of her dream. We are going to be a family . . . at last.

"No, we didn't really know each other very well," Casey agreed with matching quiet. She needed time to collect her swirling thoughts before she could delve into a discussion about that time. For years just the memory of Julia could summon the uneasy

140

emotions. And now seeing Julia herself . . .

"It is lovely to see you, Casey," Julia repeated. Then, wanting to put the conversation clearly in the present, she added, "You've done so well."

*So have you, Julia. You are married to the astonishing Jeffrey Lawrence, a man whose eyes fill with longing and desire simply at the sight of you.* There had been no desire in Jeffrey's eyes, not even a flirtatious flicker, when Jeffrey met *her,* but when he turned to greet Julia, the love in the ocean blue had made Casey tremble. Casey's thought continued, bringing with it painful reminders, *You've done better than me, Julia . . . as always.*

While Edmund made drinks, Casey raved about SeaCliff—the magnificent views, the splendid privacy, the fresh layers of Laura Ashley wallpaper, the charm of the cottage.

She was buying time, dazzling as she could on automatic pilot while her mind spun and she tried to calm herself with bourbon. Every so often she would glance at Julia, hoping she was merely a mirage that would vanish as she had vanished once before.

Julia smiled shyly, an uneasy smile, her mind spinning, too, trying to convince herself that the conversation would stay away from the past. After all, she and Casey had barely known each other, she reminded herself. It was amazing that Casey even recognized her. Julia hoped the conversation wouldn't drift to the past, but the damage had already been done. Jeffrey was so angry. Why?

Jeffrey's mind filled with vivid memories of two conversations—a recent one with Edmund about Casey's impressive credentials, including her education at the exclusive and academically rigorous Carlton Academy, and a distant one when Julia told him, as they made their wedding plans, that graduating from high school and going on to college didn't matter, as if her schooling had been ordinary, unimportant, not exceptional.

But Julia had been at Carlton with Casey.

As Julia sat in bewildered silence and Jeffrey waited to learn more secrets about his wife, Casey dazzled and drank bourbon and tried to calm the unwelcome emotions that pulsed through her at the sight of Julia.

*Julia* . . . her nemesis, her archrival, her bitter enemy in a war Julia hadn't even known they were waging. *Julia* . . . who uncovered feelings, flaws, in her that Casey didn't want to know even existed.

*Damn her! Damn Julia for making all those feelings come back to me!*

Casey hated the feelings, hated Julia for causing them, and hated herself for being unable to conquer them despite her incredible will to be perfect.

Katherine Carole was Kirk Carroll English's firstborn child. She was not the son her father wanted, and that terrible disappointment became permanent when the doctors told her parents that because of her difficult birth she was the only child they were destined to have.

Katherine Carole English was never "Kathy" or "Kitten" or "Katie." For a brief time she was "K.C. Junior," a whimsical name with an uneasy edge, and then finally, gratefully, she became Casey.

To Kirk Carroll English, worth was measured by achievement. Perfection was the standard. Winning was everything and second was no better than last. There were no rewards for success, only condemnation for failure. Casey dedicated her young life to trying to please her perfectionistic father. She never wholly succeeded, despite her remarkable accomplishments, because she could only be a daughter, not the son he wanted.

Casey was born with brains, beauty, and the legacy of generations of wealth and privilege. She fine-tuned her gifts with unrelenting discipline. She earned all A's, never cheated on diets, and never procrastinated about her exercises. She studied the expressions of her beautiful face, mastering the alluring ones until they became instinctive and extinguishing the ones that weren't stunning, confident, or provocative.

Casey drove herself relentlessly, afraid of even the slightest blemish on her flawless record of success, and her hard work inevitably paid off. Something inside Casey, a renegade voice, sometimes balked at the hard work and urged her to relax her vigil just a little. It would be safe. She would still be the best.

But Casey never relaxed, and when Julia Phillips suddenly appeared at Carlton, an unwelcome and unexpected intrusion, she realized that everything that had gone before hadn't been hard work at all. Her successes had been deceptively easy.

It was so simple to be a gracious winner when all you did was win.

Julia was a scholarship student, an "extremely gifted" girl who had been discovered languishing in a public high school in Berkeley. Until Julia's arrival, Casey had been the brightest in her class, and the youngest. But Julia was brighter—better—and she was even a year younger than Casey.

Because of Julia, Casey discovered that her need to win was as essential to her life as her need to breathe. Without winning she would surely suffocate, wouldn't she? She would surely die a desperate, gasping death.

Casey *needed* to win. But no matter how hard she worked, she was no longer the best.

Julia was better. Julia was brighter and could even have been more beautiful had she understood the power of her intoxicating sensuality. But she was so shy, so naive, so unaware of her beauty—so unaware

143

of everything!—that Casey easily retained her distinction as the most beautiful girl at Carlton. Had Julia been aware of her beauty, it would have been a bitter contest: Casey's radiant golden beauty against Julia's dark sultry allure.

Casey retained the distinction of being Carlton's most beautiful, but she lost the other all-important crown she had held for so long. She was no longer Carlton's brightest.

On every exam, every essay, every national test, Julia was better. Not a great deal better, a point, two points, but better. The margin was large at first—Julia was much better and the teachers in the school who had doted over Casey almost forgot about her—but Casey dug in, working harder, pushing herself beyond exhaustion, and gradually narrowing the gap. The scores became close, very close, but still Julia was always better.

And Julia, brilliant, otherworldly Julia, who spent the noon hours dreamily reading the romances of Charlotte Brontë and Jane Austen instead of flirting or making friends, didn't even know they were at war. What if Julia was the best and she wasn't even trying? What if Julia started to *try?*

The war Casey waged was a cold war, a war of spying, a war in which her mind toyed with sabotage, clever, devious ways to throw her opponent off track.

Perhaps a boyfriend for shy, naive, beautiful Julia. Wouldn't love be a distraction? Mightn't that affect her concentration?

The boys at Carlton would have done anything to win favor with Casey. Confident, dazzling, sexy Casey was the queen bee. She urged the boys to become involved with Julia, and they tried. But they couldn't "relate" to her. "She's from a different planet, Case!" they exclaimed, bewildered, disappointed that they had failed Casey. "Sorry, Casey, but she's really a space cadet." Julia was from somewhere else, an outer planet or a distant era of gallantry and romance.

Finally Casey decided to approach Julia herself, not to become a friend but as a way to spy behind enemy lines. She asked Julia to come to her mansion in San Francisco's prestigious Presidio Heights after school and to the beach parties on the weekends. Julia was startled by the invitations, and shyly grateful, but she declined, giving as her reason that she had to work after school and on the weekends.

*To* study? Casey demanded.

*No,* Julia repeated quietly, her lavender eyes so innocent, *to work.*

Casey didn't believe her. Julia didn't *work!* Surely she spent every second studying, never playing, rarely sleeping. That was how she won the war.

One afternoon Casey drove her BMW behind the car and driver hired by Carlton to chauffeur its star pupil between Berkeley and Atherton. If she could catch Julia in a lie, that would be a sort of victory, wouldn't it?

But Julia wasn't lying. Fifteen minutes after the car left Julia in front of a tiny, dilapidated house two miles from Telegraph Avenue, she reappeared wearing a brown-checked uniform and walked a mile to the hamburger stand where she worked, Casey learned, three evenings a week and every other weekend.

Unfamiliar, ugly, frightening emotions pulsed through Casey's beautiful body and horrible thoughts danced in her mind. The emotions were hatred and jealousy and frustration. And the thoughts . . .

Casey couldn't win by trying her hardest. She *was* trying, and Julia was still better.

Were there other ways to win? Other ways to defeat Julia? What if something happened to her?

What if she got in an accident, went into coma, maybe even *died?*

Casey hated the thoughts! She hated herself for thinking them and sometimes even wishing them! And that made her hate Julia all the more. Casey never imagined a role for herself — she wouldn't allow her mind even to dabble with those thoughts — but she wished ruin for Julia, wished for some fate . . .

And then it happened. Casey won by default. During the spring of their senior year, Julia simply vanished. At first she was mysteriously absent from class every other Friday and Monday. Then, in May, she disappeared and never returned. Carlton's headmaster told the class that Julia left for "personal reasons." She had taken oral examinations before she left to satisfy graduation requirements. Although Julia would not be at graduation, she would receive credit, but not grades, for the coursework for that spring.

Which meant that Julia graduated *second* behind Casey. Casey was the valedictorian. Casey, not Julia, addressed her classmates — the brightest high school graduates in the country — and confidently told them of the great promise their futures held.

Casey won, but it was a bittersweet victory tainted with horrible truths she had learned about herself and her desperate need to win.

That summer, before she started her freshman year at Berkeley, she spent long hours trying to gain perspective and prepare herself for the next phase of her life. Never again would she allow herself to be consumed as she had been by the competition with Julia. *In college, and in law school, and in the practice of law, there will be other Julias,* Casey told herself. *Face it, Casey, you're not the best, not always. You won't always win, no matter how hard you try.*

She disciplined her mind to those truths and prepared herself to handle failures and to lose as graciously as she had always won. But it was all an exercise.

For the next ten years there were no more Julias—not a Julia or a Julian, not a woman or man who posed a threat to her success. She graduated first from Berkeley and first from Hastings Law. And she won a record number of cases during her three years with the D.A.'s office in San Francisco.

For ten years Casey's life was deceptively easy again. Julia was simply a disquieting memory, a phantom, a ghostly symbol of darkness in perfect golden Casey, a *flaw* that haunted still.

Gone, but not forgotten.

What had happened to Julia? Where was she? What was she doing? Writing? Of Julia's enormous talents her ability to write had seemed her greatest gift. *Please let her be a writer,* Casey prayed. *Please don't let her be a lawyer.*

Casey could imagine Julia doing both, writing and practicing law, because Julia could do anything—everything. What if Julia was at Harvard Law School? Casey compulsively looked for Julia's name on the staff of the Harvard Law Review and then on lists of graduates and practicing attorneys and was relieved, but not wholly comforted, when it wasn't there.

Julia was *somewhere.* What if Casey and Julia met again one day, battling on opposing sides in a court of law? Who would win?

Casey knew.

Julia would win.


And now, on a rose-fragrant terrace on a balmy June evening, Casey was face-to-face with Julia, her ancient enemy, and with the even greater enemy—whatever it was inside her that made her very survival dependent on winning. The uneasy emotions

147

swirled, but Casey imposed reason on them, mind over emotion, fact over fantasy. Here was Julia and she was *not* a lawyer, *not* a threat.

On impulse, warmed by too much bourbon and the momentary victory of reason over emotion, Casey decided to end it forever. She would exorcise the dark demons by exposing them to the red-gold sunlight that filtered through the trees.

"There's something I need to admit to Julia," Casey said bravely. She looked from a worried Julia to an intrigued Edmund and teased softly, "Edmund, the way you mixed this drink! The bourbon is forcing me into a confession."

"When you ask for bourbon on the rocks, there isn't much mixing involved, Casey," Edmund countered lightly.

"Oh." Casey smiled. "Well, from here on, I'd better have Diet Seven Up all by itself."

"What's your confession about Julia, Casey?" Jeffrey asked evenly, his voice revealing nothing but casual interest to everyone but Julia. While he waited for Casey's answer, he poured himself a second large glass of Scotch.

"Casey . . ."

"Julia, it's nothing about you, nothing bad. How could it be? It's about me, and not a very big deal." Casey took a soft breath and then confessed to Julia's wary lavender eyes, "It's just, well, I really resented you in high school."

"Resented me? But you were always so nice to me."

*Nice? Julia, couldn't you tell that that was a ruse? Couldn't you see how much I hated you?*

"Well, I resented you, a silly schoolgirl rivalry, because you were so terribly bright."

The story was Julia's story, Julia's brilliance, more than Casey's jealousy. But in singing Julia's praises Casey was admitting, finally, graciously, that Julia

148

was the best.

And it felt . . . wonderful. Casey's audience never guessed at the depth of the emotions behind the story. They heard only gracious praise for Julia, a fond reminiscence, not the retelling of a war.

A revisionist history, Casey realized. But wasn't history often mellowed by time and perspective? Wasn't it really in essence a girlhood rivalry, something to be outgrown, laughed about, and finally forgotten? Maybe she could even learn to like Julia. Maybe they could become friends.

Wouldn't *that* be a victory?

Edmund and Paige listened, smiling fondly, not the least bit surprised at this information about their shy and brilliant friend. In the middle of Casey's story, as she was regaling them with Julia's SAT scores—"rumored to be the highest in the country"—and Julia's offers of full scholarships to Harvard, Yale, Stanford—"You name the school, they wanted her!"—Jeffrey poured himself a third drink, walked to the edge of the terrace, and faced the sea.

"Everyone always thought you would be a writer, Julia. Are you writing?" Casey asked when her story was finished.

It took Julia a moment to realize the question had been directed to her. She drew her troubled eyes briefly from Jeffrey's taut body and answered distractedly, "Oh. No."

"*Yes,*" Paige corrected with a smile. "For years Julia has been enchanting the children of Southampton with the most wonderful stories. Fortunately, she has written them down."

"For Merry and Amanda and the other children."

"They could—should—be for the world. All Julia needs to do is find an illustrator."


Jeffrey and Julia performed beautifully during

149

dinner, even though her heart screamed *Why are you angry, Jeffrey?* and his heart felt as if a knife was in it, twisting with each beat, burrowing ever deeper.

"How long will you be at SeaCliff, Casey?" Julia asked politely.

"Until Labor Day. I'll spend the last week of August in my apartment in the city, moving in and taking the Bar, but I'll be back for the weekend and the party at the Club."

"The party," Paige clarified with a warm smile, "is in Casey's honor."

"And is very nice of you." Casey knew that the lavish party that Paige and Edmund were planning at the Southampton Club was more than niceness. It was good business, the proud introduction of the newest member of Edmund's prestigious law firm to the most powerful men and women of Southampton and Manhattan.

"When do you get the Bar results?"

"Early October."

"However, she starts work the day after Labor Day," Edmund added with a look that confirmed what they all knew: Casey would pass the New York Bar with ease. "Among other things, Casey's going to litigate Elliott Barnes versus the State."

"Really?" For the first time during dinner Jeffrey's interest was more than just forced politeness.

The State of New York versus Elliott Barnes was already headlines, a high-profile and an immensely controversial case. Elliott Barnes was an attorney who had successfully won a conviction against one of New York's most influential politicians on charges of bribery and racketeering. Barnes was a local hero for about a minute before the tables turned and suddenly he was facing allegations of tax evasion and fraud. Everyone expected the charges to be dismissed, obviously trumped up, but the District Attorney had decided to prosecute.

150

The firm of Spencer and Quinn, confident of Elliott Barnes's innocence, was going to provide his defense. And Casey English was going to do the all-important litigating for what was destined to be one of the city's most talked-about trials.

"Really," Edmund answered Jeffrey's question. "Big case."

"It certainly is." Jeffrey turned to Casey. "You've just spent three years working for the D.A.'s office in San Francisco, and now your first trial here will be against the Manhattan D.A."

"I may be sitting on a different side of the courtroom, Jeffrey," Casey said softly, and smiled a beautiful confident smile, "but I will be on the same side, the winning side, of the law."

"How many more secrets, Julia?"

They were in their romantic bedroom suite at Belvedere and it wasn't what it should have been. Jeffrey hadn't reached for her dress the moment he walked in the door as he promised he would.

Everything had changed. His voice was quiet but terrifying.

"Secrets?"

"Lies."

"Jeffrey, I don't understand."

"Really? Isn't that surprising for someone as bright as you?"

"Please tell me!"

"You had a full scholarship to one of the most competitive private schools in the country—*in the world*—and yet you told me that graduating from high school and going to college didn't matter."

"That wasn't a lie, Jeffrey! It didn't matter! I only went to Carlton because they offered me the scholarship."

"You were the top student in the class."

151

"I did my best. I owed them that because they were so nice to me."

"How did you graduate, Julia? By mail? Did you hide your diploma from me when it arrived?"

"Jeffrey, no! During the week before our wedding, they gave me oral examinations. They probably sent my diploma to my aunt. I never saw it."

"You never told me you graduated."

"You told me you didn't care! But you did, didn't you? You wish I was like Casey or Paige."

"*No*. No. All I have ever cared about was that you tell me the truth."

"That *is* the truth. Jeffrey, why can't you believe me?"

"Because of all the lies we have lived and are living still."

"What lies are we living still?"

"You tell me, Julia. They are your lies. Tell me!"

But she only stared at him, trembling at his rage, her lavender eyes so innocent and so bewildered. Jeffrey knew how innocent her lovely eyes could look even as they lied, and as he waited for her to speak, he suddenly felt the terrifying power of his anger and the even more terrifying wish to hurt as he had been hurt. He was like a wounded animal, strong and wild with pain, liable to attack even those he loved.

"Where are you going?" Julia asked, a whisper of despair, as Jeffrey grabbed his jeans and running shoes from the closet.

"I need to get away from you."

Jeffrey hurriedly changed his clothes in the oak-paneled library. Then he went outside and started to run. He had run for a mile through the dense forest before he realized he was heading toward the cliffs above the sea, to the place where he had sought answers as a boy and where he had found an answer three years ago . . . when he decided to come home to be with Julia because she was more important than all the other dreams.

His footsteps were guided by the moon that had watched their intimate loving four nights before, and last night, but the moon wasn't full anymore and there were dark shadows.

Just like the dark shadow that had fallen over their love. Tonight Jeffrey learned that there wasn't just the one flaw—the secret he knew Julia kept even though he didn't know why—there were other flaws, more secrets, more necessary deceptions and important lies.

Why was it necessary for her to hide Carlton from him?

When Jeffrey reached the bluff he saw the lights at SeaCliff. During dinner they had all promised Casey she would have absolute privacy. She could sunbathe nude as she studied in the hammock above the sea if she wished, or run naked on the white sand beach. No eyes would see her. Tonight she could be undressing with the curtains open to the moonlight . . .

But Casey had pulled the curtains and Jeffrey saw only shadows. It was just a minor invasion of her privacy, but for a fleeting, desperate moment Jeffrey felt an urge to invade even more.

*Tell me, Casey, who did Julia love at Carlton? You saw Merry when she came to the dinner table to say good night to us. Does she look astonishingly like someone you have seen before? A teacher perhaps, whose career would have ended in scandal had his affair with the brilliant sixteen-year-old become public? Or the headmaster who granted Julia graduation after she completed private oral exams?*

Did Casey English know the reason for Julia's deception?

153

Perhaps, but Jeffrey would involve no one else in their very private life.

He ran down the winding trail to the beach and along the sand until every cell in his body screamed from exhaustion and begged him to stop. But he didn't heed the agonized screams. He ran even farther and even faster.

Three hours later, long after the lights had been turned out in SeaCliff, Jeffrey returned to Belvedere and to Julia.

She was in their bed shivering beneath the satin comforter even though the summer night was balmy. She listened as Jeffrey showered and prayed that the next sounds wouldn't be the sounds of him dressing again as he prepared to leave.

But Jeffrey didn't leave. He walked quietly to their bed.

Their marriage had no rules for fighting, no rituals to follow when they quarreled, because they didn't quarrel. And it didn't occur to Julia to pretend she was asleep, to turn her back to him, to pout or *play,* because Jeffrey was her heart, her love, her life. Instead of turning away, Julia faced him, bravely meeting his eyes, ready to try again to answer his confusing questions.

Jeffrey asked the same questions. And Julia gave the same answers, the only answers she could give, because they were the truth.

"Why didn't you tell me that you were a student at Carlton, Julia?"

"Because it didn't matter to me. All that mattered was for me to be with you."

"And to have Merry." Jeffrey's voice was quiet, controlled, but still the words sounded so accusatory.

"To be with you. And to have Merry. Yes." Julia paused, then asked softly, hesitantly, "Jeffrey?"

154

"Yes?" Tell me, Julia, please. Tell me the truth.

"Are you going to leave us?"

"Leave you?" Jeffrey echoed quietly, stunned by the question and the fear in her soft voice. Leave *you?* It was he who felt so vulnerable and so betrayed. Julia owned his heart, all of it, but he didn't own hers. "I will never leave you."

As he spoke the words Jeffrey wondered if now he had begun to lie to her.

*Someday, for my own survival, my Julie, I may have to leave you. I can't trust your love and it's killing me.*

They loved so carefully the next day, with soft caresses and gentle smiles. Each wanted love, only love, always love, and as they searched for ways to make their love strong and whole again, each remembered the promises of love they had made on their anniversary a month before.

"This is going to be a very busy summer," Jeffrey told her apologetically when he called from work on Monday afternoon. "I really must go to Europe to cover the President's visit to the Eastern Bloc countries, and the bicentennial of the Bastille, and the Economic Summit in Paris."

"Not to mention the nightly broadcasts, whatever else may happen, and special reports. I know, Jeffrey. I understand," Julia said softly, sadly. Jeffrey was telling her that he wasn't going to make time for them to be a family. Even though he had seemed to enjoy Merry's first riding lesson he really hadn't, not enough to make the effort.

"No, honey, you don't understand. This summer will be very busy, and it may be impossible for me to make definite plans, but I'm going to take a vacation during the second week of September. I just called Southampton Country Day and found out that Mer-

155

ry's classes don't resume until the eighteenth, so we'll have the week before school starts to be together." Jeffrey had tried to find a week before then, a time when he wouldn't be traveling with the President and someone else could anchor *The World This Evening,* but he couldn't. The *real* fathers had long since scheduled their vacations for July and August. "I'm all yours that week, Julie. Do with me what you will."

"Really?"

"Really."

"That means you'll be home for Merry's birthday. Oh, Jeffrey, thank you."

"You're welcome, darling."

"You owe me a honeymoon," Julia whispered softly after a few moments.

"You can collect any time."

"I applied for a passport today."

"Did you?"

"Yes. I thought, maybe in October or November, after Merry's been back in school for a while . . ." They were brave words, spoken from her heart, because she loved him so much and had made a loving promise to him to conquer her fears.

"Whenever you say, Julie, whenever you're ready," Jeffrey told her gently. "I love you."

# Chapter Nine

Casey spent the morning following the dinner party at Somerset planning her summer at Sea-Cliff. She made a comprehensive study schedule and compulsively outlined her other schedules as well—when she would exercise, when she would eat, *what* she would eat.

This was the disciplined way in which Casey lived her life, how she succeeded, how she was perfect. Every morning and every evening, no matter how early or late or how tired she was, Casey did the exercises that kept her thighs trim, her waist slender, her calves tapered, her arms taut, and her breasts high and proud. Casey only permitted the right foods, in small amounts, into her sleek and sexy body, and she carefully maintained a perfect tan. Sun in excess was bad, Casey knew, but she knew, too, that a slight golden hue accentuated her radiant red-gold hair and created the confident illusion that her successes were so effortless that she had endless hours to spend lazing in the sun.

Everything Casey did was carefully calculated for success . . . and it all paid off.

She calculated the words and inflections she would use in court, rehearsing and rehearsing until the meticulously scripted words flowed so naturally that even her legal opponents marveled at her gift of effortless, perfect speech. The words she spoke in the courtroom weren't left to chance and neither was the way she looked.

Casey's "look" changed from case to case depending on the crime, the judge, the jury, the opposing counsel, and the mood of the trial. The salary earned by young attorneys in the D.A.'s office was modest, but virtually everyone knew that Casey was an heiress whose monthly income from trust funds was far in excess of her yearly income from work. Casey didn't pretend to be impoverished. She wore designer clothes—Chanel, St. Jillian, Le Crillon, and Dior—with jewels by Tiffany and Shreve and watches by Ebel, Chopard, and Blancpain. Casey sometimes even wore "accessories" over her vision-perfect forget-me-not blue eyes, clear glass framed in tortoiseshell or wire-rim or the eyewear fashions of Anne Klein.

Her spectacular hair completed the look. She would pull the fire into a severe chignon, or loosely weave a thick red-gold braid, or let it fall free, a cascade of gold kissed by the sun, *depending . . .*

Before Casey stepped into the courtroom she spent tireless hours learning everything she could about the case, studying the applicable law and preparing the best defense. And she spent additional tireless hours preparing herself, her flawless flow of perfect words and the important message she conveyed by the way she looked.

Casey's decision to look beautiful—soft and feminine—for the Nob Hill Rapist trial was a decision that was closer to her heart than to her brain. She would wear chiffon and silk, she decided, in all the pastel shades of spring. And she would wear her dazzling spun-gold hair long and free.

Because the case was really about a freedom, wasn't it? she asked herself. Wasn't it really about woman's freedom to be beautiful, if she wanted, and soft, if she wanted, and feminine, if she wanted? Wasn't it really about a woman's freedom to be anything she wanted to be without fear?

Casey's summer in Southampton should have been easy. She simply had to follow her carefully calculated schedules for success. She had been given a promise of absolute privacy. There would be no intrusions, no distractions. So easy.

Except there *were* distractions and intrusions. Her privacy was invaded from within, from thoughts that swirled in her head and lured her into dangerous territory . . . *Julia.*

*Why do I keep thinking about her?* Casey wondered insistently. *Julia is ancient history, a demon purged.*

Julia was no longer a threat, except that Julia had won. Jeffrey Lawrence, who could have had any woman on earth, had chosen Julia. And it was so obvious how much he loved her! Casey had seen Jeffrey's love for Julia the second Julia appeared on the terrace. And Casey had watched his eyes throughout the evening and seen such love, such tenderness, and something else very deep, a desire so intense that it was almost pain.

To be loved that much! To be loved that much for who you were.

Julia's beauty and serenity had blossomed with

Jeffrey's love, but she was simply a womanly version of the shy and brilliant girl who had unwittingly tormented Casey in high school. Julia hadn't changed. She had simply found a man, a remarkable man, who loved her deeply for exactly who she was.

*Will I ever be loved for who I am?*

Many men had fallen in love with her, of course. Rich, handsome, powerful men who were unafraid of her success, bewitched by her beauty, and seduced by the provocative words and alluring smiles that she rehearsed as compulsively as she practiced her performances in court.

But had those men really fallen in love with her or only with the talented actress whose every performance was flawless? And why did she never fall in love with them? And why, despite her triumphs, her successes, her letter-perfect performances, did she never feel a rush of joy, a tremble of desire, a quiver of happiness?

What if Casey and the talented actress were the same woman? What if that was really who she was? *All* she was? Just perfect, forever joyless, destined to live a passionless, disciplined life of schedules that were programmed for success, and permitted virtually no free time for Casey.

Free time? Time to be free?

Wasn't there perhaps—*please*—another Casey? the intruding thoughts wanted to know. Hadn't there once been a little girl who loved to run on the beach and play tag with the waves and chase the sun? Was that happy girl lost forever or was there still within her a Casey who could abandon her law books because the snow-white sand beckoned?

Yes, there was. The little girl existed still, and

now she scampered down the winding trail to the beach, and the sand felt so soft and warm beneath her bare feet. Then she was running along the beach chasing the fiery beacon of the setting sun, half a mile, then a mile, not breathless, not aching, only buoyant . . . dancing . . . *free*.

Then the beach suddenly ended, abruptly, in a massive wall of steep cliffs. The beach was gone except for a delicate snowy ribbon of white sand that stretched into the sea. If she wanted to see the sun set—which she did—she would have to find a way up the steep cliffs. Or, perhaps, if she stood on the farthest reach of the snowy ribbon of sand there might be a view . . .

Cascy chose the sandy peninsula. She stood at its very tip on a sea-slick boulder and strained to catch a glimpse of the falling sun. But the fireball was hidden behind the wall of cliffs. As she stood on the boulder, huge rolling waves kissed the rock, splashing her with a warm shower of salt.

Warm . . . *hot*.

But the wet heat on her face, mixed with the sea, was the salty hotness of her own tears.

*Tears?* Casey never cried. But she was crying now in this breathtaking place where she had come because a lovely distant memory, or perhaps a future dream, had urged her to chase the setting sun.

Were her tears because she had failed? Because the fiery star was setting out of her sight? Or were the tears because she was chasing something even more important and more elusive—herself, her happiness, her freedom—and that, too, was beyond her reach?

\* \* \*

Patrick inhaled the warm salt air and felt the exhilarating feeling of peace.

Peace was a rare but so welcome visitor in the turbulence of Patrick's life. Peace was an overnight guest, a bewitching and beguiling one-night stand, the deceptively tranquil calm at the center of the swirling storm.

There had been moments of peace before. Patrick had tried hard to preserve them forever, but they had always vanished. He hadn't expected peace again — ever. But here it was, a gift to treasure until the inevitable moment when he was once again forced to flee. He marveled at the gift that had come so unexpectedly, a glimmer of sunshine through a storm-gray sky, just three months before.


On that March day Patrick had been at a truck stop in New Jersey looking for work. He would find the driver of a moving van who needed a second driver for the transcontinental journey, or someone who had just arrived from the West Coast, a solitary worker who needed help unloading his van. This had been Patrick's life for almost five years, traversing the country, living from job to job, with a new name and without a home.

But, of course, Patrick had never had a home.

As he drank a cup of coffee he had glanced at a copy of *The New York Times*. On impulse he turned to the want ads. It was a small form of torture, a grim reminder of his destiny. He could never get a real job because that required an identity, an authentic name with a social security number and birth certificate to match. There had never been jobs that appealed, anyway, until now.

*Riding instructor needed immediately. South-ampton Club. Experience required. Call . . .*

Patrick's heart raced as he read the ad. If he could ride again . . . It would be so very close to peace, almost like having a home.

Southampton Club. Patrick had never competed in a Grand Prix event held in Southampton. But had he ever competed against a rider from the exclusive Club? No, he was quite certain that he never had. It was safe. No one would recognize him.

Experience required. Patrick had never taught riding, but he was a champion equestrian. He could lie about his experience, give false references, and hope that "immediately" meant that someone at the Southampton Club was desperate.

Someone—the manager—was desperate. Spring break—an event that used to be a week but now seemed to stretch from mid-March to mid-April—was about to begin. In a matter of days the children and grandchildren of Southampton would appear at the stable expecting lessons and trail rides and the man who was supposed to teach riding this year had just taken a position elsewhere.

Three hours after Patrick made the call to the number in the ad, he was in the manager's office at the Club. He tried to schedule the interview for the following day so that he would have a chance to make himself presentable. He would spend all his hard-earned money—two hundred and twenty dollars—on an acceptable Ivy League haircut and proper country club clothes. Patrick knew the costumes and customs of the very wealthy. He could wear the elegantly tailored clothes beautifully and speak the polite language flawlessly. He had fitted in once, an elegant chameleon, adapting so con-

163

vincingly that everyone assumed that he, too, had been born with wealth and privilege, attended prep school in the East, then Harvard or Yale, and vacationed in the usual playgrounds in Europe. He could do it again to get this job. But the manager at the Southampton Club didn't give him time to buy clothes at Brooks Brothers or even to trim his coal-black hair.

Besides, Patrick thought defiantly as a commuter train carried him swiftly from New Jersey to Southampton, the best riders in the world wore jeans, not jodhpurs, when they practiced.

He knew about the wealthy because he had been among them once, cleverly disguised. And he knew about the best riders in the world because he had been one of them once, too.

"You've taught riding?" the Club's manager asked. He eyed Patrick skeptically but was obviously pleased that the voice had a refinement that was missing in the too-long hair and threadbare jeans.

"Yes."

"Where?"

"All over."

"The job is only for a month." The manager decided not to push for credentials. He needed someone beginning tomorrow. After spring break was over he would have two months to search for a more appropriate replacement before the summer season began.

"Will I be paid in cash?"

"If you like."

"Yes. And since the job's only for a month, I will need to stay here. I can sleep in the stable and shower in the members' dressing rooms before dawn."

"There's an apartment in the stable. It's small, but it has all the necessities. You can stay there."

The manager expected complaints about Patrick James — and prepared his retort, "only for a month" — but all he heard for the new riding instructor was praise. Patrick was a patient, tireless, excellent instructor. Even the threadbare jeans, denim work shirts, and battered boots met with approval. In fact Patrick's cowboy look became *fashion*. The expensive hand-knitted equestrian sweaters from Miller's, the linen jodhpurs and silk turtlenecks of Ralph Lauren, and the hunting boots by Beverly Feldman languished unworn in closets of the fabulous estates, forsaken for generic blue jeans, cotton shirts, and nondesigner boots. Even the "sporting" jewels — diamonds, sapphires, emeralds, and rubies set in equestrian motifs — remained in wall safes behind Impressionist paintings.

Patrick devoted tireless hours to teaching at the stable and, in his spare time, to earn additional money, he worked as the bartender for the lavish parties given at the Club.

At the end of spring break the manager asked Patrick if he would stay on indefinitely. Patrick accepted the offer and had no concern about its vagueness. He made his relationship with the Southampton Club even less binding by refusing a straight salary in favor of a percentage of each lesson he gave, paid in cash, every two weeks, and job-by-job payment for the bartending he did. He would live without charge in the studio apartment in the stable and his meals would be leftovers from the Club's gourmet kitchen.

Since he was not officially an employee of the Southampton Club, no paperwork was required.

He never filled out a formal job application, never signed a contract, never provided names of references. The Club could fire him without notice and Patrick could leave without warning.

The manager hoped that neither would happen, but he wondered. Patrick was so different from the men he usually hired to supervise the summer sports—yachting and tennis and swimming—men who themselves frequently became intriguing summertime diversions. Patrick was handsome, very handsome, but despite his elegant speech, there was a wildness about him. The manager was quite certain that the rich and beautiful women of Southampton would want the wild and handsome riding instructor. But would Patrick be discreet? Would he respect the *rules?*

The women did want Patrick, as women always had wanted him. He had wanted women, too, some of them, the ones with whom he chose to share himself. Sex had always been a wonderful pleasure, a treasured freedom, a gift of intimacy, a solemn and joyful choice . . .

Until five years ago when Patrick chose to say no to a beautiful young heiress. He didn't want her, but she wanted him, and her rage at his refusal cost him everything—his freedom, his dreams, his chance for a lasting peace.

For five years Patrick had run. And now, because he had to ride again, he was back among the rich and powerful people he loathed. And the rich, beautiful women of Southampton, like the heiress who had cost him his dreams, wanted him—as a possession, a trophy, a plaything for their pleasure—when they chose, *because* they chose.

Once Patrick had chosen to say no and that

choice had cost him everything. And now? Now he had nothing more to lose—except this precious peace. If he said no, he would have to be prepared to flee again.

And if he said yes? If he satisfied their whims? If he accepted their expensive gifts? He had nothing more to lose—except his self-respect and his fragile freedom to choose.

Patrick chose to say no to the women in Southampton who wanted him. To the petulant young heiress in Kentucky, his no had been gentle and kind, and still it had backfired. Now his no's were sullen, defiant, laced with contempt, and that backfired, too, because it made the seduction more challenging, the game more intriguing, the prize more valued. Patrick's contempt was alluring, his defiance seductive, his wildness appealing and erotic. The rich, beautiful women wanted to tame him.

Then, quite by accident, Patrick discovered the secret to his survival in Southampton.

"Patrick, do you give private lessons? At night?"

"No." Usually that was all he said, his voice hard and cold, his gray-green eyes disdainful, but on that night, perhaps because the woman was not so demanding as the others, he added gently, "I'm sorry. I really can't."

"Oh. Are you involved with someone?"

"Yes." He watched the transformation in her eyes at his lie. There was a softening, a little envy, a little admiration.

"And you are faithful to her?"

"Yes." That wasn't wholly a lie. Patrick knew that if he ever did fall in love he would be faithful.

He discovered then that fidelity was an ideal to

167

these women who wanted him for their pleasure—the married women whose unfaithfulness sprung from unhappy marriages and the unmarried women who wished for love. He told them he had a lover to whom he was faithful and they left him alone. And he survived among the rich and privileged. More than survived . . . he found peace.

*Peace.* Peace among the people he hated. So strange to find peace here.

Patrick gazed at the crashing surf and long stretch of beach and felt the immense eager power of the black stallion beneath him. In a moment he would urge the magnificent horse to chase the setting sun, but first he wanted to etch the image of the scene in his mind. Tonight when he returned to his apartment at the stable he would begin to paint this breathtaking picture of sky and sand and sea.

Whenever he could, he came to this beautiful white sand beach at sunset, and he had discovered another idyllic place from which to greet the dawn. The owners of the estates had so much land, so many breathtaking vistas from their mansions, that the wonders at the edges were all but forgotten. Patrick discovered the wonderful remote places as he rode along the trails that connected the Club to the estates, trails that meandered through dense forests, along precipitous cliffs, and across vast expanses of fragrant meadow . . . and they became his private sanctuaries.

But today he was not alone. He made the surprising discovery as he approached the steep cliffs a mile beyond the vacant cottage. There was a woman standing at the tip of the peninsula.

The peninsula. Patrick had spent many evenings watching the ever-changing drama of the slender ribbon of sand. Its size, its shape, indeed its very *existence* were defined by the waves and the tide. At low tide the sand was an extension of the beach, a snow-white comma punctuating the sapphire sea. But as the sea began to flood, the rocky tip became divorced from the rest of the beach and the peninsula became an island encircled by water swirled by a lethal undertow. At the highest tides, the full-moon tides, the land disappeared completely, swallowed by the swollen sea.

The island could vanish quickly, like the sun into the sea, a gradual descent until the very last and then a free fall.

The tide was rising now and the woman, a stranger to Patrick and the treacherous peninsula, was probably lost in the magical beauty of the sea. Patrick rode across the river of water that had begun to divide the peninsula from the beach. The channel wasn't deep yet, and perhaps this evening's tide would not completely submerge the island, but she needed to be warned of the possible danger.

"Hello!" Patrick called as he neared.

Casey hadn't heard him approach. The pounding hoofbeats were muffled by the soft sand, the noise of the crashing surf, and the confusing thunder in her mind. But she heard the male voice above the other sounds. It would be Edmund or Jeffrey. And whichever handsome man it was, he would be smiling at her, an apologetic smile, because she had been promised absolute privacy.

She would be smiling, too, when she turned to greet him. Not that he would be able to tell she'd been crying, she realized with relief as her hands

169

moved to wipe her tear-damp eyes and felt the sea-kissed wetness of her cheeks. The surprising tears, she discovered, were well camouflaged by the splashes of the sea.

The warm drops that had thankfully concealed her tears had, however, made her light cotton blouse quite transparent. The drenched fabric clung to her, revealing her provocative shape and the sensuous details of her breasts. Casey realized her nakedness before she turned and knew, too, that the mane of hair that tumbled down her back was dry still. She gave a gentle toss of her head as she turned, and the red-gold hair danced in the fading sunlight, fire lit by fire, until the silky strands fell in a luxurious cape over her round, damp breasts.

Like "The Birth of Venus," Patrick mused. The mane of red-gold hair modestly concealing a perfect body as it rose from the sea instantly recalled to his artistic mind the exquisite painting by Botticelli. Perhaps this barely clothed virtually-revealed vision *was* Venus being born in this enchanted spot on Long Island.

"Oh!" Casey's cheeks flushed pink.

Her embarrassed "Oh!" should have been a "Hello" softly purred. Casey had a soft purr, carefully practiced and trained to appear whenever she met a stunningly handsome man. But now, for this stunningly handsome stranger with gray-green eyes and coal-black hair, the purr wouldn't come.

Because the seductive purr belonged to the other Casey? *The other Casey?* Yes, you know, the Casey who doesn't cry. The Casey who would never have abandoned her schedule to chase the setting sun. The Casey who, had she decided to chase the setting sun, would never have let the fireball out of her sight, nor dashed to a dead end of sand, nor become sea-soaked, nor most assuredly *ever* have cried.

Whatever the reason tonight there was no softly purred "Hello," only flushed pink cheeks and an awkward "Oh!"

"What are you doing here?" she asked.

"Well, I guess I'm here to rescue you."

"Rescue me? From what?" *From myself? From the other Casey?*

"The tide."

"The tide?" Casey echoed. Was she dreaming? Was he really a knight in shining armor who had come to rescue her from a watery dragon? A knight, perhaps, yes, but he had forsaken his shining armor for a denim shirt opened to the warm ocean breeze.

"Come with me now," Patrick commanded solemnly.

Casey felt a tingling rush, so unfamiliar, so wonderful, and a sudden wish to be commanded by him, to make his solemn, seductive eyes glisten with pleasure, to play whatever game he wanted to play.

"All right."

"Do you ride?"

"Yes," Casey answered uncertainly. She had taken riding lessons at the Carlton Club in Atherton, but that had been years ago and she had never before ridden bareback. "Sort of."

"Climb on behind me and hold on."

"OK."

Patrick moved the horse beside the boulder and held the powerful black stallion perfectly still while Casey mounted.

"Hold on," Patrick repeated.

Casey obeyed by curling her arms loosely around his waist. When they reached the channel, deeper now and more turbulent, the stallion lurched as it high-stepped into the water. Casey felt the sudden tension in the animal's strong body and reflexively clung more tightly to Patrick, pressing against him, feeling his power, his tension, his strength.

The stallion crossed the channel in a burst of power. Once they reached the safety of the beach, Patrick calmed the horse quickly, then dismounted and circled his strong arms around Casey's waist as she slid to the sand.

"That wasn't a game," Casey whispered softly when she looked back and saw what was happening to the peninsula.

"No."

"The place where I was standing is almost gone." Had the enchanted moments of the gallant knight and mythical dragon really been life and death? Casey wondered. The question scared her because she had been so oblivious to the danger. What if he hadn't been riding by?

"Yes, but the higher ground may not sink tonight. The moon was last full ten days ago, so the tide isn't as high. You might just have been stranded until the sea began to ebb. If you're a strong swimmer you could have ridden a wave to shore." *Or if you're really Venus.*

Patrick couldn't swim. If he was caught on the peninsula on a full moon night, a night when every grain of sand dove into the sea, he would surely drown . . . unless, perhaps, it was a night when the sea was more laughing than angry and he could cling to a piece of wood and the friendly currents would carry him toward shore instead of

172

dragging him below to the dark depths.

Casey could swim. She could have made it ashore without him, couldn't she?

"It wasn't a game," she repeated quietly, trembling as a sudden icy shiver of fear swept through her.

"I don't play games. Are you cold? Would you like my shirt?"

"No, thank you. I'm fine." The evening air was warm. The sheer cotton fabric she wore would dry quickly away from the ever-dampening spray of the sea and she would be concealed again. Not that his eyes were drifting to her breasts, her hips, her slender sea-wet thighs. The intense gray-green remained focused on her face, smiling, curious, patient.

"OK."

"Who are you?" Casey asked, curious, too, and less patient than he. *Who are you that knows the phases of the moon and the secrets of the sea?*

"Patrick James. And you?"

"Casey English."

"So, Casey English. What are you doing on my beach?"

"I'm spending the summer at the cottage on the cliff."

"Oh. Only the summer?"

"Yes. Just before Labor Day I'll move into the city."

"To do what?"

*To play games,* Casey thought. *To be a magnificent actress who dazzles the world with brilliant performances, wonderful costumes, sharp legal acumen, and flawless rhetoric.*

Patrick said he didn't play games. What if, with him, she didn't play, either? What if she wasn't

173

Casey English, heiress, attorney, grand master at playing games and winning? What if she was just the girl who had danced after the setting sun? What if she was just Casey, just herself, whoever that was?

"To work. I'm just a working girl." Casey realized she needed an explanation for why she was spending the summer at SeaCliff. She had never used the word "boss" before. She never thought of Edmund, or the D.A., or *anyone* as her boss. They were simply colleagues, more experienced than she. But now she said, "My boss owns the cottage. I can do the work I'm doing for him this summer there."

"That's very nice. You weren't working this evening."

"No." Casey hadn't told him the unimportant truths about herself—her immense wealth and her stunning successes—but if she really wasn't going to play she had to tell him the important things. "I was chasing the sun, but I lost it over the cliffs," she admitted softly.

Patrick hesitated only a moment. It was his private place, but he would happily share it with this woman who had come to the beach for the same reason as he. When her journey toward the sun had been blocked by the cliffs, she had turned fearlessly to the sea. But when the same thing had happened to him on a night in April, he had chosen to find a way up the cliffs because he belonged nowhere near the lethal waves.

"There's a path up the cliffs. It's steep, but it leads to a meadow where you can watch the sun until it falls into the trees. Would you like me to show you?"

"Yes. Please."

Patrick tied the stallion's reins to a branch at the base of the path, far from the waves, then led Casey through a lush green maze of ferns and forest to the meadow.

The enchanted meadow. Patrick's meadow was an ocean of wildflowers surrounded by towering pines and bathed in the fading rays of the golden sun. The sun danced above the pines, a fiery pirouette, twirling ever lower and finally disappearing into the green but leaving behind a magnificent farewell gift — a pastel sky of pink and gold.

Casey and Patrick watched the spectacular adieu of the summer sun in awed silence. There was nothing to say, no words to describe the beauty, the peace, the wonder.

No words, but Casey suddenly felt the heat of tears. *No!*

"What's wrong, Casey?"

"I don't know," she whispered the truth. Then she offered a lie. "Maybe a delayed reaction from what almost happened on the peninsula?"

But Patrick wouldn't allow the lie.

"You were crying before," he said gently.

"Yes." Casey started to apologize for her tears, but Patrick's expression stopped her. He looked concerned that she was crying, concerned about her, but not uncomfortable with the tears. Patrick's comfort with her inexplicable emotions made Casey feel wonderfully safe, wonderfully free. As if it was all right to cry. As if it was all right to be vulnerable and imperfect. "I didn't know why I was crying then, either."

"Do you always have all the answers?"

*Yes, always.* Always before . . .

"I guess not." Casey smiled a lovely soft smile, a smile she had never smiled before, a smile she

175

had never practiced in front of the mirror until it was perfect. She had never seen this imperfect wobbly smile—and would have banished it if she had, even though in its vulnerability and softness it was more beautiful than all her flawless, confident smiles. "I would like to know this answer though."

"I'm sure you will in time. Tears aren't all bad, you know."

"No?" Casey asked hopefully. She *didn't* know. For twenty-seven years Kirk Carroll English's daughter had known only that tears were bad, always bad, an unacceptable sign of weakness and an intolerable flaw.

"Not to me. I think tears are like rain, sometimes unwelcome, sometimes nourishing." Patrick smiled and added, "It depends on whether you're a parade or a flower."

That brought a soft laugh. Earlier he had not permitted her to drown in the salty sea, and now he was not permitting her to drown in her salty tears. He spoke with a smile and a gentle tease, but the words were serious, too.

"So, which are you, Casey? A flower or a parade?"

The old Casey was a parade. And the new Casey? A fragile flower reaching bravely for the sun?

"I don't know," she whispered. *But I have to find out.*


"I need to get the stallion back to the stable before dark," Patrick said as the pastel sky faded to gray.

"The stable?"

"At the Southampton Club. Why don't I walk

you back to the cottage?"

"Oh. Thank you."

Patrick led the way back down the trail from the meadow to the beach. They paused briefly when they reached the sand and gazed at the peninsula. It was an island still, a small mound of gray in the middle of the swirling sea. The sand was gray, not white, proof that it had been kissed by the tide, but it wasn't possible to tell now whether the kiss had been a gentle, chaste caress or a deep, consuming one.


"Thank you again for rescuing me," Casey said when they reached the trail to SeaCliff.

"You probably would have been fine."

"I'm sorry about the tears."

"You are?"

*No, because there was something wonderfully purifying about my tears and the emotions that flowed with them . . . and there was something even more wonderful about the way they didn't bother you.*

"No," Casey admitted softly.

"I'd better go. Without the moonlight the path through the forest will be very dark. Good night, Casey."

"Good night, Patrick."

She watched as he became a shadow in the twilight and then disappeared into the forest.

Who was he? she wondered. Who was this dark handsome stranger who knew the mysteries of the moon and the sea and was so wise about her tears? A poet? A writer? Or was he, perhaps, an attorney who was spending his summer studying for the Bar but permitted himself free time to gal-

177

lop a prized stallion along a snowy beach?

Patrick belonged in Southampton, of course. He was a member of the Club and teased confidently about her being on *his* beach even though he surely knew the white sand belonged to Edmund and Jeffrey. When Casey had first heard his voice she had assumed he was Edmund or Jeffrey, but Patrick was only like them—rich, aristocratic, successful, powerful. Like Edmund and Jeffrey, and like her.

But Casey hadn't told Patrick those unimportant truths about herself. Instead she had told him the important things, and she had let him see her tears, and she had felt so safe with him and so free.

But now, as Patrick's shadow faded into the gray of the night, those wonderful fragile feelings faded too.

Patrick was going, *gone* . . . and he would not return.

She should have played! She should have dazzled and seduced and performed!

She shouldn't have shown Patrick her vulnerability, her confusion, her tears . . .

# Chapter Ten

"Hello, Diana."

"Chase."

Diana hadn't spoken to Chase for over five weeks, not since he left "to decide." In the two weeks since the divorce papers had been filed, they had been communicating through their attorneys. They had "his" and "her" attorneys — neither from Spencer and Quinn — although the entire divorce could have been handled by a single lawyer. The uncontested dissolution of the marriage of Diana Shepherd and Chase Andrews was quite simple, merely a matter of the equitable division of their immense fortune.

Quite simple, and going so smoothly one hardly realized it was being dissolved.

*Dissolved.*

How Diana wished the pain would be so easily dissolved!

She had hoped Chase would call. She needed to hear his voice. She needed to know if there was anger and bitterness. The loss of Chase's love was painful enough without the bitter legacy of anger.

*Chase could have chosen a better time to let*

*you know,* Jeffrey Lawrence had observed that evening in her office. The celebrated anchor's tone hadn't mocked—not then—but the words had taunted nonetheless.

Had Chase really chosen the eve of the most high-profile surgery of her career to issue a less than subtle reminder that it was her dedication to her career that had destroyed their love?

It seemed so vituperative, so hostile, so unlike Chase. Admittedly he was unused to being thwarted. Yet, when he had been confronted by a situation in his private life, in his love, that he could neither control nor change, he had finally had to leave to decide—and there had been gentleness, a wistful sadness, not anger. And the dialogue through the attorneys had been civilized, amicable, without a whisper of bitterness. Chase wanted Diana to have the Park Avenue penthouse that was a safe five-minute walk to Memorial Hospital. And he didn't want any part of her Heart, at least not the plastic one . . .

"How are you, Diana?"

"I've been better, Chase. I'm going through a divorce. It's quite painful."

"I know," Chase agreed softly. "And it doesn't help to have the undivided attention of Manhattan's most malicious gossip columnists, does it?"

"No. They haven't really found much, have they?"

"There's nothing to find, Diana."

*I know,* Diana thought. The ravenous search for skeletons, the intense search for the *other woman* in Chase's life, would come up empty. Chase hadn't been unfaithful to her, nor she to him.

Or had she? Wasn't it her secret fidelity to a

distant love that had destroyed their marriage?

"Is the settlement all right with you, Chase? You don't mind that I keep the penthouse?"

"The settlement's fine. I don't mind at all about the penthouse. I want you to be safe."

"Thank you."

"Diana, I was in Paris when the papers were filed. I met with the attorney before I left and we agreed he would file as soon as the documents were prepared. I didn't even know about the surgery on the Soviet ambassador until after I returned."

"I hoped there was something like that."

"I'm very sorry."

"It's OK. It was going to happen sometime. You've had your share of questions from the press."

"Yes, but I haven't been ambushed on live television."

"Well. It's over. I'm just glad the timing was accidental."

"I promise you it was." Chase paused, took a soft breath, and then continued, "Diana, I'd like to see you. I have something to give you."

"I have something to give you, too, Chase."

"Tonight? In an hour?"

"In an hour."


What did one wear to say a final good-bye to the man who was supposed to be her husband forever? Was there proper attire for such an occasion? Could even Emily Post provide guidance about the etiquette?

Chase had known and loved Diana in everything

181

and nothing—the designer gowns she wore to the April in Paris Ball, the bright cheery dresses she wore under her white coat at the hospital, the wool skirts and cashmere sweaters she wore for their hideaway weekends in Maine, the silk negligees he removed so eagerly. Chase had known her and loved her in silk and denim, satin and tweed, lace and cotton, and, the way he loved her best, in nothing at all in the privacy of their bed.

Diana decided to look beautiful, as beautiful as the fatigue and strain of the past few weeks would allow. She chose a sapphire silk sheath, one of Chase's favorites, caught her dark-brown curls in a sapphire velvet ribbon, and chilled a bottle of Dom Pérignon. While she waited on the penthouse balcony, she gazed at the glitter of Manhattan and thought about the marriage that was over.

It should have lasted forever. That was what she and Chase had planned. They had been so sure of their love, so confident that their hearts beat in perfect harmony and always would. Chase loved the fact that Diana was a dedicated and brilliant surgeon. He was so proud of her and her remarkable career. And Diana loved Chase's magnificent buildings and was so proud of him, too, for his unwavering commitment to quality and beauty. They shared a passion for their careers, and they shared a breathless passion for each other.

*There is nothing to find,* Chase had said. Diana knew it was true. Chase needed no other woman to give him pleasure. And she had no need for anyone but Chase. Chase was the only man who had ever been able to make her forget about Sam.

*Sam.* For ten years after Sam left her, Diana's relationships, her attempts at love, had been tainted by his memory. In those years when the loneliness became too great, she had been like the mythologic Diana, goddess of the hunt, relentlessly searching for a new love in hopes of escaping the painful memories of the love she had lost. There had been men who wanted Diana and loved her. But she had been unable to return the love because Sam was there still, a twilight shadow, long and dark, preventing the sunny joy of a new love and making even the loving as desperate as it had always been with him.

Until five years ago when Chase Andrews entered her life, and her heart, and her bed. When Chase made love to her, his tender lips and gentle hands banished all thoughts, all memories, all pain, and she was lost—and found—in the magnificent and powerful commands of her own desires.

Chase wanted Diana, only Diana, always Diana. And she wanted Chase, the wonderful man who had rediscovered in her the softness and passion and laughter that had been hiding for so long in the shadows. They wanted each other, only each other, and they joyously made plans for forever.

Then Chase changed the plans.

No children, they had agreed, a solemn vow before they were married. Chase's buildings would be his children, his immortality, and Diana had her career, her hearts. They had talked about having children, about *not* having children, and Diana had been so sure that Chase's decision was firm. She would never have married him if it hadn't been, because she knew she would never have children . . . she would never have *another* child.

When Chase told her he wanted children, all the

183

painful memories of Sam and Janie flooded back and began to shadow her love with Chase as they had shadowed other loves before.

Diana had never told Chase about Sam, and she had never told him, either, about Janie, Sam's gift of love, the beloved daughter who had died. Chase and Diana didn't tell each other about past loves, and there was no need to tell Chase about Janie, to share that sadness with him, because they weren't going to have children.

But six months ago Chase changed his mind, his heart, and they became entrenched on opposite sides of an abyss that grew and grew, darker and deeper, a giant wedge in their wonderful love.

Diana almost told him about Janie. But it wasn't fair to ask Chase to give up his dream of children because of her tragedy, was it? No, and that was certainly what Chase would do if he knew. Chase would stop pushing, but it wouldn't make his dream go away. And maybe, at some future time, the deep desires of his heart would urge him to start pushing her again.

*You had a lovely daughter who died, Diana,* he would say so gently. *But can't we have our own children? It wouldn't diminish your love for Janie or take away her precious memory.*

Then Diana would have to face the other truth. She loved Chase Andrews enough to spend her life with him. But she did not love him enough to have his children. She would not allow herself to love that much—as much as she had loved Sam— ever again.

So Diana only said, No, Chase, no children, and he was left to assume that the reason was her career. They talked and pleaded and cried. And fi-

184

nally Chase simply had to decide. Life with Diana and without children? Or life without Diana and sometime, with someone new, life with children?

Chase had made his decision, as fifteen years ago Sam had made the same one: *I can live without you, Diana, and that is what I choose to do.*

Chase had dressed, too, to look especially handsome for her. He wore a charcoal suit, one of her favorites, the dark-gray exactly matching his smoky eyes.

"Hi." It was a small word, but Chase's eyes embellished it, giving it layers of meaning and emotion—happiness to see her because he had missed her . . . sadness when he remembered why, and that it would be forever . . . uncertainty because was he really sure? . . . and desire because she was so beautiful and he loved her still.

"Hi." Diana's greeting was a mirror of his, all the layers, all the emotions, all the desires. "Come in. Would you like champagne?"

"Sure."

They clinked crystal to crystal, a silent toast to whatever—a smooth dissolution, happiness sometime, sometime again.

"I'm sending you on a three-week trip to Europe," Chase said as he withdrew a thick envelope from his jacket pocket and handed it to her. "Beginning September eighth. I assume that with this much advance warning you can schedule the time away."

"Yes, but Chase . . ."

"You have to go, Diana. Everything's already booked and paid for."

"You're probably sending me first class, aren't you?"

"Every step of the way."

Diana smiled softly. Chase knew her so well! He knew that she would never book a luxury vacation for herself, even though she could easily afford it, and he knew that she needed time away, time to think, time to heal. Where more lovely than Europe in autumn? By September she wouldn't be so raw, would she?

No. Diana knew from experience the salutary effects of time. Not that time necessarily healed . . . but it certainly numbed.

By September she would be a little numb, numb enough to face the thought that echoed in her mind, a relentless strident echo: *You have failed. You are not enough for the man you love . . . again.*

The thought demanded analysis. In September, in London and Paris and all the other wonderful places on her luxurious vacation, Diana would confront the thought and search for answers.

"Thank you."

"You're welcome."

What Chase had given her was a gift, and what Diana had for him was a gift from another time, from the beginning of his love, a gift which she now had to return.

"I thought you would want this back," she said quietly as she removed the four-carat diamond from the pocket of her silk dress.

"It's not necessary, Diana."

"But better, don't you think? Better if you have it back?"

Diana offered the diamond, a treasure that had

been in his family forever, and finally Chase took it. He took the ring and he took the fingers that held it, the calm and talented fingers of steel that now were trembling. He gently drew her to him and even more gently began to kiss her.

Diana felt the familiar rushes of desire at his touch and wondered if they were really going to make love. Their minds had said good-bye and their hearts were learning to live with the death of their love, but did their bodies need to kiss a final breathless adieu, a lingering farewell to five years of uninhibited passion and desires fulfilled? Would that make it more real, more final, more dissolved? A last loving dissolve into molten gold?

The kiss deepened, but Diana couldn't lose herself in it. Wouldn't this be too painful, too great a torture? Tonight's loving wouldn't end in a joyous reconciliation, would it?

Diana pulled away and gazed into his eyes. She saw desire—and sadness—in the seductive smoke. Chase was saying good-bye and . . .

"I can't do this, Chase."

He gently held her face in his hands and gave a wistful smile that matched the sadness in his eyes. "I know." After a moment he added softly, "Diana, I am so sorry."

"I know."

Then Chase was gone forever. After he left, Diana stood above the glitter of Manhattan, quite alone, the bright lights below blurry from her tears.

July Fourth marked the tenth day since Patrick had rescued Casey and disappeared into the shadows of the night.

*He's not coming back,* Casey told herself. *Why would he?*

Casey had looked at herself in the mirror of her bedroom at SeaCliff after Patrick left and assessed the ravages of the sea and her tears. Very ravaged, she decided as she gazed at her wind-tangled hair, crumpled clothes, and oh-so-vulnerable blue eyes. She looked like a waif, alluring maybe in a wild sort of way.

But even if there had been an erotic appeal, it couldn't erase the inexplicable emotions. Even if Patrick had been drawn to the perfect body eloquently revealed beneath her scant seasplashed clothes, he swiftly overcame the attraction with the memory of her uncertain words, her wobbly smile, and her far from dazzling tears.

Patrick James obviously wasn't interested.

But Casey didn't so easily abandon her new self. She studied compulsively, of course, and exercised, and ate almost nothing, but every day she ran on the beach and played tag with the waves and wished good evening to the sun as it disappeared behind the cliffs. Casey bid adieu to the fireball from the base of the cliffs, never following the fern-lined path to the meadow. The meadow was Patrick's enchanted place. He might be there, having taken an overland route through the forests to avoid her . . . and she had already driven him from "his" beach.

Casey felt more than thought. Answers didn't come, not in coherent phrases, but feelings began to surface from the depths of her soul, feelings she could not abandon and would not discipline away, unfamiliar but so welcome feelings of happiness and joy.

She was studying when Patrick knocked on the cottage door on the evening of the Fourth.

"Patrick."

"Hello, Casey. How are you?"

Patrick had his answer in her happy-to-see-him smile, but he asked the question to give himself time to adjust to seeing her again. He had been thinking about her, warning himself to stay away because she was soft and lovely and he could offer her nothing but remembering that loveliness and wanting desperately to be with her.

Casey had been in his thoughts, and he had begun making sketches of her, too, trying to capture the breathtaking look of awkward surprise and lovely vulnerability he had seen when she had turned from the sea to him. Patrick was a talented artist, and his artistic mind had made vivid images of that enchanted moment, but as he gazed at her now he realized that this time his immense talent had failed him. She was even more soft, more lovely than he had remembered.

"I'm fine, Patrick."

"I wondered if you would like to watch some fireworks with me."

"Yes. At the Club?"

"No. The real thing, in the meadow."

"I would like to very much."

They walked down the winding trail from the cottage to the sand, and when they reached the beach, Patrick retrieved a blanket he had set on a piece of driftwood.

"No horse?"

"The sunset is only the first act. I thought you might like to stay for the rest of the show."

189

"Oh, yes."

They watched the breathtaking fireworks of nature, the falling sun, the rising stars, the almost-full moon. And they listened to sounds of the summer night, the music of crickets, the songs of the nightbirds, and the gentle rustle of leaves as the balmy evening air wove through the maples.

"Such vastness," Casey whispered as she gazed at the inky sky glittering with an infinity of stars. "It makes me feel so insignificant." *It makes my dazzling accomplishments seem so trivial.*

"Really? I feel significant just being a part, however small, of the grandeur."

"Oh, Patrick. What makes you so wise?"

"I'm not wise, Casey."

"You seem to know what's important and what's not."

"Do I?"

"Yes." Casey smiled shyly and then asked softly, "What is the most important thing in the world to you?"

"My freedom," Patrick answered without hesitation.

*Freedom,* Casey thought. *Yes, Patrick, you are wise.* "Freedom to do what?"

"Freedom to watch the majesty of the stars and the sea, and ride on a white sand beach, and . . ." Patrick stopped abruptly because his thoughts, or perhaps his heart, had added a freedom that he had never even missed before. It was a magnificent privilege that had been taken away along with all the other privileges of freedom, and it hadn't mattered until now. But now it was the most precious freedom, the one he would miss more than all the rest put together.

"And?"

Patrick didn't answer. He only looked into her lovely blue eyes and smiled a gentle, wistful smile and thought, *And the freedom to love.*

Patrick kissed her good night. It was midnight, and they were at the door of her cottage. He had frowned slightly before the kiss, as if he wasn't sure, even though she saw desire in his eyes. It was a gentle kiss, a soft touching of lips, the most tender of hellos. As his lips greeted hers, Patrick wove his strong fingers through her silky red-gold hair, caressing with exquisite delicacy.

*You don't have to be so careful with me, Patrick!* Casey thought. *I'm experienced.*

But her experiences hadn't begun to prepare her for the unfamiliar and exciting sensations that swept through her at his touch. In fact, her experiences had only made her wary. She played the games of seduction magnificently, winning the hearts and desires of the most handsome and powerful of men. The rich and famous men wanted Casey, and she wanted them—until they touched her. Casey felt nothing when they kissed her and less than nothing when they made love to her—bewildered annoyance at their pleasure, smoldering anger that they expected her to be grateful as their hands and lips expertly urged her to sigh with ecstasy, and an immense sense of failure despite the triumph of her seduction. There was supposed to be more, wasn't there? Casey saw in their eyes that for them there was much more—joy and plea-

191

sure—but she felt nothing except a horrible feeling of imperfection and the even worse ominous belief that she was as cold as ice.

But Casey wasn't ice with Patrick.

He kissed her, and she kissed him, and she wanted more. She wanted to follow the commands of his gray-green eyes wherever they took her. But he stopped the kiss and gazed at her with eyes that told her so eloquently of their desire—and something else . . . a lingering worry.

*Patrick, I'm not a virgin,* Casey thought. *Or am I?*

*What the hell am I doing?* Patrick wondered. *She is so lovely, and I want her so much, but what right do I have to love her? What promises can I make to her? What certainties can I offer her? None, except the certainty that my life will be spent in hiding.*

"Patrick?" Casey's voice was suddenly apprehensive, as if she wasn't sure that he wanted her. Patrick saw the lovely vulnerability and knew that he couldn't say good-bye.

"May I see you again, Casey?"

"Yes."

"I have to work late tomorrow night, so the night after tomorrow? About nine?"

"All right. What work?"

"I teach riding at the Club."

"Oh, I see."

But Casey didn't see, and after Patrick left she lay awake trying to make sense of what he had said. Patrick told her he didn't play games, but he was playing now. Perhaps this summer he was teaching riding at the Club, as a lark, but surely his usual summers were spent yachting at the

Cape, or lazing on the sun-kissed beaches of St. Tropez, or running his empire from his suite of offices in Manhattan.

Casey tried to make sense of it and when she did the realization came with a soft smile and a racing heart. She and Patrick were so very much alike. Each was rich, privileged, successful, but this summer each had chosen to cast off the cloak of wealth and success and simply *be. . .* simply be *free.*

This summer Patrick James was a riding instructor and Casey English was a working girl, and they were sharing the most important truths of all, truths about who they were, not what they achieved or controlled or owned or won.

This summer Casey and Patrick were sharing truths of the heart and kisses of fire and . . .

Casey shivered as she remembered Patrick's kiss and the promise in his sensuous eyes that when he returned in two nights their loving wouldn't stop with a kiss. Casey's shiver was a tremble of desire and fear.

Desire because she wanted him so much. And fear because she was so afraid she would disappoint them both.

Casey ordered champagne from the Country Store. The delivery cost almost as much as the champagne because Casey told them it was a rush even though all she wanted was one bottle of their least expensive brand. She was a working girl, after all. The least expensive brand of champagne stocked at Southampton's small grocery still cost twenty dollars, a dusty bottle of Mumm's unceremoniously wedged between the Krug and Dom Pérignon.

Casey never offered Patrick the champagne. She only offered him herself, a trembling offer, a gift that he accepted and cherished and loved so gently.

*Oh, Patrick, you have come to rescue me again, haven't you?* Casey thought when his lips touched hers and ignited all the magnificent sensations. But what if she couldn't be rescued, not really? What if the trembling sensations faded, iced over? The flickers of desire that came alive at his touch were becoming flames, fanned by his tender lips and gentle hands, growing hotter and hotter, but what if they suddenly disappeared?

"Patrick, hurry."

"Casey?" Patrick saw the mixture of desire and fear on her lovely face and guessed at the cause of her uncertainty. "There's no need to hurry, Casey."

"Yes."

"No."

"No?"

"No."

Gently, lovingly, Patrick proved to Casey that her desires wouldn't vanish as magically and unexpectedly as they had appeared. The fire of their love wasn't a clever trick or a sleight of his talented hands. The fire was real, from the heart, magical but not magic.

The wonderful sensations didn't disappear. They only grew stronger and more demanding as his kisses deepened and expanded, covering all of her, kissing hello everywhere—her lips, her neck, her shoulders, her breasts, and then voyaging where she had never allowed anyone before, never wished it, but where she welcomed his exquisite tenderness.

Casey wasn't ice and the magnificent sensations weren't going to disappear, but when they became so strong, so powerful, she was swept with new fears.

"Oh, Casey," Patrick whispered gently as he gazed into her eyes. He had sensed that she was a virgin—not to sex but to love—and he had been so careful, but still he saw her fear. "Don't be afraid."

"Patrick, I . . ."

"It's OK, honey. It will be lovely. I'm with you, Casey."

Patrick *was* with her, holding her, smiling lovingly into her eyes, making her feel so safe . . .

Safe enough to allow the fire to explode without shame.

*Safe enough to be free.*


"Where are your eyes?" Patrick asked softly, finally, as their breathing became calm and their pounding hearts began to slow. Casey was curled against him, her red-gold head resting gently on his chest, but she hadn't spoken and he felt her trembling still, and then the wet heat of tears. "Casey?"

When Casey raised her head, Patrick delicately untangled the fire-gold silk until he could see her eyes.

"Hi."

"Hi." Casey smiled a brave and shy smile.

"Did I tell you that I've decided you're a flower?"

"Not a parade?"

"No, not a parade." Patrick gently touched the joyful, nourishing tears that fell from her forget-me-not-blue eyes. Patrick saw joy in the blue, and then a flicker of uncertainty, a whisper of disbelief, as if what had just happened could never happen again.

Patrick kissed her and held her very close.

And after a while he showed her over and over that it was the way their loving would be . . . always.


"What's in here?" Patrick asked as he lifted the knapsack Casey had packed.

The knapsack was heavier than usual, obviously carrying something more than just the blankets and sweaters they took for their nights in the meadow. For the past month Patrick and Casey had spent almost every night together, in the meadow if Patrick could get away before sunset and in the cottage or on the beach if the sky was already dark when he arrived.

"Champagne."

"Oh."


Casey knew Patrick's silences—the peaceful moments between their quiet conversations, the intimate silence when they held each other after they loved, the breath-held awe as they watched the sun fall into the trees and the stars light up the sky. Casey knew those lovely comfortable silences, but she didn't know the silence that traveled with them now as they walked along the beach to the meadow. She only knew that it was troubled, not peaceful, and that there had been a flicker of worry in Patrick's eyes when she told him she had packed champagne.

"Is the brand all right with you, Patrick?" she asked softly when they reached the meadow and he removed the bottle from the knapsack.

"Sure. I've never tasted champagne before."

"Oh! I guess I should have asked you. I could have gotten wine or bourbon or Scotch."

For the month they had been together Casey had never given Patrick anything but herself—no food, no liquor, not even coffee when he reluctantly left her bed at dawn. And Patrick had wanted nothing more. Tonight, on impulse, she packed the bottle of Mumm's that she had purchased before their first night of love.

"I've never tasted alcohol of any kind."

"Never?" Casey echoed with soft surprise. Surprise and gentle concern as she saw the sudden pain in his gray-green eyes and the solemn worry on his handsome face. There was obviously a reason Patrick had never tasted alcohol, a reason that caused him pain, and if she could help . . . After a moment she asked quietly, "Why not, Patrick?"

As he considered her question he wondered, as he had been wondering ever since they left Sea-Cliff, if this was the night he would tell her about himself . . . about the crime for which he had been falsely accused and because of which it was his destiny to spend his life in hiding. Patrick had to tell her eventually, but once he did their relationship would irrevocably change—or end. He had planned to tell her just before she moved to the city. That way, if she didn't choose to share his destiny, she could leave gracefully, easily, murmuring softly how busy she would be with her work.

But now she was asking him why he had never tasted alcohol, and Patrick wondered if tonight he would tell her everything.

"There's never been a time in my life when I felt safe enough to drink, Casey."

*Why not?* she wanted to ask again, but didn't, because her wish was to help not intrude. She waited, smiling gently at the troubled eyes, and when the gray-green focused on her, away from whatever pain it was in the past and back to the present, she knew he would tell her sometime, but not tonight.

"How about now, Patrick? Do you feel safe?" she asked finally, softly, as her heart whispered a gentle plea, *Please feel safe with me! I feel so safe with you.*

"Very safe." Patrick smiled. "So, let's try this."

As he expertly opened the bottle, Patrick first saw confusion on her lovely face and then the worry. Worry that he had just lied to her.

"I do some bartending," he explained swiftly, wanting to reassure but shaken by a future worry of his own. *Oh, Casey, will you feel so terribly betrayed when I tell you the truth about myself?*

"But you've never tasted the drinks you make?"

"No. I've always wondered about champagne, though."

Patrick liked the taste of champagne, sipping it from the glasses Casey had packed, but the bubbly honey-colored liquid was even better mixed in a kiss with the intoxicating taste of Casey.

As Patrick drank the champagne and felt its effects, he knew he had been right to be wary of

198

alcohol. Even in this idyllic place with the woman he loved, he felt the champagne insidiously stripping him of caution, making him bold and reckless. The effect was wonderful with Casey, a safe, warm, giddy joy. But in his boyhood home in the slums, where even the children were armed, the effect might have been lethal. Alcohol was lethal there—slowly lethal when it destroyed hearts and minds and hope, and instantly lethal when it caused a moment of carelessness, a loss of vigilance, in that concrete world of war.

The champagne didn't change their loving, because their passion was always uninhibited and free, but it did loosen the inhibitions of Patrick's heart, urging him to speak aloud the words that flowed through him in silent rivers of joy.

Patrick only told Casey one truth that night. It was the truth he had planned to reveal only after he had told her all the others . . . the most important truth.

"I love you, Casey. I love you."

"Oh, Patrick, I love you, too."


"When do you move into the city?" Patrick asked before he returned to the stable the following morning.

"My things arrive from California the last week in August. I'll go in that week to get settled." *To unpack my designer clothes and get my jewels from the safe-deposit box and make certain my Mercedes arrived without scratches and take the Bar exam,* Casey thought. She wasn't worried about telling Patrick the unimportant truths about herself, and she assumed he would have a similar

199

confession, but she was in no rush to tell him. Even though they would be together still when they returned to their hectic lives of success and wealth, Casey was in no hurry to end this gentle and peaceful summer of love. "I don't actually start work until the day after Labor Day, so I'll come back out on Friday for the weekend. There's a party here that night that I have to attend." *A magnificent gala in my honor.* She gazed thoughtfully at his gray-green eyes and asked softly, "Could you come to the party with me Patrick?"

"The Friday of Labor Day weekend?"

"Yes."

"I'm afraid I can't."

"Are you sure?"

"Yes. I'm sorry. I have to work late. But why don't we plan something definite for the following night?"

"I'm free."

"Good. Let's plan on dinner then."

"A picnic in the meadow with more champagne?"

"Whatever you like."

## Chapter Eleven

*Southampton, Long Island*
*August 1989*

"Rained out?" Jeffrey asked with a smile when Julia appeared in the doorway of the library.

The day, the last Sunday in August, had begun with heat and humidity, but by midafternoon sheets of rain fell from the opaque skies. Merry was at a slumber party. Jeffrey and Julia had agreed that each would work, he in the library, she in her rose garden, until dinner.

"Rained out. I think I'll go to the grocery. Is there anything special you'd like?"

"You."

"For dinner."

"Same answer."

"You can have me after dinner."

"Promise?"

"Of course."

"Good. Then what I'd like for dinner is something we can eat very quickly."

\* \* \*

"Daddy? Can I please talk to Mommy?"

"She's at the grocery, Merry."

"When will she be home?"

Jeffrey heard the edge of panic in the small voice on the telephone and thought, *Not soon enough.* He asked gently, "What's wrong, honey?"

"I need to come home. Could you ask Mommy to come get me, please?" The last word trembled.

"Yes, of course, but it may be a while."

"Maybe I should call Aunt Paige and Uncle Edmund."

"Why don't I come get you? Merry?"

"Oh. OK."

"I'll be there in"—Jeffrey thought about the distance from Belvedere to the Montgomery estate and decided he should be precise—"six minutes, OK?"

"OK."


Danielle Montgomery would not have walked Merry out to the car had the driver been Julia and she certainly wouldn't have offered even the hint of an apology. Merry was being overly sensitive, that was all. But the parent was Jeffrey, not Julia.

"Jeffrey, please accept my apologies. I should have checked with Julia, but of course we didn't expect rain. I thought we'd be at the pool all afternoon. Most nine-year-olds have seen it, anyway."

Jeffrey nodded absently to Danielle. His concern was Merry. Tears were threatening in her dark-brown eyes and she looked so small, so helpless, so afraid. And trying so hard to be brave.

202

The six-minute drive back to Belvedere was silent. Jeffrey kept glancing at her, smiling gently and sympathetically, but she couldn't speak. Her energy was focused on her fight against her tears; and, besides, she was obviously so very uneasy with him.

Why wouldn't Merry be uneasy with him? She didn't know him. As Jeffrey had driven to the Montgomery estate he realized that the brief phone call had been the first between them. And now as he drove cautiously on the rain-slick roads and glanced cautiously at the little girl who so valiantly battled her tears, he realized that he and Merry had never been alone together.

When they reached Belvedere, Merry dashed out of the car and into the mansion to find Julia. Her frantic search took her from room to room. Jeffrey followed the sounds of Merry's soft and desperate calls of "Mommy? Are you here?"

"Merry?" he asked gently of the trembling figure that looked so small in the great room, where the unsuccessful search had ended and the tears could be held back no longer.

Merry looked up at the sound of Jeffrey's voice. When he saw her face, Jeffrey drew a soft breath. Merry looked so lost, so fragile, so much like Julia had looked on the evening she confessed to him that she was only sixteen. And just as he had wanted to do with her mother ten years ago, Jeffrey felt a consuming wish to banish Merry's fears, to keep her safe and happy always.

"Tell me what happened, honey." Jeffrey knelt in front of her on the plush carpet.

"There was a movie. We watched it because it

203

was raining, and it was so sad."

"What movie?"

"It was called *Old Yeller*."

*Old Yeller*. In a rare motherly moment Victoria had dutifully taken nine-year-old Jeffrey to see *Old Yeller*. All children saw *Old Yeller*, Victoria had heard, and all children were supposed to love it. But it had made him so sad. Jeffrey never told anyone, not even his grandparents, and he had hidden his tears. But now the long-forgotten sadness swept through him.

Had he known Merry was going to be shown *Old Yeller*, Jeffrey—as Merry's father?—would have said No, just as Julia would certainly have said No had she known. Julia spent her life protecting her daughter, enveloping Merry in a warm, soft cloak of love, sheltering her from life's sadnesses as long as she could.

"When I was a little boy, Merry, just about your age, I saw *Old Yeller*." Jeffrey spoke softly to the lovely, sad brown eyes. "And it made me very sad, too."

"It did?" she asked hopefully.

"Yes, it did."

"Why did he have to die, Daddy?" Merry demanded as Jeffrey's own nine-year-old heart had demanded twenty-seven years before. Her question trembled and new tears spilled.

"I don't know why he had to die, honey," Jeffrey answered gently. "Sad things sometimes happen in life."

Merry nodded thoughtfully. Then she looked bravely into his eyes and asked earnestly, "The news can be very sad, can't it? And then you have

204

to tell people about the sad things that have happened. Does that make you cry sometimes?"

"Sometimes," Jeffrey admitted quietly. "Merry, how do you know about the news?"

"Because Mommy and I watch you every night."

A vivid collage of news events—events Merry should not have seen—flashed through Jeffrey's mind. The first was the indelible image of the Christmas massacre at the Rome airport when the daughter of a journalist had been murdered. That was three and a half years ago, never to be forgotten, but the news of the past four months had been filled with equally tragic horrors against children—the unspeakably evil rituals in Matamoros, the soccer-match disaster in Sheffield, the unimaginable act of the father in California who killed his young daughters, the ghastly aftermath of the Chinese students' stand for democracy in Tianamen Square.

In a matter of seconds Jeffrey thought of five tragedies he wouldn't want Merry to know about. He couldn't believe that she did know about them, that Julia would have allowed it.

"You watch the news with Mommy?"

"We watch you. Mommy always watches first and records the parts I can see. I used to be able to watch more, when I was little, but now I understand more so I get to watch less." Merry explained this paradox without confusion. It was obviously something she and Julia had discussed. "But I can watch all of your Special Reports when they are about politics or the economy."

Jeffrey smiled, but his emotions were suddenly very shaky and stunning questions suddenly

205

swirled in his mind.

Merry watched the news to see *him?* Her *daddy?* It was Julia's wish that they become a family, but did this lovely, sensitive little girl have expectations of him, too? Did she need his love?

Jeffrey had assumed that Merry had no expectations of him. He knew that her life was filled, overflowing, with love. Merry had Julia's wonderful love and she had, too, the almost parental love of Edmund and Paige. This summer, on the few occasions when he had been home to join the frequent picnics at Somerset, Jeffrey had been so aware of the years of love and laughter and friendship and trust that bonded Merry and Julia with Edmund and Amanda and Paige. Jeffrey was peripheral to their circle of love; he always had been. Now, as he tried to join the circle, because he had given Julia a promise from his heart that he would try, he felt awkward, uncertain, and so out of place. He was welcomed, of course, but he was a stranger to the history of laughter and love that bonded them all, an outsider, and an imposter . . . because he did not belong at picnics with fathers and daughters.

But, over the summer, as he had watched the little girl with brown eyes who was so lively and laughing with Edmund and so silent and shy with him, how desperately he had wished that he did belong.

"Merry?"

"Mommy!" Merry's eyes lit at the sight of her mother and she dashed to greet her. "You're home!"

"Yes, darling." Julia knelt as Jeffrey had, to be

206

at the same level as the dark-brown eyes. Julia tenderly stroked Merry's golden-blond hair and asked softly, "What happened?"

"They showed us a movie. It was called *Old Yeller.* It was very sad and I wanted to come home. Daddy came to get me. He saw it when he was little and it made him sad, too." Merry had been speaking to Julia, her trusting eyes focused on the mother who had been there always, a safe, gentle, loving haven, but then she turned, smiled shyly at Jeffrey, and added softly, "Daddy saved me just like he saved that little girl in Beirut."

"Thank you," Julia whispered softly to Jeffrey. Then she took Merry's hand. "Come help me in the kitchen, Merry, so Daddy can finish his work."

"I'm finished. Can I help, too?"

"Of course. You and Merry can set the table."

"I could show you how to make chocolate-chip cookies, Daddy, if you want," Merry offered quietly.

"I would like that very much, Merry."

Jeffrey's voice was quiet, too, but his heart was restless. He wanted to know this lovely little girl. He wanted Merry to know that she could trust him, too, as she trusted Julia and Edmund and Paige. He wanted her to know that she could count on him if she needed him.

*Is that all you want?* his racing heart demanded. *Or do you want even more? Don't you really want to become a family?*

*Yes.* That was what he wanted. He had promised Julia he would try and it had been a promise of love laced with uncertainty.

But now . . .

Jeffrey didn't know if Merry wanted him to be her daddy, if she needed more love in her life, but he would be there for her if she did, if she would allow it, if they could overcome their awkward shyness for each other.

As Jeffrey smiled at the dark-brown eyes that had bravely offered to teach him how to make chocolate-chip cookies and Merry smiled back, he suddenly believed that anything was possible.

*I know Merry cannot be your daughter. But you can love her as your own as I have cherished her as my great-granddaughter. The only obstacle, my darling Jeffrey, is in your heart.* As Jeffrey walked into the kitchen with Merry and Julia he remembered Grandmère's wise and loving words and thought, *You were right, Grandmère, because no truths have changed, but a great heaviness has been magically lifted from my heart. And where that leaden obstacle used to lie I now feel such joyous hope.*

"I'm going to miss you," Patrick whispered as his lips softly nuzzled Casey's neck. They were in the living room at SeaCliff watching the rain fall to the sea. Patrick stood behind her with his arms wrapped gently around her waist.

"I'm going to miss you, too. Five nights. You haven't changed your mind about Friday?"

"I really can't, Casey. I'm sorry. I wanted to talk to you about our dinner on Saturday. I thought maybe we should go to a restaurant instead of the meadow. There's a place in Southampton called Chez Claude."

Chez Claude. Paige had told her about the expensive and romantic French restaurant.

"Probably can't wear jeans or shorts there."

"We can eat somewhere else if you like."

"I have party dresses." *Just like you have tailor-made suits and silk tuxedos.* "And I'd love to have dinner with you at Chez Claude."

"I'll make a reservation then."

"Wonderful." Casey turned in his arms to look at his face. His voice had been so quiet, so solemn, and she wanted to see his eyes. They were solemn, too, so she asked softly, "Why do you look so grim about a candlelight and champagne dinner, Patrick?"

"Because we need to talk."

"About how we can see each other after I move into the city."

"Yes." Patrick kissed her lips, tenderly sealing that promise. *We will see each other after you move, my love, if you still want to see me once you know the truth.* "But, Casey, there are other things I need to tell you."

"There are things I need to tell you, too, Patrick."

Patrick feared what he had to tell her. Would Casey be terribly hurt that he hadn't told her sooner? Would she feel angry and betrayed? Would she want to escape from him? He wanted to make it very easy for Casey to say good-bye. That was why he had decided dinner at a restaurant—neutral territory in the real world—rather than in their enchanted meadow of love.

Casey didn't fear what she had to tell Patrick, nor did she fear what Patrick was going to tell

209

her. They already knew the most important truths about each other. The details—their mutual confessions of lifelong wealth and successful careers—were trivial. Casey saw that Patrick was worried about what he had to tell her and guessed that his worry was because he had been playing games and felt a little guilty, as she did, that the confession hadn't come sooner. If that was what worried Patrick, it was something they would laugh about.

And if it was something else?

It still didn't worry her.

She loved Patrick, and she knew that he loved her, and nothing else mattered.


By three the following afternoon the movers were gone and Casey was left to unpack boxes and settle into her luxury apartment overlooking Central Park. She unpacked her law books first because they were old friends, though she had never realized it before. She had become an attorney to please K.C. English. But this summer, as she thought about the important and unimportant things in her life, Casey realized that she really believed in what she did. Being a good lawyer was important to her. She didn't have to be the best attorney on earth anymore. She had to be something even more important—she had to be the best attorney *she* could be.

The law books were familiar and welcome friends. So, too, were the expensive McGuire wickers with their pastel cushions because the light and elegant California-chic furniture reminded her of SeaCliff.

But Casey frowned as she hung her designer clothes in her spacious closets. The linens by Lauren and the silks by Dior and the chiffons by Chanel were so different from the light cottons she had worn all summer—the wonderful, simple outfits that Patrick removed with soft sighs and gentle, eager hands. The designer clothes belonged to the old Casey, the talented actress who performed flawlessly but without happiness or joy. When she clothed herself in the expensive fabrics would the new Casey suddenly disappear?

"No!" Casey said aloud, speaking to the gorgeous clothes and giving them fair warning. The new Casey would be there still beneath the elegant layers of satin and silk. *It will just take Patrick a little longer, lovely, delicious moments, to undress me.*

Casey smiled confidently at the beautiful clothes and finally selected two dresses that would return with her for her final weekend in Southampton. For the party in her honor at the Club, she chose Cassini sequins. The famous designer hadn't created the stunning cocktail dress expressly for Casey English, but it was as if he had. The sequins were pale blue and soft violet—the precise pastels of her forget-me-not-blue eyes—and they shimmered against a background of sunlit gold lamé. Casey decided to wear the dazzling dress on Friday because that was the night she had to dazzle.

On Saturday, for the candlelight dinner with Patrick, she selected a dress by Laura Ashley. It was the color of rich cream, a soft romantic dress of ruffles and lace that looked like a country wedding dress from a different era. Casey had bought it in

211

Union Square a week before she left San Francisco and had never worn it. It had been an impulsive, surprising purchase because the look wasn't her, but now she smiled at the beautiful dress and thought, *It is me. Maybe, even then, even before I left San Francisco, I knew there was another Casey.*

"May I help you?" the young woman asked with unconcealed disapproval when Patrick entered the exclusive Yankee Peddler men's clothing store in Southampton.

"I need some clothes."

*Yes you do,* the woman thought.

Patrick only really needed to buy something presentable for dinner Saturday night. He could come back, if Casey still wanted to see him after she knew all about him, to purchase additional slacks, shirts, and sweaters to wear when he visited her in Manhattan. Casey *would* want to see him still, wouldn't she? Didn't it make sense, and didn't it show confidence in their love, to buy an additional outfit or two right now?

Patrick had enough money. He had worked long hours over the summer, teaching riding lessons and bartending at the many parties at the club. Some nights the extra work had kept him away from her, as it would this Friday, but he knew that as soon as school started the riding lessons would diminish, and perhaps the parties would, too, so he had worked to earn enough to last all winter, enough to be able to travel into the city often to be with her.

212

There had once been a time when Patrick dressed as if he belonged among the rich and privileged. Now, with unerring instincts, he assembled outfits of impeccable taste and understated elegance, and when he emerged from the dressing room to view himself in a three-way mirror, the saleswoman gasped.

"I know who you are!"

"I doubt it," Patrick replied calmly, although his heart pounded anxiously. He knew that except for his long—for Southampton—coal-black hair, he looked as he had looked all those years when he blended in flawlessly at the posh country clubs that hosted the Grand Prix show jumping events. He had been quite well camouflaged in denim and cowboy boots, but what if this woman *did* recognize him?

"No, I'm sure." She smiled coyly and then announced triumphantly, "You're a model for Calvin Klein, aren't you? I know I saw you in a recent ad in *W*."

Casey looked at herself in the mirror as she dressed for the party in her honor at the Club. The dazzling Cassini was all wrong. The sleek sheath of sequins looked terrible against the paleness of her bare arms. Her once carefully golden-tanned skin was pale now, despite the sunny Southampton summer, because her days had been spent indoors studying so that her nights would be free to spend with Patrick. It had been a summer of moonlight, not sunlight, and how Patrick loved the whiteness of her pale skin as it was caressed

213

by the moon!

Patrick would probably tell her the dress looked magnificent, a stunning contrast to the creaminess, and perhaps that was true.

It wasn't the dazzling dress that was the problem, she realized finally. It was the expectation that she had to dazzle. That was what was all wrong.

Tonight, amidst the most rich and powerful men and women of New York, Casey English was expected to charm and enchant, to speak perfect, clever, confident words, to bewitch and control. She would have to be on her toes, *à point,* performing a graceful *pas de deux* in every conversation. But she didn't want to dazzle. She wasn't even certain that she could anymore.

Casey frowned at the dress that was a symbol of the dazzle that was no longer her and decided that on this night she needed other symbols, symbols of the new Casey, symbols of Patrick and their love.

She would wear her hair long, she decided, as she had worn it all summer. And she would weave wildflowers into the red-gold silk as Patrick had done so often in their meadow. Casey hadn't paid attention to how Patrick braided the flowers into her hair—her attention was distracted by the quivers of desire that pulsed through her at his touch—but she had seen what it looked like hours later, a spectacular tangle of hair and petals after a night of love.

Tonight she would wear wildflowers in her hair and it would be as if Patrick were with her.

But Casey couldn't get the flowers to stay in her

214

silky hair. Somehow Patrick's strong and gentle fingers had woven works of art from wildflowers and hair, but her fingers were clumsy. The flowers slipped and fell, or showed more stems than petals, and even though Casey tried again and again, she failed.

And it was getting late, later. She was already late.

Finally, in frustration, Casey took her magnificent red-gold mane and with fingers that had been too clumsy and trembling to secure wildflowers in the fine silk expertly twisted it into a smooth, rich swirl on top of her head and secured the elegant crown with a barrette made of solid gold.

In those moments her fingers had belonged to the old Casey, and they had assumed control with swift and assured confidence. The old Casey hadn't returned in full force, however, and Casey didn't want her to. Still, as she drove her gold-tone Mercedes sport coupe toward the Club, speeding because she was almost an hour late, she wished for a few flickers of the old radiant confidence.

*Just be yourself,* she told her racing heart. *Your new self. Just be the Casey that you love and that Patrick loves.*

*But what if I can only really be myself with Patrick?*

## Chapter Twelve

"Paige, I'm so sorry!" Casey exclaimed as she walked into the foyer at the Club. Paige was there, obviously waiting for her to arrive, her face more concerned than annoyed.

"Fashionably late, Casey," Paige reassured swiftly. "Is everything all right?"

"Oh, yes. It's just that I've spent the summer slipping into shorts and tops in under two seconds and my timing is off."

"Well, you look absolutely gorgeous."

"Thank you."

Edmund joined them. Like Paige, Edmund's smile graciously conveyed a message of welcome and no apologies necessary.

"How was the Bar exam, Casey? Passable?"

"They asked the right questions, Edmund."

"Just the few points of law you happened to review?"

"I guess." Casey laughed softly.

"So, are you ready to meet some people?"

"I guess," Casey repeated quietly, without a soft laugh this time because a rush of panic swept through her.

There weren't just *some* people mingling in the elegant rooms of the Southampton Club, there were well over two hundred. The bejeweled and coutured guests wandered from the lavish buffet in the Azalea Room to the garden terrace where a band played slow, sensual melodies of love and there was dancing beneath the moon.

*These people will be your clients,* Casey reminded her racing heart. *And you will do the best you can for them. That's all that is necessary. You don't have to perform and dazzle.*

Casey didn't perform, but she *did* dazzle with her unaffected loveliness, her polite smiles and soft murmurs of "Thank you" as she received compliments for her past accomplishments. With each new introduction, she began to feel a little more calm and a little more hopeful. *I can do this. I can be myself.*

Until she saw Patrick.

Strands of colorful lanterns had been festooned across the garden terrace. As the lanterns swayed in the balmy breeze, they cast light into distant corners of the terrace, illuminating the shadowy edges—including the place where the outdoor bar had been set up.

Casey knew Patrick in faded jeans and cowboy boots. And she knew his strong, lean body even better in nothing at all. Now he wore tight black pants and a red jacket, the generic uniform of a servant at a swank country club. Patrick was the bartender, a cut above the similarly dressed valets who parked cars and the waiters who circulated with silver platters of gourmet hors d'oeuvres and took orders for drinks. The waiters gave the drink orders to Patrick and he swiftly made the cocktails for the rich and famous men and women who had assembled to honor *her*.

Patrick was a servant at the party in her honor when he should have been her date!

*I teach riding at the Club. I do some bartending.* That was what Patrick had told her and it had been the truth.

And she had told him *I'm just a working girl*.

*Just* . . . Casey had said "just" as if in apology that she wasn't something better, but Patrick had never apologized for what he did. Patrick had never said "I *just* teach riding."

Casey had assumed he was something else. Something more? Something better? Because Casey English could never fall in love with *just* a riding instructor?

The old Casey couldn't have.

But the new Casey could and had.

It didn't matter what Patrick did!

Casey stared at him from across the terrace, willing his gray-green eyes to meet hers, but he was busy mixing drinks for her future important clients. Patrick was busy and so was she, graciously meeting the influential and powerful men and women even though she wished they would all vanish so that she could be alone with him.

She desperately wanted to go to him and tell him that it didn't matter, to reassure him, if he needed reassurance.

But it was Casey who needed reassurance. Casey whose heart raced with fear.

It didn't matter to her that she was Casey English, heiress-attorney, and he was Patrick James, riding instructor and sometime bartender . . . but she feared that it might matter very much to him.

* * *

Patrick knew the instant Casey walked onto the garden terrace. He sensed her presence even though he didn't look up to meet her gaze. He had been expecting her. By the time she arrived he had overheard enough conversations to know all about the Casey English the world knew, but who he didn't, the enchanting heiress, the sensational trial attorney, the dazzling golden girl who played magnificently and always won.

Patrick had always been so wary of the rich, beautiful women who wanted him for their pleasure, as a possession, a trophy, a plaything. Always so wary . . . and yet it had never occurred to him that Casey had been playing. But she had. The beautiful heiress-attorney and the riding instructor. Had he, and their starlit nights of loving, been merely a sensual reward for the long days spent studying in the cottage?

*Oh, Casey,* Patrick thought sadly. *I had no idea that you were playing with me. You played so well . . . and you won. Because I fell in love with you, Casey English, I really fell in love.*

"Champagne?" Patrick asked when Casey finally escaped the glitter of the party to join him in the shadows. "We don't have anything under a hundred dollars a bottle, I'm afraid. Or are you done playing Lady Chatterley?"

Casey had steeled her racing heart for anger in his gentle voice, but what she heard was even worse. Instead of the fire of anger, proof of emo-

219

tion, proof that he cared, she heard only a detached coolness. Even the mocking question "Are you done playing Lady Chatterley?" was posed with the polite tone of a servant, as if there had never been anything between them, as if they were strangers. And when his eyes were illuminated for a moment by the light of a swaying lantern, the gray-green was mostly gray, a smoky veil that revealed nothing, a cloud that blocked her vision to his heart. The opaque gray eyes, like his terrifyingly calm voice, made him so very far away from her . . . and so very far away from the gentleness of their love.

"I wasn't playing Lady Chatterley, Patrick. And I thought that you . . ." Casey stopped, realizing that completing the thought, her belief that he was rich and successful, too, might push him farther away, if that was possible.

But Patrick finished the thought for her. "You thought *I* was slumming with *you?* The aristocrat and the working girl? No. Sorry to disappoint you, Casey."

"It doesn't disappoint me, Patrick. But I've disappointed you, haven't I?" she asked softly. *Oh, Patrick, I know I have hurt you! Please talk to me!*

"Let's just say that you were wrong about me and I was wrong about you."

"You weren't wrong about me."

"No? Well. It doesn't matter. Let's just say then that *you* were wrong about *me* and leave it at that."

"Leave it?" Casey echoed with rising fear. She fought the fear and continued hopefully. "Yes, of

220

course, we can't really talk now. But, Patrick, could we meet later, after the party, so I can explain?"

"You don't need to explain."

"But I'd like to," she answered quietly. Then she added softly, a tentative whisper of hope and fear, "Tomorrow night at dinner."

"I don't think so, Casey."

A waiter appeared then, with drink orders, and Patrick returned to his task of mixing drinks for her guests, as if she weren't even there . . . and finally Casey withdrew from the silent shadows and returned to the party.

Patrick was angry, he had to be, and hurt, even though he had seemed terrifyingly calm, as if he had already made the decision that their love was over, a decision that wasn't even terribly difficult to make.

Was he never going to let her explain?

*Yes,* Casey assured herself with shaky confidence. *Of course he will. He needs a little time, and this isn't the place to talk anyway. We'll see each other again, later, won't we?*

Casey filled her heart with brave assurances and stole hopeful glances at him, searching for a flicker of warmth. Patrick resolutely avoided her hopeful gaze, but he was a powerful magnet still.

Finally, in a desperate act of survival, Casey turned her back to the shadowy corner and faced the area of the terrace where couples danced beneath the moonlight. As she turned, Casey's gaze fell on Jeffrey and Julia. She hadn't seen them until now, and now she watched as they danced, and Jeffrey's blue eyes caressed Julia with

221

exquisite messages of love.

*Julia.* Tonight Julia wore her hair long and free, as Casey had wanted to but failed . . . and there was more. Artfully woven into the long strands of black silk were lovely delicate wildflowers . . .

Julia had been able to do what Casey had not. Just as always. Julia was better.

*I tried to be like you this summer, Julia, to be loved for who I really am inside. And I got so close, so very close to happiness and freedom, and now . . .*

*Now I have to get away.*

Casey knew she couldn't escape to SeaCliff, not yet, but she desperately needed a little privacy, a little time, a few quiet moments in the roses away from Patrick, and away from Julia.


"Pardon me, Mr. Lawrence?" The valet sent to find the famous anchor spoke quietly and awkwardly. It would have been easier to interrupt Jeffrey Lawrence if he had been discussing the war being waged against the drug lords in Colombia, not dancing slowly with his beautiful wife.

"Yes?"

"You have a phone call from your exchange."

"Oh. Thank you." Jeffrey smiled reassuringly at the valet and then apologetically at Julia. Calls from his exchange almost always meant he would have to spring into action, go into town to anchor a special broadcast or even fly to the site of the tragedy. "I'll be back, darling."

After Jeffrey left, Julia was alone in a sea of faces that were familiar but not friendly unless

222

Jeffrey was with her.

*I really should talk to Casey,* Julia thought.

Julia had had the same thought many times over the summer but hadn't acted on it. Of course Paige had reported that Casey was busy and seemed to be enjoying her solitude, but that wasn't the reason Julia hadn't called.

The reason was the uneasy memory of Jeffrey's bewildering anger after the dinner party in June. The anger had been prompted by Casey, an unwitting symbol of Julia's past, and since then Casey had become an unwitting symbol of that night, and Julia had made no effort to see her.

But it would be safe to see Casey now, because now that night was merely a blurry, bewildering memory, the tiniest ripple in the vast calm of their love, almost a mirage.

Jeffrey and Julia had survived that night. Their wonderful, joyous love was strong and whole again.

And in the past five days there had been magic.

The magic had begun on Sunday when she returned from the grocery and found Merry and Jeffrey in the great room. The three of them had spent the entire evening together. Merry had showed Jeffrey how to make chocolate-chip cookies, and during dinner her shy and sensitive daughter *talked* to him. Merry was a chatterbox with Julia, a fountain of words and insights and questions and thoughts, but she had always been too shy to speak her thoughts to Jeffrey.

But Sunday night Jeffrey had lured Merry from her shyness the same way that years before he had urged a shy Julia to speak by asking gentle, inter-

223

ested questions and welcoming her soft answers with a warm smile and loving blue eyes.

Sunday night had been magic, and the magic didn't vanish with the light of day. Each morning all week Jeffrey had left for work a little later than usual, lingering over breakfast, talking to Merry, and leaving reluctantly because it would be twenty-four hours before they would see each other again.

They hadn't made plans for this weekend, except that Jeffrey would be home. That might change because of the call from the studio, but even if the news of the world demanded that he be away this weekend, beginning next weekend and for an entire week they would be together. Already Julia and Merry had begun to make plans for the Vacation with Daddy. Merry, excited and shy, wanted to be so certain they made plans that Jeffrey would enjoy. The first three days of the vacation were going to be spent in Manhattan with the Spencers "doing" New York. "Will Daddy want to see the Statue of Liberty? Does Daddy like ballet? Mommy, are you sure?"

As Julia smiled at the recent memories, and the memory of their gentle summer of love, she knew that Casey could not be a threat to their happiness. It would be safe to talk to her now, safe for Jeffrey to find them together in the rose garden when he returned. Safe and polite, because Julia really did need to say good-bye to Casey and wish her well.

But Casey wasn't in the rose garden. When Julia reached the top of the stairs that led to the garden, she saw Casey disappearing in the distance past the pond toward the yacht basin. Julia didn't follow. Jeffrey would know to look for her in the rose garden but not beyond. Julia watched until Casey vanished from sight, then, as she turned to see if Jeffrey was returning yet, she saw a face in the shadows that was familiar and friendly.

"Good evening, Mrs. Lawrence," Patrick said when Julia approached. He smiled warmly at the beautiful young mother who watched her daughter's lessons so intently, her face a gentle blend of worry and pride.

"Good evening, Patrick. The girls are very excited about the show, I mean the *gymkhana*."

*Gymkhana* was Patrick's word. And it was a perfect word, the girls discovered when they found it in the dictionary—"a show for equestrians consisting of exhibitions of horsemanship and much pageantry." That was what they were planning, Merry and Amanda and Patrick, and the wonderful new word made their plans even more special and exciting. The pageantry and horsemanship was scheduled to take place the day after they returned from the long weekend in New York. All the parents would be watching because Jeffrey would be on vacation, and even though Edmund had to work he promised to be there by four on that Tuesday, September twelfth, Merry's birthday. The girls' riding ability would be a surprise for Jeffrey and Edmund who hadn't seen them ride since the first lesson, but Merry and Amanda wanted the gymkhana to be a surprise for Paige and Julia, too. For the past week no mothers had been allowed to watch the rehearsals.

"I think you'll enjoy it. Merry and Amanda are

225

both very good riders."

"They're jumping, aren't they?"

Merry and Amanda had made Patrick promise not to tell their mothers about the big surprise. Patrick had promised, but Julia looked so worried . . .

"Small jumps, Mrs. Lawrence. Very safe."

Julia gave a soft sigh.

"Really," Patrick repeated gently. "Very safe."

"Have you ever read *Gone with the Wind*, Patrick?"

"No. Why?"

Before Julia could answer, Jeffrey appeared.

"Here you are."

"Jeffrey, you remember Patrick, Merry's riding instructor."

"Yes. Of course," Jeffrey replied politely, acknowledging Patrick with a brief nod and a smile. "I have to get to the studio, Julie."

"Something in Medellin?" she asked softly as her heart whispered a silent prayer, Please don't tell me you have to fly to Cartagena.

"No. It's not Colombia, it's the Middle East. There's been a midair explosion of a commercial airliner over the Mediterranean."

"Explosion?"

"A bomb," Jeffrey answered solemnly. "Do you want to stay longer? I can have the limousine pick me up here."

"No, I'm ready to go."


Casey left the party at midnight. Some of the guests were still dancing beneath the stars but

226

most had left and she had stayed fashionably long enough. *And,* she thought, *maybe if I leave, the party will end more quickly and Patrick will be free to come to me.*

When she arrived at SeaCliff, Casey removed the famous Cassini sequins as quickly as possible and changed into familiar shorts and blouse. She wrote a note to Patrick asking him to join her in their meadow of love and left the note on the cottage door.

Had he really decided, without allowing her a voice at all, that their love was over? Because she was rich and he was poor? Because she was a successful high-powered attorney and he had to tend bar to supplement the meager amount he earned teaching riding? Was it pride?

Or was it something more important, something she couldn't so easily reassure?

Perhaps what mattered most to Patrick was her deception. *I don't play games,* Patrick had told her that from the very beginning. And he hadn't been playing, but *she* had.

But hers had been such an important pretense! It was so important that Patrick love her for *her,* who she really was, not for her dazzling successes, her immense wealth, her well-scripted flawless performances.

*I don't play games.* Patrick had told her that truth. And Patrick, who didn't play games, had told her something else, the most important truth . . . *I love you, Casey.*

As she gazed at the twinkling stars and listened to the sounds of the night, praying she would hear the rustle of ferns as he made his way to her, she

227

let those hopeful words echo in her brain. *I love you, Casey.*


It was reckless, but he felt reckless. Nothing to lose, nothing *more* to lose.

It was torture, torture and joy, and he needed the joy.

Long before dawn, Patrick removed the jumps from the shed where they were stored behind the riding ring. He had used some of the jumps before, setting the rails no higher than three feet for the lessons he gave. Now he removed all the jumps to make tall fences and massive walls and he set the rails as high as they could go, high enough to challenge even a champion.

There were two champions living in the stable at the Southampton Club now — Patrick and Night Dancer. The coal-black stallion had arrived at the Club in July, a valuable show jumper recently retired from the Grand Prix show-jumping circuit and purchased for a twelve-year-old girl who wanted to learn to jump. Patrick recognized Night Dancer and knew from a month of teaching lessons to the horse's new owner that the once-champion could still leap over six foot walls.

It took Patrick two hours to set up the jumps and ten minutes to saddle and bridle the horse. And then there was joy for horse and rider, the exhilarating freedom of floating over jump after jump, the wondrous power of flying.

And there was torture, too, for Patrick, because jumping again reminded him of all he had lost and of a time when his life had held such promise.

James Patrick Jones's life had begun without promise. He had no father and his mother could not care for him. Although James spent most of his young life away from his mother, his vivid images of her — her auburn hair and emerald-green eyes — were bright threads woven into the colorless tapestry of the concrete slums of Chicago.

Sometimes the green eyes would be glazed with drugs and unseeing and James would be taken from her to live in an orphanage or foster home. In weeks or months she would reappear, her eyes clear and sparkling with tears as she was reunited with the son whom she would all too soon forget again and neglect.

When James was eleven, his mother vanished forever. He never knew if she died or if she simply lost her fragile interest in him, because her addictions to drugs and men and pleasure and pain were so much more compelling than her life with her young son.

James learned to survive with his mother, and without her. When he was with her, he committed the minor, necessary crimes of survival — stealing food when he was starving, and clothes or blankets when the icy Chicago winter threatened to kill. When he was without her, in the endless series of foster homes, James learned to survive, too, by being wary always, wary of violence, wary of peace, wary of love.

He lived in a dark-gray world of hopelessness, decadence, and violence, but his young mind saw lovely colors even in the gray and gentle images, even amidst the violence. His artistic mind saw the images and his talented hands made the visions real. While other children found escape in drugs and alcohol, James found private solace, private joy in his painting.

He survived through his art and by being very wary always.

When he was fourteen, James decided that there must be better places on earth. It was a valiant leap of faith, but he bravely promised himself that there *had* to be.

One night he simply ran away from the new "home" where he had lived for less than a month. Two days later he was in a heaven filled with radiant colors and immeasurable beauty—the luxuriant emerald hills of Kentucky. He found work in a stable. He had never been near horses before, but he felt an immediate love for the magnificent, gentle creatures. James rode one morning, bareback and without fear, and discovered a talent as wonderful and instinctive as his art.

His gift, his natural ability to ride, did not go unnoticed. Wealthy men and women paid him to jump their prize horses. James won ribbons, mostly blue, and trophies, mostly gold, and earned recognition in elite equestrian circles as one of the best riders in the world.

James's life in the slums of Chicago was far behind him, but it might come back to haunt him if the rich people for whom he showed the valuable horses ever knew his record of minor crimes. He decided that to survive among them he needed to become like them, adopting their patrician manners and refined speech and clothing himself in elegant clothes. James adapted beautifully, and although he avoided answering questions about his background, it was simply assumed that he was "East Coast"—Greenwich perhaps, St. Paul's probably, Yale or Harvard likely.

In January of 1984, Judge Frederick Barrington hired James to show his champion horses for the year the grande finale of which would be the Los Angeles Olympics. During that year, when he wasn't traveling to events on the Grand Prix show-jumping circuit, James lived in the gardener's cottage at Barrington Farm, the judge's bluegrass estate outside of Louisville.

James knew that the judge was a widower, but he didn't know that Frederick Barrington had a daughter until June when seventeen-year-old Pamela returned for the summer from the exclusive girls' school in Geneva where she had spent the year. Pamela was very beautiful, very spoiled, and very petulant when she didn't get precisely what she wanted when she wanted it. Pamela's petulance was usually short-lived because her demands were always promptly met and her whims were always swiftly gratified.

Seventeen-year-old Pamela wanted twenty-five-year-old James. But James didn't want her. She was much too young, much too spoiled, and it was much too dangerous. James would do nothing to jeopardize the first peace and happiness he had known in his entire life. Politely, gently, diplomatically, he resisted her advances.

But Pamela wouldn't take no for an answer. She had no experience with No and never planned to

231

have any. And when it became clear that James would not accede to her wishes, her response was rage and revenge . . .

On that night in July, he was painting in the cottage when Pamela knocked on the door. Her long-nailed, exquisitely manicured fingers curled around a half-empty bottle of bourbon from which she had quite obviously been drinking.

She announced coyly that she had just made love with one of the many "boys"—the heirs her age who lounged by the pool at the mansion all day every day—but now she wanted a man. She wanted James.

He resisted her advances gently. But Pamela persisted, fueled by the confidence that she would get what she wanted, as she always had, annoyed that he would even dare to say No. When she tried to force the bottle of bourbon to his lips, James roughly pushed it away. And when she wove her fingers tightly, possessively around his neck and tiptoed to kiss his lips, he pulled away. As he freed himself, one of her long, sharp fingernails dug into his neck and left a deep scratch that bled.

Finally, her eyes blazing with anger, Pamela left the cottage. James was very sorry that he had caused anger but very relieved that she had gone away.

Ten minutes later he heard the shattering of glass followed by frantic screams. James rushed outside and followed the sound of the screams to the front porch of the mansion.

Pamela was on the porch, her clothes torn and dirty, gasping for breath as tears spilled from her

232

frightened eyes. As James moved to help her, the judge appeared. Pamela fell into her father's arms and cried hysterically, "James raped me, Daddy! He *raped* me!"

James listened to Pamela's words with astonishment and then horror. Surely the judge, whom James respected very much, and who even sometimes called him "son," would realize . . .

But James saw the rage in the judge's eyes and knew that to survive he had to run.

As he fled, the still night air that already had been broken once by Pamela's cries was pierced again by shrillness, by the screams of police sirens and the frenzied barking of dogs—harsh, strident, ominous signals that they were frantically searching for him and that the peace in his life was shattered forever.

James fled with nothing except the clothes he was wearing. The rest of his clothes, the little money he had earned, the riders' trophies he had won, the documents—birth certificate, driver's license, passport—that were proof of who he was, and his paintings were all left behind in the cottage. James was forced to abandon his possessions. And he was forced to abandon something much more precious—his freedom and his dreams.

He knew he would never again soar over jumps, a champion rider on a champion horse, perhaps he would never even be able to ride. And never again would he be James Patrick Jones.

He would have to change his name, he knew, and spend the rest of his life in shadows. There was no doubt in his mind that if he was caught, his next home—the most permanent home of his life — would be prison. It would be the word of a man with a record of minor crimes in the jungle of Chicago against the word of the precious daughter of the revered judge.

James Patrick Jones became Patrick James. For five years he lived from job to job, always a different employer, crisscrossing the country, forming no relationships, and leaving no trail.

Then, last March, he answered the ad for a riding instructor in *The New York Times*. He rode again, and that brought such peace even among the heiresses who reminded him of Pamela Barrington. He rode, and he started to paint again, and just before sunset on an enchanted night in June, the greatest surprise of all, the greatest peace, he met Casey English and fell in love.

And tonight, over candlelight, he had planned to tell Casey everything.

What if he had told Casey his truth before she told him the truth about herself?

His Casey, the lovely, unpretentious, vulnerable woman he loved would believe him. She would protect his secret identity even though in so doing, in knowing the whereabouts of a wanted felon and concealing that information, she would jeopardize her entire legal career. *His* Casey would do that, and it would cause her great harm.

And what about the other Casey, the heiress who had been playing with him, the brilliant trial attorney whom he didn't know but whose most spectacular legal triumph to date was the conviction of the Nob Hill Rapist? Would *that* Casey believe the innocence of a man with a record of crimes of survival as a boy who had fled the scene of the "crime" and remained in hiding ever since? Or would that Casey call the police?

Patrick didn't know, and it didn't matter. Because, no matter which Casey were real, the love of Patrick James and Casey English was over.

It had to be.


Casey wandered through the maze of stalls looking for a door that might belong to the apartment where Patrick had told her he lived. The stable was quiet except for the scurrying of mice and the gentle whinnies of horses. Even the grooms had not yet arrived to begin their daily chores. As she walked through the stalls near the riding ring, she heard a new noise, the soft thud of hooves on sod. She followed the noise to the ring.

Patrick was there. Casey stood in the shadows and watched as he sailed over the mammoth jumps. As a teenager Casey had watched the best riders in the world compete at Grand Prix events held at the Carlton Club. Casey knew very little about show jumping, but she had been trained since childhood to recognize perfection, and it seemed to her that Patrick must surely belong to the most elite group of world-class equestrians.

She remained in the shadows until Patrick and the champion horse had finished flying over all the treacherous jumps and he had reined in the powerful animal and was whispering quiet words of praise as he patted the stallion's strong neck. Then she left the shadows and began the brave walk toward him.

"Casey." Patrick spoke with quiet calm even

though the sight of her made his heart race.

Last night, when they spoke, the light of the lanterns had been behind her, illuminating the glittering sequins and the red-gold crown but not her lovely face. Last night, Casey's eyes had been hidden in shadows, and he had spoken to her as if she was someone he didn't know, a rich, beautiful woman who had used him for her pleasure, a woman who had played with him and for whom he could so easily feel contempt.

But now there were no shadows, and she was his lovely Casey, her long red-gold hair still damp from a shower, her blue eyes uncertain, vulnerable, needing his love.

As Patrick dismounted, he reminded himself sternly, *Your love can only harm her. And if she is not the lovely Casey to whom you gave your heart, she can only harm you.*

"Patrick, I'm so sorry I didn't tell you. I was going to tell you tonight. I didn't think it would matter."

"But it does."

"Why?"

"Many reasons." It had to be over, it had to be, but Patrick saw the exquisite pain in her lovely eyes, the bewildered sadness, and he wanted so much to hold her and make it gentle for her.

Casey saw the tenderness in his eyes, the familiar gentleness that hadn't been there last night, and her heart trembled with hope.

"Patrick, hold me, please."

"Oh, Casey, no." His voice was gentle, a soft but necessary protest. *If I hold you, lovely Casey, I won't be able to let you go. And I have to let*

236

*you go.*

The softness in Patrick's voice gave Casey even more hope. Bravely, so bravely, she wove her trembling fingers around his neck and into his black hair and tiptoed so that her lips could touch his.

"Please, Patrick, make love to me."

"No."

"No?"

Patrick heard the surprise in her voice, as if he was not allowed to say no, and reminded himself that there might be a Casey he didn't know, a spoiled heiress who always got what she wanted, a Casey English who might be very like Pamela Barrington. *Make love to me, James,* Pamela had demanded as she wove her long fingers around his neck and tiptoed to touch his lips.

Pamela's long, painted fingers had woven tightly and possessively around his neck, leaving blood when he pulled free, and Casey's hands were delicate and tentative, but still she clung to him, even though he had told her no, and he filled his mind with images of Pamela and the memory of what she had done to him and all that she had taken away . . .

"I don't want you, Casey."

Casey pulled away then, with a soft gasp. Her delicate fingers didn't draw blood as they left his neck, and it was she who was wounded, so terribly wounded, by his words and the sudden harshness in his voice.

"Last Sunday you couldn't get enough of me, Patrick," she reminded him quietly, a soft, bewildered plea.

"I've had enough now."

237

"Patrick," Casey whispered, a whisper of pain, a whisper that made his heart ache. "We love each other."

"Love?" Patrick heard the cruelty in his voice, necessary cruelty. If he could make Casey hate him, perhaps it would be easier for her to forget his love.

"Yes, *love*. You said you loved me."

"I was drunk on cheap champagne."

"A little high, maybe, the first time. But you've told me over and over."

"It was what you wanted to hear. We had good sex, Casey, that was all."

His cruel words caused such pain! Patrick almost relented, almost whispered, *Of course I love you!* But as he fought the powerful urge, he saw a transformation in her blue eyes . . . and he knew that he had been right to be very wary of the Casey he didn't know. As he watched, the pain and hurt vanished and were replaced by icy determination and terrifying rage.

"Who are you, Patrick James?" Casey demanded as her cold blue eyes left his briefly to gaze meaningfully at the jumps.

"You know who I am, Casey."

"No, I don't. You played games, too, Patrick. There was something you were going to tell me about yourself tonight."

"Nothing important. You know all about me."

"I don't think so." Her angry eyes sent a final message, a warning. *But I will find out.*

After Casey left, as he dismantled the jumps,

238

Patrick told himself over and over that there was no way that she could discover his true identity. He had covered his tracks so well and had been so very careful until the reckless indulgence of this morning. Casey had seen him jump and she had wondered if his talent was something special, something extraordinary.

But it was such a tiny clue, wasn't it?

Yes. Except that if anyone in the world was bright enough and determined enough to pursue his destruction, it was a spurned Casey English.

The instinct for survival that had driven him from the slums of Chicago in scarch of heaven and had later told him to flee that paradise for his life of shadows sent urgent warnings now. *You have to run now, today!*

Patrick sighed softly. He would run, he had to, but not yet, not quite yet. He was so tired of running.

## Chapter Thirteen

The crisis that had taken Jeffrey away from the party for Casey, the bombing of the commercial airliner over the Mediterranean, signaled the beginning of a week of terror. The unprecedented violence centered in the Middle East, but its energy and venom ricocheted, erupting in brutal acts of terrorism around the globe.

For forty-eight hours the entire planet was on alert.

Then suddenly there was calm. Was it the ominous calm before the next lethal storm? Or the stillness of death, a grim sign that there were no hearts left to fight? Or was it something else, something good?

The phoenix that arose from the ashes *was* good, a promise of peace, a hopeful beginning. Astonishingly, the ancestral enemies agreed to meet at a negotiating table with the leaders of the most powerful nations as arbiters. The ancient foes would talk and maybe, just maybe . . .

The historic peace conference was scheduled to begin in London on Monday.

wonderful vacation. *Are you really really positive that Daddy will want to go for a carriage ride, Mommy?*

And now Merry would be so terribly hurt, a hurt much greater than all the silent disappointments of the past when Jeffrey was home but still so far away, because this time Merry had begun to believe.

And now . . .

Now Julia was consumed with powerful and dangerous emotions that were beyond reason.

"Oh, Jeffrey, you are never going to forgive me, are you?"

"Forgive you for what?" Jeffrey asked, stunned by the question and the unfamiliar anger in her lavender eyes.

"For having Merry. Even now, after ten years, you wish Merry had never been born."

"That's not true."

"It *is* true! You wanted me to have an abortion, didn't you?"

"My God, Julia *no!* How can you even think that?"

"Because it's true. I saw it in your eyes when I told you I was pregnant."

"No you didn't," Jeffrey repeated firmly, urgently, truthfully. He knew what Julia had seen in his eyes—tormented anguish as his mind formed vivid images of her with another man, a wish that there had been no other lover, sadness that that secret love had given her a baby he never could give. In those swirling moments as he had tried to adjust to her devastating revelation, he had surely wished that her pregnancy was a lie, an innocent

243

ploy to get him to marry her, but he had never wanted her not to have her baby. "I never wanted you to have an abortion. Julie, please, you must believe that."

Julia barely heard Jeffrey's gentle plea because her own angry words had taken her, too, to the memory of that evening, and now that memory turned Julia's anger inward, where it belonged, to herself.

Merry would be hurt because Jeffrey couldn't keep the lovely promises Julia had made to her, but the fault was hers, not Jeffrey's. On that evening in May, when the part of her mind that was tethered to the grim lessons of her loveless life warned her to run because his stormy eyes told her so eloquently that he didn't want his baby, Julia had listened instead to her heart. Her bright mind had told her to flee, to protect herself and her unborn child, but her heart had offered promises, *Someday Jeffrey will love his baby,* and she had listened to the confident wishes of her heart because she loved him so much.

Julia had believed the whispers of her heart, but it was such a selfish belief, fueled by her desire to spend her life with the man she loved . . . but at what cost to her other precious love?

"Jeffrey." Julia spoke quietly now, her anger at him dissipated and even the anger toward herself lost in her immense sadness for Merry. "Please don't hurt Merry. It's not her fault that I became pregnant."

Jeffrey started to reply—"I would never hurt Merry!"—but Julia's other words almost stopped his heart.

"Whose fault is it, Julia?" Jeffrey paused then added very quietly, "Not mine."

"No, Jeffrey, not yours. It's my fault," Julia admitted softly, remembering the sixteen-year-old girl who had pretended to be experienced because the thought of him telling her to leave filled her with an emptiness greater than all the losses of her young life. "I'm to blame. I'm responsible."

"What else, Julie?" he asked gently of the beautiful eyes that had blazed with anger and now softened with bewildered sadness. Julia had just told him the beginning of the truth. At last she had admitted aloud that there had been another lover. Jeffrey needed to hear the rest. Then it would be over and the ancient wound could heal. "Tell me darling. The truth."

The world had just witnessed swift volleys of violence, an eruption of anger from ancient, painful wounds, and from the ashes of that bitter fury had arisen great hope.

Jeffrey's heart filled with hope now even though he still reeled from the words Julia had hurled at him and still ached as he thought of the silent anguish that had given her words such angry life. Had Julia really believed, all this time, that he had wanted her to have an abortion?

As he waited for Julia to speak, Jeffrey's heart raced with hope and he made a decision of love. He wouldn't go to London. He would spend the week with Julia and Merry, gently and tenderly healing the ancient wounds.

*Tell me the rest of the truth, Julie,* Jeffrey urged silently as he smiled at her troubled lavender eyes. *Tell me the truth so that our wonderful love can*

245

*be at peace.*

When Julia finally spoke it was a whisper of sadness, an anguished truth that destroyed all hope for peace.

"I should never have married you." *I should have raised our lovely daughter by myself. I could have told her how wonderful her daddy was and she would have been spared all the hurt and disappointment.*

As Jeffrey stared at Julia in stunned disbelief, a thought taunted, *You always wanted her to tell you the truth and part of you always feared that when she did your heart would be shattered into a thousand pieces.*

His heart was in a thousand pieces now, each tiny piece bleeding and screaming with pain. A deep instinct for survival guided Jeffrey to the top drawer of the bureau in the foyer to remove the keys to his Jaguar. He had to get away *now*. His passport was in his briefcase and he had clothes and luggage in his apartment in town. Jeffrey thought there could be no more pain, but he remembered the last time he had gotten the keys to his car, ten days ago when he had answered the frantic call of the little girl who was not his.

"Jeffrey . . ."

He heard the soft whisper, but he didn't turn around before he left. He couldn't.


"Where's Daddy?" Merry asked eagerly the next morning. She had gone to bed with the promise that Jeffrey would be home later that night and that she would see him in the morning before he

246

left for a final day of work before his vacation.

"Oh, darling, Daddy had to go to London because of the peace conference. It made him so sad that he had to go, but there was nothing he could do."

"I understand, Mommy."

*I know you do, my darling,* Julia thought as she gazed at her terribly-disappointed-but-trying-to-be-brave little girl. Her very bright daughter *did* understand, rationally, despite her great sadness. How Julia wished that she had been so rational last night!

"Why don't I ask Patrick if we can videotape the gymkhana?" Julia suggested hopefully even though the suggestion made her own heart weep. Merry had spent her life seeing her father on videotape and now . . . "Then when Daddy gets home we'll show him the tape and tell him all about our weekend in New York."

*When Daddy gets home.* But what if Jeffrey wasn't coming back? He had been so angry when he left.

Of course Jeffrey had been angry! And of course he had left! What did she expect? In her own anger, anger at herself more than him, she had said such terrible things.

*I must go to him and explain the emotions behind the terrible words. I will go,* she vowed. *As soon as I can find a way I will go to London and talk to my love.*


Diana looked at her image in the mirror with unconcealed criticism. She was in the ladies' room of the first class lounge at JFK. Only her dark curls appeared unsubdued by the events of the past few months. Her hair was longer, rich and lustrous, a soft, luxuriant frame for the face that had become so thin since June. Her drawn face made her sapphire eyes even larger, and they looked haunted, mysterious, perhaps even intriguing. But Diana knew the truth behind the haunted, luminous, blue eyes; and there was no mystery, no intrigue, simply pain.

This morning, blue-black circles rimmed the sapphire, a fresh layer, one layer deeper, because she had been called in at three A.M. to operate on a man with a gunshot wound to the chest. Diana hadn't been on call, not officially, not on the eve of her three-week vacation in Europe, but she had been unofficially on call almost constantly since the night she had received the divorce papers from Chase.

*You haven't been taking very good care of yourself,* she mused critically as she stared at her fatigued image in the mirror. The past few months had been filled—compulsively full—with work. There had been little food, little sleep, little privacy, and no time to think. *Hiding from something, Diana?*

The compassionate physician in Diana felt an instinctive urge to reassure the woman she saw in the mirror, *You should be nice to yourself, pamper yourself a little.*

Chase had booked a vacation to pamper, first-class, five-star, the best suites, a vacation that could be afforded by only the wealthiest in the world.

Diana's accommodations would be luxurious, befitting a queen, but the pampering would be an illusion. During the long nights in beds with silk sheets and feather pillows, Diana would be wakeful. Her brilliant mind, undistracted by the frantic pace — *escape* — of her work, would focus all its energy, compulsion, and curiosity on a thorough examination of *her*. Diana, the skillful physician, would take a detailed and probing history of her own life and do an intimate physical on the part she knew best . . . the heart.

Not *the* heart, her own heart.

Diana sighed as she swept a defiant curl away from her face with a gold barrette. *We'll be talking a lot,* she silently promised the face in the mirror. *Heart-to-heart talks.*

Diana had to discover how her cautious footing had led her not once but twice to a love that she believed would last forever but which had faltered and died.


There was still an hour before boarding would begin for her flight to London. She poured herself a cup of tea and found a comfortable chair in a corner of the first class lounge. From her vantage point she could watch the activity of planes on the tarmac and the activity of people in the lounge.

Diana sipped tea and succumbed to the fogginess of her sleepless night. When she was working, she could clear the fog, willing it away, but now she let the fogginess envelop her in a warm, comforting blanket.

*Comforting,* she admitted begrudgingly, *because*

*you're letting your fatigue be an excuse not to think, not to begin the journey into your past.*

*I will begin tomorrow,* Diana vowed. *After a good night's sleep at the Dorchester I will begin the careful meticulous task of reviewing the signs and symptoms of my life that should have been clues to the diagnosis of what I have become: a stunning success professionally and a stunning failure in my private life.*

For now, the fogginess was just fine.

Except that Jeffrey Lawrence just walked in.

He was undoubtedly going to London for the peace conference, obviously flying first class, probably on her flight.

A strong and confident woman would walk over to him, stare calmly into his intense blue eyes, and apologetically confess to temporary hysteria in his office.

That was what a strong and confident woman would do, someone like who Diana would be in three weeks.

For now, she simply wanted to avoid him. She reached for a magazine that lay facedown on the coffee table beside her. She frowned slightly when she turned it over and saw the artist's flattering portrait of a beautiful and confident woman with huge sapphire eyes, a Mona Lisa smile, and unruly dark-brown hair curling sensuously from beneath the turquoise surgeon's mask . . . a portrait, ostensibly, of her.

The magazine was the September fourth issue of *Time* and she was the cover story. Diana hadn't yet read the words that accompanied the flattering image on the cover and didn't read them now. She folded the cover back, not that anyone would recognize her from the portrait, and flipped quickly through the pages about her. Pages and pages. Diana was amazed by the length of the article, a chronicle of her career, her immense success, her scientific stardom by age thirty-six. Most of the words, of course, were devoted to the Heart — which was why she had agreed to the article — complete with smiling photographs of many grateful recipients.

Diana flipped swiftly past the cover story and swiftly, too, past the news of the world. It was last week's news, before the unprecedented carnage began, but the world was filled with astonishing violence and tragedy even on a "quiet" week. She turned more pages in a determined journey toward the lighter stories to be found in Theater, Arts, Books, and People.

But en route to the lighter stories, Diana found her name in print once again, this time in Milestones. If only numbers of words were the measure of success, Diana mused, then the pages and pages of words in the cover story celebrating her immense success would surely offset the few pithy words that articulately documented her immense failure . . .

"Marriage Dissolved. Dr. Diana Shepherd, renowned heart surgeon and inventor of the Shepherd Heart (see Cover Story) and Chase Andrews, billionaire real-estate developer. After five years and no children."

*No children.* Diana stared at the words for several moments, then sighed softly and turned the page to People.

The People section would be safe, glamorous shots of celebrities, paragraphs about films wrapped, parties attended, intriguing couples, people she had heard of but didn't know.

But the People section wasn't safe — because Sam was there.

*Sam Hunter returns home.* Last week, six-time Grammy award-winning songwriter and singer Sam Hunter moved from London, where he has lived for the past fifteen years, to California, where he has purchased a beachfront home in Malibu's exclusive Colony. The Dallas-born music superstar has just signed a three-album contract with Capitol Records, and although there are no firm plans for a U.S. tour, a spokesperson for Hunter did not exclude the possibility. When asked why the singer-songwriter decided to end his fifteen-year self-imposed exile, the spokesperson commented, "It was time." The extraordinary popularity of Hunter's poetic songs of love is reflected by his remarkable "crossover" success — a record ten of his titles have held number-one positions atop the hit parades of Pop, Rock, Country, and R&B. The most recent single, "Dance With Me," has been in top slots for the past ten weeks and his latest album, *Promises of Love,* has already gone platinum.

Diana read the short paragraph five times even though she knew its contents by heart after one reading. There was nothing more to be learned from the words on the page, but there were fifteen years of life between the lines.

Diana slowly closed the magazine and placed it on the coffee table. Her voyage into the past would begin today, this moment, because the voyage was, after all, about Sam Hunter.

Sam Hunter, who had entered her life on a sunny autumn day in Dallas in 1970.


Diana sat at one of the many tables in the foyer of Theodore Roosevelt High School. It was noon, and the foyer was crowded with students visiting with friends and wandering among the colorful tables piled high with items for sale — senior pins and school sweaters, dance tickets and book covers, cookies and fudge.

Diana sat at a table, selling nothing, waiting patiently for volunteers to sign up for the talent show she was planning. Talent shows weren't new to Roosevelt High School — the Revue was held every spring and was always successful — but Diana's show was to be held on the Wednesday evening before Thanksgiving. The proceeds would benefit Dallas's recently completed Children's Home, a much-needed safe haven for neglected and abused children. The autumn talent show was Diana's idea. She had already won the support of the faculty and student council. Now she simply had to hope that some of the many talented students at Roosevelt would donate their time to the project.

Diana had to hope, because it wasn't in her nature to arm twist or cajole. She sat quietly at her table, hoping not selling, wishing she had something to contribute beyond her ability to organize.

In her next life she was going to be able to sing! She loved the wonderful songs of the sixties. Music was a constant chorus to her happy life, a joyful, ever-present accompaniment even during the hours she spent studying to earn the A's that inevitably appeared on her report cards. Diana knew all the words to the wonderful songs, and sang them softly to herself, but she wasn't a singer. Her gifts lay elsewhere—in her bright mind, her boundless generosity, and her instinctive wish to share the joy and cheer of her life with others who needed joy.

Diana couldn't perform at her talent show, but she could make it a great success if enough talented students volunteered. So far, during this first noon hour spent at the table in the foyer, the response had already been better than she had dared to hope.

"Hi."

"Hi," Diana answered with surprise. Why was Sam Hunter, Roosevelt's star quarterback, stopping at her table? The sign she had painted clearly read "Talent Show Sign-Up".

"I would like to volunteer for the talent show."

"Oh!" Diana knew Sam Hunter's talent—throwing touchdowns. For the past two years he had led Roosevelt's Roughriders to the state championship. He was a celebrity, not just at Roosevelt but in all of Dallas. His participation in the show would guarantee community interest. If Sam Hunter wanted to throw passes on stage, Diana decided, that would be fine. "OK. Great."

Sam looked at her for an expectant moment then finally said, "I sing."

Before Diana could reply, Sam's girlfriend appeared. Cheryl was a pretty, sexy cheerleader.

"Well, here you all are, darlin'."

"I'll be with you in a moment, Cheryl."

"I thought we were going for a drive." Cheryl's provocative pout sent a clear message that it was the parking not the driving that appealed.

"We are. As soon as I'm done here."

"Let's go now," Cheryl urged.

She added seductive emphasis to her suggestion with long, delicate fingers that played briefly with the buttons on Sam's shirt, then drifted meaningfully to his belt buckle. As Diana watched Cheryl's bold intimacy, her cheeks flushed pink with embarrassment and she wished that she could disappear.

Cheryl was not embarrassed, of course, and Diana couldn't interpret the look in Sam's dark-brown eyes. But he stopped the intimacy, gently but firmly. The strong fingers that curled over Cheryl's wrist were lean, as Sam was, not massive like the other players on the football team.

"I'll meet you outside in five minutes, Cheryl."

"I'll be waiting."

"So, . . ." Sam began after Cheryl left. "What do you need to know? My name is Sam Hunter."

Did he think she didn't know who he was? Admittedly Sam and Diana had never met before. It was more than just the size of Roosevelt, five hundred students per class, it was the fact that Diana Shepherd and Sam Hunter lived in completely different worlds.

The handsome star quarterback belonged to, perhaps led, the "in" crowd, the small, elite clique whose members, like Sam and Cheryl, were attractive, confident, and sexually sophisticated. Diana's group was academically sophisticated but socially naive. She and her friends won championships in debate and mathematics, not football and cheerleading, were devotees of *The Hobbitt,* the Beatles, and Khalil Gibran, and scored among the nation's best on SAT's and National Merit exams. On weekends Diana and her friends assembled as a group, not in couples; and during the slumber parties the girls frequently held, they bemoaned their sexual naiveté but assured themselves with easy laughter that sex would happen, love would happen, everything would happen.

Diana and Sam had never met, but *of course* she knew who he was.

"Yes, I know. I'm Diana Shepherd."

"I know. I voted for you."

"You did?"

"Of course. You were the best candidate."

"Thank you."

Diana's opponent in last spring's election for student body president belonged to Sam's crowd, but apparently Sam had listened to the campaign speeches and decided, along with an overwhelming majority of the school, that Diana should be the first girl student body president in Roosevelt High's sixty-year history.

"You're welcome. So, what else do you need?"

"I need to have you audition." Of course even if Sam Hunter couldn't sing a note, even if his music "talent" matched hers, Diana would want him to participate, wouldn't she? "To know what you'll be singing, where it will fit in best."

"OK. When are the auditions?"

"After school next week. Oh, that conflicts with football, doesn't it?"

"Yes," Sam replied quietly. "Is there another time that would be possible for you?"

The talent show was Diana's brainchild, but the other student-body officers had agreed to attend all the auditions so that the final selections could be made by committee. Now Sam Hunter, star quarterback, school hero, probably the biggest draw for community attendance at the show, was asking if Diana could give him a special audition.

Sam Hunter *was* special, of course. Surely he knew that, even though his dark-brown eyes seemed more apologetic than arrogant.

"Sure. Any time. When would be good for you?"

"This week's game is Friday night, so Saturday morning or afternoon?"

Saturday evening was out, Diana assumed, because Sam and Cheryl would be celebrating the Friday-night victory at the dance in the gym.

"I work at the hospital Saturday afternoons, so I guess Saturday morning."

For the next three days Diana wondered anxiously what she would say to Sam Hunter during the short drive from her house, where he said he would pick her up at ten A.M., to Lincoln Park, where he suggested that the special audition take place. She and Sam had nothing in common, of course, and he probably viewed the happily innocent world of Diana and her friends, if he even knew about it, as hopelessly unsophisticated and perhaps even silly.

Diana searched for possible topics of conversation and found two: Cheryl and football. Football, she decided. She studied back issues of *Strenuous Life,* Roosevelt's weekly newspaper, and learned about Sam's record-setting seasons. Then she rehearsed what she would say about his career, to sound knowledgeable and interested, and assuaged as much as possible her worries about awkward silences.

But there was another worry that was not so easily assuaged. How would she act impressed by Sam's singing even if she wasn't?

Diana rehearsed the words she would use to fill the uneasy silences, but on Saturday morning, before there had even been a silence, Sam asked her a question.

"The talent show is for the Children's Home?"

"Yes."

"I thought it was already built."

"It is. It opened about six months ago. The funding is pretty good to cover the basics, but we can use the money made from the talent show for special events and outings."

"We?"

"I'm a volunteer."

"Is that what you're doing this afternoon?"

"No. Today I work at Children's Hospital. I spend Tuesdays after school at the Home." Diana paused, and when Sam didn't speak, she made a suggestion that bridged his interest in football and her interest in the children. "Maybe, sometime, an outing for the children could be to a Roughrider football game."

Sam didn't take his eyes from the road. He was, Diana had observed with surprise and relief, a very good and very cautious driver. His eyes remained on the road, but they became solemn at her suggestion.

"I can't imagine that children who have been physically abused would enjoy watching something as violent as football."

Diana searched for a polite reply—something that wouldn't reveal her true lack of interest in the sport that was Sam's future but which she too found to be violent—but before she found the right words they had reached Lincoln Park.

Diana hadn't needed to rehearse the words she would say to Sam about football. And she hadn't needed to worry about how she would act impressed even if Sam couldn't sing.

She did need words—and never found the perfect ones—to tell Sam how she felt about his singing. He sang her favorite love songs more beautifully, more emotionally, than she had ever heard them sung before. Sam's strong, talented fingers worked delicate magic on the guitar.

And his sensual dark eyes, and soft rich voice, and gentle smile worked magic on her heart.

Without even asking what she wanted to hear, Sam simply sang the love songs Diana loved the best—"Yesterday," "Kathy's Song," "In My Life,"

"April Come She Will," "If I Fell," "The Sound of Silence," "Bridge Over Troubled Water," "Something," "It's Only Love."

"Why haven't you been in the school's talent show before, Sam? You're so . . . you play so well."

"This seemed like a worthy cause. Do you think you'll be able to use me?"

"I think," Diana bravely told the dark-brown eyes that flickered with uncertainty even though he was so special, "that I'd like to make it a one-man show."

## Chapter Fourteen

Roosevelt High's Thanksgiving Revue wasn't a one-man show, but Sam Hunter definitely stole it, just as four days before he had stolen the state championship by passing a record-breaking last-second "long bomb" to the end zone.

The talent show was a stunning success, standing room only, a tribute to the worthiness of the cause and because the word was out that Sam Hunter was going to try his million-dollar hand at playing the guitar. It was quite obvious that no one, not even Cheryl, had known about Sam's talent. Except his parents, of course, but Diana wasn't able to identify them in the crowd that surrounded Sam in the punch-and-cookies reception that followed.

Then the show was over, and Sam still smiled his gentle, uncertain smile at her whenever they passed in the hallway, but they had no reason to stop, no reason to talk anymore about the order of the songs he would sing, or if he minded performing twice, opening the show and closing it, no reason to talk at all.

No reason not to return to their different worlds.

261

* * *

"Hello, Diana."

It was mid-December, three weeks after the talent show. She was in the student government office, *her* office, when he appeared in the doorway.

"Sam. Hello."

"How are you?"

"I'm fine."

"I wondered if you need other volunteers at the Children's Home. Now that football season is over I'm free on Tuesday afternoons."

"Oh! Wonderful. It doesn't have to be Tuesday. They can use help any day."

"Isn't Tuesday the day you go?"

"Yes."

"I'd like to go when you go. I thought you could show me the ropes."

"I'd be glad to. There aren't really any ropes. We just play with the kids and try to make them feel safe and loved."

That was candy-coating, of course, because there were some children who were painfully withdrawn and terribly mistrustful. But even those children made progress with time and the professional help of the counselors, psychologists, and doctors who worked at the Home, and their timid, grateful smiles made it all worthwhile.

"Will Cheryl be volunteering, too?"

"Cheryl? Oh. No."

At first Sam was very uncomfortable with the children. But they weren't uncomfortable with him. Even though he didn't think these children would be interested in football, Dallas was a football town and he was a folk hero. Football was Sam's entrée, but it was Sam himself, his gentle uncertain smile, the wonderful songs he sang, that melted the ice, swiftly and permanently.

In February, Diana found the courage to ask him something she had been thinking about for several weeks. Would he be willing to sing for the children who were inpatients at Children's Hospital? Diana rehearsed all the ways to make it easy for him to say no—he was so busy, he already so generously gave his time every Tuesday, she might not be able to arrange it anyway—but Sam instantly said Yes, of course, he would be happy to.

The evening of singing was scheduled for the second Thursday in March at seven P.M. in the hospital auditorium. The children from the Home would be there, too, because Sam was their friend.

Sam told Diana he would pick her up at six-fifteen. That would give him more than enough time to check the amplifiers in the auditorium and visit with the familiar small faces in the audience before seven.

As six-fifteen became six-twenty, Diana began to fight little worries. Five minutes late. *Only* five minutes!

Then ten. Then fifteen.

Diana found a listing for a Sam Hunter in the phone book with an address that was in the area for Roosevelt High.

*He's trying to call me,* she thought when she dialed the number and reached a busy signal. Diana quickly hung up and expected her phone to ring any second.

But Sam didn't call. At six-forty Diana dialed

the number again, again busy, and then the hospital to say they would be late. She could go on to the hospital, of course, but she was just a spectator, someone in the audience who loved Sam's singing as much as the children did. Sam was the show, her one-man show starring Sam Hunter at last, but where was he?

Was he with Cheryl? Was she distracting him, bewitching him with charms that made him forget time and commitments to small children who were sick and sad and needed joy in their lives?

No, Diana thought. Sam wouldn't do that!

But how well did she really know him?

They talked, of course, on Tuesdays, as they drove together to and from the Home. But then it was Sam who asked the questions and Diana who gave the answers. She told him, because he asked, that she was going to be a pediatrician. Even though she knew it could be terribly sad to see the small, innocent faces bewildered by the harms that had befallen them—inexplicable sickness and even more inexplicable abuse—her own sadness was minor to the good she believed she could do. She wanted to ease their pain, to make them smile, to find the laughter that rang like crystal when it was filled with joy.

Diana hadn't asked Sam about his dreams—she hadn't yet summoned the courage—but there were other things, important things that she knew from what she had observed. She knew that he was very gentle with the children. Sometimes his smiles were as shy and as uncertain as theirs, but these children who had so little reason to trust felt very safe with him. He wouldn't disappoint them.

But then it was seven, then seven-fifteen, then

seven-thirty. The line was still busy at the Sam Hunter number that might not even be his and Diana's own phone rang as the activities coordinator called to ask questions Diana couldn't answer.

Sam's show was supposed to last until eight-thirty. The children stayed until then, and sang anyway, and at eight forty-five the coordinator called a final time to see if Sam was going to reschedule. Diana said she had no idea, and the evening ended without explanations or promises.

But the evening wasn't over for Diana. Her anger had long since been replaced by concern. Something had happened to Sam. Even though he was a cautious driver perhaps there had been an accident . . .

*Please let him be all right.*

He finally called at ten P.M.

"Diana, I'm sorry."

"Where are you?"

"Home."

"What happened, Sam? Were you in an accident?"

"No. I just couldn't make it. I'm terribly sorry."

Once Diana knew Sam was safe, her anger returned and raged unopposed.

"How could you have done that to them?"

"I'm sorry."

"Have you any idea how disappointed they are? Did you think about the children who know you and are so proud of you?"

"Can we reschedule?"

"How do I know you won't do it again? What guarantee can you give me, and them, that some-

265

thing or *someone* more important won't come up next time? I don't think you have any idea of how damaging this was. These children trusted you, and trust is so fragile for them, and you've just shattered it!"

"I'm sorry, Diana."

"So am I, Sam."

Then there was nothing more to say, no reason to say a polite good night or good-bye, so sometime in the silence that followed, Diana hung up, not with a slam but with a sad, quiet disconnect.

Only after did she realize that Sam had offered no defense, no reason, no excuse. It was inexcusable, whatever the reason, of course. He must have known that.

Sam wasn't at school the next day. Diana learned from the records kept in the principal's office that the number she had been dialing was his. Had he and Cheryl had a lovers' quarrel and then a reconciliation over the phone that took the evening—*stole* the evening—from the children?

Diana spent the weekend fuming about what he had done and decided that she was going to find him on Monday and demand an explanation.

Sam found her first. He was in the hallway outside her home room when the bell sounded. Diana drew an astonished breath when she saw him, her anger suddenly stunned by worry. What was wrong? Sam looked quite ill, his skin very pale and his dark eyes clouded and distant.

"What's wrong, Sam?"

"Nothing. I just haven't slept well because of what happened. Diana, I really am terribly sorry. I

266

would very much like to reschedule. I want you to know that you can trust me."

"Then help me understand why it happened."

"It just did."

"And it won't happen next time?"

"No."

Diana watched his cloudy eyes as he uttered the assurance and wasn't convinced. And, she decided, neither was he. Whatever mysterious thing had happened, he couldn't guarantee that it wouldn't happen again, even though he didn't want it to.

Sam didn't tell Diana what had happened. But it was no mystery. The entire school knew. Sam and Cheryl had broken up.

The concert was rescheduled for mid-April. Sam apologized to the children at the Home and solemnly promised he would be there next time.

During the three weeks before the concert, he and Diana spent Tuesdays at the Home, as always, and, as always, rode together in Sam's car. But for those three weeks they rode in awkward silence. Each was cheerful in the hours they spent with the children, but they had nothing to say to each other. Everything was on hold, waiting to see if Sam would disappoint the children again.

But Sam didn't disappoint. When he arrived to get her, five minutes early, on the night of the rescheduled concert, he smiled the first unencumbered smile of the past three weeks—as if he was relieved, too.

Sam was supposed to stop singing at eight-thirty, but the show continued for another magical hour. And then there was more magic because he

267

didn't take her home right away. Instead he drove to Lincoln Park and they sat on the grass under the spring moon and he sang to her. That April night he sang all her favorite songs of love and one she had never heard before, one that was more beautiful than all the others, beautiful and sad, a bittersweet song of love and longing.

"What's it called?"

" 'Loving You.' "

"Who wrote it?"

"I did."

"Oh," Diana breathed. A beautiful and sad love song for Cheryl, the love Sam wanted but could not have. What if Cheryl had called tonight and wanted to reconcile? Diana shuddered. There might have been sadness again, not magic.

"I was going to sing it for you last time."

"Last time?"

"Three weeks ago."

"You wrote it before then?"

"I've been working on it since January."

"It's very beautiful."


"Loving You" was only one of the beautiful, original love songs Sam sang to her that spring. Every Tuesday after they said good-bye to the children at the Home, Sam and Diana went to the park.

He sang to her, and on a moonless night in May he kissed her. He kissed her on their Tuesday evenings after that, kissing between songs and then abandoning the songs and just kissing her, long, deep, warm kisses that made Diana forget everything except him.

268

No one knew about their love. Even though he kissed her and sang her songs of love, Sam and Diana never had an official date. But one starry night, in their private corner of the park, he asked her to the senior prom.

When Sam was five minutes late on prom night, Diana vowed simply not to look at the clock. When he was fifteen minutes late her heart began to ache and she prayed silent prayers, *No, not again* and *Please let him be all right.*

When he finally arrived, forty-five minutes late, she saw that he was not all right. Although they brightened when he saw her, his dark eyes were cloudy.

"Sam, what's wrong?"

"Nothing." *Nothing I can tell you about.* "I'm sorry I'm late. You look very beautiful."

"Thank you." *And you look so handsome and in such pain. Why, Sam? Do you wish you were taking Cheryl?* Diana crushed the thought quickly, helped by his gentle smile and the tender kiss he gave her after he pinned a corsage of white orchids on her dress.

She felt so wonderful in his arms as they swayed to the music they loved. Sam held her close to him, closer and tighter, but then suddenly he would stiffen and she could feel that he wasn't breathing and when she searched his face she saw that it had become ashen and tense as if in pain. After a few moments he would breathe again and smile a thin smile and pull her back very close to

269

him.

Waves of nausea, Diana decided as she watched Sam's silent battle. He must have a stomach flu.

They left the prom early because they wanted only slow dances and the moonlit privacy of their own special place in Lincoln Park.

"Aren't you going to bring your guitar?" Diana asked as Sam began to lead her to their secluded spot without opening the trunk of his car.

"No. No singing tonight."

No singing. Diana's mind whirled. *Just kissing? Just loving? Just dancing to our own music of love under the moon?*

They danced, their bodies kissing as their lips did. Once, when her arms tightened around his chest, Sam winced and pulled away, just a little, but after a few moments he began a soft serious journey of kisses down her neck.

"Make love to me, Sam," Diana whispered bravely.

Diana had never made love. It was 1971, the era of free love. But Diana was uninfluenced by the mores of the time or the pressures of her peers. She had long ago decided that she would be a virgin until her wedding night. She would make love then with the man she loved, her husband and the father of the children she would have. Three children, Diana thought, maybe four, because she loved children so much and all the children she would care for at work wouldn't be enough.

She was uninfluenced by mores or peers. But Diana listened to the songs of her heart. And now those songs told her joyfully that it was right, wonderful, to make love with Sam.

"Oh, Diana," Sam answered softly. "I can't."

"Because of Cheryl?"

"Cheryl? God, no. Not because of anyone but you."

"Me?"

"Because you are so lovely and so precious and so beautiful." *Because your vision of life is joyous and pure and I don't want to cloud that magnificent vision with the truth.* "And so innocent."

"I don't want to be innocent."

Sam smiled a tender loving smile. Then, after a few moments, his handsome face grew solemn.

"Darling Diana, after tonight we'll never see each other again."

"Never?" Diana had known that after tonight it would be difficult for them to see each other. In two days she was flying to Bethesda for a summer research fellowship at the NIH. By the time she returned in late August, a brief visit before going to Boston, Sam would already be in Los Angeles practicing with the football team. They were going to colleges a continent apart—she at Radcliffe, he at Southern Cal—but they could write, couldn't they? And they could see each other at Christmas and spring break and summer. "You won't be in Dallas for Christmas?"

"No. My father just got a coaching job near Denver."

"Coaching?"

"He coaches college football."

"Oh." Diana hadn't known Sam's father was a coach, or anything about his mother, or if he had sisters and brothers. She really knew very little about Sam Hunter except that the thought of never seeing him again filled her with sudden fear.

*I could live the rest of my life and never again feel the way I feel with you—the happiness, the joy, the trembling desires that make me so brave.*

"Oh, Diana," Sam whispered gently when he saw the tears and sadness in the lovely sapphire. He kissed her tears and held her very close. "Don't cry."

"I'll miss you."

"And I'll miss you." *You have kept me alive. I wonder what will become of me without you.*

# Chapter Fifteen

*Cambridge, Massachusetts*
*September 1974*

Diana left the desk where she was studying to turn the stack of records on her stereo. The records were old favorites, familiar study companions from high school that had endured during her three distinguished undergraduate years at Radcliffe and were with her still as a freshman at Harvard Medical School.

As she walked back to her desk she paused at the window of her small Hilliard Place apartment, smiled at the large, wet drops that splashed against the pane, and thought, *Cozy.*

A cozy rainy night to spend studying the anatomy of the thorax to the music of the Beatles.

When her telephone rang at eleven she assumed it would be a classmate frustrated by the spinning pace of today's lecture in biochemistry and wanting to borrow Diana's compulsive and comprehensive notes. A classmate—or Alan. Alan was a second-year law student whom she had dated for about a year, and with whom she had made love even though she knew he wasn't the man she was going to marry. Diana hadn't known that when they had first made love four months ago, but she knew it now and she needed to tell him directly.

*If it's Alan, even though it's late and a school night, I'm going to invite him over and tell him,* Diana vowed bravely as she walked to the phone. As she lifted the receiver she hoped very much that it would be a classmate calling about biochemistry.

"Diana? It's Sam Hunter."

"Sam."

"Remember me?"

"Oh, yes, I remember you." *And I never believed we wouldn't see each other again.* Not that this call meant they were going to see each other. Sam's voice sounded close, but Diana knew where he was — in Los Angeles preparing for the game against Washington State on Saturday. Diana knew the football schedule for the University of Southern California. She watched the games that were televised and read about the ones that weren't. She knew all the details of Sam's stunning career, and she knew the widely held prediction that this year he would lead his team to the national championship and in the process win the Heisman Trophy.

"How are you?"

"Fine. Wet."

"Wet?" Her heart raced as she gazed at the rain pelting against her window. It never rained in California, did it? "Where are you?"

"In a phone booth across from a place called the Coop."

"In Cambridge," she whispered. *Only four blocks away. Why?*

"Yes. I'd like to see you, Diana. Could we meet for coffee sometime, or breakfast or lunch or dinner?"

"Where are you staying?"

"I'm not sure yet."

Sam had just arrived. The final ride in his transcontinental hitchhike had let him off a soggy half mile away from Harvard Square. He knew Diana was still in Cambridge. He had checked before he left Los Angeles. From the undergraduate office he learned that she was in medical school, and from directory assistance he got her phone number.

Sam had money for a hotel—he had sold his car, his textbooks, everything but the clothes in his knapsack and his guitar—and should have called her once he found a room and changed into warm clothes. But he couldn't wait. He had to hear her voice.

Now that he had, he wanted desperately to see her. And she wanted to see him.


"Hi."

"Hi." His lips, slightly blue from cold, smiled his tender uncertain smile, and raindrops splashed from his hair onto his cheeks.

While Sam took a shower and changed into dry clothes, Diana made hot chocolate and turned the stack of her favorite records.

Then Sam was there, dancing with her, beginning where they had left off on a moonlit night in June. Beginning where they had left off and this time finishing their dance of love.

On that June night the rhythm of their dancing had been slow and graceful, a leisurely kissing of bodies. Now there was urgency, almost desperation, a reckless and furtive need to be together.

As if this was a stolen moment.

As if, even though their passion and desires were all-consuming, there could be an intrusion on their loving.

As if, even when they were melted together by the immense fire of their love, they could still be torn apart.

From the very beginning there was desperation in their loving, desperation for each other and desperation to hold onto the love. As if it wasn't real, couldn't last, wasn't meant to be . . . even though their hearts sang with joy.

"I just couldn't play football anymore," Sam told her three days after he arrived.

"You were supposed to win the Heisman Trophy this year."

"How do you know about that?"

"I know everything about your career. Test me. Ask me how many passes you completed last year and whose record that broke."

"How do you know?"

"Television. The sports page of the *Boston Globe. Sports Illustrated.*"

"Really?"

"Of course." Diana smiled. Then, as her fingers delicately traced the jagged scars on his body and dipped gently into a concavity in the right side of his rib cage she added softly, "I'm glad you gave up football. Aside from how much more wonderful it will be to follow your singing career than your football stats, your body has had enough abuse."

"Enough abuse, yes. But it could take some more love."

* * *

"How many babies shall we have?" Diana asked one day in late October as they strolled in Boston Commons amidst the Saturday afternoon activity of children gleefully scampering through piles of fallen leaves.

"As many as you like. You'll be such a wonderful mother."

"And you'll be such a wonderful father." Diana smiled and asked, "Have you thought about names?"

"For our babies?"

"Yes."

"No, I haven't." Sam smiled lovingly at her. Then his dark eyes grew serious and he added, "I guess I would like to name one of our daughters after my mother. Her name was Jane."

"Was?" Diana echoed softly. They had spent hours talking about their love, the love songs he had written for her in high school, their dreams, their future, and Diana's loving family. But, even though she urged gently, Sam resisted talking about his family. "Your mother is no longer alive?"

"No."

"What was she like, Sam?"

"Very gentle. Very brave." Sam sighed softly and his eyes were far away. "She died in a car accident when I was six." *She died trying to save my life.*


Three weeks after Diana learned about Sam's mother, she learned about his father.

She was in the apartment studying and listening to one of the tapes Sam had made for her. The tapes were medleys of love songs, Diana's old fa-

277

vorites and the ones she loved even more—the breathtaking songs of love Sam had written for her. In the middle of one of the tapes of love was a twenty-minute instrumental called "The Chime Song." During his years in Los Angeles, Sam had spent many Sunday afternoons at the missions in Southern California listening to the chimes that rang from the bell towers. "The Chime Song" was a canon of all the beautiful chimes, tumbling one on top of the other, a breathtaking cascade of music and a triumph of Sam's talented fingers.

On that November night, Sam was at the Two Lanterns, the "in vogue" coffee house on Boylston where he waited tables and sang. When Diana's doorbell sounded at eleven she looked through the peephole before opening the door. Sam would be home soon, and at first glance she thought it was he having forgotten his key. But it was only someone who looked like Sam.

Diana smiled warmly as she opened the door. She was about to say, because they looked so alike, "You must be Sam's father. How nice of you to visit us." But her brain sent a surprising but forceful warning, Beware. The man looked like Sam, the dark handsomeness, the lean, taut body, the long-lashed brown eyes. No, the eyes were different. Sam's eyes were warm, gentle, loving, and this man's eyes were hard and cold. "May I help you?"

"I'm looking for Sam."

"Sam?"

"Are you Diana Shepherd?"

"Yes."

"Then you do know Sam Hunter."

Diana gave a brief frown, then smiled.

"Sam Hunter, yes, of course. We were at

278

Roosevelt together in Dallas." She tilted her head and asked, "Are you his brother?"

"I'm his father."

"Oh! What can I do for you, Mr. Hunter?"

"You can tell me where Sam is."

*Don't blush. Hold his gaze. Sound honest.* Diana had no experience with lying, didn't believe in telling lies, but on this night the deepest of instincts made the lies come easily.

"I have no idea. I'm sorry."

"When was the last time you saw or heard from him?"

"Let me think. It must have been the night of the senior prom. We had never dated, but we knew each other. I didn't have a prom date and Sam was kind enough to take me. Mr. Hunter, is something wrong? Has something happened to Sam?"

Sam's father started to smile, and Diana relaxed just a little, but it was only a cruel trick to throw her off guard. As she was beginning to wonder if she had been all wrong to be wary of him, his smile became a mean sneer and the cold, hard eyes turned wild.

Diana felt a shiver of ice sweep through her, the terrifying realization of danger that comes with a frantic message to flee. Diana couldn't flee, and as her mind struggled to prepare for his next round of questions and her next round of lies, he grabbed her.

And all the waves of fear that had swept through her before were only tiny ripples compared to the terror she felt as his massive hands dug mercilessly into the delicate flesh of her arms.

"I don't believe you, missy," he hissed, a vicious sound that was more animal than man. "He's

279

here, isn't he?"

"No! Let go of me! How *dare* you touch me!"

"How dare I?" He laughed an ugly laugh, then pulled her close to his snarling face and repeated meanly, "How *dare* I?"

Diana smelled the alcohol on his breath, and it triggered an important memory. During her undergraduate years at Radcliffe, she had worked as a volunteer in the emergency ward of Boston City Hospital. She had seen patients who were wild from alcohol or drugs and had marveled at the calm and reasoned way the doctors and nurses imposed control. She had only been a witness to the approach, never tried it herself, but . . .

"Mr. Hunter . . ." she began quietly, trying to make her voice calm and soothing, but having no idea if she succeeded because the sound was lost in the thunder of blood pulsing through her brain. "I honestly don't know where your son is. I do know that you are drunk and that you are hurting me, even though I'm sure you don't mean to. If you don't let go I will have to scream and my neighbors will instantly call the police. I'm sure you don't want that."

"Oh, you're sure I don't want that, are you?" he mocked with eyes that showed no fear.

Diana's threat was gently offered, and almost idle, because most of her neighbors in the solidly built apartment building were elderly and had long since gone to sleep behind their almost-sound-proof walls. But words were all Diana had against his immense strength, and now her mind sent even more frantic warnings, *"The Chime Song" is playing now, but in less than a minute it will be Sam's voice singing in the background, and in ten or fifteen minutes Sam will be home.*

"So, Mr. Hunter, do I call the police?"

"Be my guest. I'm leaving. I'm sure we'll have a chance to visit again sometime. I look forward to it."

His final words were a warning, painfully punctuated by his massive fingers that dug even deeper, almost to bone. Then he released her roughly, gazed insanely at her for an endless terrifying moment, then laughed an evil laugh and mercifully left.

As Diana closed the door, the trembling that had been a terrified quiver suddenly shook her entire body, and even though she took large gulps of air she felt as if she was suffocating. Trembling, suffocating, but still needing to be certain he was truly gone. Diana staggered to the window and watched with grateful relief as he got into his car and drove away with a squeal of tires and flagrant disregard of the stop sign on the corner.

The monster was gone . . . for now.

Without even grabbing a jacket before venturing into the icy November air, Diana started out the door of her apartment to run to the Two Lanterns to warn Sam. Earlier she had opened the door to an almost familiar stranger, and he had caused silent terror; now as she opened the door and saw a hauntingly familiar form through the blur of her tears, she screamed.

But it was Sam, not his father, and suddenly his strong, gentle arms were around her, holding her as she sobbed, and her terror was magically vanquished. She was with Sam, wrapped in the gentle wonder of their love, and she felt so safe.

"Diana, my darling, what's wrong?" Sam asked

281

as her sobs quieted. He feared the answer; he had seen the bewildered terror in her lovely eyes. "Diana?"

"Your father was here."

That night Diana learned that not all the scars on Sam's body were from years of battle on the football field. Most were the result of another war, a lifetime spent living with a violent and irrational father. Sam's deepest scars, some visible, some not, were vestiges of unexpected and unpredictable outbursts of violence that were triggered by nothing except that in his father's warped mind Sam had done something deserving of punishment.

"For a very long time, Diana, I tried to figure out what I was doing wrong, what I had done to anger him and how to prevent his rage."

"But you weren't doing anything wrong."

"No. I did everything he wanted me to do. His dream was to be a great football star, but he never was, so he transferred the dream to me. And I fulfilled that dream for him, until now. Until now, until this act of defiance, I was a model son." *And still* . . .

"The night you were supposed to sing at the hospital the first time," Diana whispered softly. How well she remembered that night, her anger alternating with concern, Sam's apology without explanation and his cloudy eyes and face that looked like death even four days later.

"That night . . . I called you as soon as I could."

"Oh, Sam. But you insisted on rescheduling for three weeks later." *Even though you weren't certain the same inexplicable thing would happen again.*

282

"Why?"

"Because of you. And the children. And me. I have no idea why my father didn't want me to do the concert at the hospital the first time. Three weeks later he thought it was great. He was—is—completely irrational. He always has been. My mother tried to protect me from him when I was little, but she was a victim, too."

"Was he driving the car when she died?"

"No. *She* was. He was chasing us. I was six and I had done something, walked in the room or didn't, spoke or didn't . . . who knows? Anyway he went after me and she tried to intervene. He turned on her, but somehow she grabbed the car keys and me and we tried to escape." Sam sighed softly. "I remember that drive so well. It only lasted five or six minutes, but she kept telling me over and over that she loved me and that we weren't going back and that we would be together, away from him, forever. I knew we were going to crash and I wasn't afraid because I knew we would go to heaven, she and I, and we would never see him again. But only *she* went to heaven."

*And you spent your life in a living hell,* Diana thought as her heart filled with a new and powerful emotion: *rage.*

"Oh, Diana, how did he know about you?" Sam asked with obvious anguish. He had loved her in high school, and even though he never imagined a future with her—a future at all—Sam kept their precious love hidden, a secret and most wonderful part of his life that his father could never touch, never contaminate, never destroy. "He was never very interested in my social life, except for occasional vulgar locker-room teases about sex, but still

283

I didn't want him to know anything about you. Even though I was in love with you that spring, I dated other girls and went to the parties with my crowd."

"But you took me to the prom."

"Yes. Our first and last date. I planned to tell him I was taking someone else, if he asked, but he never did. Until tonight I believed he knew nothing about you. But he must have found out afterward. He must have made a point of finding out."

Diana thought about the night of the prom, when Sam had arrived forty-five minutes late, and his body stiffened as if in great pain.

"He must have made a point of finding out because he sensed it was important to you, because you went out that night even though . . ." Diana fought the sudden emotion in her throat and finally whispered gently, "Tell me what happened."

"What happened, my beautiful Diana, was that I wanted to make love with you, but I couldn't." On that starry night Sam's ribs had been broken and every breath felt like a white-hot poker stabbing into his chest. Sam couldn't make love to Diana that night, but he had to see her, one last time, because she had been a beacon of happiness in the storm of his life.

*But I can make love with you now, my darling,* Sam thought. *And that's what I want . . . one final gentle night of love before I must leave you forever.*

Their loving that night was different, confident and not desperate, as if it had been the dark secret of Sam's father that had always made it so furtive.

284

They loved slowly that night, so gently, so tenderly
. . . the leisurely unhurried loving of a love that
would last forever.

But in the morning, as dawn lightened the dark
November sky, Sam held her and spoke the words
he knew he must speak.

"I have to go, Diana."

"Go?" she echoed with soft surprise. Then, com-
prehending, she added quietly, "Oh, you're going to
see him, aren't you? You're going to tell him that
you will never return to football, no matter what
he wants, and you're going to warn him that if he
ever bothers us again we will call the police."

"Oh, my love, I wish it were so easy. My father
is not afraid of the police."

"No, Sam, it was after I threatened to call them
that he left."

Sam smiled lovingly at her. Diana's belief in
goodness was so strong, her joyous heart so loving,
that now she was choosing to deny what had really
happened. She had told him every terrifying detail—including the way his father scoffed at her
threat to call the police—but now she was softening
her memory, as the memory of a frightening nightmare blurs with the light of day, because the evil of
his violent father was such an aberration that she
could not, or would not, believe it was real.

But even if lovely Diana chose to soften the
memory—and Sam wished someday she would forget it altogether—he would never forget her terror,
or her gasping sobs, or the disbelief in her lovely
eyes as she stared at the ugly bruises on her arms
where his father had so brutally held her.

Sam knew the true danger of his father. He
knew that his search for the son who had finally

defied him would be relentless. His father would be like an animal stalking his prey, but, unlike an animal, and far more menacing, once his father found him he would shadow his life, as he always had, appearing in the middle of the night to cause terror and deriving great pleasure from the power of the torment. The threat would be constant, punctuated by flurries of violence, and someday, as it had been for the loving mother who had believed they could escape, the violence might once again be lethal. Someday the father, whose fragile control on his rage became more tenuous as he got older, might arrive with the guns and knives that were his prized possessions.

Sam was not afraid of his father. There had been times in his life, many times, when the fear of life was far greater than the fear of death. If he could stay with Diana, live their love and have their children, and know that when his father returned he could simply give his own life to protect his love and their babies, he would have stayed.

But Sam knew that wasn't possible. He would not ask her to live a life clouded with fear, much less a life in which physical harm might come to her and their babies. He wanted only happiness and joy for lovely Diana. Which meant that as long as his father was alive, their love could never be.

"Darling Diana, my father left because he decided to leave," Sam told her gently. "Not because you threatened to call the police."

"So you're not going to see him?"

"No." *Because if I saw him now I might kill him,* Sam thought, hating the thought but fearing that the image of Diana's terror and her bruises might compel him to fight back as he never had before. It wasn't cowardice or fear of death that prevented him from greeting violence with violence. It was the fact that that would make him no better than his father, and it might be proof of what Sam feared the most, that some part of his father's madness, some trace of his poison, flowed in his veins.

"Then where are you going?"

"I'm not sure. I just need to get far away from you, and then call him, tell him where I am, and make him think that's where I've been ever since I left Los Angeles."

"Then you'll come back here."

"No, my precious love, I'm never coming back. I can't. Don't you see, darling? Our love isn't safe. You have to forget about me, Diana. You have to find a safe and joyous love and be happy."

"Sam, *you* are my love! Our love is stronger than your father! I'm willing to take the risk."

"But I'm not willing to take it for you."

Sam left, as he had left once before, with a sad and solemn vow that they would never see each other again. But, just as before, Diana didn't believe him. She knew Sam would return to her and their love. She knew it even before the wonderful discovery that their final night of loving had created a new little life. Their baby, Sam's gift of love, was a memory and a promise. He would come back. He had left a part of him, a joyous living symbol of their love.

"We're very healthy and happy," Diana lovingly assured her parents for the hundredth time during

287

their week-long visit to Boston in June. It was her hundredth reassurance because it was in response to her mother's ninety-ninth pronouncement that she and Diana's father, both eminent archaeologists, were not going on their long-planned dig in North Africa after all because Diana's baby was due in August and they weren't scheduled to be back until September. Diana added with a soft laugh, "Go!"

"It will be very difficult to reach us, Diana."

"I won't need to! Besides, Mother, first babies are often born late, aren't they? I'll probably still be quite pregnant when you return." Diana's voice softened as she spoke of the tiny life growing inside her. "This lively little one and I are going to have a very peaceful summer studying my second-year coursework so we'll have lots of time to play in the fall."

Diana named their daughter Jane, after Sam's mother, as she and Sam had joyfully planned on an autumn afternoon in the Boston Commons.

Janie arrived in early August, an easy delivery, a labor of love, a healthy, happy gift of life. She had Sam's dark-brown eyes and the dark-brown hair of both, and she was beautiful and smiling and soft and such a miracle . . .

"The defect is extremely rare, Diana," the pediatric cardiologist from Massachusetts General Hospital told her when Janie was three days old.

Only three days old, but the small lungs that had been fine at birth were suddenly struggling valiantly for air!

The doctor explained what was wrong with Janie's tiny heart and Diana understood perfectly be-

288

cause she had received honors grades in anatomy and physiology and embryology—in all her freshman classes at Harvard Medical School.

"So she'll need surgery," Diana said firmly.

"There's . . ." *Nothing we can do.* "There isn't a surgical procedure for this anomaly, Diana. I'm so sorry."

Diana understood those painful words perfectly, too. Her lovely Janie needed a new heart, and medical science could not give her one. Heart transplantation in adults was quite new, and quite disappointing, and even in the centers where transplants were still done, transplantation in a neonate was unheard of.

Medical science had nothing to offer Diana's infant daughter. The heart that she and Sam had given their precious child of love was broken and could not be fixed.

Janie spent the only month of her life in the small apartment on Hilliard where her mother and father had loved. There was still such love in that apartment! Diana held her little daughter, kissing her, loving her, whispering words of love.

"I love you my little Janie, oh my little girl, I love you so much."

Diana whispered soft, soothing words of love and she told Janie about her wonderful daddy and they listened to Sam's tapes over and over.

And Diana sang to her. And for that month of love Diana—who loved music but had never been able to carry a tune—sang with perfect pitch.

Janie died in Diana's arms, a peaceful death, a final breath and then no more.

\* \* \*

Diana's parents arrived in Boston two days after their granddaughter's death. The happy letter Diana had written the day after Janie's birth reached their remote camp in Africa just before they began their journey home. Diana's parents gently, then urgently, tried to convince their beloved daughter to take time off from medical school and return to Dallas with them.

But Diana insisted that she was fine. She encircled her heart with a wall of steel, resumed her classes, and for the second year in a row received honors in all courses. She insisted that she was fine, even though the joy was gone from her sapphire eyes and her lovely face was taut, and so wary, ever vigilant, as if on guard for further pain. For the first year following Janie's death, Diana didn't allow herself to think, or grieve, or acknowledge the wish that was the only glimmer of hope in her dying heart—the desperate wish that Sam would return.

On the September night that marked the first anniversary of Janie's death, Diana sat in the darkness of the apartment where such great love had lived and died. The darkness was silent at first, but after an hour or two, without even thinking about what she was doing, Diana began to listen to one of the tapes of love Sam had made for her.

Then the darkness was no longer silent, and sometime later, the sound of love songs was interrupted by the ring of her telephone.

"Hello, Diana."

"Sam." She hadn't cried until now, hadn't allowed it, but the warmth and gentleness of his voice cradled her, as if he was there with her and she was safe in his arms, and he was rescuing her

290

from the pain that had been too painful even to admit. Diana closed her eyes in the darkness and allowed herself to be enveloped by his gentle voice and the memory of the loving eyes. "Where are you?"

"In London. I've been here ever since I left Boston."

"Have you seen your father?"

"I've talked to him," Sam replied quietly.

He had called his father the moment he arrived in London, and, at first, as weeks passed and his father didn't appear, Sam's heart filled with the wonderful hope that it was over, that his father realized his son would no longer be his victim. But then the calls began, some threatening and crazy, some terrifyingly normal and almost fatherly. Those calls, the almost normal ones, were the ones that shattered all hope. Because as he listened to the questions about his personal life, his *women,* Sam knew that his father's madness had not abated, nor had his rage at his defiant son. His father was simply searching for other ways to punish Sam, a cowardly bully searching for more fragile victims.

His father's madness had not abated. In fact, Sam realized, it had become worse, more calculating, a time bomb still, ticking, ticking. Every sound, even the sounds of silence between calls, underscored the solitary life Sam was destined to lead, *must* lead.

But still he thought about Diana every day and night, missing her, loving her, fighting the powerful need just to hear her voice. For almost two years he had resisted—because what was the point in calling?—but tonight his heart had won the constant battle. Tonight he felt a strong, invisible tug, as if she needed him, too . . . but of course it was just his own need.

Perhaps he needed to hear that she was happy, that she had found a safe and joyous love. Perhaps if he knew that, he could stop dreaming about a time that could never be, a time when their love could live in more than dreams and memories and songs of love.

"Nothing has changed, Diana," Sam whispered finally, softly, his gentle voice filled with sadness.

"You're not coming back?"

"No. I just wanted to see how you are . . ." His words faded because they sounded so feeble, such a tiny corner of what he really wanted.

"I'm fine, Sam." Diana's voice was suddenly strong as she reflexively spoke the words she had spoken for the past year to anyone who dared be concerned about her.

"How is medical school?"

"It's good. I began my clinical clerkships early so I'll actually be graduating a year early."

"Just like college. Brilliant Diana," Sam whispered softly, so proud of the woman he loved. What a wonderful doctor Diana would be, what joy she would share, what good she would do with her bright mind and loving heart. How often he had wondered, in thoughts that were more dreams than reality, if he and Diana could live a hidden life of love. But she would have to give up so much, and even then there was no guarantee that his father wouldn't find them, and he wanted her to give up nothing.

Sam knew what he could offer Diana—his love, his heart, his life . . . and a lifetime of fear. He wished so much more for her! He knew, an aching knowledge, that there would be other men, safe loves, who would love her and give her all the happiness and joy she deserved.

"What about you, Sam?" Diana asked after several moments, her voice softening in response to his, and softening, too, because she loved him still, always, even though he wasn't coming back to her. "How are you?"

"I'm fine, too," he lied softly.

"Are you singing?"

"Yes. In pubs." Sam paused and then added quietly, with a trace of disbelief, "And a month ago I signed a two-album contract with BMI."

"Oh, Sam. That's wonderful." Diana smiled lovingly as she imagined the dark-brown eyes she loved so much, uncertain eyes, even though he was so special, because his lifetime of punishment had taught him that no matter how much he excelled or achieved, he was still flawed and unworthy.

"The first album will be released next summer."

"Will I be able to get a copy, a hundred copies?"

*I'll send you one. I'll bring you one.* Sam fought the wonderful thought. He knew this was the last time he could call her. She had been waiting for him, even though he had told her not to, because she remembered the last time he had said good-bye and then appeared three years later. Tonight, before they said good-bye, he needed to be sure that she understood there could be no future for their love.

"Yes, if you want to," Sam answered after a moment. "The album will be released simultaneously in North America and the U.K."

"They think it's going to do well, don't they?"

"That's what they think."

"And it will. I'll just have to get my copies before they sell out. I'm very proud of you, Sam."

"I'm very proud of you, too, Diana."

Diana's heart filled with new hope at the gentleness of his voice. For the past few moments they had been discussing their dreams. The last two years had vanished, and they were together again, dreaming together, sharing the greatest dream, their lifetime of love.

"Please come back to me, Sam."

"I can't, darling. I can't."

"You mean you don't want to," Diana whispered as the hope faded and anger rushed in to fill the sudden void.

"Oh, Diana, I want to. I love you so—"

"Love? You don't love me Sam, not really! When you love someone you don't leave them. You make plans to spend your life with them—you *do* spend your life with them—and nothing else matters." *If you had loved me you would have been with me, loving our baby with me, loving her and holding her, and then we would have held each other after she died* . . . "You don't tell someone you love them and then vanish for no reason."

*For no reason.* Sam ached at the words. He missed her desperately, every second of his life, but never, not even for a second, did he doubt his decision to leave her. Diana still didn't understand the true lethal danger of his father, and that meant she didn't understand, either, that he left her because he loved her so much—too much.

"My God, Diana," Sam whispered. "Please don't ever believe I don't love you with all my heart."

The anguished emotion in his voice stopped her anger, or perhaps it was time for the anger to stop.

For the past year the steel wall around her heart had kept her emotions locked away. But tonight, the impenetrable fortress had come tumbling down, and the emotions had spilled out, a tumbling cascade over which she had so little control. The emotions spilled, falling one on top of the other—love . . . anger . . . sadness.

But Diana wanted control, just a little, because she wanted only love on this night with Sam. She would have a lifetime to live with sadness and anger . . . and the bitter truth that Sam didn't love her enough to find a way back to her. For now she clung to the softness of his voice, allowing herself to be wrapped for a final time in its warmth, feeling safe and loved. Because Sam *had* loved her— just not enough—and that wasn't his fault. She needed to live in his love now, whatever he could give her, for as long as it was there.

They talked for almost three hours, talking and sharing the silences, both knowing the good-bye would come, both wanting the gentleness to last forever. There was even laughter in the darkness, small bursts filled with surprise because it had been so long since either had laughed.

And then, when they knew it was almost time to say good-bye, there was such gentleness and Sam asked the question he had been wanting to ask ever since he realized that his lovely Diana doubted his love.

"Will you listen to my songs, Diana?" he asked, his voice soft and calm even though he desperately needed to hear her answer "Yes." Diana didn't understand the true danger his father posed, and he hadn't wanted to spend these precious hours giving her the details of horror that would convince even her lovely heart. But he wanted to convince her of his love, to make her believe how much she had been loved so that she could carry that confidence to her future loves. If she listened to his songs of love, songs that would always and only be written to her, then she would know.

"Yes, of course, Sam. You know I will."

Twenty minutes later they said a final good-bye. And then the warmth was suddenly gone, as if it had never been there, and she was alone in the cold darkness of her apartment and her unprotected heart screamed with pain as she confronted the harsh, bitter truth . . .

Sam had loved her, but not enough, and she was alone.

Sometime before the dawn lightened the autumn sky, Diana calmly removed the tape from the cassette player and gathered all the other tapes Sam had made for her. She didn't rip the once-precious tapes into a thousand pieces, because she felt sadness, not rage. Instead she simply put them in the trash in the basement of the apartment building. Then, as daylight broke, shattering the once-enveloping darkness and erasing even the shadowy memory of the gentle voice an ocean away, Diana put the wall of steel back around her heart . . . where it belonged.


"What a tragedy. This was going to be Sam Hunter's year to win the national championship."

"Something happened to Coach Hunter?"

"Yes. Haven't you heard? He was killed yesterday."

"Killed?"

The two male medical residents who were discussing the shocking news about the nation's top football coach turned in the direction of the soft female voice that had echoed *killed?*

All three were in the nurses' station on the Bullfinch Ward at Massachusetts General Hospital. Diana was in the fourth year of her surgical residency and had been asked to consult on a patient with possible cholecystitis on the general medical ward. It was late November, six years since Sam had left, and four years since the late-night call.

"Killed," one of the medical residents confirmed.

"Do they know who killed him?" Diana asked quietly. The death of Sam's father would not be a tragedy unless somehow *her* Sam was involved.

"Sure. It was one of his assistant coaches. I saw the poor guy interviewed this morning. He feels terrible, of course, but it was an accident."

"An accident?"

"They were all hunting together."

"Oh, I see," Diana whispered with relief, and not an ounce of guilt. She was a doctor, devoted to saving lives, committed by a solemn oath to life's sanctity, but she greeted the news of the death of the monster with hope that was almost joy.

*Our love is safe now, Sam. If you love me, you will come back to me.*

But Sam never returned. He could have found her easily because she remained in the apartment on Hilliard throughout her surgical residency at Mass General. Why did she stay in that place

297

where so much had died? Was she waiting for Sam? Or was the effort of living her life, merely moving from day to day, already great enough that she simply didn't have the energy to find a new place to live?

Diana didn't analyze. She simply survived. She gave up her dream of being a pediatrician without thinking about why and set her brilliant mind to becoming a heart surgeon and inventing hearts that would save precious little lives without thinking about why, either.

Of course she would listen to his songs, Diana had told Sam in the darkness of night when she was wrapped in the warm gentleness of his voice. But it was a promise that could not survive the harsh light of day. Once Diana's heart had filled with joy at the sound of music. But now music, all music, triggered painful reminders of all she had loved . . . and all she had lost. And she listened no more.

The world heard Sam Hunter's magnificent songs of love, but Diana never did. If she had been listening, she would have known that he had loved her too much not to leave her, that he wished more for her than what his love might bring. Diana would have known of Sam's magnificent love, and, after his father died, she would have heard the most beautiful love songs of all, songs that called to her by name, in lyrics gift-wrapped in tender hope, gentle pleas for her to come to him if she loved him still.

*If she loved him still.* Most of Sam believed that in all the years they had been apart Diana had surely found a new love. He had wished love for her and had told her not to wait for the love that might never be. And that was why he reached out to her with his music, and not his loving arms, because it had been so many years, too many years, simply to appear on her doorstep, a confusing bittersweet memory from her past. If she loved him still, if by some miracle she had not found a new love, she would hear his songs and let him know. And whether she heard and no longer wanted him, or wasn't listening because she had found someone new, Diana's silence gave him his answer.

Eventually, as the hope faded in silence, the love songs written by Sam Hunter had a new theme, a sad theme, the poignant and poetic farewell to a great love that once had been but was no longer.

For a very long time Diana's heart was numb. Then it was ice. And finally, defiantly, her cold heart strained for a little warmth, even a few flickers. She allowed visitors into her heart, but she would not permit the visitors to find a home there.

Until Chase. Diana welcomed Chase into her heart. She even believed that she had given him all of it. Then Chase told her he wanted children, and Diana realized there was a part of her heart that she could not give. There was a part that would belong always and only to Sam and Janie. When Chase trespassed on that precious part, their love was over.

Diana's private life was filled with failure, but her professional life overflowed with great success. She invented a new heart, a magnificent creation that would save small lives—like the life of her precious daughter whom she had been unable to save—and the world sang her praises and crowned her the brilliant and beautiful Queen of Hearts.

As if hearts were her kingdom. As if she had some special knowledge about their mysteries and was an expert on love.

*Queen of Hearts.* How she hated the name! It was so wrong, so very wrong . . .

Because she had failed in her love with Sam and with Chase.

And because she had failed, the greatest failure of all, to save the life of her beloved Janie.

*Part Three*

# Chapter Sixteen

*John F. Kennedy International Airport*
*September 1989*

Something pulled Diana from the memories of Sam and Janie in time to catch her flight to London. As she rushed to the plane that would carry her to the luxurious three-week vacation in Europe Diana wondered why she was traveling at all. What was the point? The necessary journey was in her heart. She wouldn't even notice her splendid surroundings.

Diana's preassigned seat in first class was 2B, a nonsmoking seat on the aisle. Jeffrey Lawrence was in 2A.

"Doctor."

Jeffrey's greeting was polite, civil, without the trace of a taunt. Diana steeled herself for a haughty reminder of their last encounter and her "unacceptable" behavior, but his handsome face was solemn and nonjudgmental. And there was something else in the dark-blue eyes.

No doubt the famous anchor had seen grisly footage and heard grim reports that had not been shared with the world. Was it the vivid memory of those unspeakable horrors that darkened his eyes still, despite the hope for peace?

No, Diana decided. The turbulence in the ocean-blue depths was quite a different pain, quite a private pain.

Diana responded instinctively with a wish to help but not to intrude. She smiled a soft smile, a flicker of warmth, and said with a gentle lilt, "Hello, Anchor."

Diana would have said more, would have given Jeffrey the apology she owed him, but as she stowed her carry-on luggage beneath the seat and fastened her seat belt, he looked away, far away, out the window and beyond. And by the time the plane lifted off and Jeffrey withdrew his gaze from the sun-bright sky, Diana had retreated to her own private thoughts.

They didn't speak, but each held books opened in the middle and stared at the words as if riveted by the story even though neither read or even turned a page. Jeffrey drank Scotch, straight, more than one, and Diana sipped champagne. Both declined the gourmet lunch.


*You have to apologize to him before you leave the plane,* Diana told herself sternly.

*As soon as the movie is over,* she decided. The cabin would still be dark, nicely shadowed, and soon after, no matter how awkward their words, the plane would land at Heathrow and she would never see him again.

"Mr. Lawrence?"

"Yes?"

"I owe you an apology for what I said to you that evening in your office. It was inexcusable of me to accuse you of breaking your word. I'm very sorry."

"Don't be." After a moment Jeffrey added quietly, "You had a perfectly legitimate excuse."

"I did?"

"Yes, your heart . . ."

Jeffrey didn't finish his sentence because his attention was suddenly distracted by a flight attendant who was standing in the aisle behind Diana.

"Yes?" Jeffrey asked.

"I'm sorry to interrupt. I need to speak with Dr. Shepherd."

"Oh." Diana turned her attention from Jeffrey to the flight attendant. "Yes?"

"We have a medical emergency in the back of the plane. I can page for a doctor over the public address system if you'd rather not get involved. There probably are other doctors on the plane, but we have a passenger list for first class and I noticed your name so I thought . . ."

"It's no problem."


The "patient" was a five-year-old girl with frightened brown eyes and a terrible stomachache. Her name was Becky and she was traveling alone, an "unaccompanied minor" returning home to her mummy in London after spending a month in the States with her father.

"Hello, Becky." Diana knelt in the aisle beside the little girl and smiled reassuringly at the frightened eyes. "My name is Dr. Shepherd and I'm here to help you. OK?"

"OK," Becky agreed softly.

"Good. Your stomach hurts?"

Becky nodded.

"Can you show me where?"

It took Diana only a few minutes of quiet conversation and very gentle physical examination to make the most probable diagnosis.

"I need to speak with the pilot," Diana told the flight attendant when she was finished. "And could you arrange for me to sit beside Becky for the rest of the flight?"

"Of course. The plane's full, but I can work something out."

"Why don't you put her in my seat and I'll sit here?"

"Oh." Diana turned in the direction of his voice. She hadn't realized until then that Jeffrey had followed her to the back of the plane. "That would be very nice. Thank you."

"Should I carry her up front?" Jeffrey asked.

"Yes, please." Diana smiled and added softly, "Thank you, Jeffrey."

"Hi, Becky." Jeffrey knelt as Diana had so that he was level with the dark-brown eyes. Dark-brown eyes that bravely fought tears. Dark brown eyes that reminded him of a little girl he didn't know but had wanted so very much to get to know. "Don't be afraid, honey. I know for a fact that Dr. Shepherd is one of the best doctors in the world. If I was sick I would want her to take care of me. I'm going to carry you to the front of the plane so she can keep an eye on you until we land. OK?"

Diana listened to the conversation and was impressed by Jeffrey's gentleness. She remembered the famous Beirut episode and guessed that he had an instinctive love for children, as she did. And there was something else they had in common, something in the depths of the dark-blue eyes, a ripple of excruciating sadness despite the smile for Becky.

There was something about little girls with dark-brown eyes that caused them both great pain.

Jeffrey and the flight attendant settled Becky in his seat and Jeffrey sat beside her until Diana returned from the cockpit. He vacated the seat as soon as Diana appeared and she walked with him as far as the galley that separated first class from coach.

"I think it's appendicitis," she explained to Jeffrey as moments before she had told the pilot. "The history is classic. Her abdomen is soft, which is a good sign. The appendix probably hasn't ruptured. There will be an ambulance waiting at Heathrow and a surgical team available at a nearby hospital when we arrive."

Diana sat beside Becky, talking softly and reassuring her as her experienced eyes and hands subtly monitored the girl's vital signs—the color and temperature of her skin, her respiratory rate, the radial pulse in her small wrist.

The ambulance was waiting when the plane landed and the medics and Becky's mother boarded as soon as the door was opened. Diana provided concise information to the medics, reassured Becky's anxious mother, and because the tiny veins had gone into hiding and Becky trusted her, Diana expertly inserted the necessary large-bore intravenous needle into her small forearm.

"Will you do the surgery, Dr. Shepherd?" Becky's mother asked.

"Oh! No . . ."

It wasn't just the red tape of licensure and the

sticky politics of arriving at an unknown hospital and doing a cameo. Diana had operated, command performances, in operating rooms throughout the world. But those were heart surgeries and this was an appendix. Diana hadn't done abdominal surgery in years.

"You don't operate on children?"

"Only heart surgery. This surgery needs to be done by a general surgeon. It's much better for Becky."

By the time the IV was in and Becky was on the stretcher, the other passengers had long since disembarked. Except for Jeffrey. He had returned to the first class cabin to get his carry-on luggage but waited until Diana was ready to leave. Then he gathered her bag, too, and carried it for her as they walked to baggage claim and Customs.

"Where are you staying, Diana?"

"The Dorchester."

"So am I. Shall we share a cab into town?"

"Oh. Sure."

It was a silent cab ride. Both Jeffrey and Diana had been running on empty before all the worry about the little girl with dark-brown eyes. Both were exhausted, too tired to summon the energy to chatter gaily about the sights of London as they sped past them. They rode in silence, but unlike earlier, the silence now was almost comfortable, almost comfortable enough for Diana to break the peaceful stillness to ask Jeffrey to finish the sentence that had been interrupted by the flight attendant. Almost comfortable enough to ask, *What was my legitimate excuse, Jeffrey?*

But Diana didn't ask. She and Jeffrey were both very tired and there had been such sadness in his eyes before when he had started to tell her. Better

to leave it alone. Better just to say good-bye to
Jeffrey Lawrence with a final thank-you and a
warm smile.


Jeffrey couldn't sleep. Perhaps he should not
even have tried. It was early evening and the outside world was only just beginning to fade into
darkness. But he had barely slept all week, and
last night in his apartment in Manhattan he hadn't
slept at all.

After a frustrating hour, he gave up. He showered, dressed, and began to review the notes he
had brought for his reporting of the peace conference. Tomorrow he would spend the day at the
network's London bureau going over a detailed
plan for the coverage of the historic summit.

But he didn't need to review his notes. He knew
precisely what he wanted — the maps, the graphics,
the time-lines, the photographs of leaders and hos-
tages — and he knew the history of the conflict. In
the years he had lived in the center of the fire,
and in the years since, he had spent long hours
thinking about the eventual peace.

He put down his notes and poured himself a
large glass of Scotch from a crystal decanter. The
alcohol burned his empty stomach, a deep, sizzling
sear.

Too much Scotch. Too little food. Too many
nerves. Too much pain.

And nothing he could do to ease the pain.

*I should never have married you.* For over
twenty-four hours the devastating words had
echoed in his brain. Jeffrey couldn't banish Julia's
words, the truth at last, from his memory. He
would have to live with the harsh echoes and ex-

cruciating pain, a fragile creature without a shell, raw, exposed, hoping to heal swiftly but knowing it would take a very long time.

Jeffrey paced restlessly in his elegant suite and finally, on a sudden impulse, called the hospital where Becky had been taken. After that call, he made a second and even more impulsive call.

"Diana, it's Jeffrey. Are you awake?"

"Yes!" Diana laughed softly. "I'm too tired to sleep."

"I'm the same. I do have some good news. Becky is out of surgery and doing well. It was exactly what you predicted — appendicitis without rupture."

"Oh, good. Thank you for checking. I was just about to call myself."

"Are you in the mood for dinner?"

"Sure. I guess."

"Is that a definite no?"

"It's a definite yes. But you need to know that in addition to being too tired to sleep, I'm too hungry to eat."


"Would you like something to drink?" Jeffrey asked when they were seated beneath the mirrored ceiling in the Bar, the Dorchester's cheery blue-and-white-tiled restaurant.

"Just milk."

"Warm?"

"Maybe later."

Jeffrey ordered two milks. When the drinks arrived he raised his glass and she raised hers, and as the crystal touched in a gentle chime, it was Diana who whispered the toast.

"To peace." She tilted her head and embellished

310

softly as she watched his eyes, "To world peace and to private peace."

"To world peace and to private peace."

Jeffrey held her gaze, smiled a wistful smile, and felt an astonishing impulse to tell her about Julia. Astonishing because his love was so very private.

*Why would I be tempted to share the truths I have never told another soul with Diana who I don't even know? Is it because I was an unwitting witness to the death of her love and now fate has made her an unwitting witness to the death of mine? Is it because the sapphire eyes are sending a promise that they will be very gentle with the secrets of my heart? Or is it because on the same day in November thirty-six years ago . . .*

*It's probably because I'm so damned exhausted and maybe still a little drunk.*

As Jeffrey fought the astonishing impulse to tell Diana everything, Diana waged a similar silent battle. Why on earth would she be tempted to tell stunningly successful Jeffrey Lawrence about the failures of her life?

*Because I think he would understand. And because I think he would be gentle.*

Jeffrey and Diana suppressed the remarkable impulses and spent the next thirty minutes discussing the historic peace conference and what Jeffrey thought and hoped it might mean. And then they shifted to her reason for being in London.

"Business or pleasure?" When Diana didn't answer right away and he saw sapphire confusion, Jeffrey pushed gently, "Doctor?"

"That's a surprisingly tough question, Anchor. Neither business nor pleasure, I guess."

"What then?"

311

"I'm here to spend the next three weeks trying to make sense of the first thirty-six years of my life."

"Oh, that."

"Yes." She laughed softly. *That.*

Diana didn't elaborate on her personal journey—even though the gentleness in his eyes and voice gave the carefully suppressed impulses sudden life and energy. Instead she gave him a detailed description of her luxury vacation, the cities she would visit and the fabulous hotels where she would stay—the Ritz in Paris, Loew's in Monte Carlo, the Lord Byron in Rome, the Excelsior in Florence, the Cipriani in Venice.

"And then, two weeks from Sunday, a five-day cruise through the Greek Isles."

"Wonderful," Jeffrey said quietly as Diana finished reciting the details of her itinerary. It *was* wonderful—almost precisely what he would have chosen for the honeymoon he had always promised Julia.

"What was my legitimate excuse for insulting you in your office that evening, Jeffrey?"

Dinner was over and they were almost done with the warm milk Jeffrey had ordered as a nightcap and Diana decided simply to ask. At first she wasn't sure he would answer. His dark-blue eyes deepened a shade, and the anguished pain she had seen earlier surfaced from the depths. Diana was about to withdraw the too private and too painful question when he spoke.

"Your heart was breaking." Jeffrey gave a shaky smile and added quietly, "Not that I'm an expert on broken hearts."

"No?"

"No. Only a novice. But what about you, Diana? Surely you've reviewed the world's literature on the subject. What do the great medical minds have to say?"

"They are strangely silent."

"But what do you think? Can a broken heart be mended?"

"I think it mends itself in time."

"As good as new? Or even better, like a broken bone? When I fractured my collarbone three years ago, the doctors said the healed bone would be stronger than before."

"I don't think a mended heart is ever as good as new because the scar never goes away. But a mended heart may be tougher, more wary." Diana frowned slightly. "I'm not sure that being tougher is better for a heart."

"Except that it won't break again."

"Oh, but it will. Perhaps it won't break in exactly the same place, because the scar there is strong, but the heart is made of a thousand fragile places."

*So, Jeffrey Lawrence,* she thought, *when you finally heal from the anguish that is tormenting you now, and if you allow yourself to love again, the pain can happen all over.*

Diana knew they were dancing very close to the heart and that it was a dangerous dance for them both, but Jeffrey hadn't withdrawn and she took a chance with another very private question.

"Will you tell me, Jeffrey? I'm not an expert, but I am a little experienced."

"Will you have dinner with me tomorrow night?" Jeffrey answered Diana's question with a question even though the answer that had come to him without hesitation was, *Yes, I will tell you.*

313

He hadn't spoken the words because he couldn't believe them. But the Scotch was long since gone from his body, even though the fatigue wasn't, and he still felt the astonishing impulse to tell her everything, to entrust his shattered heart to the Queen.

The following night as they dined at Tante Claire's, they shared the truths they had never shared before, anguished truths about lost loves and lost daughters.

"You don't really believe your marriage is over, do you, Jeffrey?" Diana asked quietly, after all the painful secrets had been shared and listened to.

"Julia said she should never have married me, Diana."

"She was hurt and angry. People say things in anger that they don't mean."

"Or *do* mean."

"Perhaps in that emotional moment Julia wished she hadn't married you. But ten years ago, Jeffrey, she chose to marry you. And," Diana added softly, "it sounds as though those ten years have been filled with great love."

"I thought so, Diana. I really believed our love was very strong despite Julia's secret."

"I believe that, too, from what you've told me." The words with which Jeffrey described his love were eloquent enough, but they were embellished even more by gentle longing in his eyes and tender pride in his voice. "You *are* going to talk to her, aren't you?"

"I have to. If only to hear everything, if she'll tell me. Maybe if I hear all the painful details I'll be able to hate her."

"I wouldn't count on it."

"You don't hate Sam."

"You mean Chase."

"No, I mean Sam."

"Sam is very ancient history, Jeffrey."

Just as Diana heard Jeffrey's great love for Julia, Jeffrey heard Diana's love still for Sam. Her heart was freshly broken by Chase, but that wound would heal with a scar that was strong and tough. From what Jeffrey had heard and from the way her sapphire eyes softened when she spoke of Sam, he didn't believe there was a scar in the place where Diana's heart had been broken by Sam. Her love for him lived in that place still, soft and gentle and evergreen.

"I somehow feel that the love between you and Sam isn't over."

"Has anyone ever accused you of being an incurable romantic, Jeffrey?"

"Only Julia."

"Sorry. Anyway, it *is* over with Sam. I admit that because of horrors I've seen in trauma rooms of hospitals and even on the nightly news I've come to understand that his father might truly have been dangerous. But even if Sam really did need to leave because of his father, the psychopath died ten years ago. Sam could have come back then, but he chose to stay away. End of story."

"But you don't hate Sam."

"I've tried to. But what was Sam's great crime? That he couldn't love me enough and forever? You know, don't you, Jeffrey Lawrence, where that argument logically ends?"

"Oh, yes." Of course he knew. Jeffrey knew because, like Diana, he was a perfectionist, critical and demanding. And like Diana, he placed the

315

greatest demands and expectations on himself. Jeffrey didn't blame Julia for what had happened to their love, he blamed himself. It was *his* failure to win Julia's heart, not *her* failure to love him.

"But, Diana . . ."

"Yes?"

Jeffrey hesitated. Tonight he and Diana had trusted each other with so much and been so gentle with that trust. He wanted her to believe that the words he was going to speak were because he cared very much, but he feared they might offend. Once before he had angered her with an offer of help.

But that was before they were bonded, as they were bonded now, by the secrets of their hearts.

"What, Jeffrey?"

"If you want to spend your life believing it was some failure in you that Sam couldn't love you enough — fine."

"OK." *I will*.

"But, please stop blaming yourself for Janie's death."

"Jeffrey . . ."

"It's time for you to forgive yourself, Diana."


"I think I'd better go home, darling," Julia told Merry at eight on Sunday morning.

They were in their suite adjacent to the Spencers' suite at the Plaza. The day before, the five of them had attended the matinee of Jerome Robbins's *Broadway* at the Imperial Theater and then had an early dinner at the Tavern on the Green. This morning, they were planning brunch in the Plaza's Garden Court and a carriage ride through Central Park before the ballet. Tomorrow they would do more touristy things—the World Trade Center and the Statue of Liberty and the Empire State Building—and return to Southampton in time for a good night's rest before the festivities of Tuesday—Merry's birthday and the gymkhana.

"I'll go home with you, Mommy."

"No, Merry. You stay here and enjoy the rest of the time with the Spencers. I'm just going to curl up in bed and sleep. I want to be completely well when you get home tomorrow afternoon."

*I will be completely well because I will have seen Jeffrey and our love will be whole again.*

Julia smiled lovingly at her daughter. Merry had been such a trouper yesterday, but Julia had seen occasional waves of unguarded sadness as Merry undoubtedly imagined how much more fun it would have been if only Daddy had been with them.

*Daddy will be with us next time, darling,* Julia vowed silently. *He has to be.*

"I'm sure it's just the flu, Paige," Julia said when she spoke with her fifteen minutes later.

"Were you ill yesterday, Julia? You didn't look quite right."

"I guess I was getting it yesterday. Today's worse. I'm going to Belvedere, disconnect the phone, and try to sleep it off. May I leave Merry with you?"

"Of course. But, Julia, maybe we should all go back."

"No. I'll be best on my own."

"Do you have nausea?"

"What? Oh, yes," Julia admitted truthfully, one of the few truths of the morning. She had eaten so little in the past few days that her stomach wished never to eat again.

317

"Julia, maybe you're pregnant."

"Oh, no, Paige. It's not that."


For sixteen years Julia's sleep had been tormented by the recurring nightmare of a fiery explosion in midair followed by a death spiral into the cold, dark sea. At first only her parents lived in the nightmare, but then Jeffrey did, and Merry.

The nightmare didn't vanish with dawn or wakefulness. It was always there, a dreadful fear, and every time Jeffrey flew, Julia fought the vivid lethal images.

Her fear had prevented her from traveling with him, even though he wanted her to, even though it might have made their love stronger.

As Julia boarded the overwater DC-10 she didn't think about the dream-shattering catastrophe above Cartagena sixteen years before, or her terrifying nightmares, or even about the recent tragedies that had befallen DC-10s in Sioux City or Tripoli. She did not remind herself that she was about to be enclosed in a coffin of fire.

Instead she boarded calmly and without fear.

Julia was no longer afraid of flying, because no fear was as great as the fear of losing Jeffrey.


"I figure you're either going to spend the entire afternoon studying the mummies or you couldn't care less."

"Couldn't care less. How about you? Either all day studying the Magna Carta or . . ."

"I thought I'd take a look at the Magna Carta and maybe the mummies." Jeffrey smiled in silent acknowledgment of the issue around which they

318

were skirting. They had decided to spend Sunday afternoon exploring the wonders of the British Museum. That decision had been made together and easily. But each knew it wouldn't be easy to wander through the museum together since each had a different pace and different interests.

"So, Anchor, where should we meet?"

Jeffrey studied his guide book of the museum for a moment then suggested, "How about the Horological Room?"

"The Horological Room?"

"Clocks. Clocks, it says here, invented before and after the pendulum."

"That sounds quite comprehensive. And quite interesting."

"Good. So, clocks at five?"

"Perfect. Cheerio."

Jeffrey saw Diana from a distance at the Elgin Marbles and they peered together at the Rosetta Stone. But that was at three-thirty and he didn't see her again until their five o'clock rendezvous.

Diana arrived a few minutes early. As she wandered from clock to clock, she was enveloped by the ticking. It was so calm, so primal, perhaps like what a baby heard in its mother's womb, the comforting reassuring heartbeat.

At five, as all the clocks struck the hour at the same moment, the comforting ticking gave way to a symphony of sounds.

*Chimes.* And suddenly Diana was inside "The Chime Song." Each chime spilled onto the next, as Sam had made them do with his talented fingers, layer upon layer, a magnificent cascade of beautiful melodies.

319

Diana couldn't run. She was in the center of the room surrounded by an invisible wall of music that had become an inescapable prison of memories.

Jeffrey arrived just as the chiming began. He watched the transformation in Diana, her beautiful face losing its soft, bemused smile and freezing into a look of bewildered terror. It all happened very quickly. In a matter of moments the chiming was over and the clocks lapsed again into peaceful, rhythmic ticking. The frenzy was over, calm restored, but Diana was left ravaged.

Jeffrey put his arms around her and held her. After a few moments, he took her hand and led her silently out of the museum and into the late-afternoon sunshine.

"When Sam lived in California," Diana explained when she could finally speak, "he spent Sunday afternoons listening to the chimes in the bell towers of missions. He wrote a song, a canon of all the chimes, one on top of the other . . . it was just like being in the clock room."

"I'm sorry," Jeffrey said quietly.

"I used to play the tape of 'The Chime Song' for Janie when she needed to sleep. How she loved it! She always fell asleep with a look of such peace." Diana's words ended in a tremble and tears filled her sapphire eyes.

"Diana, I'm so sorry."

"It's not your fault. You didn't know. And it didn't occur to me even when I was in the room."

As the taxi turned onto Park Lane, nearing the Dorchester, Julia raised her eyes from the hands that were tightly clasped in her lap and looked out the window to the Sunday afternoon activity in Hyde Park. The sight of frolicking children, nannies pushing carriages, families enjoying the fading rays of the warm autumn sun, and young lovers strolling hand in hand reminded her of the distant Saturday afternoon in Ghirardelli Square that had been the beginning of the love between her and Jeffrey. Julia's heart filled with hope at the lovely memory. Perhaps later, after they talked and their love was whole again, she and Jeffrey could take a romantic walk in the park.

*But Jeffrey already was taking a romantic walk in the park.*

Jeffrey . . . and Diana Shepherd. Julia recognized the famous heart surgeon from the live press conference in June and from this week's *Time*. During the past week, in the late-night hours when she was alone and awake—missing Jeffrey and worrying about the events of the world—Julia had read the cover story. And she had marveled at the genius of Diana.

And now Jeffrey and Diana were among the Sunday crowd in Hyde Park and they were picture perfect, a stunningly attractive couple strolling together, his arm draped gently over her shoulders, their entire attention focused on each other, listening to the intimate words each whispered and smiling softly as the autumn sun cast their happiness in a golden glow.

As Julia watched, Diana stepped in front of Jeffrey, stopping him. Jeffrey's handsome face came into Julia's full view . . . and it was as if Jeffrey was looking at *her,* gazing at *her* with the gentle tenderness she knew so well and needed so desperately. But today Jeffrey's look of love was for Diana, not for her. And then Jeffrey did something

321

else that had always been, Julia believed, for her alone—very delicately he touched Diana's face and moved a strand of her dark-brown hair so that he could see her eyes more clearly.

If Julia had discovered Jeffrey making love to Diana, that scene would not have been as devastating to her heart and her love as this intimate scene of tenderness and affection. Julia knew that before she met him, Jeffrey had had many lovers. She knew that he had been able to enjoy the sensual pleasures of sex without the emotion of love. If he had angrily stormed away from Belvedere and into another woman's bed, a frenzied, irrational moment of lust in response to the frenzied, irrational words she had hurled at him, she would have been terribly hurt, but their love might have survived.

But what she witnessed now in Hyde Park wasn't lust. It was tenderness, affection, *love.* Julia knew the look and feel of Jeffrey's love, and now she saw him look at Diana and touch Diana the same gentle, loving way.

The love between Jeffrey and the talented and famous Queen of Hearts wasn't even a new love, Julia realized with anguished sadness. There was such familiarity in their intimacy.

How long had they been lovers? Was their affair the real reason that the dinners that Edmund and Paige so resolutely tried to arrange kept getting mysteriously canceled at the last minute? Was Jeffrey the reason that Diana's marriage to Chase had ended?

Julia remembered the night in June when Jeffrey had returned late after his interview with Diana. He had been troubled that night, a quiet uncertain despair, and he had needed her so urgently.

Had he, on the eve of the announcement of Diana's divorce, suddenly been torn between his two loves? Or had he and Diana truly just met on that night, but had he known immediately that there was something special between them, as ten years ago he had fallen so swiftly in love with *her?*

Ten years ago, Julia's lonely and innocent heart had made a gentle plea, *Please love me for as long as you can.* And over the years, urged by the gentleness of his eyes and his words and his touch and his smile—gentleness Julia now saw for Diana—she had believed in Jeffrey's love and in her own ability to hold it.

She had actually become confident of Jeffrey's wonderful love. Confident enough to believe that their bountiful love would overflow to their daughter. Confident enough to ask Jeffrey to take time from his important dream to begin to live her dream that they would be a family.

As she watched the tender intimacy between Jeffrey and Diana in Hyde Park, Julia felt her dreams die—all her dreams, her own dream of love with Jeffrey and her dream of his love for their daughter.

There was a time, before she knew she was pregnant, when she might have been willing to share Jeffrey's love with another woman. Perhaps even now, if hers was the only heart involved, she might have lived with Jeffrey's betrayal. Or perhaps not; because hadn't the unloved little girl become a woman who believed in herself and her own generous gifts of love?

It didn't matter what she might have done, because hers was not the only heart involved. Her lovely Merry had waited so patiently for her father's love. Julia had believed with all her heart that someday Jeffrey would love his daughter. She had believed in him, and she had believed, too, that his great love for her would spill over to the child of their magnificent love.

But their love wasn't so magnificent, so bountiful, after all.

The dreams were over. Julia would not allow any more disappointment for the sensitive little girl who had waited so patiently for a father's love that would never be.

Hours before, she had boarded an airplane with resolute calm. Now, with the powerful determination of a mother bear driven by the deepest instincts of love to protect her precious cub from further harm, she quietly instructed the taxi driver not to stop at the Dorchester but to return to Heathrow instead.

Jeffrey had put his arm around Diana's shoulders because she had become very quiet again as she lapsed into painful memories of the infant girl who had loved the chimes. She had smiled a wobbly, grateful smile when Jeffrey touched her, and he kept her focused on the present with a question.

"Are you having dinner with me tonight?"

"You don't think it would be too much of a drag to appear in public with a teary woman?"

"Actually, I was thinking about dinner in my suite because I'll probably be getting calls from the bureau all evening. Thus," he continued with a soft tease, "begging the issue of being seen in public with a teary woman. Which, for the record, I wouldn't mind at all."

It was then that Diana had stepped in front of him, stopping him, and Jeffrey had gently moved a strand of tear-damp hair from beside her sad sapphire eyes.

"You're a very nice man, Jeffrey Lawrence."

"And you, Dr. Shepherd, are a very lovely lady."


The dinner in Jeffrey's suite was indeed interrupted by many phone calls from the bureau. But the calls didn't interrupt animated conversation, only thoughtful silence. Jeffrey and Diana were quiet, reflective, because they knew they were saying good-bye. Diana was flying to Paris in the morning and Jeffrey was beginning his coverage of the peace conference.

The surprising, wonderful interlude, the magical weekend suspended in time and untethered to the cautious rules that had guided their private lives, was coming to an end. But there were important legacies. Each felt more hopeful. The dark secrets had been exposed to the deep golden rays of the autumn sun and that gentle glow somehow made the secrets less menacing and less able to destroy.

Each would go on.

Diana would continue the journey into her past. And even though Jeffrey would no longer be there to guide her away from the consuming infernos of self-blame, he had taught her not to fall into those traps. Diana would remember his wise and gentle lessons and be kind to herself.

And Jeffrey would talk to Julia and try to save their precious love. Because of Diana's encouragement and hopefulness, Jeffrey believed there was a way to make his love strong and whole again. There was a way and he would find it.

* * *

When Jeffrey walked Diana back to her suite, he looked at her for a long time before he kissed her.

It was meant to be a good-bye kiss. But even though their hearts had greeted each other with such trust and such joy, Jeffrey and Diana had never even kissed hello. So the kiss became more hello than good-bye, warmer and deeper than either had planned, a tender greeting that came with powerful rushes of desire.

"Not what the doctor ordered?" Jeffrey asked softly when Diana pulled away.

"I don't know, Jeffrey, is it?" Diana had taken her lips from his, but she had not revoked her trust or her confidence that they would be honest with each other always.

"I've never been unfaithful to Julia."

"That doesn't surprise me. You love her very much."

"I've never even thought about being unfaithful before now."

"Despite innumerable opportunities?" she teased lightly. They weren't going to do this. She couldn't and neither could he, and they both knew it.

"Next life?"

"You have a date."

"Be good to yourself, Diana."

"Be good to yourself, too, Jeffrey."

## Chapter Seventeen

Jeffrey's fingers trembled and his heart raced as he dialed the number to Belvedere.

It was Tuesday evening. He was in his suite at the Dorchester preparing to write the copy for the broadcast that would go live to the East Coast at midnight.

Tuesday. September twelfth. Merry's tenth birthday.

Jeffrey wanted to wish her happy birthday and tell her how sorry he was that he would miss the gymkhana and promise to spend an afternoon, many afternoons, watching her ride when he returned.

Finally the overseas line connected to the Southampton exchange and Jeffrey heard the distinctive ring, so familiar and so welcoming. For over thirty years that ring had connected Jeffrey to a loving voice.

*Please let her soft voice be loving now.*

How many times had he called Julia, if only for a minute, just to say, "Hello, Julie, I love you"? How many times had he heard joy in her voice and her soft reply, "I love you, too, Jeffrey"?

What a luxury that had been! *Somehow* he would find a way back to that joyous love.

"Hello?"

Her voice was soft, but so very far away.

"It's me. How are you?"

"Fine."

"Julie, we need to talk." *We,* Jeffrey said gently, even though it was his desperate need, a need made more desperate by the sound of her soft voice. How he needed her. How he needed to love her. How he needed to see love and laughter again in her lavender eyes. "I should be home Saturday."

"I don't think we need to talk, Jeffrey."

"No?" Jeffrey's question was hopeful and wistful. Hopeful. *You mean we don't have to talk, we can just go on with our love?* And wistful. *Shouldn't we talk, darling, once and for all? Shouldn't we expose all the wounds and nurse them tenderly and allow them to heal?* The pain would be greatest for him, hearing about Julia's secret love, but what could be greater than the pain of losing her?

*I never loved you, Jeffrey.* Those words would cause a greater pain. But Julia would not speak those fateful words because she *had* loved him, *did* love him, didn't she? Their entire love had not been an illusion, had it?

"There's nothing to say, Jeffrey."

"Oh, honey, I think there's a lot to say."

"No, Jeffrey." *I'm not strong enough to hear your gentle, apologetic good-bye.* "It's over."

Julia's voice was small and soft, and their voices were carried into space before they reached each other, but Jeffrey heard the ominous message in her tone with terrifying clarity. It sounded as if she was saying good-bye.

"What's over, Julie?"

Jeffrey held his breath and almost asked the question again because the silence was so long. But finally she spoke, or the devastating words finally made it back from space, having languished longer there, as if they had sensed a home in that black emptiness.

"Our marriage."

"Our marriage? Julia, please tell me why."

"You know why, Jeffrey."

"Tell me." How quickly he had forgotten the lessons he had taught Diana! How quickly the gentle wisdom she had echoed to him when they said good-bye—"Be good to yourself"—had vanished! Now he was asking for more pain. Now he was asking to hear the words he had convinced himself Julia could not utter: *I never loved you, Jeffrey.* "Tell me."

Why was Jeffrey doing this? Julia wondered sadly. Was he testing to see if she knew about his new love? Why couldn't he just be relieved that she had so easily let him be free? Was he still torn, just a little, even though it had been so obvious to Julia that he had already made his choice?

"Julia?"

"Because there is someone else," she whispered finally, her voice hardening to fight her tears. She kept the fragile, icy control by remembering the image of Jeffrey and Diana in Hyde Park, and while she still had the strength of that dream-shattering memory, continued swiftly, "Will you come out on Saturday to get your things? It would be best if we weren't here, so if you could tell me when—"

"There's nothing I need." *Except what I can't have.* There were treasures at Belvedere, priceless treasures, but neither the woman nor the little girl belonged to him.

Sometime in the silence the phone line disconnected. Neither knew who had hung up first, or if the line, sensing the anguished silence, had severed on its own.

As Jeffrey felt the full effect, the staggering emptiness, he thought about the reasons he had called — to find a way back to their wonderful love and to wish Merry happy birthday. He had done neither, and he would never do either again.

He had lost the other half of his heart.


Julia knew her marriage was over the moment she saw Jeffrey with Diana. For the past two days she had prepared herself for the call she knew would come, rehearsing her words, emptying her heart, trying to force numbness where there was so much pain.

But she hadn't been prepared for the gentleness in his voice, the sadness, even though it was he who had found a new love, and it made the pain even worse.

Thirty minutes after the phone call ended, Julia forced herself to move. She had to get ready to go to the stable — the girls were already there — to watch the gymkhana and then birthday dinner at Somerset and then a lifetime of loving her precious daughter and trying to make up for all the lies. *Daddy loves you, Merry. He is just so terribly busy. His work is very important.*

Fairy tales! Just like the fairy tales Julia had invented to numb the pain of her childhood because her own parents didn't love her. Julia had filled Merry's life and her heart and her hope with the same foolish fantasies. And now, in the years to come, Julia would have to explain gently, lovingly, to her daughter that she had been wrong, and that it was her fault, not Merry's, not Jeffrey's, *her* failure to hold Jeffrey's love.

\* \* \*

Jeffrey stared at the wedding band that was a symbol of their love, the intertwined ribbons of white and yellow gold forged together forever by fire. Now the band was simply a glittering symbol of all that he had lost.

*Once you put the ring on my finger I will never want to take it off,* they had told each other the day before they were married.

Jeffrey never *had* taken it off, and he didn't want to now. But he had to. The pain of seeing it on his finger still would be greater than the pain of never seeing it again, wouldn't it?

Diana had taken her rings off so swiftly. At the time, because he didn't know her then, Jeffrey had decided it was a sign of iciness, the swift surgical excision of Chase from her heart. But Jeffrey knew Diana now and he realized, even though they hadn't discussed it, that she had taken off her rings for the same reason he had to: the rings were a shining, defiant symbol of her great failure to hold a love that meant so very much.

After Jeffrey removed the elegant wedding band, he stared at the nakedness of his ring finger. The skin that had been covered by the gold was so white, so long away from sunshine, a pristine symbol of the innocent and joyous hopes of a just-born love. The pure white skin was a painful symbol, a grim reminder of what he had lost, just as the gold had been.

And there was more, a reason that the pain might live forever. On that distant day, when it was too late to have the rings engraved before their wedding, Julia had whispered softly that the engraving in gold didn't matter, because the words were engraved in their hearts.

As Jeffrey put his wedding band in a dresser drawer in his luxurious suite he felt a deep twisting ache, a scream of pain as the words that had been so lovingly engraved now became open weeping wounds.

"Oh, Julie," he whispered, speaking the words aloud. "I will always love you."


Julia and Merry hadn't made specific plans for the Vacation With Daddy beyond the weekend in Manhattan, the gymkhana, and Merry's birthday dinner on Tuesday.

"Even though he's on vacation, he'll probably have to study," Merry had suggested solemnly.

"Probably," Julia had agreed softly. Her lovely, sensitive daughter was so shy and uncertain about the father she didn't know but who she needed and loved. For so long Jeffrey had been a phantom beyond her reach. And even though recently, in fragile, wonderful moments, he had begun to notice her, Merry was not bold enough to schedule every moment of his vacation to be with her. So they hadn't made special plans beyond Tuesday, and it was just as well because the disappointment of carrying out the special plans anyway, without him, was excruciating.

Wednesday was a relief, a day for which there had been no expectations. Julia suggested thinking of something special to do, just the two of them, or with Paige and Amanda, but Merry declined.

"You still have the flu, Mommy. Amanda and I can just go to the Club and ride and swim."

Wednesday, Thursday, and Friday were like all the other summer days, and on Saturday Paige gave the last slumber party before school for all the girls in Amanda's class at Southampton Country Day.

Normally Julia would have joined the party, enchanting the girls with her wonderful stories. Her stories had matured as the girls did, fairy tales still, not romances yet, but more sophisticated with each passing year.

But Julia didn't join the party on this Saturday.

"Does Jeffrey get home today?" Paige asked when Julia brought Merry to Somerset but declined Paige's offer to come in.

"What? Oh, yes."

"Well, assuming he doesn't whisk you to the hospital the instant he sees you, I'm going to take you to see a doctor on Monday."

"I'll be fine, Paige, really. I'm better every day."

"You don't look better."

"I am, though."


It wasn't true. Julia was worse, dying a little more each day, unable to stop the pain that gnawed at her heart.

She had to get control for Merry's sake.

After she returned to Belvedere, she paced from room to room searching for answers but finding only ghosts. It was a blustery autumn day, graying quickly with storm clouds. With every rush of wind, Julia's heart raced. Was it Jeffrey's car? Had he decided to come and get some of his things this afternoon after all? What if Diana was with him?

Julia couldn't be here.

She reached into a distant corner of her dresser drawer and found the jeans she had worn the day she met Jeffrey; jeans that had been there from the very beginning of their love; jeans that had been removed by him with expert hands and a soft laugh of desire after she had taken off her blouse and sweater.

Julia dressed in the old baggy jeans and a blouse, sweater, and tennis shoes. Then she went downstairs and outside through the French doors to the rose garden where Jeffrey had spent a spring morning transplanting roses and then had promised to return to see the magnificent summer blooms.

*Face the ghosts,* Julia told herself. *Go to all the magical places and exorcise the ghostly memories of love.*

On that lovely joyous day in May she and Jeffrey had walked through the dense forest to the cliffs above the sea. Julia followed that path now, staggering along the narrow deer paths, tripping over fallen logs, her eyes blinded by tears as she made the journey that had once been a journey of love. When she reached the cliffs, she gazed at the dramatic spectacle of the storm clouds over the Atlantic. The autumn sky was scowling, unhappy with what it saw on earth, and the sea was angry, too, gray-green and turbulent, boiling and fuming.

The meadow where Jeffrey and Julia had made love in a sea of wildflowers was barren now, the flowers past bloom and the grass brown from the hot summer. Brown, but slick from the huge raindrops that fell from the gray-black sky. Julia stumbled down the steep trail that wound past SeaCliff to the beach and walked to the edge of the sea. The surf crashed, powerful and pounding, but Julia was mesmerized by the gray-green energy and strangely unafraid.

She had always been so afraid of the sky and the sea, but she had banished the ghost of the sky when she flew to London, and now she stared bravely at the turbulent sea and smiled a soft, dreamy smile.

Good-bye, ghost!

The place where she stood at the water's edge was as far as she had gone with Jeffrey on that springtime day of love. But now she looked down the beach to a white ribbon of sand that stretched into the ocean. The distant peninsula was surrounded by the swirling water, almost an island except that it was safely connected to shore by a snow-white isthmus of sand.

She decided to go to the peninsula, a place she had never been before, a place that might have terrified her even with Jeffrey at her side.

She would go there because it was a symbol of what her life would be from now on — going to new places without Jeffrey and conquering her fears.


When Julia reached the tip of the peninsula she stood on a boulder. Her slender body was tossed by the wind and pelted by the rain and the sea. She wavered a little in the powerful storm, weak from little sleep and less food, but she was determined to hold her ground against the gusting wind and swirling sea.

The sea that crashed and churned at her feet was a magnificent kaleidoscope of green and white. The sea had once been an enemy, a cause of fear, but now, even in its storm-tossed strength there was a friendliness. Hypnotic and beckoning, the foamy green whispered to her, urging her to journey to its emerald depths and promising a peaceful forever sleep.

It would be so easy to fall into the sea! The sea beckoned and the wind pushed and she was already enveloped in wetness, the sea, the rain, her own tears.

*So easy.*


When Patrick emerged from the forest onto the beach, he saw what had happened to the day since he left the cobblestone courtyard at the Club. The leafy ceiling of forest had shielded him from the rain, but during that protected journey the gray-black sky had opened. The rain spilled and the wind hissed and the sea roared.

The drama of the sky and the sea energized the powerful stallion beneath him and filled Patrick, too, with a sudden rush of energy. This evening he would paint this drama in green and gray. Patrick painted in the lonely nocturnal hours that used to be filled with love. Casey was still with him in those late-night hours, a tormenting memory, and he only made the torment worse by trying again to paint her portrait, to capture the breathtaking image of vulnerability and surprise as she turned from the sea and met his eyes. The image was as illusory as Casey had been—a mirage, a dream, something that had never really existed at all except in his imagination and his heart.

Patrick looked down the beach through the curtain of raindrops toward the peninsula where he and Casey had met. The peninsula would vanish today because the harvest moon was full and the sea was high and angry. The ocean would swallow the land soon and swiftly in a gigantic gulp, and he would watch that powerful drama from the safety of shore.

As his gaze fell on the farthest reach of the frail finger of sand, Patrick drew a sharp breath. It looked as if someone was standing on the lethal land.

Surely it was just a mirage, another illusion of the peninsula, a trick of his memory and his rain-blurred eyes. Patrick strained for clarity through the rain, but clarity didn't come nor did the image fade. With a rising sense of panic he squeezed his strong legs against the belly of his horse. The stallion responded instantly, eagerly, pricking his ears to the wind and pounding his hooves on the rain-firm sand.

As Patrick neared his fear was confirmed. A woman stood precariously at the tip of the soon-to-vanish peninsula.

In June, Patrick had discovered another woman standing there but this wasn't *déjà vu*. The sea had been friendly that evening, warm and calm, not swollen and angry, and then when he reached the peninsula there had been only a narrow ribbon of emerald water at its neck. Now the danger was real and imminent. Already there was a turbulent channel of water between the peninsula and the beach. The land would disappear today, swallowed whole, and even if the woman was a strong swimmer, the powerful undertow would pull her to the watery depths.

The land would disappear and so would she.

And, perhaps, so would he.

Perhaps? No, it was a certainty. Once he committed himself to trying to save her, either both would live or both would die.

Patrick did not hesitate. He could not watch her die.

The stallion balked the first time he approached the treacherous channel, sensing danger instinctively and veering violently away. Patrick gave a soft sigh. The woman would die, he would die, the horse would die. Or they all would survive.

"C'mon," he coaxed gently, his voice apologetic but firm. "C'mon."

As the water swirled and pitched, its soggy tentacles touched the stallion's withers and caused new panic. The horse lurched but maintained his footing, moving swiftly and powerfully to the temporary safety of the land across the channel—the peninsula that was now an island.

"Mrs. Lawrence!" Patrick called as he neared her and recognized her.

"Patrick?"

"You have to come with me now."

Patrick moved the horse beside the boulder where Julia balanced so precariously, then sat back on the withers of the stallion and extended his arms to her. Julia was confused but compliant. Patrick pulled her on — she was so light and so unresisting! — wedging her between his body and the strong neck of the horse. He gathered the reins, wrapping his arms around Julia, and curled his legs over hers to hold them both on the stallion's bare back.

"Wrap your fingers into the mane and don't let go," he instructed as he turned the horse with a pivot and cantered back toward the channel.

The stallion entered the now-familiar channel with only momentary hesitation, but even in the few minutes they had been on the island, everything had changed. The water was deeper now, deeper than the horse, and the currents had begun swirling around the island in a cyclone of water sucking down to the depths.

When the horse lost his footing, because the floor of the ocean had vanished, they all sank for a moment. Patrick's legs clamped over Julia's, but he still felt her slipping. He dropped the reins, wrapped one arm around her waist and curled the strong fingers of his other hand into the horse's mane.

It was a matter then only of whether the powerful stallion was stronger than the sea and whether its instinct for survival was greater than its terror. Patrick and Julia were simply passengers in a voyage of death or survival, their fate wholly dependent on the strength of the frightened animal and the grace of the sea.

At first, in the endless moments when the horse lost his footing, they were swept away from the sanctuary of the shore. Then, as the mighty legs began to pump, treading water, they were afloat, bobbing above the watery grave, but still voyaging toward the horizon and a smothering death.

"C'mon, boy," Patrick whispered gently to the creature who was fighting for its life and theirs. His whisper was laced with apology. Patrick knew he had no right to risk the gentle creature's life. "C'mon, *swim*. You can do it."

The horse responded, a long, slow battle, gaining a few feet and then being carried back, out to sea, but advancing again, and finally, miraculously, touching sand, finding footing, then lurching in the waves that crashed onto the shore and, at last, in a powerful rush, plunging onto the beach.

When they reached the safety of shore the horse stopped, its lungs gasping and its powerful heart pounding, just as the lungs and hearts of its riders gasped and pounded. After several moments Patrick reached to pat the horse's neck and reclaim the reins. As he leaned over, he touched Julia and felt her silent shivers. They were all chilled, but Julia was by far the most fragile. He had to get her to the warm safety of Belvedere.

Patrick knew well the trails that connected the estates of Southampton and chose the most direct route to the mansion, not the deer paths Julia had followed. As they rode, he held her securely in front of him, his chest touching her back, feeling her ice-cold shivers and sensing the tension of her silence. Julia didn't speak, didn't provide answers to the questions that danced in his mind.

What had she been doing on the peninsula? How could she have been so oblivious to the danger?

She looked ill, tired and haunted, worse even than she had looked at the gymkhana when Merry told him she had the flu. If she was ill, or even just recovering, why would she be here on this cold, stormy day?

Something else was wrong, something that made her shiver from a chill that was deeper and colder and more ominous than the residual chill of the ocean and rain and the near-brush with death.

Something even worse. *Something worse than death.*

Was it Merry? Patrick wondered as they neared Belvedere. There were no lights on in the elegant mansion and Patrick felt as if he was delivering her into the jaws of a dark monster, not the welcoming arms of a safe home. Her husband was probably in London still, but where was Merry on this stormy Saturday? If something had happened to Merry . . .

If something had happened to Merry, Julia Lawrence would look like this, Patrick knew, because he had watched Julia over the summer and had seen her immense love for her daughter, her motherly worries, and her gentle pride.

When they reached the cobblestone drive, Patrick dismounted, then circled Julia's waist and lowered her carefully onto the ground. She swayed a little when her feet touched the ground, but she recovered quickly and smiled a wobbly smile.

"Thank you, Patrick. You saved my life."

Patrick looked at her haunted lavender eyes and thought, *No, your life is still in jeopardy.* He wanted to offer to help, but she was withdrawing, backing away toward the mansion.

"Thank you," Julia said again before she turned and disappeared into the dark house.

Patrick was tempted to follow her, to ask what was wrong, but she obviously wanted to be alone, and he had a solemn responsibility to the animal that had saved them.

The heroic stallion was quite unscathed, not even chilled by the time they reached the warmth of the stable. Nonethcless Patrick carefully dried the rain and sea from the horse's coat before showering himself and changing into dry clothes.

He spent the evening in his small apartment. The outside world was quiet now, the storm's fury spent for the moment, but the silence didn't calm the worried memories that swirled in his brain. He couldn't forget Julia's haunted eyes, her icy chill, the dark mansion, the look of death.

Finally, at ten P.M., he opened the stable office, found the directory of Club members, wrote down the telephone number of Jeffrey and Julia Lawrence, and returned to his apartment to make the call.

Julia was in the master suite, in bed but not asleep, lying awake in the darkness and listening to the stillness of the night. The sound of the phone startled her. Her thoughts went swiftly to Merry but were calmed before she answered. Merry was with Paige, safe with Paige. If anything had happened to her this afternoon, if she had fallen into the sea, if Patrick hadn't saved her, Merry would still have been loved. Paige and Edmund, Merry's godparents, would care for Merry. Paige would be a loving mother and Edmund would be a loving father and Merry would even have a sister.

If she had fallen into the sea, Merry would have a mother, a father, and a sister — so much more than *she* had been able to provide.

When the phone rang Julia had been wondering if it might have been better for Merry if she was

341

asleep now, forever, in the green depths of the sea.

"Hello?"

"Mrs. Lawrence? It's Patrick."

"Patrick."

"I just wanted to see if you're all right."

"Yes. I'm fine. Thank you. Thanks to you."

"Good."

"Yes. Thank you." Julia repeated the polite words, but despite repetition they didn't carry conviction.

"Is something . . . ? Has something happened to Merry?"

"What? No. Merry's fine."

"Oh. Good. Well. I just wanted to be sure you're all right."

"Yes. Fine. Thank you again."

"Well. Good night."

"Good night."

After he hung up, Patrick said aloud, "You are not all right."

And after she hung up, Julia whispered quietly, "Thank you for caring, Patrick."


"How do you feel, Mommy?" Merry asked when she arrived home from Somerset at noon the next day.

"I'm better, darling."

"Good! Is Daddy home yet?"

"Oh, Merry," Julia sighed softly. She tenderly stroked Merry's long golden hair and knelt so that she was close to her daughter's wide brown eyes. "Honey, Daddy isn't going to be living here anymore."

"He isn't? Why not?" Merry asked the question, but Julia saw almost instant comprehension in her very bright daughter's eyes. Comprehension that brought such sadness.

"We've decided it's best if he and I don't live together any longer."

"You and Daddy are getting a divorce?"

Julia hadn't even thought about the mechanics of what this meant. She had only been trying to live with what it meant to her heart.

"Yes. I guess so."

"It's because of me, isn't it?"

"Oh, Merry, no! Why would you even think that?"

"Because that's the reason with some of my friends."

"Oh, darling, it has nothing to do with you. Daddy loves you very much. He will always love you." Julia had to force confidence in her voice even though she had experience with this lie—it was the lie she had told Merry all her life. Julia had believed with all her heart that Jeffrey would be a loving father to his daughter. And even though she now knew it wasn't true, would never happen, Julia had to maintain the lie a little longer until she could control her own emotions enough to be strong for Merry.

"This is why you've been sick, isn't it?"

"Yes."

"Because it makes you so sad."

"You're a very smart girl." Julia smiled lovingly. *So smart, so sensitive.* "It makes me sad, but I'll be OK. *We'll* be OK. We can talk about it whenever you want, whenever you have any questions, all right?"

Merry nodded. She would have many questions, the same ones over and over. *Why? Why? Why?*

"So, darling, how was your party? Is everyone excited about beginning third grade tomorrow morning? We can have your class over tomorrow afternoon if you want."

"I would rather just be with you."

"OK," Julia answered softly as tears filled her eyes. "I love you so much, Merry."

"I love you, too, Mommy." Merry wrapped her arms around Julia and squeezed tight. When the hug ended, Julia gazed into Merry's eyes and saw flickers of worry, a signal that Merry had a question she wasn't sure she should ask.

"Ask me, darling," Julia urged, knowing that those questions, the ones her thoughtful daughter might hesitate to ask, were the most important ones.

"Will we still watch Daddy give the news?"

"Of course, if you like."

"I think we should, Mommy," Merry said solemnly, "because I'm sure Daddy's going to come back to us."

Julia and Merry spent Sunday playing card games in front of the fire, watching favorite movies, baking chocolate-chip cookies, and talking. The next morning, two hours after Merry had left for her first day of third grade, Julia put a dozen of the giant cookies in a hand-painted tin box and drove to the Club.

With school back in session and the lingering drizzle, the stable was as empty as the day in June when she and Paige had first met with Patrick. Julia retraced the steps of that day, familiar steps now, and found Patrick in the stable office. Patrick didn't hear her approach because she wore tennis shoes, not high heels.

"Patrick?"

"Mrs. Lawrence. Hello." Patrick stood up from the desk and smiled. She looked a little better, he

344

decided. *Still very fragile, but maybe a little stronger.*

"I just wanted to thank—" Julia interrupted her own thank-you because something he had said seemed so wrong. "You should call me by my first name."

It would cause horrified gasps throughout Southampton. It simply wasn't done. He was a servant and she was a lady. Not that anyone considered her a lady, Julia knew, and she knew, too, that it wouldn't be the first horrified gasp she would cause. How she hated the pretensions!

"All right. Do you prefer Julia or Julie?" Patrick asked, because he had heard her called both. Paige Spencer always called her Julia, but Patrick remembered clearly that Jeffrey had called her Julie the night of the party.

"Julia."

"OK," Patrick agreed softly, even though he preferred Julie. Julie was the right name for her, spoken the loving, gentle way Jeffrey spoke it, but now "Julie" seemed to make her sad lavender eyes even sadder. "Julia."

"I came to thank you again. And . . ." This time Julia stopped because she was suddenly embarrassed by the silliness of her impulsive gesture, such a trivial offering for saving her life.

"And?"

"I brought you some chocolate-chip cookies."

"Thank you," Patrick said softly as he took the hand-painted tin. He was very touched by her innocence and shyness. Such shyness that now, her mission completed, Julia was starting to withdraw. "Why don't we each have a cookie, Julia? With some coffee?"

"Oh." Julia hesitated, almost tempted.

But the temptation was because she knew what

lay ahead of her after she left the stable. She knew the painful loneliness that awaited her at Belvedere. Once the silence of the huge mansion had been so peaceful, a lovely, expectant silence that would be joyfully punctuated by one of his many calls—"Hello, Julie, how is your day? I love you, Julie"—but now the silence was just an oppressive reminder of the dreams that had died.

Julia dreaded returning to the empty mansion and she dreaded, too, the stop she had to make first. She had to go to Somerset to tell Paige—if Paige didn't already know about the affair between Jeffrey and her good friend Diana.

"No, thank you, Patrick. I have some errands. I just wanted to thank you again."

"You're welcome. And Julia? You've thanked me enough, OK?"

"OK. Well, I guess I'll see you tomorrow at four for Merry's lesson."

"Good. I'll see you then. And . . . Julia?"

"Yes?"

"If you ever would like to talk, I'm here and not very busy now that school has started."

The lavender eyes didn't look offended, only shyly grateful, and she whispered again, "Thank you, Patrick."


"Oh, no, Julia. It can't be. You and Jeffrey . . ."

"It's over, Paige. You really didn't know?"

"I knew something was troubling you, but I never imagined it was your marriage."

"You didn't know that he was in love with someone else?"

"No, Julia. How would I know that? I don't believe it anyway."

"You'll see, Paige." *Paige would see. The world*

*would see.* Jeffrey and Diana didn't need to be discreet any longer. Julia stood up, suddenly restless, even though her only destination was one of lonely pain. "I have to go."

"Why don't you and Merry have dinner with us tonight, Julia? Edmund is in Boston on business. It would be just us four girls."

"I'm not sure, Paige. Let me ask Merry."


Merry didn't want to have dinner with Paige and Amanda. She just wanted to be with Julia and watch Jeffrey's broadcast.

"Daddy looks sad, Mommy," Merry said quietly as they watched the Monday evening telecast of *The World This Evening.* "I'm very sure that he misses us."

It was agony for Julia to see Jeffrey, to know that he was back in the country, in Manhattan, only sixty miles away, but gone from her life. Julia didn't know if it was sadness she saw in his dark-blue eyes, but she agreed with Merry that Jeffrey looked different. Maybe it was simply that she saw him differently because of the pain in her heart and the tears that misted her eyes.

*He* is *different,* Julia reminded herself. *He is someone else's love.*

*Even though I still love him with all my heart.*

# Chapter Eighteen

"Is everything all right, Jeffrey?"

"Sure." Jeffrey turned his attention from the copy he was writing for Thursday evening's broadcast to the executive producer who had appeared at his office door. "Why do you ask?"

"The viewers are worried about you."

"Really," Jeffrey replied quietly. The *viewers?* Was his pain that obvious? Was he wearing his heart on his shirtsleeve? He, who was so famous for his objectivity that even his own political affiliation and personal stance on major issues were remarkably hidden beneath his unwavering commitment to the doctrine of journalistic impartiality? "What are the viewers saying?"

"That you seem a little flat. Last week, when you were in London, it seemed like a combination of jet lag and the exhaustion of covering the conference. But this week . . . They are concerned, you understand, not upset."

There had been many calls and letters of concern about the popular anchor. The change was quite noticeable although no one could precisely label what was different—just as it had defied diagnosis when it was there.

*It* . . . the subtext from the heart, the wonderful

subliminal intimacy for Julia.

Now Julia was gone and so was the intimacy. The intimacy had always been subconscious, a direct connection from his heart to his face, an emotional path that bypassed his brain. It had been there when Julia lived in his heart. Now she was gone and Jeffrey's ocean-blue eyes no longer sparkled with joy and his voice no longer softened with loving tenderness.

Jeffrey knew how he felt inside, so raw, so empty, but he believed he had been performing well. Quite obviously he had not.

The viewers noticed something was different about their favorite anchor and contacted the network in hopes of learning the cause of the change. The executive producer, indeed the entire crew, had noticed the change in Jeffrey, too, but they had a major clue to its cause.

"Jeffrey, we've been keeping the camera off your hands all week."

"Off my hands?"

"Your wedding ring."

"You're telling me you think the viewers would notice that I'm no longer wearing a ring?"

"Instantly."

Jeffrey sighed. Not only had the viewers noticed a flatness, the crew had noticed that his wedding ring was gone and were covering for him, hiding his hands, forestalling the inevitable revelation that his marriage was over until he was ready to deal with the curiosity that such a revelation would ignite.

"Maybe I'll take next week off."

"Why not? You missed your vacation two weeks ago. I'm sure John can fill in."

\* \* \*

After the broadcast, Jeffrey dialed a number that connected him to the once so familiar and welcoming ring of the Southampton exchange. The call was not to Belvedere, but to the adjacent estate.

"Hello, Edmund? It's Jeffrey."

"Jeffrey."

"Have you spoken to Julia?"

"Yes, both Paige and I have."

"So you know."

"Yes. We're terribly sorry."

"Thank you. Did Julia explain what happened?"

"She said that there is someone else."

"Yes." Jeffrey didn't ask Edmund if he knew the name of Julia's new love. It didn't matter. What mattered was that Julia had already told Edmund and Paige. It meant that she quite clearly had no second thoughts about her decision. "Edmund, has Julia asked you to file for a divorce?"

"No," Edmund answered truthfully. Julia hadn't asked that of him, but they had, at Edmund's gentle urging, at least discussed the issue. Edmund wanted to be very certain that she would come to him if there was going to be a divorce. He wanted to avoid for Julia, especially for Julia, the kind of excessive publicity that had befallen Chase and Diana because the attorney handling the case hadn't been sensitive enough to defer filing until after the surgery on the Soviet ambassador. The divorce itself would be terribly painful for Julia. Edmund wanted to avoid any additional anguish for her. "Julia hasn't asked me to file, Jeffrey. Are you asking me to?"

"Oh, no, Edmund. I'm not going to be the one who files."

"I see." Good, Edmund thought. Perhaps, then, the divorce would never happen, because that was precisely what Julia had said: *I'm not going to be*

350

*the one who files for divorce, Edmund. I'm sure Jeffrey will be calling you.*

On Saturday morning Jeffrey took the Concorde from New York to Paris. At Charles de Gaulle he connected to a nonstop Alitalia flight to Venice's Marco Polo-Tessera Airport.

Diana was in Venice at the Cipriani. Tomorrow afternoon, if he was remembering her itinerary correctly, she would begin her five-day luxury cruise through the Greek Isles.

*What am I doing?* Jeffrey asked himself as the launch took him from the Piazza San Marco to the island of Giudecca and the lavish Cipriani. *Just flying halfway around the world to see if Diana is free for dinner tonight.*

And if Diana wasn't free? If she had met someone in her travels or if she was lost in her private journey and didn't want to be disturbed?

Jeffrey trusted the sapphire-blue eyes to tell him.

"*Sì, signore,*" the concierge at the Cipriani replied when Jeffrey asked if Diana was registered.

"Could you ring her room for me?" Jeffrey asked as he moved to the ivory-and-gold telephone that sat on the marble counter.

"*Certo.*"

Diana wasn't in her suite then and still didn't answer when Jeffrey tried again an hour later after he had settled into his room and showered and changed. Refreshed and restless, he decided to explore Venice. Before leaving the hotel he made a reservation for dinner for two in the hotel's elegant dining room and left a note for her at the reception desk: "Diana, dinner here at eight tonight? Or next week in Manhattan? Jeffrey."

The launch from the hotel returned Jeffrey to the Piazza San Marco. He didn't climb the famous campanile or wander through the Doges' Palace or view the Byzantine mosaics in the Basilica. He had spent many hours marveling at the wonders of the City of Canals in the past, many hours during which he had wished Julia had been there to marvel with him.

Today he forsook the historic landmarks and just meandered through the maze of bridges and canals that was Venice. He followed no map but made clear decisions at each corner, turning left or right or continuing straight ahead as if there was a correct answer, a definite path to follow. But he was simply wandering, and his decisions, he assumed, were merely guided by whim—the appeal of an enchanting bridge, the coyness of a wily gargoyle on a distant building, the elegance of a statue by Verrocchio, or the lure of a fresh scent from a pizzeria. At least that is what he believed until his random meander led him to Diana.

Seated at a tiny sidewalk cafe far away from the tourist attractions of San Marco and the Grand Canal, Diana was sipping cappuccino and gazing across the cobblestone street to a bronze fountain of mermaids.

Jeffrey's gait slowed, suddenly uncertain, when he saw her. He was here because of his need, because he trusted her and needed to see her honest blue eyes and hear her honest words.

His need, her privacy.

But she greeted him with a soft smile of welcome, a smile that held gentle sadness, because she saw the emptiness in his dark-blue eyes and the left hand that looked so barren without the elegant ring, and a smile that held happiness, too, because

352

she was so happy to see him. She had missed him.

"Hi."

"Hi. I . . . I came to wish you bon voyage."

"You look wonderful, Diana."

"It's the candlelight."

"It's more than that."

"Yes. I'm much better, Jeffrey, thanks to you." It had helped her so much to speak her secret pains and guilts aloud. Jeffrey had heard and understood, and he had told her what she needed to hear. *Forgive yourself, Diana.* She had heeded Jeffrey's wise advice and she was much better. "I'm not sure I would be so strong or so hopeful if I hadn't had you to talk to in London."

"You would be."

"I don't think so, Jeffrey." After a moment she asked quietly, "Are you going to tell me what happened with Julia?"

"When I called she told me our marriage was over. She has found someone else. I don't know who. It was a very brief transatlantic phone call."

"I'm sorry."

"So am I. But it's over." Jeffrey gave a soft shrug. "Tell me what you thought of the Uffizi."

"Are you going to tell me how you feel?"

"No. That's not why I'm here." Jeffrey paused. *I'm not really sure why I'm here, except it feels very right, but I am quite certain that I'm not here to talk to you about Julia.* He added quietly, "Besides, Diana, you know how I feel."

At midnight when Jeffrey kissed her at the door of her suite Diana didn't pull away as she had in London, except to pull him inside the elegant

353

room. Because it was the next life, wasn't it?

Diana trembled at Jeffrey's touch and at her own fears. Was she strong enough for this? She was freshly strong, almost whole again, but still quite vulnerable. And Jeffrey was just-wounded and so very vulnerable, too.

And they were both so lonely.

Jeffrey held her beautiful face in his hands and looked into her eyes with an expression that gently reminded her what it was that was so special about them, how honest they were with each other, how much they trusted each other.

"What are you thinking, Diana?"

"That you're a lonely man and I'm a lonely lady."

"What else?"

"That this has disaster written all over it."

"It does? Even if we're very careful with each other?"

"Probably." Diana gave a soft laugh. "Probably."

The soft laugh came with a sudden rush that carried a light message. *Don't be so drearily serious and analytical about everything!*

"Are you any good at making love, Anchor?" she teased, suddenly playful, lightening the mood, causing a sparkle in his dark eyes.

"Do you want to find out, Doctor?"

"Yes!"

They began their loving, their discovery of the only parts of each other that they didn't already know, with smiling eyes and a soft chorus of laughter and gentle teasing whispers that cloaked their fears and awkwardness in a safe, warm cape.

"You're very beautiful, you know."

"I don't know, but thank you. You're very handsome. But, of course, you know."

"I do?"

"Don't you?"

"Don't *you?*"

Their loving began with smiles and teases and laughter. As they discovered each other and felt the hot rushes of desire, the smiling eyes smiled still but flickered with new messages and the whispers became more tender and less teasing and the soft laughs came from feelings of joy not from words. And their loving was warm still and not awkward, but it was no longer safe.

As the teases faded, because they had to, the emotions that replaced them were very dangerous. Because now when Jeffrey whispered, "So beautiful, Diana, so very beautiful," he wasn't whispering about her sapphire eyes or her sensuous lips or the surprising softness of her lovely body. Now when he told her she was beautiful, he was whispering about the way his heart felt about hers.


"You're invited, you know."

"Invited?"

"To float around the Mediterranean with me."

"I really just planned to wish you bon voyage."

"And you've done it magnificently." Diana started to add something but stopped.

"Speak."

"Well. You wouldn't be intruding at all, not at all, but I know that you may want to be alone, so . . ."

"So I accept your gracious invitation."

"You do? I'm so glad."


"May I help you?"

"Oh, yes, thank you. I was looking for Patrick."

"About halfway down this row of stalls there's a

dark-green door on the left. He's probably in there."

"Thank you."

Julia had checked the stable office and riding ring and finally wandered into the stable itself where she found a helpful groom. She walked along the wide brick walkway between stalls and knocked when she found the dark-green door on the left halfway down.

"It's open!"

"Oh!" Julia exclaimed as she opened the door and realized that it opened not into another office, a tackroom, or an employees' lounge but into Patrick's private apartment.

"Julia." Patrick was as startled as she. He had expected one of the stablehands, perhaps the Club's manager, but not a Club member, not Julia. "Please come in."

The apartment was small and windowless. The door from the outside opened directly into the combination living room and kitchenette. The rest of the apartment, the bedroom and bath, was behind two closed doors.

The windowless apartment would have been dark and dreary, but it had been transformed into a painter's studio, a bright, cheerful clutter of pencils and brushes, watercolors and oils, sketches and paintings.

As soon as Julia was inside, Patrick moved to sweep a still-damp painting off the small couch and gestured for her to be seated. But Julia didn't sit. She stood awkwardly, suddenly very uncertain.

"How are you?" he asked. Patrick hadn't seen her for over two weeks, not since the day she brought the cookies. Amanda, but not Merry or Julia, had been at the lesson the following afternoon, and the next Tuesday Paige Spencer had called to cancel the girls' riding lessons indefinitely.

"Fine, thank you."

"Would you like some coffee?"

"No, well, yes, if it's easy."

"Very easy. Milk? Sugar?"

"A little milk."

While Patrick poured two mugs from a pot on the linoleum counter that separated the living room from the kitchen, Julia looked at the paintings.

"These are wonderful, Patrick."

"Thank you. Here's your coffee."

"Oh, thank you. Do you sell them?"

"No."

"What then?"

"When I run out of wall space I throw the oldest ones away."

Patrick kept no souvenirs of his life. He had kept souvenirs once, in a gardener's cottage in Kentucky, but he had been forced to leave those mementos behind and had kept none since. There hadn't been memories in the past five years that he had wanted to preserve anyway.

Except one. And on the easel in his bedroom Patrick was painstakingly painting her portrait, trying to, even though the one memory he chose to preserve was the most tormenting memory of all.

"Why do you paint?"

"It's very peaceful for me."

Julia answered with a wistful smile, as if she understood, as if she, too, had once known about peace.

"Do you think you could paint a pastel dragon, Patrick?"

"A pastel dragon?" Patrick echoed softly as he looked at her so-serious lavender eyes. Her startling question was obviously very important to her. "Maybe. What pastel?"

"Well, all shades, depending on her mood."

"Her?"

"Her name is Daphne." Julia's creamy cheeks flushed a lovely pastel, the palest of pinks.

"What does she look like aside from being a dragon of many colors?"

"I guess she looks friendly and gentle. She's a character in Merry's favorite stories and I thought it would be nice for Merry to have a picture of her. If that was something you would want to do? I'd pay you, of course."

"That wouldn't be necessary. You want me to make an enlargement from a picture in a book?"

"No. There aren't any pictures, just descriptions."

"I should read those then. Can you show them to me?"

"If you will allow me to pay you."

"I will allow you to pay me with chocolate-chip cookies." Patrick held up his hand to stop her protest. "I mean it. That's the deal."

"All right."

"Good. I guess I should read about Daphne."

"I could bring one of the stories by tomorrow. When is convenient for you?"

"This is a good time."

"Tomorrow, then, at ten?"

"That would be fine."

Julia left then as quietly and mysteriously as she had arrived and without ever touching her coffee or sitting on the couch or telling him why she had come.

*She didn't come because she knew I was an artist. She came for another reason. Perhaps to talk?* Patrick hoped that was the reason, that Julia had remembered his offer and decided to accept it.

*She is like a fragile bird,* Patrick mused after she

left. *She knows I am extending my hand to her, offering her much-needed sustenance, but she is so wary, so afraid.*

It might take a very long time to earn Julia's trust, Patrick knew, but he was infinitely patient. *I will extend my hand to you, Julia, and I will hold it very still so that you will not be frightened.*


"Here is a description of Daphne," Julia told him the next morning. She had turned to page four of the first story she had written about Daphne. The story was printed in large bold letters—"Large enough for my old eyes to read to my great-granddaughter," Grandmère had announced gaily when she bought the word processor and printer for Julia—and bound in a pink notebook.

Patrick tried to read the passage Julia pointed out to him on the page, but it was impossible. He couldn't fully concentrate with her watching anxiously and, besides, there were questions he wanted to ask.

"What is this, Julia?"

"The story."

"Where did you get it?"

"I wrote it. It's one of Merry's favorites. She's almost too grown up for it now, but Daphne is an old friend." Julia thought sadly, *And Merry needs her old friends—the gentle dragons, the frolicking serpents, the magical unicorns, and the fairy princesses.*

"Could you leave the story with me overnight, Julia? I think it would be best for me to read all of it."


When Julia returned at ten the following morning Patrick was almost done with the sketch of Daphne. He had read Julia's wonderful story over and over, learning about Daphne and the other magical characters. Then he had taken a long walk and allowed his mind to fill with images of Julia's characters and of the enchanted land where they lived.

He had returned to his apartment after midnight and had then begun to put to paper the image his mind had seen of the shy but friendly and gentle dragon.

"Oh, Patrick. This is what Daphne looks like, isn't it?"

"I think so. I was just going to give her a little color. I think her expression is happy, so—daffodil yellow?"

"Yes. Should I come back later?"

"No. This won't take long. Pour yourself some coffee and pull up a chair."

"It won't bother you if I watch?"

"Not at all," Patrick answered confidently because he didn't want her to leave. But he didn't know. His painting had always been solitary and private.

But Julia Lawrence, the fragile sparrow, did not invade his privacy. Patrick painted and she watched, and finally it was Patrick who broke the peaceful silence.

"I wondered if you would like me to illustrate the entire story. I have in my mind what Andrew looks like, and Robert and Cecily and the castle. Of course I may be all wrong."

"You weren't wrong about Daphne."

"Well. We could work together. You could tell me if you agree with the images I've painted."

"That would be so much work for you."

"I told you, Julia. Painting is very peaceful for

me. It's really not work. I loved your story. Are there others?"

"Stacks and stacks."

"I'd like to read those, too. Tomorrow, when you come, you can bring more. After I've illustrated this story, if you like the result, I can do others."

"Oh, Patrick, Merry will be so thrilled."

"How is Merry, Julia? Is she all right?"

Julia hesitated. Merry wasn't all right. Merry's optimism that Jeffrey would return had faded into quiet despair. The optimism had only survived a week because the next week, the week after Jeffrey returned from London but not to them, another network journalist gave the news on *The World This Evening* because the famous anchor was away on a well-deserved vacation. Jeffrey's vacation with Merry and Julia hadn't happened, but two weeks later he was on vacation without them.

"This is a difficult time for Merry, Patrick. Jeffrey and I aren't together anymore."

"A difficult time for both of you."

"Yes."

# Chapter Nineteen

"Edmund?"

"Oh, good morning, Casey. Please come in."

Casey walked across the plush carpeting of Edmund's office to the desk where he was working.

"Here is the brief on the Wright case."

Casey handed a thick legal-size folder to a surprised Edmund.

"Wright? I just gave you that case on Friday afternoon."

"Yes, but it wasn't difficult. The precedents were quite straightforward."

"Assuming you spent every second of the weekend working on it." Edmund smiled warmly at the brightest new star in New York legal circles. "I'm not complaining, of course, Casey, but sleep *is* permitted, and once in a while even a little free time."

"I know." Casey returned the smile and wished that it had been a confident smile of success and energy from the old Casey. But the old Casey had yet to reappear. Where was she? Where was the Casey who relished the challenging games and

362

basked in the golden triumphs? Where was the perfectly disciplined actress whose every word, every smile, every move was calculated for dazzling success? Where was the Casey with the heart of ice? The abilities of the old Casey reappeared, of course, because they belonged to both Caseys, and even though it was only mid-October and she had received word that she passed the Bar just a week ago, Casey was known already among Spencer and Quinn's most valued clients. She was terribly successful, terribly busy, and terribly unhappy.

"Is everything going all right, Casey?"

"Everything's going just fine, Edmund, thank you. I thrive on being busy." *And I permitted myself a little free time once and the emptiness now is greater than had I never allowed it.*

"OK." Edmund wasn't confident that Casey was thriving, although she was succeeding beyond even his greatest expectations. She seemed tense and strained, but he had never actually worked with her before and perhaps this was usual. Besides, in the past few months Paige and Edmund, who had always believed themselves to be in touch with the emotions and sensitivities of others, especially their friends, had spent long, bewildered hours wondering how they had apparently witnessed the disintegration of two marriages, the marriages of their four closest friends, and been so unaware of the trouble in what appeared to have been paradise. Edmund's mind drifted to the most recent bewildering break-up, and, remembering that Casey and Julia had known each other since high school, asked, "Have you spoken to Julia, Casey?"

"To Julia? No."

"Neither have we. Not for weeks. Paige has tried, of course, but Julia has withdrawn com-

363

pletely and even Merry and Amanda only see each other at school now."

"Edmund, I'm sorry. Obviously something has happened to Julia, but I don't know what it is."

"You have been working every second, haven't you?"

One had to make a concerted effort to avoid reading or hearing about the separation of Jeffrey and Julia Lawrence and the love affair between Jeffrey and Diana Shepherd. Such an effort necessarily included avoiding *W, Vanity Fair, People,* the society pages of *The New York Times,* the popular Manhattan insider's television show *Viveca's View,* and *The World This Evening,* because even the most unobservant of viewers could not help but notice the Mediterranean tan where once there had been elegant gold. The nation's leading newsman was news, and his alliance with the beautiful Queen of Hearts made it all the more titillating. Jeffrey and Diana avoided the limelight, but there were necessary appearances at charity dinners, and last weekend Manhattan's newest glittering couple had been together at the annual benefit for the Heart Institute.

Everyone knew about Jeffrey Lawrence and Diana Shepherd—except Casey. Her determined effort to be so absorbed in her work that she shut everything else out had clearly succeeded.

"Jeffrey and Julia are no longer together," Edmund clarified.

"What?"

"Apparently Jeffrey fell in love with Diana Shepherd."

"But he was so much in love with Julia!"

"Paige and I thought so, too."

"I can't believe it."

"But it's true." Edmund added quietly, "And, of course, Julia is devastated."

"Are they getting divorced?"

"I've spoken to both of them, and each seems to assume so, but neither has filed."

"Will it be a battle?"

"I can't imagine that it will. Belvedere already belongs to Julia so it would simply be a matter of dividing the remainder of the fortune and making custody and child-support provisions."

"Belvedere is Julia's?" Casey asked with surprise.

"Yes. The estate was left to her by Jeffrey's grandmother." Edmund paused, gave a soft sigh, and added solemnly, "I'm hoping it won't come to divorce. But if it does, for Julia's sake everything needs to be handled very quietly and very discreetly."

"By you."

"Or by you, Casey. It just needs to be done by someone who knows Julia and cares about her and will make absolutely certain that she doesn't get hurt any more than she already has been."


When Casey returned from Edmund's office to her own, she saw a familiar face waiting in the reception area.

"Mr. Tyler." Casey greeted him calmly even though her heart raced. John Tyler was a private detective. His services were used often by Spencer and Quinn. Casey had already involved him in two of her cases, but she knew he was here today on a project for which he was billing her directly. "Please come in."

*Find out everything you can about Patrick James,* Casey had told John Tyler a week ago.

John had predicted it would take about a week, and now he was here, precisely a week later, to give her a detailed report of Patrick's life.

"I have nothing for you," John said when they were in Casey's office and the door was closed.

"I don't understand. You couldn't find a way to talk to the manager at the Club without revealing why?" That had been a stipulation. No one was to know the real reason for the inquiries.

"Sure I could. It was very simple. One phone call. I said I was double-checking a reference Patrick James had given for a line of credit. When I started to give the social security number he had allegedly given—mine, by the way—I was told they had no social security number for him. Apparently he's not a full-time employee. He just gets paid in cash for services rendered. I gather it's a fairly small amount of money, probably a yearly amount well below the poverty level. I asked for names of previous employers, again implying that I was simply double-checking what he had given me, and they have nothing."

"Did you research other sources?"

"Of course. I ran Patrick James and James Patrick through the usual lists and came up empty. It's probably a new name. Your man is in hiding, Ms. English, and may have been for a very long time."

"In hiding?"

"That would be my best guess."

"So, that's it? There's nothing more you can do?"

"Sure there's more, but I wanted to check with you first. The manager said that Patrick does some bartending. I have a tux for my more upper-crust undercover work. I can make a two-minute

366

appearance the next time Patrick is bartending and get a very nice set of prints from a crystal glass."

"Prints?"

"Admittedly a bit of a long shot. However, in the past few years there have been major attempts to get fingerprints of wanted criminals into centralized computer systems, so if he's committed a crime recently we may get lucky."

"A crime?"

"Well, I suppose he could have been printed—as I'm sure you were—when he became an assistant D.A. somewhere, but somehow I don't think that's likely."

"Let me think about it," Casey murmured, although it required no thought. Patrick was not a criminal!

"Sure. You know how to reach me."

After John Tyler left, Casey thought about what had prompted her investigation of Patrick. She could not believe that their love had been an illusion. It just couldn't have been! Patrick's cruelty that morning in the stable had been so unlike him . . . and so desperate.

The more Casey thought about it, the more she decided that Patrick had ended their love because of whatever it was he had been planning to tell her over candlelight and champagne at Chez Claude. Casey had known that whatever it was, it had worried him before he knew the truth about her. What if, once he learned that she was rich and successful, he had decided that his secret would matter too much to her?

Casey had wanted to discover his secret so that she could go to him and tell him she knew it and it didn't matter and that she loved him. Now she would never learn Patrick's secret unless he told her. But she would go to him still, because she had to, and tell him of her love.

*I'll go to Southampton tomorrow,* Casey decided. *I owe myself a little free time. I'll go to Southampton and see Patrick. And then, when Patrick and I are together again, and before I return to the city, I will visit Julia at Belvedere to see if there is anything I can do to help.*


"I didn't care if I fell into the sea that day, Patrick."

For a fraction of a second the paintbrush in Patrick's hand was suspended in midair, so startled was he by Julia's stunning admission, but he forced himself to continue painting calmly because he didn't want to drive her into hiding with his full attention.

Julia had been in his small apartment almost every weekday morning for the past three weeks. She watched him paint the magical characters from her wonderful fairy tales and at his gentle urging talked a little about her childhood. Julia told him the facts of her life, without the emotions, but Patrick heard enough to realize how alike they were.

He and Julia were both orphans. They had raised themselves, providing their own gentleness and nurturing. Patrick had survived his harsh childhood by filling his gray world with colorful visions, and Julia had survived hers by creating enchanted kingdoms populated by friendly serpents and kind dragons. Gentle images and lovely fantasies had sustained Patrick and Julia as children. Perhaps that was why, when they were older, they actually believed they could live their dreams.

368

But Patrick and Julia, refugees from a world of hopelessness and poverty, were imposters in the world of the very wealthy even though that was where their dreams lived. And even though each had come so close to living the dreams, both had ultimately failed. The impertinent orphans had dared to reach for the fiery brilliance of their dreams . . . and each had been badly burned for the presumptuousness.

Julia had told Patrick the skeleton of her life, the bones without the heart, even though her silences and the anguish in her lavender eyes spoke eloquently of her deep sadness. And now the timid bird was trusting him with a most important truth.

"You didn't care, Julia?" Patrick echoed quietly, painting still.

"No. In a way I thought it would be better."

"For who?"

"For Merry."

"It wouldn't have been better for Merry, Julia." Patrick put down his paintbrush then and turned to her. He waited until she was looking into his eyes. "And it wouldn't have been better for me."

"Oh!" Julia's cheeks flushed. "Thank you, Patrick."

"You had to fight very hard to keep yourself from falling into the sea that day, Julia. If you had wanted to fall it would have been quite easy. Something made you hold your ground against the power of the wind and the lure of the sea."

"Something," Julia repeated quietly.

"I think you love Merry too much ever to leave her." Patrick paused. Then he took a chance, moving closer to her with his words, hoping she wouldn't back away. "And maybe you hope that

369

Jeffrey will return."

Julia didn't retreat. She only smiled a lovely wistful smile.

"That will never happen."

"No?"

"No." Julia looked bravely into his eyes. "Have you ever been in love?"

"Yes. Once. The woman I fell in love with wasn't who I thought she was."

"I guess that's what happened to me, too."

"But you still love him, don't you, Julia? Despite what he has done."

"Yes." Julia tilted her head and asked softly, "Do you still love her, Patrick?"

"Yes. I still do."

Casey parked her Mercedes sport coupe in the visitors' parking lot at the Southampton Club. She knew the way to the stable through the forest from the sea, the path she had taken the morning after the party, and now she got directions from a gardener. When she reached the cobblestone courtyard, one of the grooms directed her to Patrick's apartment.

Casey was about to knock when she heard voices close to the door—Patrick's voice and a softer one. Casey withdrew into an empty stall a few feet away and waited. Her heart had been racing all morning and she had filled her mind with hope and confidence, but now she felt an ominous sense of dread.

Patrick had found someone new.

*But you will remind him of your wonderful love,* Casey told herself bravely. *And whoever she is, Patrick will still want to be with you.*

Whoever she is . . .

But *she* was Julia. Casey's ancient enemy. Julia with Patrick.

Had Julia lost Jeffrey? Or had she simply tossed him away because she found someone she wanted even more?

Yesterday, when Casey learned of the end of the love of Jeffrey and Julia, she had felt genuine sympathy and compassion for Julia's devastating loss.

But Julia had lost nothing.

As always, Julia had won.

And of all the things Casey English had wanted in her life, of all the things Julia had taken from her, Patrick's love was the only one that really mattered.

"I'll see you tomorrow, Julia." Patrick said the words every day, but today there was deeper meaning, a promise that from now on they could speak from their hearts, if they wanted to, as they had spoken today.

"Yes, Patrick," Julia echoed softly. "Tomorrow."

Casey overheard the gentle good-bye and the promise of tomorrow. And Casey saw the pale-pink flush of Julia's creamy cheeks and the inno-cent-yet-seductive lavender eyes as she gazed at Patrick.

*Julia with Patrick.* Did Patrick and Julia lie to-gether under the stars in the meadow of love above the peninsula? It was Julia's meadow, after all, an enchanted corner of Belvedere. Patrick and Casey had loved in Julia's fragrant meadow of wildflowers, but they had been trespassing there.

And now Patrick was with the meadow's rightful owner. And what did Casey own? What was her legacy of love?

371

She owned only the feelings that churned within her now, the desperate feelings of imperfection, the flawed emotions that had first surfaced over a decade ago because of Julia. Emotions that had told her then, as they reminded her now, that somehow she had to win or she would surely die a gasping, tormented death.

Patrick watched as Julia disappeared along the brick walkway, and so did Casey. As soon as Julia turned the corner, Casey emerged from the stall.

"Hello, Patrick."

"Casey." Patrick's heart responded before his brain, a response of desire and longing, but his brain lagged only a second behind, hobbling his smile, filling eyes that wanted to smile with joy with wariness instead. "Hello, Casey."

"I've been trying to find out who you are."

"You know who I am."

"I know that Patrick James doesn't exist. Why is that, Patrick? An endless line of heiresses, perhaps, with the odd husband seeking revenge?"

"Leave it alone, Casey. Please."

*I can't,* Casey realized as she looked at the man she had loved as she had never loved before, the man for whom she would have forgiven anything, *anything,* if only he loved her, too.

But Patrick didn't love her, or perhaps he had for a while until someone better had come along.

Someone better, the best . . . Julia.

*I can't leave it alone, Patrick. I can't fight the powerful feelings that are swirling inside me.*

"I hope it is a secret that will destroy." Casey's whisper was a hiss of ice borne of her ancient but evergreen hatred for Julia and her sudden hatred for Patrick.

*It is,* Patrick thought heavily as he watched her

leave. *It is a secret that will destroy, and if there is anyone in the world who can discover it, it is you, Casey. Brilliant, clever, vindictive Casey. My love, my greatest love, who is now my most bitter enemy.*

Patrick knew he should run. He had long overstayed his welcome in this peaceful haven. But now, because of Julia, he couldn't leave. Julia was so fragile, in such pain, and she needed him.

And Patrick needed Julia, too.

He needed her gentleness.

He needed her wonderful fairy tales.


Casey walked into the law offices of Spencer and Quinn at eleven.

"Casey!" Her secretary greeted her with obvious surprise. "I thought you weren't going to be in until this afternoon."

"I just couldn't stay away. Will you please reach John Tyler for me? Now?"

"Yes. Of course."

As Casey waited in her office she felt the return of the old Casey. The old Casey announced her dazzling arrival with the once-familiar rushes of power and control. The power to destroy. The control to vanquish the lingering whimpers of her broken heart.

By the time the private detective was on the line, Casey felt terrifyingly calm.

"Mr. Tyler? I want you to get the prints."


"Diana? It's Mark Hall."

"Hello, Mark." Diana looked at her bedside clock. It glowed 3:12. Three hours and twelve minutes of sleep wasn't terrible, she mused. She was the attending cardiac surgeon on call and the busy night had begun at four yesterday afternoon with an emergency case that lasted until eleven. By the time she had returned to her penthouse it had been almost midnight. Now Dr. Mark Hall, the chief resident in cardiac surgery, was calling, and that meant they needed her help with a new patient. "What do you have?"

"A knife wound to the heart."

"Still alive?"

"We cracked his chest in the E.R. and threw a few big stitches into the ventricle. He's in the O.R. now and should be on bypass soon."

"I'm on my way. And Mark . . . very impressive job."

"Thanks, Diana."


The emergency surgery on the man with the knife wound to the heart finished, successfully, at six. Diana had time to return to her penthouse for a refreshing shower and to dress for the day and still easily make the meeting of the executive committee of the Heart Institute at seven-thirty.

The shower and clean clothes gave the illusion of a morning that followed a good night's sleep. The illusion held until halfway through the meeting when Diana realized she would have to tap deep into her reserves to find the energy necessary to spar with Dr. Tom Chandler. She had to spar with Tom today, a legitimate battle, because they honestly disagreed about the staffing for Memorial's soon to be inaugurated helicopter transport service for emergency heart cases.

* * *

374

"Long night?" her secretary asked when Diana arrived at her office at nine.

"Not as long as the meeting." Diana gave a wry smile. "How is it so far today?"

"Quiet. Something did come up yesterday after you left for the O.R."

"Oh?"

"A man called from California to schedule an appointment with you. He wouldn't give me details except to say it was important and he wanted to see you as soon as possible. He'll be here at four today."

"OK. What's his name?"

"Sam Hunter."

"Sam Hunter?" Diana echoed softly.

"He said he was in high school with you in Dallas. Does that mean he's the same Sam Hunter who's the singer?"

"Yes," Diana answered quietly, marveling at the deceptive calm in her voice. Her heart wasn't calm — it had begun to race, an ancient reflex, when she heard his name — and unanswerable questions were already thundering in her mind. "He'll be here at four today?"

"Assuming his plane is on time."

Without another word Diana retreated to her office and privacy for her swirling thoughts.

Sam. Here. Today. *Why?* Had he read the cover story in *Time* and the notice in Milestones about her dissolved marriage? Was Sam coming to tell her, after all these years, that he should never have left her? The paragraph Diana had read about Sam in the same issue had mentioned no wife, no family, no personal details at all. What if Sam was free and was coming to see her because she was

375

free now, too?

But Diana wasn't free. Jeffrey was in her life and in her heart. Jeffrey, her wonderful lover and friend. Jeffrey, with whom there was honesty and trust that had never existed before for either in their other loves. Jeffrey, with whom she had shared all her secrets, including the secret truth that Sam Hunter lived in her heart still and always would.

"Jeffrey Lawrence." Jeffrey answered the private line in his office on the third ring.

"Good morning."

"Hi." His voice softened. "How was your night?"

"A little busy."

"Meaning no sleep."

"No. I slept from midnight until three."

"Would you like to cancel dinner tonight?"

"Jeffrey, are you responsible for my four o'clock appointment?"

"What?"

"I'm scheduled to see Sam today at four."

"Sam? No, I'm not responsible, honey. Why is he coming to see you?"

"I don't know. He didn't give any details when he made the appointment."

"Are you OK?"

"I'm apprehensive. And," she sighed softly, "it would be nice to be facing this after a good night's sleep."

"You'll do fine."

"Whatever that is."

"I'm here, Diana."

"And you're willing to let the nation watch reruns of the news in case I need you just as you're about to broadcast?"

"I am absolutely willing to do that."

# Chapter Twenty

His thick brown hair had a few threads of white at the temples and the years had put tiny wrinkles beside his eyes and age had made him even more handsome, but he was Sam. His dark eyes were sensitive still and no more confident than they had ever been despite his success. His smile was uncertain, too, as it always had been . . . and so gentle.

He was Sam and she loved him still.

*He didn't want you!* Diana reminded herself as she smiled bravely at his dark eyes. *He didn't want you and he isn't here today to tell you that he wants you now.* Diana saw warmth in Sam's dark eyes, a sparkle of friendship, but not the silent messages of love that had always made her tremble—as she was trembling now, even though the messages were no longer there. Diana hoped Sam couldn't tell and hoped that her eyes, like his, only sparkled with friendship and didn't betray her love.

Sam fought the powerful feelings of love that swept through him as bravely and as successfully as Diana did.

His precious Diana. When he had first met Diana, her sapphire eyes had glowed with happiness and the confident knowledge that life was good, wonderful, bountiful. The grim truths of his life had put bewildered sadness in the lovely sapphire, and he saw sadness still, as if there had been other sadnesses in Diana's life even though he had prayed there would be no more.

How he wanted to whisper words of love to her! But he had sung such words of love to her for years. And by the time he could sing songs that promised a safe forever for their love, it was too late for them. Perhaps she had heard, and felt a wistful sadness that it had happened after all, but too late . . . or perhaps by then she had stopped listening, because she had found another love and no longer cared. Whatever the reason, Diana's silence had given him his answer.

*She didn't want you!*

Sam would never have seen Diana again except that now something, someone, mattered more than his broken heart.

"Hello, Diana."

"Hello, Sam. Please come in."

Her heart raced as she led the way to the conversation area in her huge office overlooking Manhattan.

"How are you?" Sam asked as soon as they were seated.

"I'm good, Sam. How are you? Very successful, I know."

"So are you. I didn't realize . . . I imagined you

379

in a pediatric practice in Texas. Then I saw the article in *Time*."

"Plans change." Diana shrugged. "Are you in town for a concert?"

"No, I'm here to see you."

"Oh?"

"Diana, my daughter needs heart surgery."

"Your daughter?" *You had a little girl, Sam, who needed heart surgery.*

"Yes." Sam removed several folders from the briefcase he had with him. "I brought all her medical records, Xrays, the cath report, and a copy of the cineangiogram. She's six months old. She was born with a ventricular septal defect. The doctors thought the VSD would get smaller as she grew and that it would only need to be corrected if it hadn't completely closed by the time she was six or seven. She was doing well until about three weeks ago. Now she's in congestive heart failure and the doctors at UCLA think she needs surgery very soon. Her heart surgeon there is Dr. Anthony Jones. He says he knows you."

*Yes, I know Tony. He is one of the men I slept with in those years when I was desperately trying to forget about you. One of the men with whom the relationship might have been love, but it faltered because of memories of you, and I never even told him why.*

"Tony is a superb pediatric heart surgeon. I'll be happy to provide a second opinion, Sam, but if Tony thinks she needs surgery soon, I imagine that I will agree."

"I'm not here for a second opinion, Diana. I'm here to ask you to do the surgery. There is no one on earth I trust more than you to take

380

care of Janie."

*Janie.* Diana stood up abruptly and walked to the window. Her eyes filled with tears as she stared at the snarl of rush-hour traffic below. *I tried to take care of your other daughter, Sam—our Janie—but I couldn't save her.*

"Diana?"

Diana couldn't turn around, not yet. She shifted to a topic that would stop her tears, a reminder that Sam had chosen to make a life and have a baby with another woman.

"Does your wife want the surgery done here rather than in Los Angeles?" *Does your wife know about us? Or was it such ancient history, such insignificant history, that you didn't even share it? Perhaps Sam had simply said, "Diana and I knew each other in high school. She's very bright and she loves children."*

"I don't have a wife. Janie's mother was Roxanne."

"Roxanne?"

"The British rock star," Sam replied, a little surprised. Surely Diana, who knew and loved music, would know the songs and career of the famous Roxanne. "She and I were together for about a year. Our relationship was already falling apart when she became pregnant. Roxanne didn't want to have the baby—and wouldn't have wanted to even if everything was fine between us—but I insisted."

"Roxanne obviously agreed or she would have done something about it."

"I paid her to agree. I essentially bought my own baby. It's hard to imagine that money would have mattered to Roxanne, but her drug habit con-

381

sumed every penny she earned. We agreed on ten million dollars to be paid after the baby was born, and I would get sole custody. The other stipulation, of course, was that she had to be drug-free for the balance of the pregnancy. For five and a half months, from the time I learned she was pregnant until Janie was born, Roxanne lived in an exclusive drug rehabilitation facility outside of London. I was there every day, and I always accompanied her when she went to the recording studio in London. I know she didn't use drugs during those months, except medications in the beginning that the doctors had to give her to treat the withdrawal, but I've wondered if the drugs she used in the first trimester might have caused Janie's septal defect."

Perhaps the drugs Roxanne had taken were responsible, or perhaps not. Perhaps, Diana thought sadly, it was simply Sam's destiny to have daughters with heart defects. Destiny, not genetics, because neither the anomaly in their precious Janie nor the septal defect that afflicted the little girl for whom Sam's voice filled with such love was hereditary. Both were fate, not genes, and there was a major difference between the two. The heart that had been given to the infant daughter of Sam and Diana was a heart that could not survive with what medical science could offer then. But the heart that had been created by Sam and Roxanne, if successfully corrected, would live to laugh and sing and fall in love.

After a moment Diana turned back to Sam, stronger now and tear-free, and said, "I don't know if it was the drugs, Sam. Septal defects just occur, often without any identifiable risk factors at all."

"That's what Tony said, too."

"Was Roxanne able to just give Janie up when she was born?"

"Without a backward glance."

"Is that why you left England, though? In case she changed her mind?"

"I guess that's partly the reason. I'd been thinking for quite a while about coming home."

"And now you're home with Janie and Roxanne hasn't followed you?"

Sam frowned briefly, a frown of surprise not of pain.

"Roxanne died of a drug overdose a month after Janie was born."

"Oh."

*Janie has no mother.* They both had the same thought at the same moment. The thought was filled with longing and pain and it brought those emotions close to the surface of their eyes as they looked at each other. Too close, too painful.

"Does Tony think Janie can travel safely?"

"On a nonstop flight, with oxygen available, yes."

"How soon was he planning to operate?"

"In three days, on Friday."

The more Diana heard, the more critical Janie sounded. Her condition was fragile, a delicate balance between the small heart that pumped valiantly but inefficiently and the medications she was being given. It meant that the surgery was riskier, the operative mortality even higher. Many septal repairs were almost elective—as they had hoped Janie's would be—but the surgery on a six-month-old in congestive heart failure was not elective. It was necessary and urgent, life-saving or life-ending.

"I need to review the records and speak with Tony."

"Of course." Sam stood up to leave. He didn't ask Diana when she would reach her decision—he didn't want to push her—but she saw the question in the dark eyes that obviously loved his infant daughter so much.

"Where are you staying, Sam?"

"Nowhere. I came directly from the airport. I was planning to fly back tonight unless . . ."

"Unless?"

"You need me."

*Oh, Sam, how I have needed you.*

"No. Why don't I call you tomorrow morning in Los Angeles? Eight o'clock your time?"

"That would be fine. Let me give you my telephone number at home."

Diana was in Jeffrey's office when he finished the evening broadcast. She sat on the couch, head bent, lost in thought.

"I've been worrying about you."

Diana looked up at the sound of his voice. "Jeffrey."

"Tell me." He closed his office door and sat beside her.

"Sam has a six-month-old daughter with a heart defect that needs almost immediate repair. Jeffrey, her name is Janie and Sam wants me to do the surgery."

"Oh, Diana. Do you know what you're going to do?" Jeffrey asked the question carefully, without prejudice, but he thought firmly, *You are not going to do this.*

"Not yet. I have to think about it. Can we do dinner another time?"

"Sure. Diana, I'm here to help if I can."

"You do help, Jeffrey."

Diana reached her decision at midnight. For hours her mind had spun with questions that had no answers.

Her brilliant mind could not arrive at the right answer. But her heart could. It was a confident answer and it came with a calm and clarity that matched the sparkling clear October sky.

It was the right answer, even her mind agreed, but her cautious mind offered a safety net, if he was willing.

"Hello, Diana. Do you have a case this morning?" Tom Chandler did not recall having seen her name on today's O.R. schedule, but it was six-thirty A.M. and she was in the surgeon's lounge.

"No. I came to talk to you. To ask a favor of you."

"OK." The "OK" meant "OK, ask" not "OK, I'll do it," whatever it is." Tom guessed it was something he would not want to do, a taunt of some sort, although he had never seen her sapphire eyes so serious or so unarmed.

"I'd like you to do a case with me, Tom. The patient is a six-month-old girl with a VSD. She's in failure, fairly well controlled for the moment with meds, but the surgery is semiemergent. I'd like to operate on Friday, but if that's not good for you we could schedule for the weekend or early next week."

"I can check, but I think Friday would be fine. Diana, what am I missing? Obviously I will review her records and examine her, but give me a clue. What's the worry?"

"It's not the surgery that worries me, Tom, it's the surgeon. I'm personally involved, enough involved that I can't say no but maybe too involved to really be objective about how I'll handle my emotions in the O.R."

"I didn't think you permitted emotions in the O.R., Diana."

"I try not to, Tom, just like you, but I may not be able to keep them out this time."

Tom stared at her in stunned silence. It was astonishing enough that Diana Shepherd was admitting to a possible chink in her magnificent armor, but to make such an admission to him was extraordinary.

"What would you like me to do, Diana?"

"Watch me. Take over if you think I'm not doing everything perfectly."

"You've done hundreds of septal repairs. You are regarded as one of the top pediatric heart surgeons in the world."

"So are you, Tom."

"Why me, Diana? You have a team of skilled surgeons."

"Because I know you won't cut me a millimeter of slack. And I'm counting on that."

Tom listened to her words and felt the effect of their meaning: *I'm counting on you, Tom. I'm trusting you.*

"OK, Diana," he agreed quietly. "Not a millimeter."

"You don't like the man, Diana, and I gather from what you've told me that he isn't crazy about you, either."

"But he's a wonderful surgeon, Jeffrey. He will not allow anything to happen to Janie. He may intervene too soon, but that's all right."

"You have a highly trained team of surgeons whom you trust and respect and work with every day. Why not have one of them watch you?"

"Because it's *my* team, Jeffrey. I'm the leader. I'm afraid they might hesitate to take over even if they thought I was making an error. Don't you see?"

"No, I don't."

"OK. Imagine that you had to do a live report, something so critical that even the slightest slip might cause your viewers to panic, and for whatever reason, you had doubts about your ability to find the right words. Who would you want to back you up? Correspondents from your own network who think you can do no wrong? Or an anchor from a rival network, someone like Dan?"

Jeffrey sighed softly. He couldn't fault the logic. His own "team" had taken over a week before gently suggesting that the viewers were a "little worried" about him and before almost apologetically informing him of their decision to keep the cameras off his ringless finger. Jeffrey's team had known he was in trouble, but they had covered for him, protecting him, not wanting to offend.

"The trouble is, Diana, that nothing I do, no

387

matter what scenario you want to imagine, is ever life and death. And the surgery on Janie is."

"But with Tom as a backup . . . I may not like him, Jeffrey, but I have no doubts about his ability as a surgeon, his willingness to intervene if he doesn't like what I'm doing, and his commitment to do what is best for our patient."

"Why don't you just let Tom do the surgery, then?"

"Because I realize now that this is where my life has been leading me ever since my baby died. This is why I became a heart surgeon. And I'm good, Jeffrey, one of the best. I have to do this for Janie."

"For which Janie, darling?"

"For all the Janies in the world."


"Hello, little Janie. How are you tonight?" Diana whispered softly to the little girl in the crib in Memorial Hospital's I.C.U. The dark-brown eyes that belonged to Sam's infant daughter looked up at her and her beautiful face became a smile. "Is your breathing better? Yes? Good. Oh, you are so pretty, little one. Your daddy loves you so much. Do you know that? You do, don't you? So much. You're going to be fine, honey, just fine."

It was nine-thirty Thursday night. Janie had arrived at three. Her breathing was better now, quiet and calm, proof that the medications designed to remove excess fluid from her small lungs were working.

Sam was in his room across the street at the Clairmont Hotel. Diana had encouraged him to leave at eight, the end of visiting hours, even though hospital policy would have permitted him to stay with his daughter all night.

Sam needed a good night's rest. Sam did, and Janie did, and Diana did.

Diana had firmly encouraged Sam to go to the hotel. And there was someone who was going to make sure that she, too, went home to rest.

"Hi." Diana smiled when she saw Jeffrey in the corridor outside the I.C.U. He had gone to her penthouse after his broadcast, and after an hour of waiting decided to come find her.

"Hi. How is she?"

"Ready for surgery."

"How are you?"

"I'm ready, too, Jeffrey."

"After a good night's sleep."

"Are you really going to ply me with warm milk and then tuck me in and leave?" Her voice held a slight tease, but Diana wasn't trying to get Jeffrey to change his mind. For many reasons, tonight, like last night, she needed to sleep alone.

"That's exactly what I'm going to do."


*Little Janie, little Janie, little Janie.*
The words danced in her mind, defiant pirouettes in all the corners, twirling to the sound of cascading chimes. Diana's heart raced and her emotions would not be still, and today she could not keep her ghosts from the operating room.

The ancient ghosts had invaded her thoughts, but they did not banish the thoughts that were always with her—supposed to be with her!—when she operated. The ancient ghosts danced with the necessary thoughts in a dangerous and breathtak-

389

ing *pas de deux*.

Diana tried to concentrate on the familiar wonder she always felt when she operated, and on the extraordinary wonder of operating on an infant heart. There was such purity and such innocence in the tiny organ, a pristine perfection, just as infants themselves were pristine and perfect and untainted. The hearts of adults always showed the ravages of their lives, diets that were less than ideal, and tobacco and alcohol and stress. But infant hearts were pure and clean, touched only by the hope and promise of their new lives.

Hope and promise.

Hope for Janie. A promise to Sam.

*Little Janie, little Janie, little Janie.* The words whirled and the music chimed, and even though part of her was able to concentrate, Diana felt that most of her was trembling—her heart, her emotions, and surely her *hands*.

Tom needed to take over. Any second he would, wouldn't he?

In the midst of all the swirling thoughts that made her heart tremble came one that suddenly made her heart stand still.

What if she was wrong about Tom? What if there was something so evil within him, a hatred so deep that the immense pleasure of watching her fail was worth the price of Janie's life?

"Tom?"

Diana's voice broke a silence that had lasted since the operation began. It was startling enough for Diana to speak, but the edge of panic in her voice startled him even more.

"What, Diana?"

"Why haven't you taken over?"

"Because you are doing brilliantly." Tom's answer was truthful and reverent. He had heard about Diana, the magic of her slender fingers—so delicate, so skillful, so sure—but all the words of praise had been inadequate to describe her true talent.

"Are you sure? I feel like my fingers are trembling and that I'm moving in slow motion."

"I'm very sure, Diana. Your fingers aren't trembling. You're not moving in slow motion. Really. I feel like I'm watching a most beautifully choreographed ballet."

*A ballet.* Like the ballet in her mind. Except the thoughts that twirled and danced and spun and leapt weren't beautifully choreographed. Each thought danced defiantly to the music of its own chime. Surely, eventually the frolicking thoughts would collide, tripping each other and causing a disastrous fall.

"If I stumble, Tom . . ."

"I will catch you."


But Diana didn't stumble. Despite her own trembling heart and wobbly emotions, the part of her that had spent the past fifteen years of her life training for this moment never faltered. With the confident, agile fingers of the highly trained seamstress that she was, Diana delicately embroidered the tiniest of stitches into Janie's heart, sewing the Dalcron to the small, pure tissue, sealing the hole that threatened her life, making it so that Sam's precious little Janie would have a life of hope and promise.

As the anesthesiologist got Janie ready to transport for routine post-op recovery in the I.C.U., Tom and Diana retreated to a corner of the O.R. to remove their sterile gloves and gowns.

"Tom, I don't know how to thank you."

"I did nothing."

"Yes—"

"*No*. Diana, you are really a helluva surgeon."

"I owe you, Tom."

"No you don't." Tom frowned briefly then heard himself say something almost as remarkable as the surgery he had witnessed. "Maybe we each owe each other a second opinion."

"OK." Diana smiled at the man who, in her opinion, had always been hopelessly arrogant and egotistical. Tom didn't look hopelessly arrogant and egotistical now, and Diana said quietly, "I like my second opinion much better."


When Diana walked into the surgery waiting room and saw Sam, all the emotions suddenly surfaced in her sapphire eyes.

"Diana?" he asked anxiously when he saw her tears.

"She's fine, Sam," Diana reassured swiftly. "Janie's going to be fine, a healthy little girl."

"Really?" Sam's dark eyes filled with tears of joy. He started to reach for her, to hold her, but he stopped and only whispered emotionally, "Thank you."


Janie convalesced quickly. Her young body responded robustly to the sudden increased flow of well-oxygenated blood and the disappearance of the fluid from her lungs. By the end of a week she was ready to return to her home in California. The wound in her chest was a perplexing discomfort but not an obstacle to soft squeals of joy whenever she saw her father and not an obstacle to being cuddled in Sam's loving arms.

Janie's dark-brown eyes lit with happiness whenever she saw Sam, or heard his voice, or sensed his presence. And, in that week, she learned to smile at the sapphire eyes and soft voice that came to see her so many times during each day and very early in the morning and late at night.

Diana saw Janie more often than she saw Sam, but she saw Sam frequently, too. frequently. She had imagined that seeing him daily and maintaining the almost stiff distance between them would desensitize her to his effect. But it didn't happen. Her heart set a new pace every time she saw him. A new pace and a painful one.

Only once in the seven days before Janie was able to return to California did the words Sam and Diana speak to each other drift even a little into the past.

"You are such a wonderful father, Sam."

"I was never sure that I would be."

"Really?" Diana asked with surprise. So many times they had talked about the children they would have and Sam hadn't seemed uncertain at all.

"Yes. I worried that some legacy of my evil father might exist within me, some poisonous gene that had been lurking in darkness." *I knew I would be a wonderful father for our children, my love, because you would be there to protect me even if there was a darkness inside me. But on my*

393

*own I wasn't sure and I was very afraid.*

"But there is no legacy of evil."

"No," Sam agreed softly. If a seed of evil or a trace of his father's poison lived within him, that darkness had been conquered by his immense love for his infant daughter. "No, there isn't."

That week their words only drifted once into the past, a brief allusion to Sam's violent father but not even a whisper about their gentle love. As if there had never been a love at all.

And then it was time to say good-bye.

"Good-bye, little Janie," Diana whispered softly to the smiling brown eyes that were snuggled so safely in Sam's arms. After a moment she looked up and said quietly, "Good-bye, Sam."

Then Sam was gone and Diana felt a great sense of loss but an almost greater sense of relief. Now, perhaps, the heart that Sam had owned for the past fifteen years would be hers again, hers to have and hers to give away.

In time, when they both were ready, Diana would give her heart to her wonderful Jeffrey.

*Her wonderful Jeffrey.* During the week that Sam and Janie were in New York, Jeffrey had stayed close enough to support her and love her and listen to her when she needed him, but he had stayed far enough away—not intruding and never demanding—to give Diana a chance to find love again with Sam if that was meant to be.

And if she and Sam had rediscovered their love?

Jeffrey would have been happy for her. Her wonderful friend and lover would have been sad-dened at the loss of their closeness and trust and love, but Jeffrey would have been happy for her.

Just as, even though she would miss him terribly, Diana would be happy for Jeffrey if he could find a way back to his love with Julia.

## Chapter Twenty-one

Casey discovered Patrick's true identity on Thanksgiving Day. John Tyler had gotten Patrick's fingerprints without difficulty—a brief tuxedoed appearance at a wedding reception at the Club in late October—but the prints were a "no match" with the hundreds of thousands on file.

But Casey didn't give up. Driven by the tireless energy of revenge against Patrick *and* Julia, she pursued the only other possible clue: Patrick's extraordinary ability to ride. Casey obtained old issues of *Horse, Show Jumping, Equestrian,* and *Grand Prix,* going back five years and then ten. Her luxury apartment was cluttered with stacks of the equestrian magazines and she spent countless hours going through each magazine, peering at small photographs of champion riders with faces frustratingly shadowed by caps.

Casey's countless, determined, disciplined hours finally paid off.

The photograph, taken eight years before when he had just been crowned Grand Prix Rookie of the Year, was shadowy, but it was definitely of Patrick.

Casey looked at the picture of the young champion and felt a rush of happiness for the obviously pleased and triumphant Patrick.

*Happiness for Patrick's triumph? Not happiness at your own triumphant discovery? Now you know his real name and can find out his secret! Now you can destroy him!*

*Leave it alone, Casey. Please.* It had been a quiet plea and there had been fear in his fearless gray-green eyes.

Casey hadn't left it alone, but now, as she held the key to Patrick's destruction, her heart made the same gentle plea. *Leave it alone.*

Casey heeded the whispers of her heart for ten days, but it was a battle that her heart ultimately could not win. Her need for revenge against Patrick *and* Julia was too powerful. The gentle whispers of her broken heart could not stop the inevitable course that had been set in motion the moment she saw her ancient enemy's innocent-but-so-seductive lavender eyes smiling at Patrick.

On December fourth Casey hired a new private detective, not John Tyler, and instructed him to find everything he could about James Patrick Jones.


"She is absolutely shameless," Addy Hamilton observed haughtily.

"A lady would be discreet," Danielle Montgomery concurred with matching disdain.

"No one has ever accused Julia Lawrence of being a lady."

"What are you saying about Julia?"

"Oh! Paige. I didn't realize you were here."

"Here" was Emily's, Southampton's charming and expensive gift shop. The shelves at Emily's were cluttered with the usual gifts of crystal,

397

porcelain, and silver, but because it was almost Christmas, an elegant assortment of music boxes, wreaths, and ornaments had been added to the already bountiful shelves. Paige had been looking at an intricately embroidered tree skirt only one aisle away in the small store, but Addy and Danielle hadn't seen her beyond an expensive, imported, hand-carved crèche that was displayed on a top shelf.

Danielle and Addy withered a little under Paige's stern sky-blue gaze, although each had the same thought. Surely Paige and Julia, if they had ever been friends, were friends no more. The enchanted afternoons for the children of Southampton at Belvedere with Julia hadn't happened at all this school year, and now Amanda spent her afternoons playing with their daughters, not with Merry.

"I overheard you saying something about Julia," Paige repeated finally.

"Well, Paige, you might as well know. Julia has been having a rather obvious affair with the riding instructor at the Club. He has a room, a *bed,* at the stable, and Julia spends almost every weekday morning there."

"Julia and Patrick?"

"It's true, Paige."


"Paige."

"Hello, Julia. May I come in?"

"Oh, yes, of course. Has something happened to Merry?" Julia asked anxiously, surprised by Paige's unannounced arrival at Belvedere and then concerned as she saw the sympathetic worry on her face. Julia had just returned from the stable.

What if someone from Southampton Country Day had tried to reach her and called Paige when they couldn't find her?

"No, Julia," Paige reassured her quickly. "I just wanted to talk to you. How are you?"

"Fine."

"Good." Paige smiled warmly but she thought, *You don't look fine, Julia.* She looked fragile. Beautiful, of course, but very fragile. What if Patrick, the sensuous and menacing panther, was taking advantage of beautiful Julia's fragility and loneliness? "Julia, I heard today that you've been seeing Patrick."

It took Julia a moment to understand what Paige was saying. When she did, she was astonished. Paige, and apparently others in Southampton, believed she was having an affair with Patrick! Believed it and condemned it.

"Is there something wrong with Patrick, Paige?" Julia's eyes blazed with sudden anger. "I can't believe the small-mindedness of this place! It's wonderful, *lovely*, that Jeffrey Lawrence left me and his daughter for the magnificent Queen of Hearts! But when I become friends with the riding instructor—who, by the way, they all want—suddenly the patrician glowers begin. What Jeffrey did was wonderful and what Patrick and I are doing is . . . I don't believe Patrick James would leave his wife and child for another woman. It was Jeffrey who broke our wedding vows, Paige, not me. It was Jeffrey who broke our hearts."

"Oh, Julia."

"Do you think it's wonderful, too, Paige? Are you relieved that Jeffrey is with Diana?"

"How can you ask that?"

"Diana is your friend."

"*You* are my friend, Julia." *My dear friend whom I had always hoped to introduce to my other friend Diana because I thought you two would like each other very much.*

"Really? Did you think it was a gesture of friendship to tell me that Southampton is shocked that I spend every morning with the riding instructor? That I've *offended* the ladies? I have been hated here since the moment I arrived, Paige. I couldn't care less what they're saying about me. Being with Patrick helps me get through the day."

"Couldn't I help, too, Julia? May I go outside and ring the doorbell again and start over? I came because I've missed you and I've worried about you and Merry. If you and Patrick are lovers, more power to you. I'm going outside right now, OK? If you don't answer the doorbell I'll be sorry, but I won't blame you."

Paige was halfway across the great room when Julia's voice stopped her.

"Paige, wait." Julia gave a soft, grateful smile. "I've missed you, too. I just haven't been able to see you."

"Because of Diana?"

"In part, I guess, yes. You've seen them together, haven't you?"

"We saw them at the benefit for the Heart Institute six weeks ago, but that's the only time. We haven't seen them socially, Julia, and we're not planning to."

"But you should if you want to, Paige. You and Edmund are Jeffrey's friends—and hers. You shouldn't feel caught in the middle of this."

"We don't feel the least bit caught in the middle! Don't you know that Edmund and I are completely on your side? Yes, we consider Jeffrey and

Diana to be friends, but, Julia, you and Merry are part of our family."

"Thank you." Julia tilted her head and asked with soft amazement, "Do you really believe that Patrick and I are lovers, Paige?"

"It's none of my business."

"I can't imagine ever being with anyone but Jeffrey," Julia said quietly. *Someday,* some far away day, she would have to imagine it, wouldn't she? Or was she going to spend her entire life being faithful to a dream that had died? "Would you like to know what Patrick and I do every morning?"

"Only if you want to tell me."

"I'll show you." Julia crossed the great room to a mahogany bureau. From the bottom drawer, beneath a soft layer of linen placemats, she removed a stack of the original sketches Patrick had made of her fairy tale characters. The sketches were too large for the "books" Patrick was illustrating for Merry, but Julia was going to have them framed. "Patrick's an artist, Paige. He's illustrating some of my stories. We're trying to finish at least one by Christmas. I say 'we,' but it's really Patrick. He paints, and I watch, and we talk."

"My God," Paige breathed as she looked at the sketches. "This really is Daphne, isn't it? And Robert and Cecily and Andrew."

"I'm glad you think so. I hope Merry and Amanda will, too."

"Amanda?"

"I thought she might like one of the framed sketches. And the bookbinder I spoke to says he can make more than one copy of the stories."

"I know Amanda would love that, Julia. These are truly wonderful. You've found an artist whose

401

talent matches the magic of your imagination."

"He really is talented, isn't he?"

"Yes. Have you talked to him about getting these published?"

"Oh, no."

"Why don't you? If Patrick agrees, I have a friend who I know would love to see them."

Julia had never cared about publishing her stories, but it would be an opportunity for Patrick to share his wonderful talent and supplement his meager income.

"I *will* ask him. Thank you, Paige."

"For coming over and telling you the ladies don't approve?"

"For coming over. For not leaving when I accused you of not being my friend."

"I *am* your friend, Julia. If there was any way I could help you and Jeffrey get back together . . ."

"There isn't, Paige. It's all over but the paperwork. I keep expecting Edmund to call and tell me Jeffrey has filed for divorce."

"Jeffrey hasn't filed. Isn't that a hopeful sign?"

"It just means he's been busy."

"Julia, your marriage isn't over in the eyes of the law and it isn't over in your heart."

"But it *is* over, Paige," Julia said firmly. "I'm just so very worried about Merry."

"Amanda misses her terribly."

"I don't think Merry is ready to be with Amanda yet. I've encouraged her to see Amanda, of course. But, Paige, how can I urge Merry to be with her best friend when I've withdrawn from you?"

"This all takes time, Julia. And Merry is with her very best friend because she's with you."

"Yes, my Merry and I are best friends. We've

become even closer because of this, but I feel so helpless. She is in such pain and I can't make it better for her." Julia shook her head and added quietly, "Jeffrey never spent much time with Merry, but he was so important to her. I had no idea this would be such a loss for her."

*But I should have known because of how I felt when I lost my parents.*

"Jeffrey hasn't seen Merry at all?"

"No." Tears misted Julia's sad lavender eyes. "I don't think he ever will."

"Oh, Julia. How can I help you? I could speak with Jeffrey, or Edmund could."

"No, Paige, please promise me that you won't."

"OK. I promise." Paige shifted tack as an idea came to her. "Julia, why don't you and Merry join us for Christmas? We're going to Maui. Amanda and I are leaving on the seventeenth and Edmund will be flying out on the twenty-third. We would love to have you and Merry come with us." Paige smiled a coy, conspiratorial smile and added lightly, "And Patrick, too, of course."

"Thank you, but I don't think Merry will want to. I'm afraid that part of the reason Merry can't see Amanda is because of Edmund, because Amanda has a daddy and Merry doesn't."

"Edmund loves Merry very much. Maybe it would be helpful for her to be with him. Anyway, think about it. It might be a good change."

"I'll talk to Merry."

"Good. And Patrick really is welcome to join us."


Merry didn't want to go to Maui for Christmas with the Spencers. She didn't offer a reason and

Julia was torn between trying to get her sensitive daughter to talk and not suggesting ideas Merry hadn't considered.

Julia didn't ask, *Is it because you think Daddy might come home for Christmas?* She didn't want to plant that desperate hope. Not that Christmas held memories of Jeffrey. Christmas was a time of wonder and happiness and love because of Grandmère and Amanda and Edmund and Paige. On Christmas, as with all events in Merry's life, Jeffrey had usually been uninvolved.

On December seventeenth, twelve hours after Paige and Amanda left for Maui, Patrick joined Merry and Julia for dinner at Belvedere. Merry hadn't seen Patrick since September because she stopped her riding lessons—as she stopped all of her after-school activities—after Jeffrey left. Julia assured Merry that Patrick wasn't upset that she hadn't been riding and that he wanted to see her.

Merry wanted to see Patrick, too, but the evening was almost cancelled anyway because Merry had been very tired all week and on Sunday awakened with a stomachache. She felt better by late afternoon, she said, so Julia didn't call Patrick to cancel. After dinner, Julia and Patrick gave Merry an early Christmas present.

"Mommy!" Merry exclaimed as she opened the book and saw the title page. The title of her favorite story was printed in elegant script, and beneath the title was a colorful picture of a smiling, blushing-pink Daphne.

"Patrick did the paintings."

"Patrick, you did?" Merry's eyes grew wide.

"I did. It was easy because your mommy's descriptions are so good."

"I can't believe this! Wait until Amanda sees!"

Julia felt a rush of emotion, tears and happiness, as she watched Merry and heard her talk about Amanda again.

"We can make another book just like this one for Amanda if you want, Merry," Patrick told the glowing eyes.

"You can?"

"Sure."

"And we can mail it to her so she'll get it for Christmas," Julia added. "Or we could even take it to her."

As Merry considered the suggestion that they join the Spencers in Maui, Julia thought she saw a "maybe" in the sparkling dark-brown eyes.

*"Oh."* Merry's smile faded.

"Merry, darling?"

"My stomach still hurts."

"Would milk help? Maybe if I warmed it?" Julia cradled Merry gently as she spoke.

"I think if I just lie down and go to sleep."

"Do you want to settle here, on the couch, near us?"

Merry nodded. She didn't want to be too far away from her mother.

Julia got soft feather pillows and a down comforter and tucked Merry gently onto the couch.

"Patrick and I will be in the kitchen talking about doing more stories if you need us, darling."

"More stories?"

"More stories." Julia kissed her forehead. It was cool, not hot, not feverish. "Good night, my love."

"Where are you going to sleep, Mommy?"

"After Patrick leaves I'll get some blankets and curl up on the other couch. OK?"

"OK. 'Night, Mommy. 'Night, Patrick. Thank you."

"Coffee?"

"Sure. Shall we do dishes?"

"I'll do them in the morning. Oh, Patrick, Merry was so pleased! Thank you so much."

"You know it's been wonderful for me."

"But not profitable. Paige thinks we should show them to a publisher."

"I don't know, Julia."

*"Mommy!!!"*

Julia and Patrick rushed into the great room toward the scream of terror from Merry. She was sitting up, gazing at a dark stain on the down comforter.

Blood. Blood from the stomach that ached and gnawed.

*"Merry!"* As Julia wrapped her arms around Merry, her head touched her daughter's. The forehead that had been cool was now damp and clammy.

"Where's the nearest hospital?" Patrick asked as he leaned over to pick Merry up.

"In Southampton, about three miles."

"I'll carry Merry, Julia, and you drive."


"She has an ulcer," the doctor told Julia and Patrick several hours later.

Patrick and Julia had been given intermittent reports throughout the evening: *Her blood pressure is fine and her bleeding has slowed. We need to do some X rays of the stomach. If those don't give us the diagnosis, we'll have to look into her stomach with an endoscope. We'll be admitting her to the Intensive Care Unit so we can monitor her*

406

*vital signs closely as soon as she's done in Radiology.*

The bulletins had been delivered with calm reassurance—Merry was stable and the diagnosis would soon be made—but punctuating the reassurances were troubling questions. Has Merry been taking a lot of aspirin? Has she been under stress? And then, questions that suddenly seemed very ominous, Has she had bleeding from her gums? Does she bleed excessively from minor cuts? Has she had an increase in infections? A decrease in energy?

"An ulcer," Julia echoed. That her precious daughter had a gnawing wound in her delicate stomach from the stress of how her life had changed filled Julia with great guilt. But the diagnosis of an ulcer seemed less frightening, something from which Merry would recover, than the diagnosis that might have prompted all the ominous questions about bleeding and infections and fatigue. To Julia that diagnosis sounded like leukemia.

"The ulcer is quite small, Mrs. Lawrence. There's no evidence that it has penetrated into adjacent organs and the bleeding has stopped. It should respond very well to medications and rest." The doctor's expression changed slightly as he continued, "It appears, however, that Merry has an additional problem . . ."

The additional problem was not leukemia, but the symptoms were similar for a similar reason: Merry's bone marrow was not making its necessary cells—the red cells, white cells, and platelets—as it should.

"It's called aplastic anemia. It means that for some reason the bone marrow has stopped production. Sometimes this is a suppression caused by a virus, or a drug, or exposure to a chemical, and sometimes, especially in girls Merry's age, it's idiopathic, meaning it happens without a cause that can be identified."

"Is emotional stress a cause of aplastic anemia?"

"Probably not by itself."

"How is the anemia cured?" Julia asked the question, knowing it was naive, hopeful, unrealistic.

"If the bone marrow is suppressed because of an external cause, like a virus or a drug, it may recover completely on its own. If the suppression is idiopathic, there is the potential for cure through bone marrow transplantation. Either way, for the moment we need to be prepared to support Merry's blood counts with transfusions."

"Transfusions?"

"We have very good screening tests, Mrs. Lawrence," the doctor swiftly assured the sudden, knowing look in Julia's intelligent eyes.

"Yes. I know." Last spring Jeffrey had done a special report entitled "How Safe is the Blood?" The report explored the safety of blood banks, the newest tests for antigens, the extraordinarily low risk of infection from screened volunteer blood. Julia knew all the data because she and Jeffrey had both read the articles and discussed the topic in detail, but still . . . "You could give her my blood, couldn't you? I'm very sure that my blood is safe."

"I think mine would be safe, too," Patrick added quietly.

"Are you Merry's father?"

408

"No. I'm a friend."

"Does Merry have any siblings?"

"No, why?"

"I was thinking about the question of bone marrow transplantation. Related donor transplants have the best success rates. Siblings are ideal because there is a possibility of an identical match, but the immunologic match with parents can also be very good. Since you're a potential bone marrow donor for Merry, Mrs. Lawrence, we won't want to use your blood for transfusions."

"Because?"

"Because we don't want Merry to develop an immunological reaction to the components of your blood that aren't identical to her own. I'm actually ahead of myself, though, because I want to talk to you about transferring Merry to the Pediatric Hematology Center at Memorial Hospital in Manhattan. If she needs marrow transplantation, that's one of the best places in the country, and if she doesn't, if her marrow comes back, I still think you'd feel better having her watched closely by specialists."

"What about testing me to see if I can give her my marrow?"

"That should be done there."

"When did you want to transfer her?"

"First thing tomorrow morning."

"It's a good match, Mrs. Lawrence," Dr. Phil MacGregor told Julia late the following afternoon. "However, I would like to test Merry's father, too, in case his marrow is a better match."

"I see."

"Is that possible? Is he local? If not, if he lives

409

near another major transplant center, we could have it done there."

*Is it possible? Yes, it has to be, somehow I will make it possible. Is he local? Oh, yes . . .*

"He lives in Manhattan." *He lives in Manhattan with one of Memorial Hospital's most famous doctors.*

"Why don't I talk to him, Julia? I am not one bit afraid of the great Jeffrey Lawrence." Patrick added quietly, "And you are."

"It's just that he has always been so angry about Merry."

"You're afraid he'll be angry with you for asking him to test his blood to save his daughter's life? You think he might say no? He can't be that much of a bastard."

"Patrick, he's—"

"I know. He's not a bastard at all despite what he's done to you and Merry. I know you love him still, Julia, which is yet another reason you shouldn't go see him."

Patrick was right, of course. If she went to see Jeffrey she might become emotional, perhaps even angry, and that wouldn't help Merry.

"I think I will ask Edmund to talk to Jeffrey. Jeffrey and Edmund are friends and I know Jeffrey has great respect for Edmund. Maybe there's even a legal way to ensure that he gets his blood tested."

"Julia, the Spencers are in Maui."

"Not Edmund, unless his plans have changed. Paige said he wouldn't be joining them until the twenty-third."

"Then I think it would be a very good idea to

410

talk to Edmund," Patrick agreed quietly.

He had been thinking about calling Paige himself. He had urged Julia to call the number in Maui that Paige had left, in case she and Merry decided to join them, as soon as the diagnosis of aplastic anemia was made. But Julia had said no. Patrick hadn't pushed, even though he couldn't shake the ominous worry that there might soon come a time when Julia would need the support of all her friends.

Patrick had been with Julia since the moment Merry became ill. He had waited at Belvedere while she packed a suitcase for herself and her daughter, and she went with him to the stable while he packed the clothes he had bought last summer, the stylish clothes for visiting Casey in Manhattan. They both rode in the ambulance with Merry when she was transferred to Memorial Hospital. Patrick was with Julia and Merry all day at the hospital, and he was with Julia in her room at the Clairmont until very late at night. They would sit in her room, talking or not, and finally, when Julia was so exhausted that she would probably be able to sleep, he would walk down the hallway to his own room.

He wanted to be with her. And, if need be, he would hold her and protect her from the beckoning depths of the emerald sea. But Patrick wasn't sure that even his strong, determined grasp could save Julia if Merry died.

Julia had two loves and three friends. She had already lost one of her loves. If she lost the other, she would need the three friends she had on earth—Patrick and Edmund and Paige.

And still that might not be enough.

\* \* \*

411

"James Patrick Jones is a rapist." The private detective punctuated the startling revelation by dropping the heavy envelope that contained his detailed report and copies of the Louisville police files on Casey's desk.

"A rapist?"

"Yet to be convicted because he has been on the lam ever since it happened. The victim, Pamela Barrington, is the daughter of a highly respected judge in Louisville. As you will see, the Louisville police file is quite thick. They've had leads from time to time over the past five years but nothing has panned out. They wanted to know why I was interested in the case. I told them, truthfully, that I didn't know and I protected your identity as my client, but—"

"I'm not about to jeopardize your career or mine by harboring a wanted felon," Casey interjected brusquely.

"I figured you wouldn't. Well. This will give you something to read for a while. James Patrick Jones had a record of nickel and dime juvenile offenses, stealing food and blankets, then seemed to be on the road for success as a champion equestrian. No one had any idea about his background until the rape."

"What physical evidence do the police have?"

"Pamela Barrington was a minor at the time. She was examined the following day by the family doctor—also a pillar of the community—who confirmed recent sexual intercourse but didn't collect samples."

"A good lawyer might get him off on that technicality."

"A better lawyer would convince the jury to believe the testimony of an innocent girl and the father who saw her terror moments after the event rather than the word of an ex-juvenile delinquent who made a career of concealing the truths about himself. Not to mention the fact that he ran and has been in hiding ever since."

After the detective left, Casey felt the full effect of the information he had given her. She had forced calm professionalism while he was in her office, but now, alone with the thick folder she would force herself to read tonight, her mind reeled.

Patrick, a rapist? Patrick, the perpetrator of the most vile crime against a woman? Patrick, who knew the secrets of the moon and the sea and the stars, and who made love so gently, so tenderly, so sensitively? Patrick, with whom she had felt so safe and so free and so loved.

And now so betrayed.

"Casey?"

Casey was pulled from her thoughts by the soft, hesitant voice, and when she looked up she saw her ancient enemy and the living symbol of Patrick's greatest betrayal. "Julia."

A distant corner of Casey's mind was struck by how fragile Julia looked, how thin, how anxious, and how her dark-circled lavender eyes were filled with sadness. But those images registered in a distant corner because mostly she saw the Julia she had always known, the enchanting seductress whose victories were so effortless.

"I'm sorry to bother you, Casey. I came to see Edmund, but he is in Washington for two days. His secretary suggested that perhaps you could

413

help me."

"Help you?" Casey echoed in disbelief.

"Yes. I wondered if—"

"Julia." Casey raised her hand to stop Julia's words. She assumed Julia was ready to file for divorce. Edmund had said that he wanted to handle the divorce or have Casey handle it to ensure it was done with discretion and care so that there would be no more hurt for Julia. Edmund was away so now his secretary had sent Julia to her to begin the paperwork that would free her from Jeffrey and enable her to be with Patrick. "Don't waste your breath. I'm not going to help you."

"I realize you are very busy, Casey."

"You realize nothing, Julia. You have always lived in a dream world. But this dream is over. This time you are not going to win."

"I don't understand."

"Patrick will."

"Patrick?"

"Please tell Patrick—I mean *James*—that I know his secret." Casey's forget-me-not blue eyes flashed triumphantly at Julia. "He hasn't told you, has he?"

"Told me what?"

"Told you about James Patrick Jones and Pamela Barrington. No, of course he hasn't told you. But I think it's time he did. Why don't you go to him now, Julia, and ask him to tell you all about Pamela and James."

After a bewildered moment, a moment in which Casey finally took her eyes from Julia and turned her attention to the work she had on her desk, Julia quietly withdrew.

After Julia left, Casey thought about what she had done. She had acknowledged aloud her ten-year war with Julia and her intention to claim a victory at last. And she had sent a warning to Patrick.

Why? Casey wondered. So that Patrick could flee? Because she cared about him still, despite everything?

When Julia returned from the Madison Avenue offices of Spencer and Quinn to Merry's room at Memorial Hospital, Merry was asleep and Patrick was sitting in a corner reading and keeping vigil over Julia's sleeping daughter. Julia caught Patrick's eye and beckoned to him to join her in the hallway. They walked in silence to one of the waiting areas on the pediatric ward. The waiting area was empty, as most of the pediatric ward was, because any child that possibly could be home for Christmas was home.

"Did you talk to Edmund?"

"No. He was away. Patrick, was Casey English the woman you loved, the one who wasn't who you thought she was?"

"Yes. Why?"

Julia told Patrick about the bewildering conversation and Casey's warning to her and to Patrick.

"I didn't realize you knew her, Julia. You were at the party in her honor, of course, but so was all of Southampton."

"I don't really know her. We were in high school together. I've always thought she was very nice."

"*Nice?* Oh, Julia."

"Your name is really James Patrick Jones?"

"Yes."

"Who is Pamela Barrington?"

"Pamela is an heiress who says that I raped her."

"But you didn't," Julia replied swiftly and confidently.

"No." Patrick smiled slightly at Julia's instant and unquestioning support. "However, you're probably the only person on earth who would believe my word over hers. Casey obviously doesn't."

"Casey's going to call the police, isn't she?"

"Oh, yes. I guess it *was* nice of her to give me a little warning since there are a couple of things I would like to do before the police arrive. I need to go to the blood bank . . . and I need to talk to Jeffrey."

"No, Patrick. You should go to the police before Casey does. You should turn yourself in and tell them you didn't do anything!"

"Lovely Julia and your fairy tales. Whether I go to them or they come to me, I will be going to prison. There's no doubt about it. Since I have some very important things to do first, I'm going to let them come to me."

"I will hire the best lawyers for your defense."

"Thank you." Patrick smiled then added softly, "But there is no lawyer better than Casey, and I wouldn't be at all surprised if she decided to become involved with this case."

"Run then, Patrick! Leave now. When you get to a safe place, call me and I'll send you money."

"No. It's OK, Julia, I'm really very tired of running and hiding." *And there is no way I would leave you now.*

He would be leaving her soon, once the police found him, and then he would place the call that Julia had forbidden him to make. Even a criminal accused of a crime as heinous as the one they would accuse him of had the right to one phone call, didn't he? Patrick would make that call to

416

Paige. In the meantime he would stay with Julia as long as he could and do whatever he could to help. "So, Julia, where to first? Blood bank or Jeffrey?"

"Blood bank," she answered without hesitation. Patrick's blood was safe and a very good match for transfusions for Merry. "I will talk to Jeffrey."


After Patrick left to donate more of his blood for Merry, Julia returned to her daughter's room. Merry was still sleeping, and probably would be for a while because she was weakened and fatigued from her anemia. Julia placed a gentle kiss on Merry's pale cheeks and made a silent promise. *I'm going to go talk to your daddy, my darling, so you can be well.*

As Julia walked down the linoleum corridors toward the elevator that would take her to the lobby, she heard the overhead page. "Dr. Shepherd. Dr. Diana Shepherd."

Undoubtedly Diana Shepherd had been paged many times since Merry had been admitted, but Julia hadn't heard it until now.

Now she heard the name and it was a whispered suggestion.

Who would Jeffrey listen to? Who would he believe? Who would he trust?

Julia, whom he had always accused of secrets and lies? Julia, for whom his desire had waned? Julia, who had borne the child he never wanted? Julia, whom he had left? Or Diana, the woman he loved? Diana, the compassionate and dedicated physician whose surgical specialty was mending the broken hearts of children?

Julia knew that as emotionally difficult as it

would be for her to see Jeffrey, it would be even more difficult to see Jeffrey's lover. But Julia didn't hesitate. Because Jeffrey would listen to Diana and that would help Merry.

Maybe, just maybe, Julia could find an ally in the Queen of Hearts.

# Chapter Twenty-two

"I wondered if it would be possible for me to see Dr. Shepherd?"

"May I ask about what?"

"About my daughter. She's very ill."

"I'm Diana Shepherd." Diana had been near the door of her office and overheard the conversation. "Please come in."

"Thank you."

Diana led the way across her spacious office to the conversation area in front of the wall of windows that overlooked Manhattan.

"How may I help you?" Diana asked when they were seated. As she asked the question, Diana looked sympathetically at the beautiful young mother with the very ill daughter and made a silent vow. *I will help you however I can.*

"I'm Julia Lawrence."

Diana heard the words but did not instantly make the connection. In the months that she and Jeffrey had been together, Diana had formed a clear image of his wife. Her image of Julia was etched from Jeffrey's silent pain, not from anything Jeffrey said. Diana imagined a beautiful, self-absorbed, and calculating woman—a modern-day

419

Cleopatra who had enchanted Jeffrey, stolen his heart, and cast him aside without a pang of remorse.

"Jeffrey and I . . ." Julia added after a moment, when it was obvious, so painfully obvious, that Diana didn't even know her *name*.

"Oh," Diana breathed. This shy and lovely woman was Jeffrey's Julia? Yes, Diana realized, because she was exactly who Jeffrey had so lovingly described the only time he had ever talked about her. That weekend in London there had been such gentleness in his voice, such love and such pride as he spoke of the brilliant and less-than-confident woman who was his wonderful love, and a wonderful and loving mother to her daughter. Until this moment, whenever she remembered Jeffrey's description of Julia, Diana had assumed it had merely been a deluded portrait of love. But now she saw that it had not. "How may I help you, Julia?"

"Has Jeffrey told you about our daughter Merry?"

"Yes." *Our daughter?* Diana's mind spun. Jeffrey had told her that Julia's innocent lavender eyes could lie without a flicker. There was innocence in the lavender, yes, but such pain and despair that Diana couldn't believe Julia was lying.

"Last Sunday Merry had bleeding from an ulcer. While they were treating the ulcer they discovered that she has aplastic anemia."

"I'm certain that Jeffrey has no idea."

"No. I wasn't going to tell him, but Merry needs a bone marrow transplant. Dr. MacGregor has already tested my blood as a potential donor. It's a fairly good match, but he would like to see if Jeffrey's might be better."

"I see," Diana replied quietly, although she didn't see. While she was deciding what to say next, her thoughts were interrupted by the ring of the private line in her office. The number to the private line was known to the O.R., her colleagues, and the nurses in the I.C.U. When it rang it usually was a question about one of her patients. "Excuse me. I have to answer that."

This time it was a call from the one person outside Memorial Hospital who knew the number.

"Hello, Doctor."

"Hi." Diana usually responded softly, "Hello, Anchor," but now her reply was stiff.

"I was thinking about last night."

"Yes." Last night. Something had happened last night, a new closeness, a melting of the vestiges of pain, a healing of the wounds in their hearts that kept their love a little distant despite their wonderful honesty and trust. Last night was the beginning of their forever. They both knew it. "I can't talk now."

"So I gather. I love you, Diana."

*I love you, too, Jeffrey.* "Same. I'll talk to you later."

As Diana walked back across the office to Julia she wondered if Julia knew who had been at the other end of the phone.

Julia's lavender eyes told her that she knew and that it caused her great pain.

*You left Jeffrey, Julia, remember?* Diana thought. *You hurt him terribly.* Yet it was Julia who looked terribly hurt, as if she didn't remember what had happened. Just as she apparently didn't know that Merry wasn't Jeffrey's daughter. Diana knew and Jeffrey knew. But Julia didn't know.

"What would you like me to do, Julia?"

"I thought if you explained to Jeffrey, maybe he would be willing to have his blood tested."

"Of course he'd be willing," Diana answered swiftly. Julia made her request quietly and calmly, but Diana felt her panic and fear. Diana knew the panic of a loving mother trying to save her dying child. She knew the desperation, had lived through it . . . although perhaps she had not really survived. "How could you possibly imagine that he wouldn't be?"

"I thought he would have told you. Jeffrey never wanted Merry."

*That's not true!* Diana thought instantly, remembering the sadness in his eyes as he talked about Merry, the distant wish for a miracle, and the more recent wish to be the father of the little girl who wasn't his but who had captured his heart.

"Jeffrey's blood will be tested today, Julia," Diana said calmly despite the swirling, bewildering thoughts. "I promise. Do I have your permission to speak with Dr. MacGregor about Merry?"

"Of course. Thank you."

Before Julia left, Diana almost gave her a gentle warning. *Jeffrey's blood may not be a good match with Merry's.* But she didn't because what Julia needed now was hope. And she didn't, either, because what if . . . ?

An hour later Diana appeared in Jeffrey's office carrying a small paper sack that contained needles, syringes, alcohol wipes, a tourniquet, and rubber-stopped glass tubes. Jeffrey greeted her with a surprised and loving smile that became quizzical as Diana removed the contents of the sack.

"May I have your arm, please?"

"You can have all of me. Diana?"

Diana didn't answer until after she had expertly rolled his shirtsleeve, applied the tourniquet, prepped the skin of his antecubital fossa, withdrawn the blood, and filled the tubes. Then she sat in a chair across from him and looked at him with thoughtful sapphire eyes.

"Julia came to my office this morning."

"Julia? Why?"

"Last Sunday Merry was admitted to Southampton Hospital with an acute GI bleed from an ulcer."

"Oh, no," Jeffrey breathed softly as rushes of emotion and concern swept through him. "How is she?"

"The bleeding has been controlled and the ulcer will heal without surgery, but there's a second more serious problem."

*"More* serious?"

"Merry has aplastic anemia."

"What does that mean?"

"It means that her blood counts are low and need to be supported by transfusions until either her marrow recovers or she gets a marrow transplant. I spoke with her doctor just before coming here. He thinks spontaneous marrow recovery is unlikely and is eager to proceed with transplantation as soon as possible. Since Merry has no siblings, the next best related donors are her mother and father. Julia is a good match, but there's a chance that the match with her father might be better."

Diana's sapphire eyes left Jeffrey's for a moment and drifted to the tubes of blood she had just drawn.

"Diana?"

"From everything you've told me, Jeffrey, it seems impossible for you to be Merry's father. But, darling, Julia truly believes that you are."

"She knows that I'm not."

"No, Jeffrey, she docsn't know that. Julia is a loving mother who is trying desperately to save the life of her dying child. She believes that you are Merry's father and hopes that your blood might be a better match than hers."

"But why did she go to you and not me?"

"I don't know. I can tell you it was very difficult for her to come to me. She was there when you called. She knew it was you and that obviously caused her great pain."

"Why? Julia left me."

"I know. I don't have any answers, Jeffrey. And there are very important questions that need answers. Julia truly believes that you are Merry's father and that you never wanted Merry."

"Never wanted Merry," Jeffrey repeated quietly even though the memory of Julia's words thundered in his brain. *You will never forgive me for having Merry! Even now, after ten years, you wish Merry had never been born. You wanted me to have an abortion, didn't you?*

Jeffrey started to protest—But that isn't true!—but he stopped. Diana didn't need to hear those words, because she knew the truth. The woman who needed to hear the words was Julia.

"What did Julia ask you to do, Diana?"

"To see if you would be willing to have your blood tested."

"Do you think she really believed that I might have refused?"

"I don't know. Maybe," Diana admitted softly, truthfully, to his anguished and disbelieving eyes.

"It was almost as if she was afraid to ask you herself."

"Afraid?" Jeffrey echoed quietly. How could Julia be afraid of him? But Jeffrey knew Julia had been afraid of him the few times that he had so angrily demanded that she tell him the truth about Merry. How he had hated the fear in her lovely, bewildered eyes! How he had wanted her only to be confident of his love! But her secrets, her lies, had caused him such pain. *Julia truly believes that you are Merry's father.* No wonder her eyes had been so innocent, so bewildered, so afraid . . .

"There are some very important questions that need answers," Diana said again. When his dark-blue eyes met hers, she added softly, "And there's something else you need to know, Jeffrey."

"Yes?"

"Julia may have left you for someone else, but she still wears the wedding ring you gave her."


At eight-thirty that night Diana called the immunology laboratory to get the results of the studies that had been done on Jeffrey's blood. She had earlier obtained the same data on the blood samples that had been run on Julia and Merry previously. Diana's experience with heart transplantation made her very familiar with tissue typing.

"Oh, Jeffrey," she whispered softly. "Merry is your daughter, darling."

"No." Jeffrey's eyes filled with tears and he couldn't speak. For a stunned moment everything was suspended in disbelief. Then, carried by thundering waves of pain, the horrible realizations began to crash down on him. *For ten years I have denied my own daughter. For ten years I have*

425

*doubted the woman I love.* "Diana, are you sure?"

"Yes, Jeffrey, I'm very sure. The match is really astonishingly good, much better for transplantation than Julia's."

Diana's words pulled Jeffrey's thoughts away from the past and made him focus on the present and future.

"So I should be the donor."

"Yes. Shall I call Phil MacGregor? He gave me his home number."


Phil MacGregor used the word "remarkable" to define the match.

"You will be willing to donate your marrow, Mr. Lawrence?"

"Of course." *I would be willing to give my heart if Merry needed it.*

"Good. Let's plan to do the transplant the day after tomorrow. Why don't you come into the hospital tomorrow morning? We need to do a battery of routine pre-op tests. Has Diana explained the procedure to you?"

"No."

"I'll explain in full detail when I see you, but, essentially, I will harvest the bone marrow from your hip bone. The procedure is done under anesthesia. It's customary to remove quite a large sample of marrow, which means cracking little bits of bone. You'll have some discomfort after, like a small fracture, but—"

"Will it be painful for Merry?"

"No. The actual transplantation is basically an intravenous transfusion. The marrow cells enter the bloodstream and quickly migrate to the marrow."

"What are the chances of success?"

"With your marrow? I would say excellent."

"A cure?"

"We can hope for that. So if you could get fasting blood drawn at the lab first thing tomorrow morning—I'll call in the requests tonight—then go to Admitting and plan to come to my office at, say, eleven?"

"Fine. Have you told Julia?"

"Not yet. I'd like to tell her tonight, though."

"Of course."

"Did you want me to call her or would you like to?"

"Why don't you?" It would be a long time before Jeffrey could control his emotions and begin to find the words he needed to say to Julia.

A long time. And Julia needed to know about the plans for the transplantation now.


"What kind of man am I?" Jeffrey demanded aloud after the long, anguished silence that followed the conversation with Dr. MacGregor.

He stood at the living-room window of Diana's penthouse. Outside, snow was falling, blanketing Manhattan in a fleecy cloak that looked so virginal, so peaceful, so pure.

"You are a wonderful, loving man, Jeffrey Lawrence."

*"Wonderful? Loving?* Can you think of anything worse than denying your own child? Do you remember how we talked about Sam's and Julia's parents and what great harm they had done to their children?"

"They knew they were causing harm, Jeffrey. You had no idea that Merry was your daughter. You told me that for ten years Julia very carefully kept you and Merry apart."

"Because she thought I never wanted Merry! Julia was protecting Merry from the pain of a father who didn't want to love his daughter. Julia knew that pain so well because of the lovelessness of her own childhood. She kept us apart to protect Merry, but she must have believed that one day . . ." Jeffrey's words were stopped by emotion and the anguished realization that Julia had been waiting so patiently, so lovingly, so hopefully for him to claim his daughter. Finally, after almost ten years, when she could wait no longer, she had made a quiet, hopeful, almost apologetic request that he make a little time in his busy life for them to be a family. "You accused me of being a bastard once, Diana. You were absolutely right."

"I was absolutely *wrong.*"

"No, *I* was absolutely wrong. God, I was so sure! Do you have any idea how many awards I have won for exceptional quality in journalism? I drive people crazy because I am so compulsive about accuracy and fairness. I have fired people for carelessness in gathering the facts. Did I ever tell you about the conversation I had with the reporter who asked you the infamous question at the press conference?"

"No, and I don't want you to tell me now. What I want is for you to remember that you did gather the facts, carefully and compulsively, and arrived at the only conclusion you could, even though you wished for something different. Jeffrey, you saw many specialists, including one a few months before Merry was born, and they all told you what?"

"That it would be virtually impossible for me to father a child. *Virtually,* not absolutely."

"But then Merry was born almost nine weeks

prematurely. And even though you'd done an in-depth report on neonatal I.C.U.'s the year before, you spoke with Merry's doctor and confirmed that she was premature—perhaps as much as four weeks—and that she had done incredibly well for a baby born that early."

"That was another miracle, Diana. Julia knew. She *told* me, so softly, her voice so full of wonder, that Merry was a miracle. And I didn't believe her. I didn't believe in the miracle even though I wanted to."

"Because the facts wouldn't allow you to, Jeffrey."

"I should have done more. I should have gotten blood tests then! I didn't even think about it because there was no doubt in my mind. And I call myself a journalist?"

"Jeffrey, darling, for the record, the kind of genetic detail done on your blood today wasn't available ten years ago. What you would have learned then was only that you and Merry shared some of the major blood group antigens—the most common ones, by the way. Until recently, blood testing has only been useful in *excluding* paternity, not in establishing it. You couldn't have known ten years ago what you know now. Now you know, beyond a shadow of a doubt, that the miracle really happened."

"Ten years too late!"

"It's never too late for love."

"You're not going to let me hate myself, are you?"

"I know you will hate yourself no matter how hard I try to stop you. I just hope you won't destroy yourself with hatred." Diana added softly, "A very wonderful and very loving man once told me to forgive myself."

"I told you to forgive yourself for the death of a daughter whom you loved so very much, and a death for which you were not to blame. But I have ignored my lovely daughter, Diana, and I *am* to blame." *And I will never forgive myself for what I have done.* "I have to . . ."

"Go. I know." Diana saw the torment in his dark-blue eyes and felt the power of his restlessness. For now Jeffrey needed privacy for his emotions. And later, sometime, he needed to be with Julia. Maybe he could find a way back to the love with his beloved Julia, who was the mother of his daughter, the woman who hadn't deceived him after all, and who still wore the wedding ring he had given her. Diana wished that happiness for him. She smiled a gentle smile and whispered softly, "Be good to yourself, Jeffrey."


Memorial Hospital was only five snowy minutes away from Diana's penthouse. Jeffrey went there first . . . To see his daughter.

Visiting hours were over and the hospital was very still but Jeffrey was used to roaming Memorial's halls after hours in search of Diana. He knew that visiting hours weren't strictly enforced, especially for parents of critically ill children. Critically ill children like Merry, and parents like Jeffrey . . . and Julia. Jeffrey slowed as he neared Merry's room, apprehensive about seeing the little girl he had denied for all her life, and suddenly apprehensive, too, about seeing Julia.

But perhaps Julia wouldn't be there. Perhaps Dr. MacGregor hadn't told Julia that she could stay beyond visitors' hours because he knew if he did that

Julia would be at Merry's bedside every second and would never get the rest that she needed, too.

Most of the rooms on the pediatric ward were dark and empty for the holidays. As Jeffrey neared the open door to Merry's room he saw a soft beam of light coming from inside.

Merry was alone in her room. She sat on her bed, propped up against pillows, reading a book with a pale-pink cover. The light above the bed cast a soft glow, circling her golden head like a halo.

Jeffrey stood in the doorway and gazed at the little angel. Merry was so pale, her skin so white — except for the many bruises on her slender arms, large purple blotches caused by intravenous lines, venipunctures, and by tourniquets and blood pressure cuffs, because without enough platelets there was oozing of blood from the delicate capillaries.

Merry looked happily lost in the story she read, her dark-brown eyes earnest and a soft smile on her lovely face. She seemed quite absorbed with the story, and Jeffrey was content to watch her forever as he tried to control his swirling emotions, but suddenly she looked up and her eyes lit with radiant joy.

"Daddy!"

"Oh, Merry." Jeffrey walked to her then and sat beside her on the bed and gently touched her golden hair, her soft, pale cheeks, her frail shoulders. He wanted to pull her to him, but he was afraid he might hurt her.

"I knew you'd come back!"

"Merry, my darling . . ."

"Daddy, why are you crying? Don't cry!"

"I'm crying because I'm so happy to see you." Jeffrey held her lovely pale face in his trembling fingers and confessed to her smiling eyes, "And I'm

431

crying because I haven't been a very good Daddy."

"Yes you have!"

"No."

"Yes! It's just that you've been very busy because your work is so important. You've had to be away from me, but that didn't mean you didn't love me . . ." Merry's words had begun confidently, an earnest recitation of the beliefs she had held most of her life, but the confidence faded as she made the bold pronouncement that Jeffrey loved her.

"I love you very much, Merry, so very much. How I have missed being your daddy!" *But how can you possibly love me?* "But why are you so wise?"

"Mommy always told me that you loved me. She said someday you would be able to spend more time with me. Mommy wouldn't lie."

"No. Mommy wouldn't lie." What a gift Julia had given him—his daughter's love even though Merry should have hated him!

"I was worried that you wouldn't come back, though," Merry continued quietly. "That's why I got the ulcer."

"Oh, darling . . ."

"I'm OK, Daddy. Really. As soon as I get my bone marrow transplant, I'll be fine."

"That will be the day after tomorrow, Merry. I'm going to be the donor."

"You are?"

"Yes, I am."

"And you're coming back to us, aren't you?"

"Oh, Merry," Jeffrey whispered. How he wished he could go back! "I'll be with you as much as I can, darling, but Mommy may not want me to come home."

"No, Daddy, she does want you to come home!

She misses you. I know that Mommy cries, too, even though she doesn't want me to see."

"Does she?" Jeffrey asked hopefully as he felt the heat of fresh tears. He forced his eyes to leave Merry's lovely face for a moment to search for a distraction. He touched the book that she had been reading and asked, "Is this a good book?"

"Yes. It's one of the fairy tales Mommy used to tell me when I was little."

*When I was little.* Jeffrey's heart ached as he thought about all the years he hadn't known his little girl. Merry was a little girl still, but she was growing up, becoming a little lady.

"I remember Mommy telling you fairy tales, Merry. I remember a dragon named Daphne and sea serpents named Cecily and Robert." Emotion stopped his voice as he remembered the car trip from Los Angeles to New York and Julia's obvious apprehension that his bright, lively daughter might *bother* him. But he had loved the fairy tales, and he had loved Merry's obvious excitement as she pointed and exclaimed gleefully, "Moo cows, Mommy!"

"This is a picture of Daphne."

"That's a wonderful painting."

"Patrick did it."

"Patrick? The riding instructor at the Club?"

"Yes. He was having dinner with us the night I started to bleed. He carried me and held me while Mommy drove to the hospital. And that's his blood." Merry pointed to the plastic bag of rich red blood that hung on the intravenous pole beside her bed and was slowly dripping into her tiny veins, giving her strength, keeping her alive.

Jeffrey's mind filled with images of Patrick, the handsome man whose blood sustained his precious daughter. Did Patrick's lean, strong body sustain Julia, giving her pleasure, making her lavender eyes shine with desire and causing the soft sighs of joy that had filled Jeffrey with such immeasurable happiness?

"Daddy, what's wrong?"

"Nothing's wrong. Just a faraway thought. Would you like me to read to you until you fall asleep?"

"Yes."

Without hesitation, as if her daddy had read bedtime stories to her all her life, Merry moved over so that Jeffrey could sit beside her and then curled against him. Jeffrey gently wrapped his arm around her small shoulders, feeling her warmth and her softness and her lovely trust. *How much he had missed.*

"What if I just tell you a story, Merry?" Jeffrey asked finally, breaking a silence that had been so comfortable, so patient, so peaceful. Jeffrey looked from the book with the wonderful paintings by Patrick into her smiling brown eyes and suggested, "What if I tell you about the first time I ever saw you and held you?"

"OK," Merry agreed eagerly as she curled even closer to him. Her sparkling eyes became solemn, and she touched the dampness on his cheeks with her pale, delicate fingers. "But, Daddy, not if it's going to make you cry."

"These are happy tears, darling," Jeffrey whispered softly. "Besides, Merry Lawrence, you were crying the first time I ever held you."

"I was?"

"Yes. I guess you were upset because I hadn't held you until then."

"And I wanted you to hold me."

"I think so, because when I did, you stopped crying right away."

"I did?"

"Yes you did." Jeffrey gently kissed the top of her silky golden hair and searched his mind for other memories of him and Merry. There were so few, so painfully few. Jeffrey didn't have many memories of the two of them together, but he had memories of Merry, sunny, happy images his mind had recorded during all those years when he saw her from a distance. Jeffrey held Merry very gently and very close and lovingly began to tell her every scene he could remember.

Merry fell asleep in his arms, smiling happily, and for a long time Jeffrey just held her as tears spilled again. Finally, he pulled away and gently lay her head on the pillow and tucked the blankets around her and turned out the light.

"I love you, Merry," he whispered softly. Then he kissed her pale cheek and whispered again before he left, "I love you."

## Chapter Twenty-three

Jeffrey paced around Manhattan only vaguely aware of the heavily falling snow, the ever-increasing chill, the festive Christmas decorations, and the joyous melodies of distant carols. He was lost in a snowstorm of memories, trapped inside a glass ball filled with snowflakes and a lovely Yuletide scene, his whole world turned upside down.

He wandered, almost oblivious to his surroundings, until he stepped off a curb without looking, and brakes screeched in the snow-slick street and a horn blared stridently, jarring him back to reality.

Reality. *Merry needs my marrow. I have to take care of myself. I have to stay alive for Merry.*

After that, Jeffrey walked in the snowstorm still, but now he walked cautiously and only in the safest areas, only amid the late-night shoppers beneath the twinkling lights of Fifth Avenue. The snow swirled, chilling him, and his thoughts swirled, chilling him, too, a deeper chill.

*I have to stay alive for Merry.* That was the first certainty that emerged from his stormy thoughts. As the hours passed another certainty surfaced. *I have to talk to Julia. I have to tell her.*

* * *

436

Merry's nurse had told Jeffrey that Julia was staying at the Clairmont Hotel across the street from the hospital. At midnight he walked into the warm lobby of the hotel, found a house phone, and asked the hotel operator to connect him to Julia's room.

Jeffrey had thought he could feel no greater pain — until a man's voice answered Julia's phone.

"Patrick?"

"Yes."

"This is Jeffrey Lawrence. May I speak with Julia?"

"Just a moment."

Would Julia take his call? Who could blame her if she refused?

But Julia didn't refuse.

"Jeffrey?"

"Hello, Julia. I wanted to be sure that Dr. MacGregor reached you."

"Yes. Jeffrey, thank you."

*Don't thank me!* his heart screamed. After a moment he assured quietly, "Dr. MacGregor is very optimistic. Merry's going to be fine, healthy."

"Yes," Julia replied softly. *Please.*

"Julia? May I see you? There's something I need to tell you."

"Oh."

*Oh.* It was only one word, and it was spoken so softly, but still Jeffrey heard her sudden apprehension. Oh, Julie, don't be afraid of me. "Please?" he asked gently. "It won't take long."

"All right."

"Tonight? I'm in the lobby of your hotel. There's a bar down here where we can meet."

"Why don't you come to my room?" Julia sug-

437

gested quietly. She knew what Jeffrey was going to tell her and she knew that she would want privacy for her emotions when he did.

"OK. But I'd like to see you alone."

"We'll be alone."

"Hi." His heart quickened as always when he saw her and he smiled a shaky smile at the tired lavender eyes he loved so much and missed so much.

"Hi. Come in."

As he entered her small room, Jeffrey prepared his heart to see a room shared by Patrick and Julia. As Julia had promised, they were alone, but there were no signs that Patrick had even been there.

"Did Patrick go to the bar?"

"He went to his own room."

"Oh."

"There was something you wanted to tell me, Jeffrey?" Jeffrey didn't answer her question right away, but the message of his dark-blue eyes was so sad and so apologetic that it confirmed what Julia had already guessed. She continued softly, needing it to be over quickly because it was so difficult to see him. "Is it that you've filed for divorce?"

"No. It's not that," Jeffrey answered with matching softness. Then very gently, very quietly, very sadly, he said, "Julia, until tonight I believed with all my heart that Merry wasn't my daughter."

"Jeffrey," Julia whispered a gentle protest, as if she knew his words were going to bring a pain greater than all the other pains that had come before. "You were so angry with me for having her."

*"No*. I was never angry about Merry. I was hurt and angry about the secret I believed you were keeping—that she was the child of another love."

"But there was never anyone else, Jeffrey. I told you that!"

"I know you did, Julia," Jeffrey whispered softly. "I just didn't believe you."

"You would have wanted Merry? You would have loved her?"

"I do want Merry. I do love her."

Jeffrey watched Julia's beautiful eyes as the realization began to settle. He knew the layers and layers of pain that would follow, wave crashing upon wave as every memory was relived twice—the way it had been and then the way it might have been.

Jeffrey watched as the first waves of sadness washed through her. The waves were already huge, but they were merely the earliest warning of the devastating hurricane that loomed on the horizon. As he watched, a second emotion appeared in the stricken lavender . . . *fear*. Somehow he had caused fear again in the eyes he had only wanted to fill with confident happiness and joy! Why fear now?

"Julia?"

"Are you going to try to take Merry away from me, Jeffrey?" Julia added quietly, "I will fight you."

"Don't you know that I would never do that?" Jeffrey saw the answer in her eyes, *No, Jeffrey, I don't know that,* and after an anguished moment he whispered emotionally, "Oh, Julie."

*Julie.* His loving name for her spoken so gently now caused her such pain. And when she tilted

439

her head because she had to look away and her
hair curtained her eyes and his trembling fingers
so delicately parted the black silk curtain, the pain
was more than she could bear. She backed away
from him and sat on the bed, her head bent, her
body curled by an enormous invisible weight, her
hands clasped tightly in her lap.

Her ringless hands.

*Julia may have left you for someone else, but
she still wears the wedding ring you gave her,* Diana had told him just hours ago. The words had
flickered in his brain, a fragile ray of sunlight in
the blackness.

But Julia *wasn't* wearing her wedding ring. Her
hands were so pale that there wasn't even a patch
of greater whiteness where once the gold had been.
There wasn't a patch of whiter whiteness, nor was
there a depression in the delicate skin. If Julia had
worn her wedding ring recently the fit would have
been very loose because her fingers were much
thinner now than the day they were married, thinner than he had ever seen them.

Jeffrey looked at his lovely Julia, already
weighted down by the truths he had told her and
bracing herself for even more pain, and wondered
if he should just leave. But there were words she
needed to hear, words he had rehearsed over and
over as he wandered through the snow.

"Julia, I promise I will leave in just a few moments, but please let me tell you everything I came
to say. OK?"

Julia nodded slightly, a resigned nod.

"I want you to know how sorry I am. I'm not
asking you to forgive me because I know that
what I've done is unforgivable." Jeffrey took a soft

breath and continued shakily. "And yet, despite everything, because of who you are, you have given me the immense gift of Merry's love. When I saw her this evening she was happy—*happy*—to see me. I don't deserve Merry's love, Julia, but I am so very grateful that you have given it to me."

Julia looked up then. She gazed at him through a misty curtain of hair and tears and asked, "You saw Merry this evening?"

"Yes. I had to. I guess I should have checked first with you, but . . . I just had to see her. I'm sorry."

"Jeffrey, Merry is your daughter. She needs you. I want you to see her."

"Thank you."

Julia gave a shaky smile and then returned her gaze to the pale, ringless fingers in her lap, fingers that had become even more white because her unrelenting clench had not allowed blood to flow into them.

After a few moments Jeffrey continued with the words he needed to say.

"I would give anything to be able to undo the past. I loved you so much, Julia, and I believe that once you loved me, too. I guess I want you to know that deep down I really am the man you thought you married. I know now that you kept me and Merry apart because you believed I didn't want her. And you need to know that I never tried to claim her because I believed she wasn't mine. I never would have intentionally hurt Merry or you, although I know I have caused you both great pain." Jeffrey sighed softly. "That's all, Julia. Your dream was to make a happy life for the ones you loved, and you did that beautifully and lov-

441

ingly for Merry and for me. I was so happy with you! You probably can't believe this, but my dream was to make you happy, too. I wanted so very much to give you all the happiness and joy that you deserved . . . but I failed miserably. I understand now why you needed to find someone new to love. I marvel that you stayed with me as long as you did. How you must have hated me for denying our lovely daughter."

Jeffrey might have said more, might have at least thanked her for listening to him, but emotion overcame him. As he gazed at her his emotions became even shakier, and finally he simply turned to leave. He had just touched the doorknob when Julia's voice stopped his hand and her words almost stopped his heart.

"I didn't find someone new to love, Jeffrey."

Jeffrey turned back to her and drew a startled breath when he saw her. Julia was sitting up now, straight and proud, the invisible weight suddenly cast away. She had parted the tangle of black silk so that she could see him clearly with eyes that were tear-free and no longer filled with sadness or fear or pain. The lavender gazed at him with hopeful wonder, as it had on a distant day in Ghirardelli when her eyes had been pulled from the sea by the silent call of his heart.

"Julie," Jeffrey whispered as a delicate tremble of hope began a brave search for even the most precarious footing in the emptiness. "You told me that our marriage was over because there was someone else."

"Yes. Because of Diana."

"Diana and I got together *after* you told me our marriage was over."

"I saw you with her in London."

"You came to London?"

"Yes. And I saw you with Diana in Hyde Park." Julia spoke with wonder, not anger. Wonder, because what if she had been wrong about what she had seen? On that autumn day, because no man except Jeffrey had ever touched her with affection and no eyes except his had ever smiled at her with gentleness, to Julia the tender intimacies she had witnessed could only have been love. But in the past few months, and especially in the past few days, her dear friend Patrick had touched her and held her and smiled at her with such gentleness. "I saw the way you looked at her and the way you moved a strand of hair from beside her eyes."

"Is that why when I did that earlier it upset you so much?"

"Yes."

"Oh, my Julie," Jeffrey whispered, a whisper of hope and joy. "Diana was very sad and I was trying to help her. We were both very sad that weekend, both mourning losses of love. We became friends, honey, good friends but just friends. I spent the weekend telling Diana how much I loved you and how afraid I was that I had lost you. And Diana heard my love for you and kept assuring me that our love couldn't be over. Diana knew in London how much I loved you. And she knows how much I love you still. She told me that when she saw you in her office you were wearing your wedding ring. Were you?"

"Yes. I took it off after you called from the lobby. I thought you were coming to tell me that you were going to file for divorce."

"Did you wear it because you hoped we would

get back together?"

"I didn't dare hope for that." Julia shrugged softly. "I just had to wear it."

"I just had to take mine off even though I never wanted to."

"Jeffrey?"

"Yes, my darling?"

"I never hated you. But how you must have hated me when you believed that I had deceived you about something so important."

"I never hated you. I only loved you. I will always love you." Jeffrey smiled gently, hopefully, and urged lovingly, "Julie, tell me what you want."

"I want what I have always wanted, Jeffrey. I want you to love me." Julia paused for just a moment and then spoke the other half of her dream, "And I want you to love our daughter."

"I love you both with all my heart."

Jeffrey held his arms out to her then, and Julia came to him joyfully as she always had, and they were together again at last, where they belonged. Jeffrey whispered her name over and over, his lips caressing her hair as he spoke, until finally he had to see her eyes.

"My lovely Julie," he whispered to the lavender that sparkled with such love and such happiness. Jeffrey cupped her face in his gentle and trembling hands and asked a question that he had tried to answer but couldn't, a question only Julia could answer. "In September you told me that you were responsible for our pregnancy. Why did you say that?"

"Because I *had* deceived you then, Jeffrey. I let you believe that I was older and experienced and in control when I was really just a virgin and completely unprepared."

"Oh, honey." Jeffrey kissed her lips softly, and after a few minutes told her truthfully, "If I had known you were only sixteen, I still would have made love to you if you'd wanted me to, or just held you if you didn't. And if I had known you were a virgin I would have been more gentle."

"You were very gentle, Jeffrey."

Julia kissed him, a gentle kiss that might have lasted forever, but suddenly she remembered something and pulled free.

"Julie?"

"Will you put my ring back on my finger?" she asked as she retrieved the elegant band from the pocket of her sweater.

"Yes, my love, in thirty minutes."

"Thirty minutes?"

"We can get married again, our own private ceremony, in thirty minutes, if you will have me."

"I will have you."

"Then I'm going to go to my apartment right now and get my ring."

"You still have it?"

"Of course I do. And I want it back on my finger, where it belongs, as soon as possible."

"Jeffrey, there's a snowstorm outside."

"Warm, lovely, beautiful snow." Jeffrey smiled. "I love you so much, Julie."

"I love you so much, too." As she gazed into his loving eyes, a slight frown crossed her face. "Jeffrey, while you're gone, I need to speak with Patrick. He's waiting for me. Patrick and I are friends, Jeffrey, not lovers. He has been very important to me since you left, and now he needs me."

"Why does he need you?"

"He has been accused of a crime he didn't commit."

"What crime?"

"I can't tell you. I need to talk to him first. I'm going to try to get him to leave, but if he won't he'll need my—our—help. OK?"

"OK." *I trust you, Julie. I'm going to spend the rest of my life trusting you.*


"Patrick, please."

"I won't be in prison forever. At least I don't think they can do that to me." Patrick frowned. Maybe *they*—under the dazzling direction of Casey English—could lock him up and throw away the key. "Then, when I'm out, I'll be free. I won't have to hide anymore."

"You will never go to prison, Patrick. I won't let anyone do that to you!"

"Please don't worry about me. Please spend every ounce of your energy on the life of love that lies ahead for you with Jeffrey and Merry. Forget about me, Julia. I dug this grave."

"You didn't!"

"Well. I'm choosing not to run or fight. I'm tired of running. First thing in the morning I'll go back to Southampton to ride and paint and take long walks on the snowy beach until they come get me. Don't worry about me, Julia, please. I'll be fine."


"Mommy!" Merry was wide-awake, bright-eyed, and eagerly waiting for Julia the following morning. "Daddy was here last night! Oh! Daddy's with you!"

"Daddy's with both of his girls forever," Jeffrey said lovingly as he kissed Merry good morning. "How are you today, Merry?"

"I'm *better!* My stomach doesn't hurt at all and I feel fine."

"I'm so glad, darling. I just wanted to wish you good morning and tell you that I'll be back. I have to go get admitted and arrange for someone to do the news for a while." Jeffrey shifted his loving gaze from his daughter to Julia as he left unspoken the other thing he had to do this morning.

*I have to say good-bye to Diana, Julie. After I say good-bye I will never see her again.* Jeffrey had told Julia that last night as they lay in bed, holding each other, gently sharing all the truths and all the fears, so that the ancient wounds could finally heal and their wonderful love could be at peace.

As Jeffrey silently reminded her now of the promise he had made about Diana, Julia smiled back, a loving, confident smile, so confident of his love *at last.*

Jeffrey was waiting in her office when she returned from rounds. One look at the dark-blue eyes she knew so well, eyes that would never lie to her, and Diana knew. She saw the gentle apology and the hope . . . apology for her and hope for his life and love with Julia and Merry.

"I'm happy for you, Jeffrey," she whispered truthfully. She would miss him very much, but she wasn't consumed by the feelings of failure she had felt when Sam and Chase had said good-bye.

"I would have spent my life with you, Diana."

"I know that." *And I know that Julia is a love that is greater than all loves. I know because your love for Julia is so very much like my love for Sam.*

Jeffrey put his arms around her and they held each other for a long time. Then, at the same moment, as if by silent signal, they both released their embrace and whispered a soft "Good-bye."

"Mr. Lawrence. Oh, Julia, I'm glad you're here, too," Dr. MacGregor said when they arrived at his office for Jeffrey's eleven A.M. appointment.

"Is something wrong? Has something happened?"

"Nothing's wrong, but maybe something has happened. The platelet and white blood cell counts done on Merry last evening and again this morning are up."

"She had a transfusion last night."

"Yes, but that would affect the red blood cell count—the hematocrit—not the white cells and platelets. Her red cell count before the transfusion hadn't fallen as much as I would have expected, but I elected to transfuse anyway because her hematocrit was very low. Even if her marrow is coming back I wanted to correct the anemia at least to a level that will give her a little reserve."

"Even if her marrow is coming back?"

"I've ordered repeat counts for this afternoon, but if they're still up I want to hold off on transplantation."

"You're saying that her marrow might recover?"

"Yes, if the aplasia was a temporary suppression from an external cause. From my review of her marrow aspirate I really didn't think that's what we were dealing with, but . . ."

"Doctors believe in miracles just like everyone else." Jeffrey quietly whispered the words that the specialist at UCLA had spoken to him four months before his miracle baby was born.

# Chapter Twenty-four

"Hello, Judge Barrington. My name is Casey English. Thank you for taking my call. I am presently an associate with Spencer and Quinn in Manhattan. Before coming here I was with the D.A.'s office in San Francisco and was quite involved with the prosecution of rape cases."

"I see. What can I do for you, Ms. English?"

"I understand that your daughter Pamela was raped five years ago. I wondered if it would be possible for me to speak with her?"

"Why?"

"Because I am still very concerned about the issue of rape, Judge Barrington, and the impact of rape on its victims."

"It would be Pamela's decision."

"Of course."

"She just returned yesterday from Paris. She's spending the year abroad but is home for the holidays."

"I would be happy to fly to Louisville at any time. I think it might be helpful for Pamela to speak with me. I've really had a great deal of experience in talking with victims. Do you know if Pamela has fears that the man will return to rape

450

her again?"

"I don't know. To be honest, we don't talk about it very much anymore."

"But the man has not been apprehended."

"That's correct."

"So she may be worried."

"I guess so. Let me talk with her this evening and give you a call tomorrow."


Casey wasn't sure what she would do if she couldn't meet with Pamela Barrington. She was supposed to have reported her knowledge concerning the whereabouts of a suspected felon to the police the moment she learned Patrick's true identity.

But she hadn't.

She had decided first to read all the documents the private detective had assembled for her. As she read about Patrick's boyhood, the details about the biological mother who alternately claimed and neglected him, the series of foster homes, the homelessness and hopelessness, Casey's heart ached.

Of course James Patrick Jones had become a criminal. Of course he hated the wealthy and privileged. Of course he felt rage and anger against women . . .

It all made sense, horrible, perfect sense. It was the classic portrait of a criminal—someone who had himself once been a victim and now left other victims in his wake of terror.

*But, but, but . . .*

Part of Casey, a place in her heart that wouldn't be silent, could not believe that Patrick had committed an act of such violence. Patrick was so gentle!

And there was something else in the Louisville police report . . .

According to Pamela Barrington, Patrick had found her that night sitting by the pond at the estate. She had always been a little afraid of him, she said, and that night he was even more terrifying because he was drunk, surly, menacingly powerful. He carried an almost-consumed fifth of bourbon, Pamela told the police. He offered her a swallow of the alcohol, and when she politely declined, he forced her to drink. Then he forced her to kiss him. As she tried to push him away she scratched his neck, drawing blood, and that enraged him all the more. He angrily threw the bottle against a boulder, shattering it, and then he raped her.

The judge's statement to the police confirmed the presence of a bleeding scratch on Patrick's neck. The judge didn't get close enough to Patrick to know whether he was drunk, but he recalled that Patrick's eyes were wild and the police found fragments of the bottle. There were fingerprints on the shattered glass, which, although the prints had never been entered into a centralized computer system, to Casey's untrained eyes exactly matched the prints John Tyler had obtained at the wedding reception in late October.

The deeply wounded woman within Casey wanted to punish Patrick for hurting her so much, for making her believe in his love then discarding her so cruelly and choosing Julia instead. And the dedicated attorney within Casey, the woman who believed in giving voice to the silent cries of victims and was truly passionate about justice, wanted to see justice done.

But the careful compulsive discipline that made Casey such an excellent attorney was very troubled by the testimony that Patrick had been drinking. On a moonlit evening in their romantic meadow of love, Patrick had told her that he had never tasted alcohol before because he had never felt safe enough to drink. And Casey had believed him because his voice was so quiet and his gray-green eyes flickered with pain and because she had witnessed his surprise when he felt the effects of the champagne.

*I was drunk when I told you I loved you.* Casey shuddered at the memory of those cruel words. But she needed to remember them, because Patrick hadn't been drunk that night, just a little high, a little giddy, but he didn't know the difference because alcohol was foreign to him.

And that was why she had to talk to Pamela Barrington. Casey had to watch Pamela's eyes as she asked the tough questions.

Casey told Judge Barrington the truth. She *did* care about the victims of rape . . . even if the real victim of this rape had been Patrick.

Casey met with the judge and Pamela in the living room of the mansion at Barrington Farm on the afternoon of December twenty-second. The mansion reminded Casey of her home in San Francisco at Christmas, the huge tree decorated with expensive ornaments, the scent of pine, the crystal vases of holly, the mounds of elaborately wrapped presents. It wasn't a nostalgic memory—

those grand Christmases hadn't been filled with joy—only an uneasy one. Casey's uneasiness grew when she met Pamela Barrington.

Because Pamela was so very much like her, a beautiful and privileged heiress who believed that life owed her everything her heart desired. Pamela's eyes clouded a little when she talked about Patrick, but there was no fear, no shame, no anguish that he had violated her. There was only anger and the intense desire for revenge. Pamela hadn't refused to meet with Casey—as a true victim might have, not wanting to relive the pain—she had welcomed the opportunity to re-create the drama. The talented, well-rehearsed actress was quite happy to give another performance.

"Did you see him drink, Pamela?"

"Yes. He had a bottle with him. He was drunk already, but he drank more in front of me and he forced me to drink, too."

"And it was bourbon?"

"Yes. Jim Beam. The police found the bottle shattered on a rock by the pond."

"Pamela, what if I told you that James Patrick Jones has a fatal allergic reaction to all types of alcohol including bourbon?"

The judge started to speak, but Casey held up her hand to stop him.

"Do you understand my question, Pamela?" Casey continued, clarifying her question as she would for a witness in the courtroom. "What if I told you that even a sip of alcohol would kill him in a matter of moments?"

Casey could tell that Pamela was searching her memory for proof that it wasn't true. But Pamela had never seen James Patrick Jones drink. It was she who had tried to force bourbon on him that night, part of her seduction, and he had shoved the bottle away, as if afraid even to have it near him, *as if it might be lethal*.

"Pamela?" the judge asked, hesitantly at first because he didn't want to believe . . . and then sternly, *"Pamela?"*

"Yes?" Pamela's eyes widened with surprise at the unfamiliar harshness of her father's tone.

"Did James rape you?"

"He didn't want me, Daddy," Pamela explained calmly, as if that was all the explanation that was necessary—the astonishing fact that James Patrick Jones had dared to say no to *her*. "You understand, don't you?"

"No. I don't understand, Pamela."

"He didn't want me!" Pamela repeated emphatically, annoyed and exasperated by the sudden obtuseness of her father. "He had to pay, Daddy, don't you see?"

*"Did he rape you? Yes or no?"*

"No! But—"

"Oh, Pamela," the judge sighed heavily, a sigh of shock and sadness for the wrongfully harmed James, and an almost greater sadness for the terribly spoiled daughter who was so unrepentant about what she had done. "All these years the police have been looking for him. And if they had found him, and if you had continued to lie, he would have gone to prison."

"I don't care! He *deserved* to go to prison!"

As Casey listened to the exchange between the defiant and remorseless Pamela and her horrified father, Casey, too, felt a deep horror.

Because she had been so much like Pamela.

Because she had wanted Patrick to pay for the unforgivable crime of not wanting her.

"Mr. Lawrence."

"For God's sake, call me Jeffrey."

"Jeffrey. Please come in." Patrick held open the door to the small apartment where he and Julia had spent so many hours. "Is Merry home? When I spoke with Julia last night she thought her blood counts might be high enough for her to be released from the hospital today."

"They were, and she's home."

"That's wonderful."

"We were very lucky," Jeffrey said quietly and with the same wonder that had filled Julia's voice years before when she had described their daughter's remarkable progress after her premature birth. "Patrick, I've come to thank you for all that you've done for Julia and for Merry, and to tell you that I will do everything possible to help you."

"I'm not a rapist, Jeffrey."

Jeffrey nodded. He didn't know that, but Julia did, and Jeffrey was going to spend the rest of his life believing her, trusting her, proving his trust and earning hers. *You'd better not be a rapist, Patrick.*

"Don't you think it would be better to turn yourself in?"

"I don't believe there's a chance in hell I can stay out of prison no matter what I do. This is Casey's show. I'm not going to spoil it for her. I'm quite sure she has a plan."

Patrick knew that Casey and the police would arrive soon. He was ready. He had spent the past few days soaring over jumps, walking along the beach to the meadow, and painting. Late last night he had finished the portrait that had tormented him for so long—the portrait of Casey, his wonderful Venus, the picture of an illusion. The magnificent portrait hung on the wall in his bedroom, a grim reminder of his folly.

"Julia and Merry and I would like you to come for dinner tomorrow night."

"For Christmas?"

"Yes."

Patrick shook his head in disbelief. Merry and Julia might want him to join them, but not Jeffrey.

"You will always be welcome in my home, Patrick." Jeffrey spoke truthfully to Patrick's obvious skepticism. "You saved my wife and my daughter. *There is no way I can ever repay you for that.*"


Twenty-four hours later, moments before Patrick was to leave for dinner at Belvedere, Casey knocked softly on the door to his apartment.

"I really underestimated you, Casey. I just didn't think you'd choose to do it on Christmas Day."

"May I come in?"

"Of course. Where are the police?"

In the moments before Casey answered, Patrick fought to calm his racing heart. It wasn't fear that caused his heart to pound. Patrick was unafraid of the police. He had accepted his fate. What caused his heart to gallop still, despite everything, was Casey. She wore a tailored navy-blue suit and her fire-gold hair was pulled tightly off her face and into a severe chignon. She looked like the consummate attorney, except for her eyes.

Her eyes were soft and vulnerable and uncertain, exactly like the eyes in the portrait that hung in the other room, a portrait that he had believed was the artist's deluded conception, the illusory memory of love.

Casey should have looked so triumphant. But instead she looked like the woman Patrick loved.

"No police, Patrick. Only this." Casey removed a large envelope from the briefcase she carried. Then she took a deep breath as her mind frantically searched for the words she had so carefully rehearsed. But the well-scripted eloquent flow of words, a brief yet complete explanation after which she could quickly leave, had vanished the moment she saw him and she fumbled as she tried to recall the important points. "This packet contains a copy of Pamela's statement recanting her accusation, the official notice from the Louisville police that all charges against you have been dropped, and a letter from Judge Barrington. I don't know what the letter says, but I do know that he liked you, Patrick, and respected you, and feels great remorse about what Pamela did. His letter should contain a check in the amount of five million dollars. It's obviously a great deal of money, but I think the judge truly believes it's small compared to the five years of your life that were taken from you and can never be replaced. The money is a gift from the judge to you, and it is not intended to dissuade you from filing a civil suit against Pamela. She's an adult now, with her own fortune, and the judge expects, and even supports, full legal recourse against her."

458

"Casey," Patrick said softly, interrupting the spill of words to which he had barely listened after the miraculous ones—*All charges against you have been dropped*—words that had been delivered to the briefcase where her vulnerable lovely eyes had been resolutely focused ever since leaving his. "How did this happen?"

"Oh. In her statement to the police Pamela said you had been drinking."

"But you knew that wasn't possible. And you got Pamela to admit that she lied. Is that right, Casey?" *Look at me!* "Is that what you did?"

"You were innocent, Patrick." Casey looked up then, into the gray-green eyes she loved so much. "You were the victim."

"You went to Louisville and confronted her?"

"Something like that."

"Casey . . ."

"Oh, your wallet and passport and birth certificate are in here, too. The clothes and riding trophies that were impounded by the police will be mailed to you. And there were some paintings . . ." As Casey spoke, her eyes drifted to the walls of Patrick's apartment that were covered with his wonderful art. Casey hadn't wanted to see the place where Patrick and Julia had loved but it was impossible to keep looking at him. "I didn't know you were an artist."

*An artist, not a rapist!* her heart cried. *Oh, Patrick, couldn't you even have told me that?*

"I have to go, Patrick. I have a plane to catch."

"Where are you going?"

"What? Oh, to Bermuda. I'll be back in a week. Please let me know if you would like me or someone from our firm to handle the suit against

Pamela."

"I'm not going to file a suit against Pamela."

"Oh, well, if you change your mind."

"I won't. I'm not interested in revenge."

*No, you wouldn't be interested in revenge, Patrick, because you are so wise and you know what is important. Somehow you know the destructive power of revenge.* Casey looked at him briefly, long enough to smile a wobbly smile, then turned to the door.

"Casey?"

"Yes?"

"Thank you."

"You're welcome," she whispered softly.

Then she was gone, and he should have run after her. But she seemed so eager to get away from him. And he was still so very stunned by what had happened.

Eventually, a surprising flicker of reality surfaced from the stunning swirl of emotions and thoughts that consumed him . . . he was expected for dinner at Belvedere.

Patrick realized, after he left his small apartment, that he hadn't looked at the documents, or read the letter from the judge, or even opened it to see if the check was inside.

None of that mattered. What mattered was that he was *free*. He was going to Christmas dinner at Belvedere as a free man.

Because of Casey.

Two days after Casey gave him his freedom, Patrick flew to Bermuda. He knew where she was staying, because he had called until he found the hotel where she was registered, and when he reached the hotel perched on a cliff above a white sand beach, his heart filled with hope. Had she chosen this place because it reminded her of a cottage above the sea where once there had been such love?

Casey wasn't in her room. On impulse, or perhaps something much stronger, Patrick walked down the steep trail to the beach below. And in the distance, on the farthest reach of a rocky point, he saw her. She stood defiantly, facing the wind and the waves, her hair a red-gold beacon dancing in the muted rays of the winter sun.

"You're just not afraid of the sea, are you?" Patrick asked softly when he stood on the rocky point a few feet behind her.

Casey hadn't heard him approach; the wintry Atlantic was thundering, and the wind whistled and roared. But she heard his familiar, gentle voice above the wind and waves.

"Patrick," Casey whispered to the sapphire waves. She spoke to the waves, instead of turning to him, because her eyes were filled with hot tears, just as they had been filled with tears on that June night when he had rescued her. "Why are you here?"

"Why won't you look at me?"

Casey turned then, without drying her tears, because she had dried them on that distant balmy night, and Patrick had known anyway.

"You gave me my freedom, Casey. Do you have any idea what that feels like?"

"Yes, I do know, Patrick," she answered quietly.

"Last summer with you, *I* felt free."

Casey had almost lost the gift Patrick had given her, *almost* drenched herself in hatred and revenge. But in giving Patrick his freedom, she had begun to believe again in the woman Patrick had discovered last summer, the lovely generous woman who she wanted to be. Her need to win wasn't as strong as her love for him. Now, perhaps, at last, she could be a gracious loser.

"Because of you, Casey, I'm free to ride again, and even compete if I choose, and I'm free to paint and even have my work published, and I'm free to travel to a foreign country and show my passport and have no fear that my real name will summon the police. Those are such wonderful freedoms, Casey, but there is another freedom that is more magnificent than all the rest."

"The one you didn't tell me about last summer."

"Yes. The most precious freedom of all, the freedom to love, the freedom to give your heart and know that your love won't cause harm. I can do that now, Casey. I can ask the woman I love if she will marry me. I thought, at least on the weekends, we could live in a cottage I'm going to build in a meadow of wildflowers."

"Julia's meadow. Now you are free to marry Julia," Casey whispered quietly, a gracious defeat, a generous wish for Patrick's happiness with her ancient enemy. "When she came to my office that day, wanting my help with her divorce, I guess, I was very rude. I need to apologize."

"It wasn't about a divorce. It was because Merry was ill."

"Oh. Patrick, I didn't know."

"I know and Julia knows, and it's OK. Every-

462

thing's OK. Well, not everything, because I still haven't heard a yes to my marriage proposal."

"Patrick?" Casey asked softly as she looked into eyes that filled with such love, such desire for her.

"Casey, I don't want to marry Julia. I have never loved anyone but you. Will you marry me, my love?"

"Oh, Patrick. Have you come to rescue me again?"

"I have come, my lovely flower, to love you forever."

"Jeffrey?" Julia found him in the library at Belvedere at three A.M. on a snowy night in the middle of January. She had fallen asleep in his arms, but had awakened to find him gone. "What are you doing?"

"I'm reading the letters you wrote to me when I was in Beirut."

"Oh, Jeffrey." Julia moved behind him and rested her hands on his shoulders. She felt the tension in his muscles, a palpable sign of his despair as he read her loving descriptions of the daily events in the life of his little girl. "Please stop torturing yourself."

"I missed so much."

"But you're missing nothing now."

"Just all the hours of every day when I'm at work."

"While Merry's at school and with her friends. I miss her during those hours, too, Jeffrey, but she's a very happy, very healthy, and very loved little girl."

"Yes she is. Because of you. Because you

wouldn't let her believe that her father didn't love her despite the evidence."

"And I was right." Julia tenderly kissed his lips. After a moment she pulled away and gazed at him with an expression that was thoughtful and a little worried.

"What, darling?"

"Merry is planning to have a father-daughter talk with you this weekend. I think you need to know in advance what she's going to propose."

"All right."

"Your daughter wants a baby brother or sister, perhaps one or two of each. She's very innocent still about babies and where they come from. I think she believes that if all three of us combine our wishes it will happen."

"Merry wants us to have another baby?"

As Jeffrey asked the question, so quietly, Julia saw the sadness in his eyes. She had worried that his reaction might be sadness not joy, sadness that the daughter he loved so much and who finally knew his wonderful love was ready so soon to share it.

"Jeffrey, Merry never *ever* talked about having brothers or sisters before. This is a sign of how confident she is of your love. She knows that nothing can diminish the bond between you, and she probably knows, too, that you have more than enough love for an infinite number of babies. Merry has always been a remarkably unspoiled and generous little girl."

"Like her mother." Jeffrey smiled, but the smile faded as a new sadness filled his eyes. "Julie, I don't deserve . . ."

"Yes you do, and your unborn babies deserve to

have you as their father."

"Well, they deserve to have you as their mother. Do you want more children, honey?"

"I would love to have more children, Jeffrey."

"There are new techniques — in vitro fertilization — I suppose we could look into . . . What? Why are you smiling?"

"What's wrong with the old-fashioned way? We've practiced birth control ever since Merry was born. Couldn't we try without for a while?"

"Yes, but Julie, I think it was truly a miracle that Merry was conceived."

"I think, my love, that all babies are miracles."

"Yes," Jeffrey whispered softly. "Oh, Julie, have I ever told you how much I love you?"

"All the time, but I never tire of hearing it."

Julia tilted her head, and a strand of hair fell into her eyes. As Jeffrey very delicately moved the black silk, he saw a fleeting flicker of sadness in the lavender.

Jeffrey knew the cause, and even though Julia was more confident of their love than she had ever been, she couldn't erase the painful memories of his affair with Diana any more than he could erase the sadness he would always feel about the past he could not change.

The memories could never be erased, but they could be softened with love. Just as Julia gently commanded Jeffrey to stop torturing himself and then spent long, patient hours listening to his torment and helping him ease it, Jeffrey gently tried to stop the sadness in her eyes when her thoughts drifted to his affair by lovingly discussing the worries with her.

Now he saw a worry that lingered even after the

fleeting flicker of sadness had vanished.

"What, honey? Tell me."

"Do you think about her?"

"Sometimes," Jeffrey admitted honestly. "Sometimes, when I feel so happy, so lucky, so overflowing with joy, I think about her. And what I think is that I wish she could have even a part of the happiness and love that we have. That's all, Julie. I just wish happiness for her."

# Chapter Twenty-five

*Manhattan*
*February 1990*

"Happy Valentine's Eve." Jeffrey whispered the words between a tender kiss as he greeted Julia when he arrived home at ten P.M.

"Happy Valentine's Eve," Julia echoed softly.

"You're listening to music?"

"Yes. I bought a wonderful collection of love songs, most of my very favorite ones, released just in time for Valentine's Day." Julia smiled lovingly at Jeffrey, who was so very romantic in the intimate privacy of their own love, but who, she knew, never listened to other lovers' songs of love. "Let me go turn the stereo off so that we can go to bed."

This was their new pattern, to go to bed as soon as Jeffrey arrived home, and it was so much more wonderful than the old pattern they had followed for years. Because now, instead of talking for hours before going to bed, they went right to their master suite, pausing to gaze at their sleeping daughter on the way, and they awakened early so that the three of them could linger over breakfast together.

467

Jeffrey followed Julia across the great room to the stereo. As she reached for the record on the turntable, he glanced casually at the ivory-colored double album with elegant crimson script, and his eyes fell on two familiar crimson words: Sam Hunter. The discovery prompted more reading, and more discoveries. The album was called *Memories of Love*, and it featured a new love song entitled 'Queen of Hearts.'

"Jeffrey?" Julia asked when she saw his obvious and surprising interest. And there was more, because, as she watched, his interested dark-blue eyes became confused, and gentle, and so thoughtful. "Jeffrey, darling, what is it?"

Jeffrey looked at her, his lovely Julie, and smiled a gentle smile. He would let it go, not mention Diana's name at all, not resurrect the still-painful memories. But Sam Hunter's newest song of love was entitled "Queen of Hearts," and Jeffrey needed to listen to it. He could come back to the great room in the middle of the night, when Julia was asleep, and listen to the song privately, and if it meant something tell Julia then . . . But there were no secrets in the love of Jeffrey and Julia anymore. There was only truth and trust and infinite faith in their magnificent love.

"It has to do with Diana, Julie . . ." Jeffrey began apologetically.

"OK."

"She was in love once, before her marriage to Chase, and for Diana, for her heart, that distant love was as strong and as forever as my love for you."

"And mine for you," Julia reminded him gently, reassuring him, knowing that he was only mentioning Diana because it was something important.

"Tell me."

"Her great love was Sam Hunter. They met in high school in Dallas."

"Oh," Julia whispered softly, with a slight frown because for some reason the revelation wasn't entirely a surprise. Julia knew well, and loved, the love songs written by Sam Hunter, especially the ones written a decade ago, which meant that although she had not known until now that Sam's Diana was Diana Shepherd, she had known for a very long time that Sam Hunter loved a woman named Diana. "Yes."

"Sam left her, and that caused great pain, and even though it was a long time ago, Diana has never really stopped loving him. Anyway, I noticed that his new love song is called "Queen of Hearts," and I wondered—"

"Sam had to leave her, Jeffrey," Julia interrupted gently but confidently. "He didn't want to, but he had to."

"What? How on earth do you know that?"

"Because it's in his songs. And all the songs are all here, Jeffrey, in this album, and there's a booklet with lyrics and dates when each song was written. We can look at them, or listen, but, darling, I'm really very sure that all his songs of love were written for Diana and that even though he loved her—I think *because* he loved her—he had to leave her."

"He sang to Diana by name?" Jeffrey asked softly.

"Not at first, but eventually. His most beautiful love song, until this new one, was 'Diana's Song.' It was released just before Lady Diana Spencer married Prince Charles. Sam lived in England at the time, and it would make sense that the most

469

beautiful of all his songs of love was written for the most beautiful and enchanting royal bride, but I always believed 'Diana's Song' was written for the same woman to whom he had been singing all along. It seemed like the happy ending to the longing that had been in his songs until then, a joyous hope that they would finally be together." Julia paused, then added quietly, "But the ending wasn't happy. Sam sang to her, but she didn't come, and after that his songs were still beautiful, and very moving, but quite sad."

"Diana never heard his love songs, Julie."

"Oh, but she must have, if she listened to the radio at all."

"But she didn't. She couldn't."

"Why not?"

Jeffrey hesitated, but for only a moment, because he knew he had to tell Julia everything.

"When Sam left her—and you're right, my lovely Julie, it was because he had to—Diana was pregnant with his baby. Sam never knew about their daughter. Her name was Janie. She was born with a serious heart condition and died a month after she was born."

"Oh, no," Julia whispered softly as she remembered Diana's gentle concern and compassion when Julia asked for her help for Merry.

"Diana's life and love with Sam, and with Janie, had been filled with music. After Janie died, and when Diana believed that Sam didn't love her enough and would never return, she stopped listening to the music she once had loved. The memories of Sam, and the daughter who loved listening to tapes he had made, were just too painful. The day that you saw us in Hyde Park, honey, when Diana was so very sad, it was because she had heard a cascading of chimes that reminded her of a song Janie had loved."

"Oh, Jeffrey," Julia whispered after several moments. "Sam loved Diana so much."

"And Diana loved Sam. She would have gone to him if she had heard his songs. She still would."

"Sam loves her still, Jeffrey. That's why he wrote 'Queen of Hearts.' He must have seen her again."

"Yes. He did see her. In October he asked Diana to operate on his infant daughter . . . Janie. It was very emotional for Diana, but something she had to do, and the surgery was a complete success. Janie recovered quickly, and she and Sam returned to their home in California."

Jeffrey gazed at Julia's lovely eyes, tear-misted and thoughtful, and hoped that Diana would not be angry that he had revealed her secrets. Jeffrey had told Julia all the truths because he believed it was necessary because of what he had to ask of Julia.

But Jeffrey didn't have to ask.

"You have to tell her, Jeffrey. You have to go to Diana and tell her."


"For my Valentines," Jeffrey said at breakfast the following morning as he handed pink-and-white gift-wrapped boxes to Julia and Merry.

"Daddy!" Merry exclaimed as she removed the gold necklace with a pendant in the shape of a tiny, solid-gold, friendly dragon. "Mommy, it's Daphne."

"This is beautiful, Jeffrey," Julia said as she held the small and perfect re-creation of her fairytale character in her hand. "How did you do it?"

"I took one of the illustrated stories to a jeweler at Harry Winston."

"He did a magnificent job."

"He did, didn't he? See how you think he did with your present."

Julia's present was a necklace, too, a necklace to match their elegant wedding bands, delicate ribbons of white and yellow gold, intertwined and then melted together by fire.

"Oh, Jeffrey."

"You like it." It wasn't a question, because Jeffrey saw the joy in her lavender eyes. "The other thing, before Merry has to rush off for school, is that I've scheduled time off for the same days that Merry is on spring vacation. Since that's only a month away I thought we should start making plans."

"You still might have to work, though, Daddy."

"No, Merry. I won't work on those days, no matter what."

"But if you had to, because it was something very important like the peace conference, that would be OK."

"It would be OK, wouldn't it?" Jeffrey gently asked his lovely daughter. Jeffrey knew the answer—"Yes, it would be OK"—because their love wasn't precarious any longer. "But it can't happen two vacations in a row, so I think we should start to make plans."


Five minutes after Merry left for school, Jeffrey and Julia walked to the foyer to watch for the limousine from the studio.

"I love the necklace, Jeffrey. And the vacation. We still haven't done our honeymoon, have we?"

472

"I was thinking we might have to postpone that until all our babies are grown. I can't imagine going on vacation without Merry, can you?"

"No, I can't."

Jeffrey kissed her for a long, tender moment. Then the limousine appeared on the cobblestone drive and he reluctantly pulled free and reached for the briefcase that contained Sam Hunter's *Memories of Love.*

"I love you, Julie."

"I want you to do this, Jeffrey." Julia smiled a loving smile, and there wasn't a flicker of uncertainty in her lavender eyes. Julia believed in Jeffrey's forever love. "I want happiness for Diana, too."


"Hello, Diana," Jeffrey said quietly when she answered the private line in her office at noon.

"Jeffrey."

"I need to see you. It's important."

"Jeffrey . . ."

"It's Julia's idea."

"Oh?"

"Are you free this evening?"

"No. In fact, I'm leaving at seven tonight for a week's vacation in Florida."

"Florida, not Malibu?"

"You know me so well. I actually had been having masochistic ideas, like dropping by for a post-op check on Janie. That's why I'm taking this vacation. I'm in need of a heart-to-heart talk with myself."

"Are there other topics?"

"Other than Sam? Well, yes, there's the directorship of the Institute. It's harder to convince myself

473

that I *must* get the appointment now, for the good of the Institute, because Tom and I are no longer enemies. In fact, I think most of me wants Tom to get the job. I've been thinking about withdrawing my name from consideration."

"I just have a feeling that everything is going to work out."

"Really? What a remarkable prediction based on absolutely no facts, Anchor."

*I do have the facts,* Jeffrey thought.

"Can you see me before you leave, Diana?"

"You mean this afternoon?"

"Whenever you're free."

"I'm free anytime. I'm just doing paperwork."

"So, your penthouse in an hour?"

"OK."

"Hi." Jeffrey smiled warmly at the familiar sapphire eyes. He saw fatigue and strain, but Diana smiled a lovely, sparkling smile of welcome for him.

"Hi." Diana tilted her head and asked softly, "This was really Julia's idea?"

"It really was. Last night, together, we discovered something that you need to know. Julia knows how very important it is and made the suggestion that I see you before I even had a chance to ask." Jeffrey's solemn and gentle eyes left Diana's for a moment to glance at a far corner of the luxurious living room. "That wall of state-of-the art stereo equipment does work, doesn't it?"

"Yes. Chase used to listen to an occasional opera."

"Good. Although it hardly matters. There's a booklet inside the album with all the lyrics," Jef-

474

frey explained as he removed Sam's album from his briefcase and handed it to Diana. Then, instead of waiting for her to make the slow, hopeful discoveries, wanting her to know *now*, he continued gently, "Sam loves you, honey. He always has."

"What?" Diana didn't even look at the album. She looked instead into the dark-blue eyes she trusted so much. Jeffrey knew of her love for Sam and would never hurt her. "How do you know?"

"Because it's all here in this just-released album of Sam's most beautiful songs of love. Sam sang his love to you, Diana. All the songs are here, all his messages of love, including his wish for you to be together again, if you loved him still, after his father died."

"He sang to me by name?" Diana asked softly.

"When it was safe to, after his father died, yes. And before that . . . well, darling, it's very obvious, beautifully, eloquently, lovingly obvious, that all his songs were always to you."

"All those years . . ." Diana whispered, a whisper of painful memories and immeasurable loss. "He loved me?"

"Yes, just as he loves you now, still. Sam's newest song, just written, is called 'Queen of Hearts.' I always thought that name was perfect for you, Diana, even though you believed it was so wrong. But Sam knows the name is perfect, too, and in this most beautiful love song he has proven that it is who you are." Jeffrey gently touched her cheek and gazed into her hopeful but still-disbelieving sapphire eyes. "I'm going to go now, darling. Don't get so lost in memories that you miss your plane."

"My plane's not until seven."

"No, Diana, it's at four." Jeffrey removed a United Airlines ticket from his jacket pocket. "It arrives in Los Angeles at eight-thirty. I decided to put you in Seat 2B."

"Jeffrey . . ."

Jeffrey smiled lovingly. "It's only a one-way ticket."

"I'm going to go see him, aren't I?"

"I hope so."

"Oh, Jeffrey, thank you." Diana smiled a lovely, hopeful smile and whispered softly, "And please thank her, thank Julia, for me."

"She asked me to do the same to you."


Diana still had the piece of paper on which Sam had written his unlisted home phone number. She had kept it, a loose scrap inside her address book, never transcribed to one of the pages but not discarded, either.

She dialed the number when she reached Los Angeles.

"Sam? It's Diana."

"Diana."

"Remember me?" Diana asked softly, suddenly swept to the memory of Sam asking the same question on a rainy night in Boston.

"Oh, yes, I remember you," Sam whispered gently, just as Diana had whispered the same words to him that soggy night. "Where are you?"

"At the airport."

"Are you coming to see us?"

"Yes."

"Let me get my healthy little girl bundled up and we'll be right there to get you."

"Is Janie asleep?"

"Yes, but she'll fall asleep again in the car."

"Why don't I just take a taxi? Wouldn't that be quicker?"

Sam was waiting on the porch near the front door so he could hear if Janie awakened, but *outside* so he could greet her as she arrived.

In October, both Sam and Diana had so carefully hidden the love they still felt. But now, in the sapphire eyes and in the dark-brown ones, the love was at the surface, radiant and hopeful and full of joy.

"Oh, Diana," he whispered softly. "How I have missed you."

"How I have missed you, too, Sam."

Sam gently touched her face, a tender caress of welcome and love, then he reached for her suitcase with one hand and her hand with the other and they walked into his beachfront bungalow and upstairs to his bedroom that overlooked the ocean. They stood for a moment and gazed at the rippling ribbon of gold cast by the moon on the inky black Pacific. Then Sam led her across the hall to the room where Janie lay sleeping so peacefully.

"Hello, little Janie," Diana whispered.

Janie didn't awaken, but her long dark lashes fluttered and her pink lips curled into a soft smile, as if she knew the familiar gentle voice had come to stay, as if she knew that from this moment on she would have a loving father *and* mother.

"She's so healthy, Diana. She can laugh forever because her lungs are so free." Sam smiled as he spoke, but his words caused sudden tears in her lovely eyes. "Diana?"

"Could we go back to your room and talk?"

477

"Of course."

They sat on Sam's bed, their faces illuminated by the moon. Sam gently cupped her sad, lovely face in his hands and tenderly kissed the tears that fell from the sapphire and waited in patient loving silence until at last she was able to speak.

"There are things I need to tell you," Diana whispered finally to his loving eyes. How sad he would be when he learned about the daughter whose small lungs had never had a chance to laugh forever. "Maybe tomorrow."

"All right."

"Tonight you need to know that I waited for you to return to me, but I never heard your songs of love. I know I told you that I would listen . . . but I didn't."

"I sang instead of coming to you, Diana, after my father died, because it had been so many years and I didn't want to intrude if you had a new love, or confuse you, and . . ."

"And because you knew that if I was waiting I would hear your songs."

"But you never did."

"No. I still haven't." Diana smiled a trembling smile. "I've only read the lyrics. Oh, Sam, such beautiful lyrics of love."

"For my most beautiful love." Sam gently kissed her trembling lips and whispered softly, "I will sing all the love songs to you, my Diana. I will spend my life singing songs of love to you . . . if that's what you want."

"Oh, yes, Sam, that's what I want."

"I love you, Diana. Oh, how I love you."

"And oh, how I love you, Sam."

Sam and Diana danced beneath the golden moon, as they had danced in their private corner

478

of the park in Dallas, their lips and bodies gently kissing as they swayed to the music of love that lived within them, the joyous melodies of their hearts and souls.

And sometime during the moonlit night, their dance became a dance of love. And so slowly, so tenderly, in a rhythm of joy that promised forever, Sam made love to his beautiful Queen of Hearts.

# SURRENDER TO THE PASSION

**LOVE'S SWEET BOUNTY**                                    (3313, $4.50)
by Colleen Faulkner

Jessica Landon swore revenge of the masked bandits who robbed the train and stole all the money she had in the world. She set out after the thieves without consulting the handsome railroad detective, Adam Stern. When he finally caught up with her, she admitted she needed his assistance. She never imagined that she would also begin to need his scorching kisses and tender caresses.

**WILD WESTERN BRIDE**                                     (3140, $4.50)
by Rosalyn Alsobrook

Anna Thomas loved riding the Orphan Train and finding loving homes for her young charges. But when a judge tried to separate two brothers, the dedicated beauty went beyond the call of duty. She proposed to the handsome, blue-eyed Mark Gates, planning to adopt the boys herself! Of course the marriage would be in name only, but yet as time went on, Anna found herself dreaming of being a loving wife in every sense of the word . . .

**QUICKSILVER PASSION**                                    (3117, $4.50)
by Georgina Gentry

Beautiful Silver Jones had been called every name in the book, and now that she owned her own tavern in Buckskin Joe, Colorado, the independent didn't care what the townsfolk thought of her. She never let a man touch her and she earned her money fair and square. Then one night handsome Cherokee Evans swaggered up to her bar and destroyed the peace she'd made with herself. For the irresistible miner made her yearn for the melting kisses and satin caresses she had sworn she could live without!

**MISSISSIPPI MISTRESS**                                   (3118, $4.50)
by Gina Robins

Cori Pierce was outraged at her father's murder and the loss of her inheritance. She swore revenge and vowed to get her independence back, even if it meant singing as an entertainer on a Mississippi steamboat. But she hadn't reckoned on the swarthy giant in tight buckskins who turned out to be her boss. Jacob Wolf was, after all, the giant of the man Cori vowed to destroy. Though she swore not to forget her mission for even a moment, she was powerfully tempted to submit to Jake's fiery caresses and have one night of passion in his irresistible embrace.

*Available wherever paperbacks are sold, or order direct from the Publisher. Send cover price plus 50¢ per copy for mailing and handling to Zebra Books, Dept. 3362, 475 Park Avenue South, New York, N.Y. 10016. Residents of New York, New Jersey and Pennsylvania must include sales tax. DO NOT SEND CASH.*